OF LOVE

MK SCHILLER

OMNIFIC PUBLISHING
LOS ANGELES

Omnific Publishing
1901 Avenue of the Stars, 2nd floor
Los Angeles, CA 90067
www.omnificpublishing.com

First Omnific eBook edition, September 2014
First Omnific trade paperback edition, September 2014

The characters and events in this book are fictitious.
Any similarity to real persons, living or dead,
is coincidental and not intended by the author.

Library of Congress Cataloguing-in-Publication Data

Schiller, MK.
  Variables of Love / MK Schiller – 1st ed.
  ISBN: 978-1-623421-31-1
  1. Multicultural — Romance. 2. New Adult — Romance.
  3. College — Fiction. 4. Indian — Fiction. I. Title

10 9 8 7 6 5 4 3 2 1

Cover Design by Micha Stone and Amy Brokaw
Interior Book Design by Coreen Montagna

Printed in the United States of America

To Patrick
for keeping us stocked on faith, laughter, and ice cream.

I wish I could say I didn't remember that day. I was sixteen, and it was the first sunny day of spring after a long, dark winter. There was sand, laughter, the lake, flip-flops, beer, and Matt Stapler's shiny green eyes. But I'd been far too pissed off to enjoy any of it. My plan for the perfect first kiss ruined…because of *his* interference.

He pulled me to the side, lowering his voice, but the words rang with such hostility, he might as well have screamed them. "You look like a slut."

How could I respond to that? I looked like the rest of the girls, in my hot pink bikini and denim shorts that slung low on my hips. Fuck him…I looked hot. I started walking away, but he grabbed my arm.

"I'm not always going to be able to watch over you."

My bitter laugh was so biting that he actually winced. "Thank God for that."

"We are not like these people. We were raised differently," he said in a much calmer voice, as if he was now trying to reason with me.

"I am exactly like them. You're not. Just because we share the same DNA, doesn't mean I'm like you in any way."

"You can say that as much as you want, but they will never accept you. Just as we would never accept them."

"Live your own damn life and stop fucking up mine. I hate you," I spat, doling out the words like cruel, heartless slaps. He didn't scowl or sneer as expected. He looked hurt. *Good.*

He stopped me from getting onto the shiny motorcycle, taking my place. I curbed my anger just enough to prevent an obnoxious scene, but inside I was seething. I wished I didn't have a brother.

Vijay turned to me and shook his head in smug satisfaction. I might have laughed at the sight of my conservative brother on a motorcycle, and the ridiculous fight he and Matt got into when Vijay insisted on riding bitch, but there was too much venom flowing in my veins. Instead, I got in my friend's small convertible and watched them pass us from my side of the car.

The screeching skid of tires snapped me from my selfish thoughts, jolting me upright. I watched in paralyzed horror as the shiny black motorcycle collided with the large SUV in front of it. It fell to the pavement, bouncing up again, looking as if it were made of elastic not metal. The rebounding motion happened not once, but three times — three heart-wrenching, tear-inducing, life-changing times.

The desperate shriek lodged in my throat, silenced as my head crashed into the dash. My ears absorbed the foreign sounds as they mingled, merging into a new song that would forever infest my mind. The loud scrape of metal against metal as it twisted, bent, yielded, and broke. The screeches and screams combined in a nightmarish lullaby as the pungent aroma of burning rubber assaulted my nostrils and broken glass rained down on me.

I had wished I didn't have a brother.

And just like that, I didn't.

Meena

1

$\mathcal{I}$ usually took my time as I walked, but today I was breaking all pedestrian speed limits. I preferred to think of myself as prepared, but Raj called me anal-retentive. Neither description fit today. I was running very late thanks to my roommate, Rachael, who had unplugged my alarm clock to charge her iPod. And what an important day it was — the beginning of the end — my last year of college.

I wasn't looking ahead in the hazardous, crowded hallway but down at the loose papers in my hands, cursing myself for not having the foresight to staple my essay. That's why the impact was so strong when my face slammed into a wall of uncompromising muscle. I reeled back but managed not to fall on my ass. The papers didn't fare as well. They drifted to the floor like white flags of surrender. I wasn't sure what had happened, except there was an intoxicating aroma encircling my head along with the imaginary birds.

Strong hands gripped my arms, holding me steady. "Are you okay?"

I looked up at him, blinking rapidly, trying to form a basic syllable. He held me at a short distance as he inspected my face with the most piercing blues eyes I'd ever seen. Of course, it wasn't the first time I'd seen them, but never this close. They looked like several shades of blue combined to form the perfect color, like all the good blues in the world, from the bright summer sky to the deep churning ocean, got together and decided to be one.

I took a step back, expecting him to release me, but instead he moved with me. He caressed my arms up and down, causing a prickle of goose pimples to invade my flesh, acting as a traitorous road map of our contact. I allowed myself a quick glance at where his hand rested under the cuff of my short-sleeved shirt. I wanted to paint the image to freeze it in time. I would call it *Cream over Coffee*. It was an apt title.

"Fine," I finally answered, happy my voice didn't crack.

"Sure? You took a hard hit."

No, I'm not okay. You're a little too beautiful to exist, and I just crashed into you like a total dumbass.

"Yes. Are you?" I cleared my throat to stall any drooling. The boy was delicious. Although my nerves suffered a momentary reprieve when he laughed at my question. I looked down at the mess of white pages strewn around us, and his laughter died.

"I didn't feel a thing," he said, and I swallowed, lifting my eyes to meet his. There was a suggestive smile tugging at his lips. "That's not true. What I meant to say is…I'm not hurt."

I refused to read anything into the remark. I watched Bollywood movies sometimes with my parents. I enjoyed them, but they were way too corny to be believable, especially the hero and heroine's first meeting. Their instant desire symbolized by long, drawn-out pauses while some romantic melody echoed and the camera shifted dramatically between them, capturing their intense, angst-ridden faces. It didn't seem so ridiculous to me now. He was seducing me with those eyes.

People passed us with hurried steps, scattering my papers even farther down the hall. *What am I supposed to be doing?* I couldn't remember, especially when he dragged his hand through that thick, sandy brown hair, pushing it away from where it lay so artfully on his forehead. It all sprang right back into place with stubborn precision, causing my throat to go dry. He didn't seem as affected, though. He looked calm and collected, unlike me who was in danger of melting into the linoleum.

Some guy bumped me with his laptop bag. I stumbled forward, but my Bollywood babe's steady hands braced me tighter, preventing another collision.

"Watch it!" he said to my aggressor with clear irritation. It wasn't the guy's fault. We were in the middle of a narrow hallway—static objects in a high-traffic zone.

He gently pushed me away from the stream of hurried students until I felt the cool, cement wall pressed against my back. I was grateful for something to lean on, but it felt like an act of protection and far too intimate a gesture for this kind of exchange. I watched like a helpless fool as he bent down to gather up my scattered pages, carefully sifting through them. Not a lot of guys would have picked up the papers let alone arranged my essay in page order. He even took time to fix the few sheets that fell victim to crumples by placing them on his knee and running his large hand against the paper to smooth them out.

People parted for him, careful to step around him. He commanded that kind of presence even in a kneeling position. A few slowed their steps to say hello, especially the girls. I did my best to ignore them and hold in my scowl. He returned their greetings in a sincere, easy-going way that I admired. His grin conveyed mischief and innocence as he handed the orderly stack back to me. God help me, I almost fanned myself with the damn things!

"I've heard Cronin takes off points if you don't use APA style," he said in a deep, raspy, masculine tone that made me shiver. How did he make something ordinary sound so sexy? His voice was a low-cadenced combination of rough gravel under a rhythmic flowing river.

"But I did," I insisted, speaking a little louder than I needed to. As he drew nearer, though, my determination crumbled and my knees started shaking. I prayed he wouldn't notice. He was taller than me, so I tilted my head to look at him, probably not the brightest idea. I could feel the heat of his body as it invaded mine in an invisible airborne assault. *What is wrong with me?* I didn't have these reactions to boys.

He's different, but why?

"Paragraphs aren't indented," he said.

I snapped out of my ridiculous thoughts. *Crap! He's right.*

"It's too late to fix it." I willed my hands to stop trembling so I wouldn't drop the papers again.

"Maybe not. When do you have class?" He looked at his watch, which probably cost more than six credit hours. It was an elegant, expensive, silver thing, modern but classic, without being flashy. It contrasted with his simple black Henley and well-worn jeans. It was strange how all the items fit him even though they didn't necessarily go together.

I looked down at my own cheap watch, grateful for the distraction from his chiseled face. I cursed myself again. "Like now." I held my papers to my chest and tried to veer around him, but he shifted, blocking me.

"Let me help you hold it together."

What? Am I that apparent? "I have to g-go," I stammered, trying to move past him again.

"Let me fix it," he replied in a quiet but authoritative voice that made me feel like one of the Pied Piper's mice. *Fix it?* Was he planning to alleviate my sexual anxiety in the hallowed hallways of the Landau Economics Building?

He reached into the messenger bag slung across his shoulder. I almost gasped until I saw the single red paperclip he held. I wasn't sure if I was frustrated or relieved. He didn't take the papers again but let me hold them while he secured it. It seemed they were conducting heat like a torch, slowly burning my fingertips.

"Now you won't have to worry if you slam into someone else before making it to class."

"Thank you, but I wasn't planning on doing that."

"Good. I like that I'm the only one you planned on hurling yourself at, M Kapoor."

He noticed the way I signed my papers. He was waiting for my whole name, but I wasn't giving it.

"I didn't plan to bump into you either."

"I guess it was my lucky day, then, Sunshine."

Sunshine? Was he really calling me that? Internal or external, there was nothing sunshiny about me. The term would be appropriate for little, freckled-faced kids with toothy smiles and pale, waif-like girls with long blond tresses. I was neither. What's more, I was snarky and sullen. *Nope, no sunshine here, buddy.* I slipped past him and walked away with speedy steps, except this time I looked where I was going.

"Hey, I think we have a class together," he shouted.

"I guess I'll see you there."

"Goodbye, girl-who-bumps-into-strangers. I only call you that because I don't know your name."

Yes, and I won't give it because hearing it said out loud by your deep, sexy voice will make me lose whatever dignity I have left.

I smiled at his description, feeling more myself as each step carried me farther away from his beautiful face, sculpted muscles, and boyish grin.

"See you later, gorgeous-boy-who-picks-up-and-arranges-clumsy-girls'-essays," I muttered under my breath when I was out of earshot.

Of course, I knew who he was. Ethan Callahan, the boy who sat in the back row of Advanced Statistics. The same boy who made frequent cameos in my daydreams. I hated that he sat in the back of the lecture hall. I only saw him enter and exit the classroom. I wanted to see him enter and exit other things…like me. *Wow, where the hell did that insane thought come from?* Maybe I had a concussion from ramming my head into his chest. *That would explain it, right?*

Except I'd been harboring these naughty ideas since I'd first seen him. Rachael would be proud. I was smut thinking, and it wasn't like me at all. In fact, the last time I'd crushed on anyone was years ago.

I was a good little Indian girl. Ethan Callahan was a dangerous detour that I needed to avoid. I refused to break my vows of being the ideal daughter, especially when I was so close to fulfilling my parents' wishes. I'd already made too many deposits into the sizeable bank of their endless suffering. The promise wasn't something I'd ever shared with anyone else. Nonetheless, it was a solemn oath, made to myself, signed by my hands, and inked with my brother's blood.

2

Ethan

dvanced Statistics was now my favorite course. *How have I never noticed how beautiful she is?*

She sat in the front row by herself, which was good and bad—good because she couldn't see me staring at her and bad because I couldn't see her pretty face. She had skin was the color of rich caramel and perfect, almond-shaped eyes that reminded me of hot melted chocolate. Yeah, she looked delicious. I wanted to run my fingers through that shiny black hair. I bet it fell to the center of her back when she had it down, but I'd only seen it worn one of three ways—tight, precise braid; high, swinging ponytail; and, my personal favorite, the loose bun. The loose bun came complete with runaway strands, begging to be played with.

Her name was still a mystery, so I just called her Sunshine. I'd never called a girl that before, but it fit because she made me feel warm, calm, and happy. I'd never seen her smile, but I knew it would be a beautiful sight. She had full, luscious lips that could coax poetry, even from a dry-witted math major like myself. *Who am I kidding?* I wasn't capable of more than a few words in the presence of that sexy mouth of hers. It was ironic how something that created speech made me speechless.

She always wore jeans and a shapeless T-shirt, but that didn't fool me. There were valuable assets under all that fabric. I'd felt those soft curves firsthand when she knocked into me. It wasn't entirely her fault, although I hadn't admitted it. She'd been looking down at her papers, walking too fast, and I'd been watching her, enjoying the view. Naturally, our gravitational pull caused a collision.

"Stare harder and you'll go blind," my buddy Alex whispered.

"You're original," I said, forcing myself to look away from her just when she started twirling a piece of that shiny hair around her finger. *Shit, when did I become a crazy stalker?*

"And you're obvious. Hope you're enjoying your dreams, because that's the only place you'll get to do the stuff you're thinking."

"Like you know what I'm thinking."

He gave me a cynical look that told me he knew exactly which head was doing the thinking.

"Why can't it happen? She's real. Isn't she?" I asked.

"She's real, but I'd give it up now."

Professor Malkin cleared his throat, staring in our direction. I clamped my mouth shut, trying to lay off the urge to torture Alex into spilling all his inside information on my Sunshine.

When class let out, I grabbed Alex's arm before he started packing up. "What do you know, Goldberg?"

Alex stared at me like he was trying to figure out if it was a serious question. I wanted to shake the answers out of him until they fell like high-hanging fruit. "She was in my chemistry class. She's Indian."

"So, why does that matter?"

"Reese Denton asked her out and got denied."

"So? That means she has good taste. Denton's a dickhead."

"She told him she doesn't date. She's conservative, which means she doesn't hang out, and she doesn't do any of the dirty things you want to do with her, Callahan."

"I just want to know her, asshole."

Alex laughed it off. "Besides, I think she already has a boyfriend."

"You just said she doesn't date."

"I know, but there's a guy she's always with. Obviously, he's Indian too."

"Just because she hangs out with him doesn't mean they're together. He could be her brother."

"What part of 'she's Indian' are you not getting? Girls like her don't just hang around guys."

"Priya dates," I said, referring to our mutual friend.

"Priya is the exception. Meena is the rule."

"Her name is Meena?" I leaned forward. Why didn't I ask him that first? Oh, it was because I liked calling her Sunshine, but Meena was nice too...very nice. "Meena," I repeated, liking the way her name rolled off my tongue. Simple but sexy. I scrawled it down on my scribble pad next to all my other moronic ranting.

"Come on, idiot. You're going to make me late for my next class."

I walked with him, but I kept thinking about her. I had to know her, or at the very least, see her smile...just once. Yeah, it was going to be my new mission. It might be a lame goal, but small steps were the easiest. That was the way I lived my life—as a path of achievable objectives that led to bigger payoffs. It was a philosophy that worked for me. It got me a near-perfect grade-point average, a slew of friends, and a future ripe with possibilities. *Maybe it would get me a little Sunshine too.*

I'd never had issues talking to girls before. Usually, they approached me. I didn't consider myself narcissistic, but I knew I was good-looking. Hell, I'd received such compliments from females all my life, but Meena was different. It wasn't her culture, or the possibility that she might have a boyfriend, but the sorrow in those large, brown eyes. I was no psychologist, but it was apparent that along with her baggy clothes, the girl wore a shroud of misery. Misery was not something I'd ever been attracted to, but in this case, I felt a strong impulse to cure her of it. With all of those thoughts in my head, and my need to organize them, you'd think I'd have been more prepared.

I waited until after our next class and raced down the aisle, taking two steps at a time so she wouldn't be so far ahead of me. "Excuse me," I said, chasing after her. She walked fast. She headed out the double doors exiting the building. I sped up to catch her and shouted, "Meena."

She stopped, pausing before turning around. She didn't seem surprised that I knew her name. She tapped her foot in an annoyed gesture, clutching her textbook as if it were a life raft. It was completely opposing body language, and definitely not the reaction I expected.

"You figured out my name."

I nodded, taking a few more steps to close in the gap between us. "Girl-who-bumps-into-strangers is just too many words."

"I guess we're not strangers, then, Ethan."

Shit! I could feel myself growing hard as my name spilled from her sexy mouth. It sounded flirty, but her posture was too stiff to support that idea. She pressed her lips together, like she was trying to keep them in place, although the corners of her mouth bent up just a tiny bit. *Come on, baby, smile for me.*

"Guess not, Sunshine."

She shifted her eyes downward. I was making her uncomfortable. "What can I do for you?"

It was a very dangerous question, and I forced myself not to blurt something sexual. I needed to find the right way to reassure her because, at this point, my window of opportunity wasn't just closing — it was shattering. *Play it cool, Callahan. She won't appreciate it if you come on too strong. It'll make her run away.*

We were a foot apart in the warm California sunshine. The breeze carried all the sweet scents of her toward me. It was vanilla, and not the fake stuff you bought in the bottle, but the actual bean, and something else…maybe coconut? *Damn, she's making me hungry!* I searched my inventory of friendly phrases for anything that seemed acceptable. *I've got nothing.*

I held my ink pen toward her. "Did you drop this?"

She looked down at the cheap pen indented with my teeth marks and back at me. Her lips curled in a slight smile. I sucked in some air between my teeth. *Did I just make her smile?* It wasn't a full smile, more like an amused grin, but fuck it, I was taking the win.

"No, that's not mine, but good luck finding the owner."

She turned to walk away, but I wasn't ready to let her go. "Are you sure? I thought I saw you drop it."

She turned back toward me, the half-hearted smile faltering a little as if the expression didn't feel natural. "I only use pencils."

"Why is that?"

"I like to erase my mistakes," she replied before rushing off and disappearing into the crowd.

What does that mean? Was it something deeper, or did we really just have a mundane conversation about writing utensil preferences? Alex was right. I was a total idiot. Even though I never had any trouble finding a date, I definitely lacked the skills to charm this honey. It wasn't going to stop me, though.

Okay, new goal. I wanted a huge smile next time, and maybe even a laugh too. I could make that happen. I was willing to work for it.

The next day, I waited for Darren outside Tresidder Union. As usual, he was running late. I spotted him, combing through his floppy mop of curly hair and looking thoroughly pissed off. That could only mean one thing. He found my present.

"You're late. Were you primping?" I asked with a wide grin. I'd found a hair straightener in the bathroom a few weeks ago. At first I thought it might be some sort of hand-held mini panini press. Once I'd figured it out, Alex and I gave him a ton of shit over it, threatening to revoke his man card. What guy straightens his hair? To his credit, Darren took it in stride, claiming that man-primping was a necessity these days.

"Funny, shithead. Mandy found the box of douche."

"I was trying to be a good friend."

He jerked his head in confusion.

"Since you grew a vagina overnight, I thought you might want to primp that new pussy." It was the most embarrassing purchase I'd ever made, but totally worth it. I only wished I'd seen him holding that package, decorated in pink flowers. "Are you all fresh now?"

"Not cool, bro. She thought I was cheating on her."

That was a dumb thing for Mandy to think, but I couldn't blame her. Darren was an asshole of a boyfriend. Still, I hadn't meant for my joke to backfire like this.

"Did she really think a girl left that in our apartment?"

"I know, right? Girlfriends can be such a bitch." He laughed like it was a clever thing to say.

I sighed, shaking my head. "I think she needs to break up with your douchey ass anyway, but do you want me to talk to her?"

"Nah, we're all good. I told her you had too much time on your hands since you didn't have a girl and all." He liked to rub that in my face, but it never affected me. I wasn't commitment-shy; I was choosy when it came to relationships.

I'd known Darren forever. We'd both decided to go to Stanford, and it only seemed natural as best friends we would room together, although I sometimes questioned that decision. He smoothed his hair once more, and I busted a gut all over again. I had a feeling the days of the mini panini press were over.

Darren narrowed his eyes. "Keep laughing, Callahan." There was a warning in his words…payback's a bitch, and mine was coming.

We walked into the bustling cafeteria. "I forgot how crowded this place gets," I said.

"Yeah, I thought these days were behind us."

We grabbed sandwiches and energy drinks, skipping long lines at the other stations.

"Dude, do you have ten bucks I can borrow?" We were already in the checkout line, so it was obvious he expected me to pay.

"Why didn't you ask before you loaded up your tray? What if I didn't have it?"

"You always have it." It was true—I bailed him out all the time. Still, his assumption pissed the hell out of me.

I paid for our food and looked around the crowded cafeteria for a seat. I spotted a vacant table and started heading toward it before it could be snatched up by blond, Birkenstock-wearing, long-skirted girls who were walking the same way. As soon as I saw *her* though, I stopped in my tracks, causing Darren to bump into me.

Meena was sitting at a table in the far corner next to a guy in a green T-shirt. *The boyfriend?* My jaw clenched, and I gripped the tray so tightly I could feel the heavy plastic bending. Envy was a rare feeling for me. So much so, I had difficulty identifying it at first.

"What the hell, Callahan?" Darren asked, pushing me forward. "All the tables are filling up." The skirts won, staking the table with their soy lattes and woven hemp purses. One smiled, pushing an empty chair toward me. I shook my head politely, thanking her anyway.

"There's someone I want to sit with. Later," I said, heading in her direction.

Darren laughed. "Oh, I get it. Don't worry—I'll be your wingman."

I really didn't want Darren as my wingman, nor did I need him, but I didn't feel like arguing about it, either.

"What girl does ladies' man Ethan Callahan have his eye on?"

I lifted my tray toward Meena, glad she hadn't spotted me yet.

"You have to be kidding, right?"

His question pissed me off. *No one thinks we could be good together…not even her.* "What the hell does that mean?"

"Don't get me wrong—she's cute, very cute, but I don't think she's right for you. Plus, she's with her boyfriend."

"I don't know if he's her boyfriend, but I'm aiming to find out."

"It's pretty obvious he is."

"Why do you say that?"

"She's either Middle-Eastern or Asian, right?"

"Middle-Eastern *is* Asian, dumbass." I only knew she was like sunshine to me and she liked pencils. *Shit—maybe I was the one in need of douche.*

"Whatever she is, he is too. Thusly, they are together." Only Darren would use a word like "thusly."

I was glad for the tray in my hand because I sort of wanted to punch him. "Did you mean that to sound as racist as it did?"

Darren chuckled. "No, man. I'm just saying that's the way these things typically work. Funny how white guys always get blamed for being xenophobic and closed-minded, when people in other cultures are usually the ones to stick with their own kind."

"Do me a favor and don't mention your little theories, okay? In fact, pretend you're mute." I would have told him to sit somewhere else, but there were few choices, and I wasn't mean enough to force his brand of assholery on the pretty, hippy blondes.

Darren shrugged. "Whatever, but don't say I didn't warn you."

We made our way to Meena's table. She looked up at me with a mix of surprised curiosity.

"Hi, can we sit here?" I claimed a space with my tray, and Meena's eyes darted between Darren and me with suspicion. "The other tables are full," I quickly explained.

"It's a free country," she said, gesturing to the empty seats.

I smirked at her attempt at casual indifference, taking the offered chair. Darren took the other.

"I'm Ethan," I said to her companion when she didn't make introductions. I did my best to keep a friendly smile even though we'd most likely be mortal enemies. "This is my friend, Darren Jones." Darren was too busy staring at Meena to introduce himself. She was hot as hell, but I wasn't expecting Darren to be so obvious.

"Hi, Darren, I'm Meena, and this is Raj."

I was hoping she wouldn't introduce him as her boyfriend, but I was disappointed she didn't give him any identification at all.

"Nice to meet you," Raj said, not even bothering to look up at us. He was reading an open book on his lap. *Must be the most riveting story ever written to keep you from noticing two guys gawking at your girl.* Then I saw the writing on his shirt: "Thanks for asking but no…I am not tech support." Damn, that was pretty funny, but he was still my mortal enemy.

"Meena is an interesting name. How do you spell it?" Darren asked.

M-I-N-E, I wanted to say, but I kept my mouth shut while she answered.

"So, what year are you guys?" Darren asked. I was suddenly thankful he was with me. He had a way of not allowing any dead space in conversation, and for the first time, I was grateful for that.

"We're both seniors," Meena answered.

"Us too. What's your major?" Darren asked.

"We're both economics majors. I have a minor in statistics." She was answering for both of them. *Is he shy?* He didn't seem to be, but it still seemed weird that he was content to let her do all the talking.

She didn't ask, but I wanted to tell her anyway. "I'm studying applied mathematics."

"Applied mathematics is a very impressive major." She broke open a bag of popcorn. *Popcorn and salad?* What kind of lunch was that? Then again, I lived on a diet of mac and cheese and energy drinks, so who was I to judge?

I shrugged my shoulders, smiling. "I've always enjoyed math."

"Yeah, he's pretty brilliant. You should ask him about his solution to the food shortage."

I gave Darren a warning look, but it was too late. He was trying to embarrass me. *Hello, payback.*

Meena stared at me, waiting for an answer.

"It's a stupid story, and besides, I was twelve."

"Stupid stories are the best ones," she said.

I ran my hands through my hair, frustrated because this wasn't exactly the best opening, but an opening nonetheless. "I may have done a science fair project where I hypothesized we could end world hunger by utilizing the theories of *Star Trek*'s food replication system."

She laughed. It was a deep, good-natured sound, almost harmonic, and it made me happier just hearing it. *Mission accomplished—even if I was the butt of the joke.* It was worth it. Raj jerked his head up, and even Meena looked surprised at the sound. I'd make her laugh all the time—it was too beautiful to keep locked away.

"What grade did you get?" she asked once the moment had passed.

"He got an A," Darren grumbled, and Meena raised her eyebrows. "Our teacher said he had enough science to warrant it. Kiss up." I grinned at him—his plan to humiliate me failed.

"That's pretty hilarious." She concentrated on her food for a minute, as did Darren. I followed suit. "Did you ever find the owner of that lost pen, Ethan?"

I chuckled, embarrassed by the stupid way I'd approached her, but also enjoying the way she said my name. She took a piece of popcorn and threw it into her mouth with perfect accuracy, chewing it slowly. It was turning me on something fierce.

"Still looking."

"What pen?" Darren asked.

"I found a pen. I thought it was hers. It wasn't."

"Meena doesn't use pens," Raj said. He'd been so quiet, I had almost forgotten he was there.

"She told me as much," I stated, meeting his gaze. He surprised me with a friendly smile.

"I don't know why. I think pens are much easier. No one uses pencils anymore except for standardized tests," Raj explained. It was funny that between the two of us, I was the jealous one. He actually seemed oblivious to the fact I'd pretty much been ogling her since we'd sat down.

"So, what country are you guys from?" Darren asked.

"Country?"

"Yeah, what country?" he said a little louder and slower as if she was hard of hearing.

Meena's lips curled into a smile, and she leaned into the table. I loved her smile, but I hated that it was a reaction meant for Darren. "I'm from the far East." Her response surprised me because she had no trace of an accent. I decided not to interrupt. I just hoped Darren would stop his line of questioning before he made us both appear ignorant.

"I figured that, but what country?" Darren prodded. I fought against the reflex to kick his shin. Darren was good at making conversation, but he could be a real dickhead.

"From a place called Mashpee. Have you ever heard of it?"

"It sounds familiar to me. Do you miss it? I mean being in a different country and all has to be difficult."

Meena was still smiling, but it was a naughty smile, which made it all the cuter. Raj stopped reading to watch her too.

"I do. It's very scenic. You should visit sometime. It borders a few bodies of water, Waquoit and Popponesset."

"Maybe I will. I've always liked traveling. This has got to be a real culture shock for you." Darren said, staring into Meena's eyes.

Despite the fact she was giving him her undivided attention, something in her posture put me at ease. Darren was addicted to flirting, even though it resulted in huge fights between him and Mandy, and he made no apologies for it, claiming it was part of his DNA. I always felt sorry for her, but I knew he'd never cheated. He was just a tool sometimes.

"Oh, it's not so different from here. The weather is different, and the people have funny accents, but we're really very similar."

"Oh yeah? It's strange you don't have an accent."

"I kind of grew out of it."

"What's the thing you miss the most about where you came from?" Darren asked, leaning into the table like they were having a private conversation.

Meena was quiet for a minute, but the corners of her mouth were curling up like she was fighting a smile. "The people are wonderful. They're hard workers and have a strong heritage. I also love the wildlife and being surrounded by water. We're almost an island, you know."

Darren turned to me, wiggling his eyebrows. I had a sinking feeling I knew what was coming. "Sounds tropical and beautiful… just like you." *He was being a douche…because of the douche.*

I wasn't jealous of Darren. It was obvious that coming on this strong wasn't appealing to her. Besides, the way she was eating popcorn was a little too distracting. I'd never thought of popcorn as a sexy food, but it was a freaking aphrodisiac right now.

At least Meena wasn't being flirty with Darren, but Raj's reaction shocked me. He had a wide grin. I hadn't expected him to challenge Darren to a duel or anything, but to smile when some guy was flirting with your girl didn't seem right either.

"Why did you decide to go to school here?"

"What's with all the questions, Katie Couric?" I said a little too sharply, but as usual, Darren ignored me.

"I don't mind. I love that he's so curious." Meena wore a huge grin now. "We have excellent schools where I'm from, but I wanted a change of scenery."

"I'm sure a degree from Stanford holds a great deal of weight there."

"It's definitely impressive, but we do have one of the best schools in the world not too far away. My parents wanted me to go there, but I decided it wasn't for me."

"I'm sure it's a great school in your country, but I doubt it has the international presence of Stanford."

"Oh, I think it does. It boasts some of the most prestigious alumni in the world. The Crimson is very highly rated."

"If it's so great, how come I've never heard of it?" Darren challenged.

I almost smacked my hand against my head when it all clicked into place. My laugh was so rowdy that people at other tables stopped their conversations to look our way. Raj laughed too.

"What's so funny, Callahan?" Darren grumbled.

"She's from Massachusetts, dumbass," I said, relishing the puzzled expression on Darren's face. "The Crimson is Harvard. The people's accent is that funny way Bostonians have of ignoring their Rs. She lives by Cape Cod...right, Meena?"

She nodded. "Yes. I'm sorry, Darren. I wasn't making fun of you. I just couldn't resist."

"You know I was asking where you were originally from, right?" Darren asked, a little too demanding. Unlike me, he couldn't stand to be the butt of jokes.

She didn't shrink back or seemed fazed. "The answer to that question is still Mashpee, Massachusetts. I was born there."

"That's not what I meant."

She straightened up, narrowing those beautiful brown eyes at him. "Why don't you ask the right question, then? You want to know my ethnicity." The straightforward way she put Darren in his place made her lovability quotient grow.

"Yes, I guess. If you want to answer this time."

"Of course. I'm not ashamed, and I never hide it, but your presumptions were far too interesting for me to reply in such an ordinary way. My family originates from Mumbai, India, and I am Hindu. There…now you know all the important things about me."

"I doubt those are the most important things about you, Meena," I said.

The smile slipped off her face when she met my eyes. "They are all the things Darren wanted to know."

"They're checkboxes on a census or standardized test," I replied, locking my eyes on hers with tractor-beam preciseness. She didn't look away. "They don't even scratch the surface of what I want to know." It felt like we were alone in this crowded cafeteria, while everything and everyone disintegrated around us. I could stare at her mysterious, beautiful face for forever and a day if she'd let me.

"What is it you would like to know, Ethan?" she asked in a half-whisper.

I smiled, hoping to reassure her. Why sugarcoat it? "Everything."

She broke our contact, looking down. Raj shifted his chair closer to her. Darren's flirting didn't rattle her, but mine made her uneasy. Maybe because it wasn't meant to be playful.

"I'm from Ahmedabad," Raj interjected in an attempt to change the subject and get me to back off.

"So, you're Hindu…You worship cows?" This time I did kick Darren under the table.

She actually smiled again, looking relieved by the interruption. "Yes, as a matter of fact, I do. They are a revered source of food and a symbol of life for us. Are you Christian?"

"Catholic," Darren replied. It was obvious he wanted to get a rise out of her. Darren had a tendency to succumb to misguided anger when he felt ridiculed.

"So, you worship a virgin?"

Darren laughed sarcastically. "Obviously you don't understand my religion."

Meena's voice was soft but full of conviction. "You pray to Mary. Praying is a form of worshipping—therefore, you worship a virgin. I was making a statement, not passing judgment."

"I wouldn't quite put it like that. I mean, it's kind of funny coming from you. Don't you guys believe in a hundred deities or something?"

I wondered how the conversation became so heated so fast. It was a runaway train, and all I wanted to do was jump on the tracks. "Darren…that's enough. You're acting like a total douche bag," I cautioned.

"I don't mind," Meena said, holding her hand out to dismiss me. "It's hard to answer that since there are many schools of thought, but yes, I suppose we do. Do you believe a man lived inside a fish for three days?"

"Actually it was a whale, just so you know."

"The New Testament says it was a whale, but the Old Testament referred to Jonah being in the belly of a great fish."

"You've read the Bible?" I asked her.

"Yes. I try to read everything that confuses me."

"Apparently it didn't clear anything up for you," Darren said through clenched teeth.

"I doubt the Bhagavad Gita would clear anything up for you either. My point is not to diminish your beliefs or state that mine are any better."

"What is your point?" Darren demanded.

"It's simple, really. All religion is grounded in forms of incredulous implausibility. That's why faith is a prerequisite for any moral belief system, isn't it?"

"It doesn't matter, does it?" I added. "Morality is not confined to religious people, and although it serves as a guiding light for many, it's not the only path. After all, I'm an atheist, and I know I'm a moral person." It was something I seldom talked about, but I wanted her to know that about me.

"Me too," Raj revealed, shocking me for the second time.

Meena smiled at me. I was glad we were in a comfortable place again. "I agree morality is not limited to the faithful. If that were the case, we could blindly trust every priest, monk, or guru out there."

"I don't know whether to be impressed or offended," Darren replied.

"You're allowed to be either or both. As I said when you joined us, it's a free country." She looked down at her watch. I noticed it before, but it still surprised me she had one. Not many people wore watches anymore. It was something we had in common—a small connection, but a connection nonetheless. "We need to get to class. Come on, Raj."

Raj stood up, causing his book to fall next to my feet. I reached down to pick it up, pausing to scan the title before handing it back to him. He stuffed it into his backpack quickly. The small exchange gave me a great deal of information. I relaxed with the realization we were no longer mortal enemies.

"It was nice seeing you again, Meena. You forgive Darren, right?" I asked, smiling like an idiot.

She stood up and walked over to Darren's side of the table, bending down so they were face to face. "Of course. As long as he forgives me. I didn't offend you, right?"

He leaned toward her, and my fist clenched, preparing to punch him if he dared kiss her. "Nah, you're too cute to find offensive."

I exhaled loudly, and they both turned toward me.

"I'll see you in class, Ethan."

I watched them walk away. Actually, I watched Meena. She leaned into Raj, and he put his arm around her. My eyes narrowed as I zeroed in on that arm.

"That was…interesting," Darren said.

"Did you have to be such a shithead?"

"Whatever. She liked me. It doesn't matter anyway. As cute as she is, she's not interested in you. Plus, he's definitely her boyfriend. And she's got him whipped. You got off lucky."

"Yeah, I'm the luckiest guy in the world."

3

Meena

I made my way to class with an anxiety I'd never felt before. I knew I would see him, and even worse, he would see the back of my head. I'd actually checked myself using the two-mirror method to make sure I was presentable. I got the impression he watched me. It sort of excited me, which was a little twisted.

Other boys had flirted with me, but there was something about the way Ethan did it—and my reaction to it—that was dangerous. He had a quiet intensity that amplified his classical good looks. His wavy, sandy brown hair and those ocean-colored eyes caused my usual rigid composure to crumble into a quivering mess of nerves. His crooked smile altered the steady beats of my heart and heated my skin. I had to gulp down a bottle of water after our cafeteria encounter. Part of me liked these new sensations, but most of me worried about it.

I was on a path, and everything was laid out for me in a neat and orderly fashion. I would graduate at the end of this school year, hopefully *summa cum laude*, and then start my interviews. Unlike Rachael, I didn't go to parties or even socialize. I was responsible… and boring too. All of my choices served a purpose, though. I didn't have time for distractions, and Ethan was the epitome of distraction.

For those reasons, I reacted icily when he sat next to me in class. He flashed that boyish grin my way, running his long fingers through his hair, making me wish for temporary blindness.

"Hello, Sunshine," he said, taking out his materials.

"You're sitting here?" I asked, more pointedly than I intended. His smile faltered, and I thawed a bit. He didn't deserve my attitude.

"Looks that way."

"Why?"

"I…ah…oh hell, why not? It's a free country, right?" *Damn, he's using my words against me.*

He seemed to like me, but I couldn't understand why. In that moment, I assumed the worst. "We're not having a test today, so there is no benefit in you sitting here."

He tilted his head. "You think I want to copy off you?" he asked, eyes widening. I looked away, but he leaned in closer. "Trust me—I don't need to copy off anyone. I was actually going to apologize for Darren."

"You don't need to apologize for him. I liked him." He wasn't expecting me to say that, so I added for no particular reason, "So did Raj."

"What's the deal with you guys? Are you together?"

His forwardness surprised me, but his assumption did not. Most people thought Raj and I were together since we always hung out. We didn't correct them either. The idea benefitted both of us.

"It's none of your business, is it?"

"No, I suppose not, but I'm curious." His amused grin only widened.

"I guess you'll have to remain curious."

"What if I told you I was concerned about you?"

"Why would you be concerned about me?"

He dropped his voice to a low whisper, leaning toward me conspiratorially. His pleasant, clean, masculine scent surrounded me, and with shame, I sniffed. "Well, if you were dating, and I don't think you are, but if you were, you should know your boyfriend's gay."

I was having trouble catching my breath all of a sudden. The pencil dropped right out of my hand. He picked it up and handed it back to me.

"How did you know?" I asked in a demanding whisper.

"There were signs."

Raj was very protective and somewhat confused by his orientation. That Ethan had guessed morphed my fear into a form of anger that surprised even me. "What signs, Ethan? Because he has a limp hand-shake? He doesn't. Because he knows how to pair colors and patterns?"

His bottomless blue eyes widened. He opened his mouth to respond, but I cut him off.

"What fucking signs? Tell me." The swearing was so rare for me that I cupped my hand to my mouth.

"Relax, Meena," he said in a gravel-laden whisper that was the perfect mixture of comfort and command. "I figured it out because of the book he was reading. My mother's a psychologist, and she recommends it to her patients who are confused by their sexual orientation. That's all."

I sucked in a deep breath. "You can't tell anyone. Promise me that."

"His secret is safe with me, but I don't understand why he's hiding it. Coming out is almost fashionable these days. We live in California, after all, and it's not uncommon."

I shook my head, backing away from him. "Not for people like us."

Ethan nodded. "So, you knew. You're not dating, then."

It made no sense to continue with the charade. "No, we're just friends."

Ethan exhaled, which was strange since it hadn't even looked like he'd been holding his breath.

"That's a relief," he said, tilting his head and smiling optimistically.

"Why do you say that?"

"Because I'd like to ask you out."

"Out where?" *Oh crap, he means a date.* I got that about two seconds too late.

He shrugged. "I don't care. Anywhere you want. Lunch, dinner, brunch, high tea, low tea, coffee, pretzels in the park, dancing in the dark, sightseeing at sunset?"

I couldn't help but laugh at his long list, but I looked away from his penetrating gaze so I could concentrate on my response and not his striking blue eyes. "Thank you, but I don't date."

"We'll go as friends then," he replied nonchalantly.

"I already have two friends." *Did I really just say that aloud?* I shut my eyes, wishing I could press the rewind button on my stupid mouth. His laugh echoed through the lecture hall. People had to be staring at us.

"Do you have a quota on friends?"

"That's the wrong word. A quota would imply a minimum. I have a maximum. I'm very busy, and I have two close friends. I don't need another, but thank you for your interest."

"You won't even let me apply for the job of your friend?" He raked his fingers through his hair, making it a perfect blend of messy beautiful, which sounded like a contradiction, but it was the only way to describe it.

"There are no openings at this time," I stated sternly. It didn't deflate his wide smile though.

"Is it okay if I check back? You know, to see if you have any vacancies? I'm really very interested in the position, and I promise not to let you down. I'm well qualified and can even provide references."

I felt heat rush into my face. Although I was tan, there were rare occasions when I blushed. This was one of them.

Professor Malkin entered just then, and everyone quieted down. He immediately turned our attention to the graphs on the overhead. This class was difficult for me, so I did my best to pay attention, but it was challenging with Ethan's clean scent lingering in the small space between us.

After class, Professor Malkin asked us to approach his desk so he could hand back our tests. Ethan stood behind me, and I did my best to ignore him, despite the fact that he was very close—about the distance of a ream of paper. My body yearned for a smaller gap, like a single sheet, while my brain wanted the expanse of the Pacific between us. I bit my lip, ordering the racy thoughts out of my head, but that only made them worse.

Professor Malkin handed me back my test. "Meena, you seem to be having trouble with this new material. I think you should come see me during my office hours."

I stared at the B- on my paper in disgust. I had to get my grades up before report cards went out. My parents would kill me. An A- was irritating, but a B-…Well, to my parents, it was one step away from dealing meth. The legend of the Asian F was true, and a B- was on the fast track to failure.

"I have class during your office hours, Professor." I lowered my head, unable to meet Professor Malkin's disappointed gaze.

"Well, then, I suggest you get a tutor. This is not your usual stellar work."

I murmured a pathetic apology, clutching my paper as I walked out of class.

"I could help you," Ethan said, keeping step beside me. My embarrassment increased exponentially—he'd heard the whole exchange.

"I don't need your help," I replied, willing my feet to move faster.

"Are you sure about that?" He managed to move in front of me, making me stop before I bumped into him. He held up his own paper with the large A sprawled across the front in big red marker. "Or maybe you just want to cheat off me?"

I gaped at him, at a loss for words. He definitely put me in my place.

"Get a cup of coffee with me, Sunshine. Let me help you."

"Why would you want to help me?" If anything, I'd been rude to him.

He smiled crookedly. "I'm applying for a pretty prestigious job. I think this will earn me some brownie points."

I couldn't help but smile. I had never been comfortable around boys, but he put me at ease with his sense of humor and easygoing personality. Unfortunately, his tall, muscular frame, wavy hair, sapphire eyes, and cocky grin did just the opposite.

Ethan and I walked to a coffee shop on campus. He ordered a plain coffee, black. I ordered green tea, iced.

"I didn't think anyone drank black coffee anymore."

"I like to keep it simple."

It took about half an hour, but Ethan was very good at explaining the concepts I'd missed. It was easy to see he was brilliant. Unfortunately, that attracted me to him even more. How could he be so good-looking, smart, and funny at the same time? It wasn't lost on me that several girls had come by to say hi to him, including our barista, which was unusual since this was a counter service place.

"Thank you for your help. I really appreciate it, and thank you for keeping Raj's secret too. This is on me." I pulled out my wallet, placing a few bills on the table. I reached for my backpack.

His voice stopped me. "That's it? I thought maybe this would get me an interview at least."

"Interview?"

"Yeah, you know, for my application. I think I would have at least made it to the interview stage."

I laughed at his brashness. "Look, Ethan, you've been very nice to me, but I'm serious when I say you won't get what you want from me, so it's better to drop it now."

He narrowed his eyes, but his smile didn't waver. "And what is it you think I want?"

I swallowed, steadying my hands. "I told you I don't date."

"I told you we could just be friends."

"I know how this works. Despite my heritage, I'm not off the boat you know."

He laughed deeply, which for some strange reason put me at ease. "Exactly, so I don't understand why you have a friendship limitation. Help me understand."

I clenched my teeth, not sure how to extricate myself from this gorgeous, strange boy who was doing horrible things to my self-control. "Okay, Ethan, you wanted an interview. I'll give you one."

He smiled eagerly, like the most adorable little boy.

"Why do you want to be my friend?"

"I think you're interesting. I like talking to you."

"If we hypothetically entered into a friendship, what is your ultimate goal?"

"Who says I have a goal?"

"There is always a goal with any endeavor."

"Maybe my goal is to make you smile more. Isn't that an admirable goal?"

I stared in stunned silence while he smiled at me expectantly. His smile was infectious though, and I couldn't help but match it.

"See? I'm succeeding already."

I sucked in a deep breath, feeling the smile transform back into the grim expression I usually wore. "Interview's over," I said, grabbing my backpack.

"What is it that precludes me from being your friend, Sunshine?"

I melted when he called me that, but I'd lay a wager he assigned that moniker to all the girls. I swallowed hard, not sure how to explain myself. "You're a really nice guy, but—"

"It sounds like you're breaking up with me already."

I gave him a cynical smile. He straightened up, lacing his long fingers together on the table.

"You're a math major," I said, "so you understand the importance of balance. Every equation has to equal out, and we don't. Not on any level. We don't fit. Not as anything. Not even friends. Do you understand?"

Ethan's eyes lit up, and his sexy lips curled in a playful smile. "I can't lie. You're turning me on something fierce with that math analogy, especially one so Euclidean in nature. Honestly, though, I can't say I understand since correlation does not equal causation. If anything, mathematics provides logic for my argument."

"How so?"

"A and B are different variables, but together they always equal C, right? A and B are rarely equal. You're implying that you and I are on opposite sides of the equation, but we're not. We are both on the same side, working toward C. C represents the culmination of our friendship. But, Meena, if we're not friends, then we'll never find C, will we? Don't you want to solve for C?" He held out his hands in some sort of invitation to me. It was so adorably sexy I almost forgot my point. *He is actually turning me on...with math.*

I shouldn't have brought up math to a math major. "Sometimes C has no solution."

"Every problem has a solution. It's just that some are so complicated they haven't been solved yet, but that doesn't mean they can't be."

"I have to go. Thanks again." I grabbed my stuff and rushed off before he had a chance to respond.

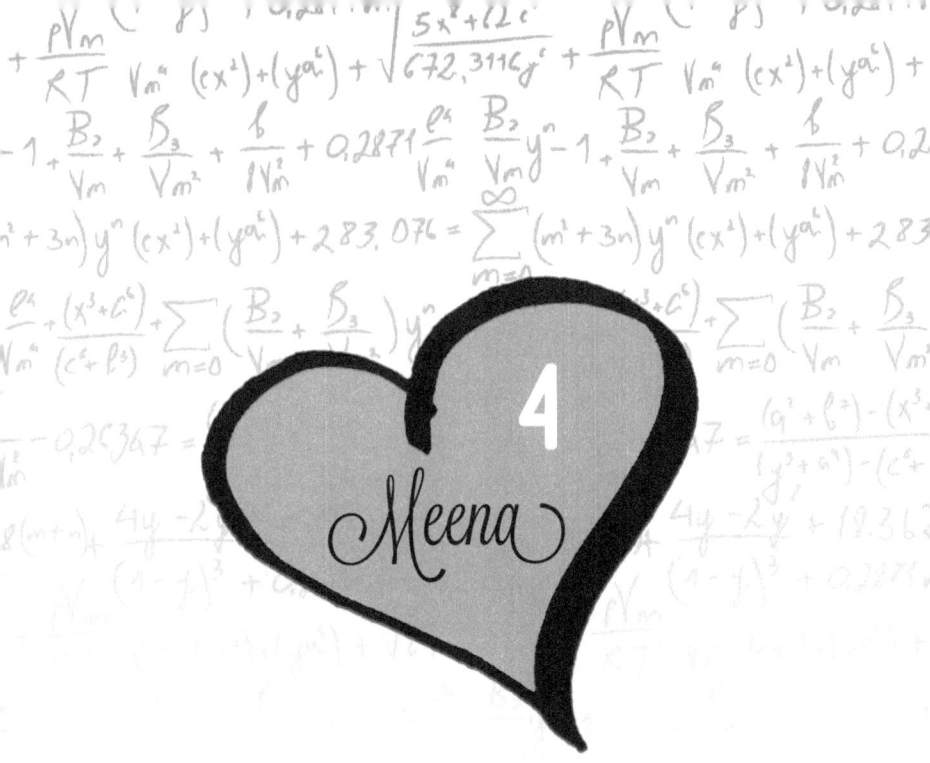

$$+ \frac{p V_m}{RT} \; V_m^a \; (\epsilon x^2) + (y a^6) + \sqrt{\frac{5x^2 + 12 c}{672, 3116 g^2}} + \frac{p V_m}{RT} \; V_m^a \; (\epsilon x^2) + (y a^6) +$$

$$-1 + \frac{B_2}{V_m} + \frac{B_3}{V_m^2} + \frac{b}{1 V_m^2} + 0.2871 \frac{\rho^4}{V_m^a} \; \frac{B_2}{V_m} y^n - 1 + \frac{B_2}{V_m} + \frac{B_3}{V_m^2} + \frac{b}{1 V_m^2} + 0.2$$

$$n^2 + 3n) y^n (\epsilon x^2) + (y a^6) + 283.076 = \sum_{m=0}^{\infty} (m^3 + 3n) y^n (\epsilon x^2) + (y a^6) + 283$$

4

Meena

"Doesn't Keith look hot?" Rachael asked, fanning her porcelain skin with a movie magazine. She leaned back on the picnic table, letting her crimson locks fall down her back.

"Sure," I agreed although I wasn't paying attention.

Raj, Rachael, and I sat at the wooden picnic table at an off-campus park, watching a rugby match. Rachael's latest boy toy, Keith, invited her. She came because she wanted to appear supportive. She'd dragged us along because she didn't want to get bored.

I had no idea why we indulged her since it was just a matter of time before she broke up with this one. She rarely stayed with the same guy for more than a few weeks. Rachael was loud, brash, and bright. She was the complete opposite of my rigidity and Raj's timidity, but that's what made the three of us work so well.

Rachael and Raj were my two best friends. Despite the fact Raj and I shared the same culture and Rachael and I hailed from the same small town, we were an unlikely trio. Still, we relied on and confided in each other. I would have told them about my feelings for Ethan, but I was having a difficult time understanding them myself, let alone articulating them to someone else.

It had been a few days since Ethan and I'd had coffee, but he had taken up all the valuable space in my head. I remembered the strangest things about him — how long his fingers were, the way his hair swept across his face, and the various shades of blue captured in his eyes. I was so captivated with these thoughts that when I saw him, I thought I was dreaming. He ran down the field in a black and white striped rugby shirt and loose shorts, flexing the muscles in his powerful legs. Although he was dressed like all the other players, I recognized his tall, muscular frame right away.

"Can't say I'm not enjoying myself," Raj said, gesturing to the field. I had to agree. We were away from the stands. It was close enough to watch, but far enough not to be heard. I doubted Ethan had seen me, which was good since I was pretty much leering. He was very athletic and had managed to score some points, or goals, or touchdowns, or whatever they called it in rugby. I didn't know, but I was still in awe of it.

"I like this better than football. No padding, but the pants could be tighter," Rachael said.

"Actually they're called scrum shorts and designed to withstand all the tackling and grabbing," Raj said. Both Rachael and I stared at him, mouths gaping. He shrugged. "I boned up."

"I'm sure you're all boned up, Rajesh," Rachael said, winking at him.

Raj's laughter was so surprising, it momentarily distracted me, but then my eyes darted across the field to find Ethan again. I was happy I came today. This way, I could watch and enjoy him without any discomfort. Any kind of relationship with Ethan Callahan was off limits. He was like an expensive work of art roped off with velvet.

Suddenly, Rachael stood up and clapped. I looked down, not wanting to draw attention to myself. "Did you see that? Keith scored."

"Meena's not looking at anyone else on that field except Ethan Callahan."

In one sweeping move, Rachael dropped down from her perch on the table to the seat next to me. "Ethan Callahan? What have you been keeping from me, karma girl?" she asked, wiggling her eyebrows suggestively.

I shrugged my shoulders. I was embarrassed, but I knew better than to give in to it.

This piece of info was like catnip for Rachael. "Do you think he's cute?"

"She does," Raj answered before I could.

"I do not!"

Raj laughed. "Then why the hell are you staring at him so hard? Are you testing your psychic powers?"

"How do you know him?" Rachael asked me.

I told the condensed version of the class we shared and our run in at the cafeteria. Raj interjected, adding unnecessary embellishments about Ethan drooling over me. Surely I would have noticed drool. Ethan was too calm and collected to have any such reaction, especially over me.

"So, answer my original question. Do you think he's cute?" Rachael asked, bumping my shoulder.

"Yes," I replied, rolling my eyes. "It doesn't mean anything."

"It means everything," she said. "You never think anyone is cute. You don't even think Johnny Depp is cute, and I've had boyfriends that could admit that." Raj started laughing, but Rachael silenced him with her snarky glare. "And, no, they were not gay."

"Are you sure?" Raj asked, raising his eyebrows.

"Trust me. You're my only turncoat." We all shared a mutual laugh over Rachael's reference to her and Raj's failed sexual experiment in determining his orientation. Actually, maybe it was a success. I wasn't quite sure. Whatever it was, it somehow bonded them. He was grateful to her, and she felt protective of him as a result. Rachael turned back to me.

"He asked me out," I said.

Rachael squealed. It was a high-pitched unnatural sound, and even some of the players noticed.

I patted her knee. "Calm down. I said no."

She frowned. "Meena, live a little. You're not off the market yet."

"I was never *on* the market. Besides, I don't like him like that. I just think he's cute, that's all. It's an observation."

Rachael rolled her eyes, and I braced for another stern lecture about how I needed to loosen up. "I know Ethan Callahan," she said, staring straight ahead. "He's the kind of guy even smart girls get into catfights over. He's sexy, smart, and athletic. I hear he's well-off, too."

She sighed wistfully, staring in Ethan's direction, "Yep, he's a total package any girl would love to unwrap, if you know what I mean."

My mouth went dry, and my hands clenched into tight fists. "How do you know him?"

She smiled with fake innocence. "I've seen him at parties. We have some mutual friends. I'd call him an acquaintance."

"How *well* do you know him?" I asked. The question came out much sharper than I'd intended, or maybe it was exactly as I'd intended.

She leaned back, crossing her legs. "You're asking if I've slept with him?"

"I guess so."

"Because I'm a slut, right?"

"Frankly, yes," I replied, crossing my arms. I didn't like the idea of Ethan and Rachael together at all.

Raj busied himself with his phone. He always stayed out of conflicts like this between Rachael and me, but in reality, they weren't hostile. We were brutally honest with each other, and neither of us approved of the other's lifestyle. Raj hid who he was, and Rachael showed someone she wasn't. I fit right into the middle of those two things. Either way, I was grateful we'd all found each other. It was in the bluntness of that honesty that our friendship bloomed.

"If I told you I fucked him, would it make you like him less?"

"I don't know. Maybe."

Rachael's satisfied grin spread from ear to ear.

"What?"

"I knew you liked him. You just admitted it."

I pushed her away. "You tricked me."

"Relax, Meena. I haven't slept with him, though I wouldn't mind."

"Rachael!"

"Don't worry—you know I'm a slut with ethics. Now that I know you like him, it's hands off. Chicks before dicks and all that."

"You're so gross!" I was about to tell Rachael she could have him because I couldn't, but I snapped my mouth shut. That was the last thing I wanted to say.

Since we were on the topic of Ethan, I'd come clean about everything. My face became serious as I stared up at Raj sitting on the tabletop. I didn't know how he would react, or if this was even the right venue for this conversation, but I'd avoided it too long. "Raj, he knows about you. I swear I didn't tell him, but he figured it out anyway. He says he won't tell anyone, and I believe him. But I wanted you to know…Ethan knows you're gay." I whispered the words even though I doubted anyone was listening. I expected Raj to freak, but he didn't seem fazed at all.

"Raj doesn't even know if Raj is gay," Rachael said dryly.

"Raj is pretty sure he's gay," Raj said.

We both gaped at him. I'd known this boy since I was a freshman, and he'd questioned his homosexuality for so long it was shocking to hear him make such a definitive statement. He smiled impishly at Rachael and me, before jumping off the bench and sitting in the small space between us. He was very thin, so he just fit into the snug area. He placed an arm around each of us. "I kissed a boy, and I liked it."

I gasped, and Rachael chuckled. "What?"

"A boy in my Macro class asked me out for coffee. Afterward, we went to his car and talked."

"You kissed him?" I asked.

"He kissed me. It was nice."

"Are you going to see him again?" Rachael asked.

"Um…actually, I just got a text from him. He wants to meet up. Would you guys mind if I bailed?" I felt him stiffen beside me, like he was trying to keep his emotions from spilling out.

"Yeah, go ahead. Keith can give us a ride back," Rachael offered. I wasn't very comfortable with the idea, but I couldn't protest. I was too happy for Raj.

Raj smacked a kiss on each of our cheeks before standing up.

"Wait, what about Ethan knowing? Aren't you upset at all?"

Raj simply shrugged, the smile on his face only deepening, showing off his dimples. "I don't think he's the type of guy to blab. He seems cool."

I let out a long sigh. Rachael and Raj both looked at me questioningly.

"Meena, stop worrying so much. You're going to get an ulcer," Raj warned.

He was right. All my muscles relaxed at once, and I felt foolish for being so tense in the first place, especially when Raj was so calm.

Rachael and I clung to each other, smiling like loons, as if we were watching our baby bird take his first flight. Because we were so distracted, neither of us noticed Keith approach with Ethan by his side.

"Hey, baby," Keith said, sitting next to Rachael. He pulled her in for a long kiss. I looked away from them, not wanting to invade their moment. Unfortunately, my eyes landed on Ethan's chiseled face, complete with boyish grin.

That was a big mistake, because I had to take a deep breath at the sight of him. His golden brown locks were slightly damp, and his face was flushed with a light sheen of sweat. His shirt clung to him, outlining the tightly coiled muscles underneath. *Crap…even his sweat smells good.* He curled his lips into a huge grin.

"Hi, Meena."

"Hello," I said, wanting to evade his eyes but unable to look away.

"Oh, Ethan, I didn't see you there," Rachael mused, disentangling herself from Keith's grip. "I forgot you know my roommate."

I tried not to react sarcastically to Rachael's innocent act.

"You guys are roommates?" Ethan asked, arching his brow. It was a common reaction, but usually people were surprised Rachael picked me. Ethan was probably surprised I picked Rachael.

"Since freshman year," Rachael announced as if it was an accomplishment. In many ways, it was. "And best friends too."

"Oh, so you must be friend number one then. I'm applying for the job of friend number three. Will you put in a good word for me?"

Keith and Rachael both gaped at Ethan. I bit my lower lip so hard to keep from grinning I almost drew blood.

"Huh?" Rachael asked.

"It's nothing. Are you ready to go?" I asked, gathering Rachael's supplies, placing them back into her bag. It was like she was going on an overnight trip with the assortment of sunglasses, sunscreen, magazines, snacks, and water bottles.

"Yeah, can you give us a ride, Keith?"

Keith put his hand on the back of his neck, rocking back and forth on his feet. He was a nice guy with a shoulder-length mane of blond hair that would have been considered a hippie cut anywhere else in the country but fit perfectly in California. I felt sorry for him.

Nice guys didn't last long with Rachael. Once she realized they wanted her as much as she wanted them, she dumped them. I never understood it, but Rachael loved a good race, especially when it involved chasing lust. It was her drug, and like most addictions, it wore off fast, so she had to up her dose frequently. She didn't date bad boys specifically, but she required a variety nonetheless.

"Sure, but I brought my motorcycle today, so I'll have to make two trips."

I stopped cleaning up to stare at Rachael and Keith. "That's okay. I can walk." I would walk a thousand miles before I got on the back of a motorcycle.

"I can give Meena a ride," Ethan said.

"Awesome. Thanks, man," Keith replied, keeping his eyes glued to Rachael's.

Rachael finally snapped out of her daze, turning to me for confirmation. I didn't want to be alone with Ethan. It wasn't that I didn't like him. In fact, it was just the opposite, and that made me nervous, but I didn't want to be a third wheel to Rachael and Keith either. In fact, I couldn't be. There was no wheel for me. Living in Stanford was expensive, and neither Rachael nor I had a car. It wasn't uncommon, and usually everything was within walking distance so it wasn't impractical, except for times like this.

"Good, it's all settled then," Ethan confirmed, smiling at me.

"Meena, does that work for you?" I was glad Rachael asked. I was beginning to wonder if I was invisible. I sometimes felt like I was.

"It's fine. I'll see you later." I handed the bag to her, and she immediately handed it back.

"Can you take it? There will be no room for it on the bike. We'll probably go for a drive." That meant I wouldn't see her for the rest of the day.

"Sure, we can take it," Ethan said, taking the bag from me. I laughed as he hung the bright pink bag covered in silly pictures of kissing lips across his broad shoulder along with his black duffle. But he didn't seem to find it uncomfortable.

"Be careful, and text me when you stop," I said to Rachael. She sighed but nodded in agreement. As soon as Rachael and Keith left, I told Ethan, "It was a nice offer, but you don't need to give me a ride. I can walk."

"It's about two miles back to the dorms." How did Ethan know I lived in the dorms? Then again, mostly everyone did, even the seniors.

Renting a place off campus just wasn't economical for most students, including Rachael and me.

"I like to walk. It's a nice day."

"Every day is a nice day in Palo Alto."

I shot him a sarcastic glance, but he was right. It was pretty much always beautiful.

"Why don't we compromise? We can go for a walk, and then I'll give you a ride."

"How is that a compromise?" I placed my palms on my hips, wiping them on my jeans. *Why are they so damp?*

"Well, you just said you liked to walk, and I'd like to give you a ride. Now, you get to do both. It's the perfect compromise. Come on — I'll show you something cool." He jerked his head toward the exit of the park, smirking at me.

He started walking, not giving me a chance to protest again, taking Rachael's silly bag with him. I stood there for a second. When I finally started following him, I had to run to catch up. *How did this happen?*

"Hungry? Want a hot dog?" he asked, gesturing to a nearby vendor.

"I'm a vegetarian."

He grinned, shrugging his shoulders. "Want a hot dog bun?"

I laughed but shook my head. "No, thanks." He walked up to the vendor anyway and ordered two water bottles. He handed one to me. I was completely parched, so I thanked him for the drink as we walked.

"Tell me about friend number one and two."

"Why do you want to know?"

"I like to know who my competition is."

"It's not like if they stop being my friend, I'll have a place for you. It doesn't work that way."

"Okay, then tell me how they managed to attach themselves to you. I want some inside information."

I laughed at Ethan's odd way of putting things. He didn't think like most people. I liked that about him. "Rachael and I are both from Mashpee."

"So, you were friends in high school?"

"No, we were in different circles." In actuality, by the time Rachael moved to Mashpee, I didn't have a circle at all. "When my father found out she was coming here, and who her father was, he insisted we room together. He managed to talk her parents into it."

"Who's her father?"

I glanced away nervously, unsure if Rachael wanted me to share this, but it didn't make sense to lie either. "Her dad's a preacher."

Ethan's blue eyes widened, and his mouth opened in surprise. "Really?"

Rachael was known as a party girl, not that she wasn't brilliant. Everyone at Stanford was super smart, but Rachael had a reputation for drinking, partying, and sleeping around. Unfortunately, it was earned.

"Yes, I know it doesn't fit. Her parents think she's a perfect angel. In fact, my parents think so too. So, as strict Indian parents, they were only too happy to have their child room with a preacher's daughter. They thought we'd keep each other in line under the devilish California sun."

"That's some sweet irony. So, you guys became friends?"

"At first, we hated each other. I tried to change room assignments right away." *It's weird how easy it is to talk to him. Too easy.*

"What changed?"

"We're extremely different, but somewhere along the way, we discovered we could be friends…best friends. I know the real Rachael, and we support each other. It works."

"I get it. What about Raj?"

"He's Indian."

"So, that's why you're friends? Are you telling me if I were Indian, I would have an automatic in?"

I laughed. "It's not that simple. He started sitting with me in the cafeteria. I had no idea what his deal was. Finally, I asked him why he didn't sit with the other Indian kids that all seemed to be best friends with each other. He just looked at me and said, 'Why don't you?' That was all it took. We didn't really fit anywhere else, so we found each other. It took him a while to trust me with his secret, and Rachael too. But now the three of us are best friends."

"Why didn't you fit anywhere else?" he asked with curious concern.

I shrugged, wondering how he managed to ask such a simple question with so much intensity. "I just didn't feel it. Neither did Raj… nor Rachael. We're kind of misfits. I don't expect you to understand."

"You're right. I've always been the most popular guy around. I have this magnetism that attracts people to me."

I gaped at him, shocked by his ego, until he started smiling.

"I mean, look how well it's working with you. You can't keep your hands off me."

I stifled my giggle, but it escaped anyway.

He paused, taking a strand of my hair and placing it behind my ear. His finger lingered there before trailing down my neck. "You have a pretty laugh, Sunshine." The giggle died in my throat, interrupted by my sudden need to calm my ragged breaths. My expression must have conveyed my discomfort because he backed away.

"Do you play rugby lot?" I asked in a desperate attempt to change the subject.

"Not really. I was filling in for someone. I like rugby, but it's not my first choice."

"What is this place?" I asked, looking around at the acres of marsh-land surrounding us.

"Baylands Nature Preserve. I love this place. It's peaceful. I have a park behind my house in New York. This is way different, of course, but in some ways it reminds me of home."

His accent wasn't quite New York. Some words were sharp with an East Coast inflection, but there was also a slow, raspy drawl at times, which I could not place. It was the sexiest combination I'd ever heard.

"This is beautiful," I said, staring at the tranquil lake.

"Mostly, it's a place to bird-watch, but you can kayak or wind surf on this lake."

"You're from New York?"

"Among other places," he replied.

"California's really different, huh?"

He shrugged his shoulders and placed our bags next to a bench by the lake. I sat beside him. "Not that different. The sun sets differently, the weather's nicer, and there's more grass, but the people, well…the people are the same wherever you live."

"You think so?"

"Yeah, people pretty much all want the same thing."

"And what's that?"

He looked at me, and I could feel my pulse quicken as I stared into his bottomless blue eyes. "Happiness."

I turned my concentration toward the swans gliding majestically on the lake. They were as graceful as Ethan was on the rugby field. I loved swans in general. It amazed me how they always traveled together, and how they formed a perfect heart when they kissed. They were the original lovebirds.

"That's very simplistic," I responded, shuffling my legs nervously.

"It's the most basic need in its simplest form, yet it's the empirical sum of all logic."

"Do you always think in terms of math?"

"I guess I do. I love math — not just solving problems, but the applications. My mind just likes the organization of it. I know it's weird."

"I don't think it's weird that you think that way, but it's strange you feel like people are the same everywhere. There's too much cultural diversity for such a simple statement."

I thought he might start arguing with me, but he just smiled.

"Do you think it's wrong to date people outside of your race?"

I almost choked on my water. I swiped the back of my hand across my mouth in the most unladylike fashion. "Where did that question come from?"

"I'm just trying to make conversation. I know you don't date, and I get that. I'm not trying to change your mind, but I am very curious about the reason."

I struggled with my words. He was patient, waiting for me to respond. I brought my legs up on the bench, wrapping my arms around them in an effort to shield myself from the penetration of his intense gaze. "There is something to be said for being with people who have the same values, ethics, and motivations. It would definitely avoid the drama of dating someone outside your ethnicity."

"You really think so?"

"I know you don't share my opinion. It's not popular."

"I don't share it, but it has nothing to do with popularity. My opposition is rooted in science. The discipline you've chosen as a matter of fact."

I turned to him, perplexed. "Come again?"

"You know the rules of workplace discrimination in economics?"

"Of course I know it. I'm an economics major."

"So, then, you know why."

"No, I have no idea what you're talking about. You're applying an economic theory to…dating?"

"It applies. Go ahead…tell me the answer to every freshman's first term paper in economics. Why shouldn't employers discriminate? I know you know this."

I shook my head, unsure of the connection.

"You've forgotten Econ one-oh-one already?"

I narrowed my eyes at him. Of course I knew the concept. I had written numerous papers on it. "You shouldn't discriminate in the workplace because it lowers your pool of potential applicants."

"And why is that wrong?"

"Because it yields less than desirable results when looking for the best qualified person."

"Exactly. I mean, if you limit yourself, then you may have lost the chance to find the ideal mate, right? An opportunity cost."

"You're using that term wrong," I replied, rolling my eyes.

He laughed and shrugged his shoulders. "Sorry, I'm not an economics major. I don't know everything."

"No, you don't." *He baits me, and I fall for it.* My plan was to avoid him, and here I was having a deep philosophical conversation about dating outside of my race. Truthfully, I didn't want to think of those things or talk about them, especially with Ethan Callahan.

"You like the swans. You've been watching them."

I was grateful for the change of subject. "They're beautiful. I like how they come in pairs."

"Let's name them. They can be our swans."

I laughed. "We don't own them."

"You don't have to own something to make it yours. I name the male Isaac."

"For Isaac Newton?"

Ethan nodded, smiling widely.

"You would name him after a mathematician."

"I'm glad you recognize Newton as a mathematician. Not many people do. What do you name the female?"

I said the first name that came to mind. "Suzanne."

"Is she a famous economist?"

I shook my head, feeling slightly more comfortable. "No, Suzanne Valadon was a famous French painter. She's one of my favorites."

"I'm at a disadvantage. You obviously know all about Isaac. Tell me about Suzanne." He appeared genuinely interested.

"She was crazy, but she found beauty in that. She was Renoir's muse for a while. I think she was the first woman to paint a nude. She would work on a single painting for ten, sometimes thirteen, years to get it right. She was a perfectionist, and she fed her cats caviar."

Ethan nodded approvingly. "Sounds like a good name for a lady swan." He gestured toward the two birds, swimming in synchronistic perfection. "Our names match."

"How?"

"Isaac was somewhere between genius and crazy too. It's a fine line. Isaac and Suzanne are good names. Swans are crazy in general…crazy mean. I was attacked by a swan once."

"No!" I giggled, cupping my mouth.

He feigned a hurt look, but his eyes were twinkling with mischief. "That's nice. Just go ahead and laugh at my traumatic childhood memory." I laughed harder. "It was my fault. I was six and very stupid. I was swimming in their territory. The males are very protective of their mates. I deserved it."

"Of course he would be protective. They mate for life. If you had hurt the female, he'd have no one. Isaac needs Suzanne."

"Isaac and Suzanne are totally safe from me. After that swan pecked my forehead, I've learned to appreciate them from afar."

The image of a curious, young Ethan pecked by a swan made me smile in the sappiest way.

"It is kind of cool…the mating for life thing," he continued. "There are so few species that mate for life."

I turned and stared at him, feeling my heart flutter by his very close presence. His hand twitched a bit, like it wanted to grab mine. Was he feeling the same charge of electricity I was? I wanted to be honest with him. After I told him, he would probably rather hang out with a swan.

"That's why I love them. They are just like me."

He didn't seem frazzled by what I'd said. He was quiet, soaking in my words. Rachael told me statements like this were the fastest way to get a guy to leave you alone, but Ethan didn't even seem surprised. "You mate for life, Meena?"

"My people do."

"Economists?" he asked with an amused grin.

"Very funny."

"Are you saying there are no Indian divorces?" His question sounded genuine.

"There are exceptions to every rule, but we do have the lowest divorce rate in the world."

"Why do you think that is?"

"It's culturally discouraged."

He nodded. "Maybe it should be here too. But is that really the only reason? It makes it sound like it's very difficult to get yourself out of a bad situation."

"It's difficult, but usually not impossible. That's not the only reason. I think the marriages, in general, are stronger and more stable."

"What makes them stronger? Religion? Culture?"

I was quiet for a moment, contemplating my response.

"Come on, the answer to the Western woes of wedlock could be solved by this very conversation. Surely, you have a theory."

"Two words—arranged marriage."

His eyebrows shot up. I had finally surprised him, but he didn't hesitate with his next question. "People still do that?"

"It's not as common as it was, but it's not uncommon either. Most Hindu marriages are the result of an arrangement."

"I don't know anyone who would want to get married like that."

I sucked in a deep breath but didn't let my eyes waver from his. "Yes, you do."

This time he choked on his water. "Seriously?" he asked, now wiping his mouth with the back of his hand.

I nodded in response.

"Why?"

"Why not? Thousands of years of culture and current statistics prove it works. It's what my parents and my grandparents did and generations before them. Why wouldn't I want to invest my future in something I know has a strong rate of success?"

"I'm no romantic, but it sounds too grounded in fact, not feeling. Where's the passion, the spontaneity, the—"

"Love?"

"Sure, love. I was going to say chemistry, but love works too."

"Those are amorous ideas that work well in books and movies, but obviously, we know from current data they don't work in the real world."

"Do you already know who you're marrying?" His hand clenched into a tight fist, and he looked away, far off into the distance.

I was discussing my arranged marriage plans with Ethan Callahan. How had we gotten here? "No, I haven't met him yet."

He exhaled next to me. "How do you know he'll be right for you?" Ethan's voice lacked its normal amusement.

"I know we'll have similar backgrounds. He'll be successful. Our families will both approve of our union. Even our stars will match up."

"Your stars? You're basing the most important decision in your life… on astrology?"

I did not appreciate the incredulous quality of his voice, even if that voice dripped with sexiness.

"It's one of many factors, yes."

"So, if he fits all that criteria, it's a done deal?"

"It's not that simple. Women aren't objects. My family's modern. I'll interview him. I can ask him anything, and I have veto power."

"Veto power?"

"Yes, I can deny anyone I don't like. It's kind of cool in a way. I can ask any question, no matter how private. I can ask them how much they make, what their deepest fears are, who they idolize. Things that might take you twenty dates to figure out, I'll know in one meeting."

Ethan shook his head, keeping his eyes fixed on the lake. "You're missing the best part, Sunshine."

"What's that?"

He ran his fingers through his hair, and it miraculously managed to fall right back in place. I had to look away from him. Ethan's voice was quiet, but his words coursed through me like a physical presence, gravelly and deep. "It's not the knowing. It's the finding out."

"It's the best of both. I'll know, and I'll find out more. You probably think I'm really weird, but I know this is right for me."

"Yes, I think you're weird, but I'm not so intolerant that I can't consider all the pros of your argument although I oppose it. Were you telling me all this to scare me off, or did you want to share a part of yourself with me?" His honesty shocked me. He seemed to understand my motivations better than I did.

"I'm not sure."

He turned toward me, smiling, but there was no joy in it. "I don't scare easily," he said. "I was attacked by a swan once."

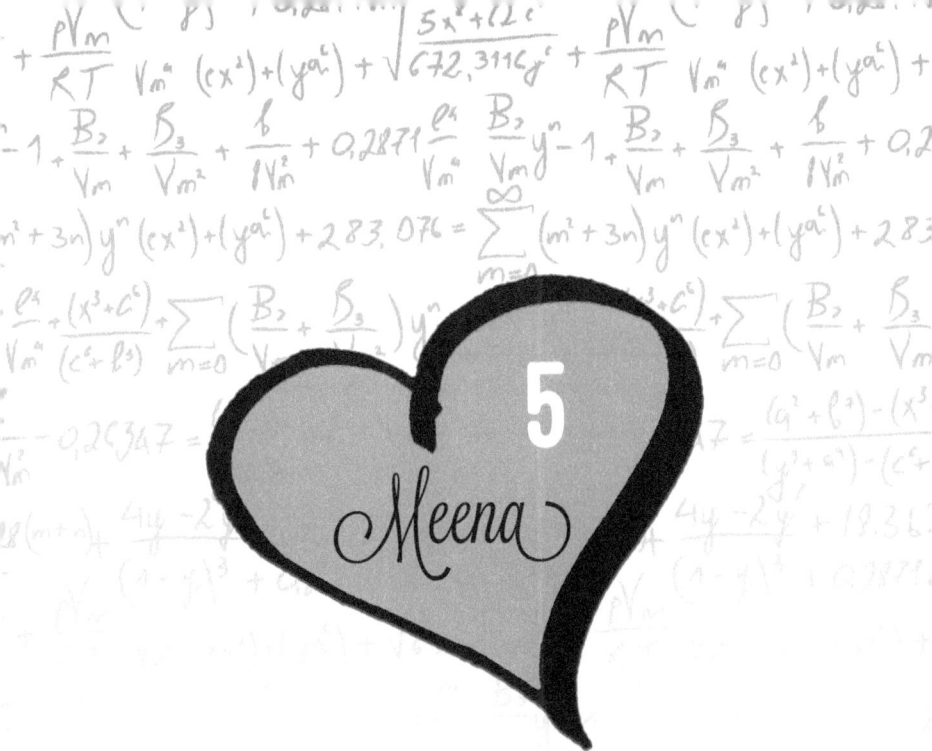

5

Meena

$\mathcal{M}$y conversation with Ethan preyed on my mind in the coming weeks. He still sat next to me in class and joked with me, but he didn't ask me out again. In many ways, I felt more comfortable with him, despite my growing attraction. I was as uptight as pressurized coal morphing into a diamond, but Ethan's carefree and fun attitude was hard to resist.

He seemed like a complete oddball. A hot, free-spirited math guy with a great sense of humor. He seemed too good to exist. He was too tempting. I could dream about him, though. That was acceptable as long as I didn't act. I justified it to myself as I made my way to my room. After spending several hours at the library, I was exhausted, ready to crawl into bed, and looking forward to dreaming.

Instead, I opened my door and let out a small shriek. There was Rachael, naked and sitting on top of a boy I didn't recognize. It wasn't Keith.

"Oh, Meena, why did you come in?" Rachael gasped.

"You didn't have the bra on the door!" I yelled. The lacy, hot pink, polka dot bra that was too big for Rachael and too small for me was our universal code for "do not disturb." We bought it together at some bargain-basement sale, figuring it would fit one of us. No such luck, but we both loved it and cursed our bodies for not fitting into the adorable thing. Rachael had found another use for it.

"I forgot. Can you give us a minute?"

"Just a minute?" the mystery man underneath Rachael groaned.

"Half an hour?" Rachael pleaded. I made a disgusted grunt, realizing they were still in the act. I ran out, slamming the door behind me, not wanting to converse with Rachael while she was…occupied.

I had never seen anything like that. I felt overwhelmingly traumatized and disturbed. As shocking as it was, though, a small part of me was intrigued. Rachael had shared so many sexual stories, I felt somewhat knowledgeable, but the School of Rachael was not necessarily the best education, and it certainly hadn't prepared me for this.

I walked to the common room, planning on plopping on the couch and watching television, but found the door locked. I didn't want to sit outside of my room. I knew Rachael's voice was loud in general, and I didn't want to hear her. I decided to go for a walk. There was a cool breeze, and maybe I could get the image of Rachael having sex with a stranger out of my head.

I started walking, admiring the campus that had been my home for the past three years. I would miss it. I was sure it was the most beautiful campus in the world. I made it to the far end, almost exiting the gate. My thoughts started drifting from the manicured lawns and perfectly clipped rose bushes to Ethan Callahan, as they so often did these days.

When he pulled up beside me in his Escalade Hybrid, I actually shrieked. Maybe, like my swan, Suzanne, I was going mad. *Is he trying to torture me?*

"What are you doing out here by yourself?" he asked before the window was even rolled down.

"Just walking." At least it was dark and he couldn't see me blushing.

"You shouldn't be out here this late."

His concern touched me, but I tried not to let it show. I didn't want to seem vulnerable. "This is a very safe campus."

"Get in. I'll drive you back."

"I'm fine."

"It wasn't a request."

I shook my head, continuing my walk, but he just followed beside me.

"Think of it as a favor," he said. "Do it for me."

"How is it a favor to you?"

"Because I won't be able to sleep tonight not knowing you're safe, Sunshine."

Does he imagine me in bed too? It was hard to be stubborn when his demand held just the right mixture of command and concern that it turned me on. After a deep breath, I opened the passenger door. I sat down on the plush seat and did my best to maintain an air of relaxation, which I sure as hell didn't feel. The Eli Young Band's song, "Just Add Moonlight," wafted through the speakers.

"You like country?" I asked him, surprised.

"Yeah, I'm from Texas. It's kind of a rule."

I was suddenly able to place the drawl in his voice. It was the husky sweetness of the southern accent combined with East Coast flair. It was as unique as him.

"You lived in Texas?"

"Among other places." He moved to turn off the radio.

"Will you leave it on? I love this song."

"You like country?" he asked, cocking his eyebrows in surprise.

I nodded. "I always have. Every song conveys a story whether it's silly or something heart wrenching. Know what I mean?"

"Yeah, I know exactly what you mean." His fingers tapped against the steering wheel, keeping time with the music.

We were just sitting in his car, listening to the radio. Yet it was the most natural exchange I'd had all day.

"What are you doing here? Don't you live off campus?"

"I was on a date. I just dropped her off." He looked guilty, but he had no reason to be. My body coiled with tight anxiety just the same.

"That's nice," I said with enough aggression to communicate it wasn't nice at all. I clenched my fists, turning my head toward the window. I didn't trust myself to speak another word. It was so obvious I was seething with jealousy, and I had no right to be.

"Which dorm do you live in?"

"I can't go back yet. Rachael's entertaining."

He paused for a moment, but he understood what I meant. "Let's go somewhere else, then."

"Where do you want to go?"

"I'll take you to one of my favorite places. It's close. You'll like it."

I didn't agree, but he started driving anyway. I wanted to ask him about his date. *Who is she? Do I know her?* In other ways, I didn't want to set foot anywhere near that topic. It was a landmine, ripe with explosive possibilities, none of them favorable.

"Does Rachael…ah…entertain a lot?" His voice didn't have judgment, but he seemed concerned in a way.

"Not a lot," I lied. "I usually go to the common area, but it was locked."

"Do me a favor and stop walking around at night by yourself. If you can't get into the common area, call me."

His generous offer left me speechless.

He drove us up to a ridge on that overlooked the cities of Silicon Valley. It wasn't far, but I'd never been here. He hopped out and came around to my side, opening my door.

"What are we doing here?"

"It's a good place to look at the stars. I like astronomy, and I figured you might like it too…you know, since you're into astrology." He smirked, offering me his hand. I took it hesitantly, but he tightened his grip, pulling me out of the car.

"I wouldn't say I'm into astrology," I replied, crossing my arms.

Ethan didn't reply, but he shocked me instead by stepping onto the passenger seat. He gracefully pulled himself onto the roof of his car. "Come here," he said, extending his arm.

"You want to sit up there?"

"It's the best view. Besides, this is certified Detroit rolling iron," he said, taking his fist and banging it like a gavel on the roof. "You won't hurt it."

I placed my foot on the passenger floor, tentatively taking Ethan's hand. A slight jolt of electricity rushed through me as he pulled me up effortlessly, grasping my waist in the process. I sat next to him in the small space between the rails.

"Lie down, Sunshine." His voice had an effect on me, lulling me into a quiet compliance that I'd never known. I followed his command. Ethan pulled off his sweatshirt, managing to almost take his T-shirt with it. I saw the tight, hard-pressed muscles underneath and forced myself not to touch them. He rolled his sweatshirt into a ball and handed it to me. "Use this for a pillow."

I placed the makeshift pillow under my head. A visible shiver coursed through my body when I realized only a few inches separated us.

"Cold?" he asked, mistaken about my trembling.

I nodded, not knowing what else to say. In some acrobatic move, he hooked his feet on the rack, lowered the top half of his body, opened the back passenger door, and closed it again. When he came back up, he held a velvety soft plaid blanket.

"Thank you," I said, taking it with hesitation.

"What?"

"Why do you have a blanket in your car?"

"In case I need it."

"Have you ever had sex on it?" I asked, staring at the soft plush material with narrowing eyes.

Ethan laughed. "Of course I have."

"Oh," I said, holding the material further away.

"It's my sex blanket. Whenever I'm in the mood, I just lay it on the ground, take off my clothes, and the ladies line up."

It took two seconds before his words sank in, and I burst out laughing.

"I've had sex on it once, but don't worry—I've washed it since then." His honesty was jarring. *Did he always tell the truth?* He pulled it over us before crossing his arms behind his head and lying down. Our shoulders grazed each other's. "Look up, Sunshine."

I gasped. The golden stars appeared to drop right out of the sky like they might fall on us. "It's beautiful. They look so close."

"I know. It makes you feel important and insignificant at the same time."

"That's a good way to describe it."

We were silent for a moment, both staring at the magnificent view above us. "Do you bring a lot of girls here?"

Ethan chuckled, turning toward me and resting his head on his crooked elbow. "No, why? You think I should?"

I couldn't fit any more of my foot into my mouth if I tried. Ethan was so close to me, and like the stars above us, he felt within reach, but he was just an illusion. We were quiet for a while, but when I shifted, I saw he was still staring at me. "How was your date?"

"It was okay."

I wanted more than that, but I had no right to ask for details, but I really wanted them.

"Did you get lucky?" I winced at the forthrightness of the question. I was acting like a locker room buddy of his or, worse, a jealous, insecure girl, which was the reality.

"You seem very interested in my sex life, Meena."

I was grateful it was dark, because I actually felt the heat color my face. "I'm just trying to make conversation," I said, repeating the same statement he'd made the other day at the lake, hoping it sounded casual.

He was quiet for a moment, and I desperately wanted to see his expression, but I kept my eyes on the stars instead.

"That's an interesting phrase. Getting lucky implies my sole objective was to have sex."

"Wasn't it?"

"I like sex as much as the next guy, but I wouldn't say it's my goal or my reason for going on a date."

I couldn't believe we were discussing his sex life. Then again, I chose the topic like the complete fool I was.

"Are you looking for 'the one,' Ethan?" I asked with a hint of sarcasm in my voice.

He chuckled. "No way. Not at twenty-two."

"I don't get it."

"Get what?"

"Why people date."

His laughter boomed out into the night air. "Did you seriously just say you don't get why people date?"

I sighed, irked by his response. "You don't get arranged marriage, but I didn't laugh at you. I don't get the dating thing. I mean, if you're not looking for sex or a long-term relationship...why bother?"

Ethan lay down on his back again and was quiet for a while. I'd almost wondered if he'd fallen asleep. Then I felt his pinky hook onto mine. It was a surprise, but it didn't make me feel awkward.

"You're a very linear thinker, aren't you? You believe that *A* plus *B* has to equal *C?*" he said.

"Doesn't it?"

"It does. The thing is there are about a million variables between *A* and *B* before you get to *C*. Nothing is as simple as a straight line. In fact, it's pretty difficult to find anything linear in life."

"What do you mean?"

He started talking, with his free hand gesturing to match his words. I watched it against the moonlight. "When you throw a pebble across the water, it doesn't dart out in a perfect path. It skips along the water, causing ripples—concentric, connecting circles." He pointed to the night sky. "The stars above us, they don't line up like an arrow on a treasure map. They hang out in clusters and groups, connecting to each other's energy. Even biologically, our heartbeats bounce. A straight line in reference to your heart means you're dead. Dating or friendship—it isn't about the product but the process. It's about forming connections and their relationship to each other. I think that's the purpose of dating or at least...my purpose. It's a connection to someone else."

"You should have been a philosophy major. You're wasting your time with this math stuff."

"It is math. All math."

"I don't think it's really math."

"It's as simple as addition or as complicated as the exponential functions of a natural logarithm. Take us for example."

"Us?"

"Yes, right now, we're having a conversation. You're giving part of yourself to me and vice versa. It's a piece of you I can take with me. Some connections make us better people, some worse, but they usually influence us in some way. They shape who you are or who you become. Do you get it?"

"Somewhat, but there's still one thing I don't understand."

"What's that?"

I turned to him, smiling. "How did you not get lucky tonight with lines like that?"

Ethan let out a rowdy laugh, tightening his pinky around mine. It was infectious, and soon we were both cracking up. We sank back into the quiet again, lost in our own thoughts.

Ethan's raspy voice spilled into the night air. "If I'd wanted to have sex, I could have."

"Why didn't you?"

He turned to face me, displaying a cocky smile and winking. His eyes took on a shimmering quality, even in the dark. "No connection."

He dropped me off at my dorm an hour later. "Do you think he's gone?" Ethan asked.

"Oh, I'm pretty sure he left a while ago." I knew enough to know that even Rachael couldn't have sex this long.

"Give me your phone."

I took my cell out of my pocket and handed it to him.

He put in all his contact info and handed it back. "Text me if he's still there. I'll wait."

"You don't have to do that."

"I know."

I nodded, opening the door. It felt wrong to leave like this without somehow expressing my feelings to him. At least something to let him know I was grateful. For what, I wasn't sure. We'd just hung out, but the exchange we shared seemed to signify something. I couldn't give in to my desires and date him or anything, but I could let him know that he meant something to me.

"Ethan, I wanted to say thanks."

"For what? I enjoyed it."

"Me too, but I wasn't thanking you for that. I was thanking you for being a friend."

He face lit up as he grinned that cute, boyish smile at me. "So, I got the job?"

"It turns out I had an opening after all," I replied, matching his smile.

"I knew my persistence would pay off."

I floated back to my dorm room. I had no idea how a conversation with Ethan could make me feel that way. Then again, it was a combination of everything. The conversation we had. The small touch of his pinky hooked with mine. Of course, there was inhaling his intoxicating scent, sharing a blanket, grazing shoulders, and staring at the stars. It was everything, and yet it was nothing but a brief moment in time. I wanted it back.

Rachael was sitting at her desk, reading a textbook. She looked up, relieved, as soon as I entered the room. "Where were you? I was worried. I texted you and went to the common room."

I pulled out my phone and took a moment to send a quick message to Ethan under the guise of checking for Rachael's text.

"Sorry, I didn't hear it. The common room was locked, so I went for a walk." I decided to keep stargazing with Ethan to myself.

"I think they shampooed the carpets today. I'm sorry, Meena. I really suck as a roommate. How mad are you?"

I shrugged my shoulders. "It depends on if you have the good chocolate."

"I got it," she said, opening her drawer and throwing a candy bar my way.

"Who was the guy by the way?"

Rachael smiled. She was completely at ease with her choices. Though I didn't agree with them, I envied her lack of regret. "Greg." She didn't give me his last name. I wondered if she knew it. "He's cute, right?"

"Um...I didn't really get a good look." I fiddled with the wrapper on the chocolate bar.

"Oh, yeah, I guess it was awkward."

Awkward? That was an understatement.

"He's okay," she continued. "I got a small O out of the deal."

"A small O?"

"You can't have the big O all the time."

I sat on my bed, shaking my head at her. "Do you ever think that's because you don't stay with them long enough for them to know what you like?"

Rachael laughed. "Nope, if a guy's a good fuck, he's good no matter what. It doesn't matter if we do it once or a hundred times. In fact, I think it gets worse the more you do it."

"How could that be?"

She was thoughtful for a moment. "It gets predictable."

"Law of diminishing returns?" I asked, using an economic reference.

"Exactly," she exclaimed, clapping her hands as if I'd made a radical scientific discovery.

I threw my pillow at her. She managed to catch it and throw it right back. "I was just kidding. That's not the right concept."

"Sounds right to me."

6

Ethan

*I*t had been two weeks since Meena and I stared at the stars from the roof of my car. Our relationship had shifted. She was more relaxed and comfortable around me. We were friends now. I wanted more, but I respected her boundaries.

We were sitting in the cafeteria after Professor Malkin's class, studying as we usually did now. Well, she was studying. I was staring at my book, unable to concentrate, stealing sly glances at her. She had her hair up in that messy bun that was killing me. *How does she manage to make it look so sexy?* She wasn't trying, and that made her even more irresistible. She had no idea how hot she was.

Other guys gave her that up-and-down look that bordered appreciation and creepiness. Hell, I was guilty of it myself. I wasn't typically a jealous guy, and when it came to Meena, I had no right to be, but I was, just the same. I had a ridiculous urge to put my arm around her to let those assholes know to step off. It didn't matter, though. In reality, Meena wasn't interested in any of them...or me. I had gone on a few dates, trying to put her out of my mind, but it wasn't helping the cause.

"Can I borrow your notes? I think I missed something," she said, looking up from her textbook. I glanced down, embarrassed I'd been caught staring at her. I slid my notebook to her. She ran her fingers down the page until she found the section she was looking for. "Your notes are meticulous."

I shrugged. "It's the math guy in me. I have a need to systematize."

"Systematize? Is that even a word?"

"I'm pretty sure it is."

"Why do you have two notebooks?"

Her observation surprised me, but then again, it wasn't really something I hid. "It helps me stay organized."

"What do you write in the other book?"

"It's nothing that has anything to do with class. I jot down distracting stuff I need to get out of my head. Shit, that kind of makes me sound crazy."

She was thoughtful for a moment. "What do you consider distracting?"

Mostly you, Sunshine. Thankfully, I had enough intelligence to know I couldn't say that. I didn't know if I wanted to explain this to her. It wasn't something I shared. In the end, though, it was me, and if you couldn't be honest about yourself, faults and all, then you were just a liar. "Everything and nothing. I have ADHD."

She gaped at me.

"You're surprised?"

"You're just so focused and orderly. It's hard to imagine."

I smiled coyly. "I don't take medication for it anymore, but my biggest problem is concentration. When I was in high school, I sucked at taking notes. I had the right ideas, but my writing was like hieroglyphics. I made good grades, but it was almost impossible to study. My therapist recommended a second notebook. I write stuff in it when it comes into my head. It helps me focus."

"You go to therapy?"

"I did. My mom's a psychologist. She believes everyone should go to therapy."

"Does it work?"

"The therapy?"

She smiled. "The second notebook."

"It does."

"So, you just write the meaningless stuff in it?"

"I wouldn't say it's meaningless. It's meaningful to me. That's why it's difficult not to focus on it. When I write it down, it's kind of like taking it out of my head for a while. It serves as a visual. It helps. That and staying active."

"What do you write about?"

"All kinds of stuff. It's a scratchpad of randomness. Like today, I wrote down that Professor Malkin needs glasses. It's not like I would tell him, but it was difficult to concentrate on his lecture with that distracting me, so I wrote it down and then I didn't think about it anymore."

She laughed. It automatically made me smile. "I think you're right. He squints."

How would she react if I told her she has several pages dedicated just to her, featuring insane run-on and fragmented sentences about the way her hair smells or the fact that I get a little hard every time she laughs? Hell, if she ever saw it, she'd think I was some kind of stalker. It was weird because I never used my scratchpad to write about girls. They never dominated my mind. Then again, she was always in my head, no matter how much I wrote.

"It must be nice to be able to release the useless stuff just by writing it," she said.

"Some things are easier than others."

"What do you mean?"

"Well, sometimes I have to shred the paper. Get rid of it somehow. It's just part of the visualization. When I don't have it with me, it makes it easier to move on. Okay, I'm sounding like a total psycho now."

She laughed, relaxing me instantly. "No, I don't think it's crazy at all. It's kind of cool how that works for you. Your brain works differently…almost more efficiently in some ways."

"Differently than most people? Isn't that the definition of a psycho?" I asked, grinning at her.

"No, different isn't bad. Although you have this issue, the left-brained math side of you has to organize it. You have to organize your chaos, and that's kind of an amazing concept. I'm sort of in awe of it. Math people always amaze me."

"I never thought of it that way." I was glad for her to know that about me, and equally happy she didn't pass any judgment. "But are you seriously telling me you're not a math person, Meena? Economics and statistics have a basis in math. I think that qualifies you as one of us."

She looked away from me, and it seemed she was going to shut down on me. I liked it when she talked about herself, but she always had a point of retreat. I waited for her patiently. If I didn't muck up the conversation with too much pressure for her to answer, she usually did.

"I'm not like you. It doesn't come naturally to me. I wouldn't qualify it as my passion."

"What is your passion?"

She looked up and smiled, like a child hiding a secret that would make them burst. I smiled back, hoping she wouldn't keep me in suspense. "Do you want me to tell you or show you?" she replied.

"Definitely show me," I said, straightening up in my seat.

She reached into her backpack, pulling out a pad of her own. It wasn't a notebook, but a sketchpad. "These aren't so great. I just did them with a pencil, but I like to draw."

She slid the sketchpad toward me. She didn't readily let it go when I took it. I gave her a reassuring smile before she finally released it. She tapped her fingers on the table nervously while I flipped through it, taking my time to observe each drawing. The level of depth and shading she was able to get with a pencil was impressive. There were drawings of simple objects like an apple to more complex sketches, like a picture of an older woman I recognized from the sub shop at the Union. Meena had captured the woman's wrinkling complexion, salt and pepper hair, and cranky expression with perfect precision. "These are really good, Sunshine."

"They're okay. Just something I do for fun," she said dismissively.

"If you sucked, I would tell you. Take the compliment."

She exhaled. "Thank you for the compliment."

"You're welcome. Have you ever used another medium?"

"I took an art class in high school for an extracurricular. I used colored pencils and watercolors. I liked it."

"You should be in art school."

She choked and laughed at the same time.

"Why is that funny?"

"I was just imagining telling my dad I wanted to go to art school. I might as well tell him I'm going to cosmetology college."

"There's nothing wrong with pursing a degree in art or…cosmetology if that's your thing. You should be doing this on a canvas using real artist supplies."

She shrugged. "There's nothing wrong with it per se. It's just not quite…culturally acceptable for me. My parents wouldn't be supportive of that decision. I mean, they would freak if I told them I was getting a liberal arts degree, let alone planning my career around this." She gestured to the sketchpad. "We settled on economics because it was the only major we could all agree on."

"Your parents picked your major?" It was my turn to be shocked.

"We picked it together. They're paying for my degree so it's only right they have a say in it."

"Yes, but it's your life." I held up her sketchpad. "This is what you should be doing." We weren't just talking about her choice in majors anymore. The sullen expression on her face told me she knew it too.

She took the pad from me. I'd upset her. "It's just a stupid hobby."

"You just said it was your passion. A hobby is something you do for fun, but a passion is something you're meant to do. You choose a hobby, but a passion chooses you."

She stuffed the sketchpad into her backpack. "Don't make me regret showing you this. I've never shown anyone."

"Not even friend number one or two?" I grinned.

"No, not even them. So, are you going to show me your scratchpad since I showed you my sketchpad?" It was a relief to see the sweet smile return to her face, but her question made me anxious.

I instantly closed my scratchpad and placed it safely into my bag. "No, it's not a passion or a hobby. It's random disorganization. Trust me — you don't want to know the crazy that lives here," I said, knocking my fist against my head.

"Well, thank you for telling me about your crazy."

"Thank you for showing me your passion."

"Meena, there you are! I've been looking all over for you. I texted you." Rachael took a seat next to us.

We were so wrapped up in our conversation we hadn't even noticed her coming. It was annoying. I only saw Meena a few hours a week, and I didn't want to share them with Rachael. Honestly, I didn't really like Rachael in general since Meena had told me about her entertaining. I could read between the lines.

What if one of those random assholes she brought home made a play for Meena? It was ridiculous, but I had an insane need to protect her.

"What's up?" Meena asked.

Rachael waved at me, before answering Meena. "I wanted to know if you were staying here again for Thanksgiving break. I was going to book my flight, but I wasn't sure if you wanted me to book your ticket too. The rates are good right now."

"I'm staying here again," she said quietly.

Her choice was surprising, so I had to ask, "Why are you staying here? The campus is going to be ghost town."

"I have homework to catch up on." She wasn't being honest, but I didn't press it, especially with Rachael here.

Rachael nodded, turning to me. "I don't even know why I asked. She never goes home for Thanksgiving."

"It's too expensive to fly, and besides, my family doesn't celebrate Thanksgiving," Meena said a little too fast to be casual. She smiled brightly at me, but it was the fake, tight smile she reserved for other people. *It isn't my smile.* "It's hard to celebrate a holiday revolving around a bird when you're vegetarian."

"Yeah, a fact I try not to hold against you," I said, trying to put her at ease.

"What are you doing?" Meena asked Rachael when she opened her laptop on the table. *Cool, at least she's pissed about Rachael sticking around too.*

"Booking my ticket. I can't put it off any longer."

"Hey, Ethan. Hello, Meena," Alex said, taking the seat next to her. Great, another interruption to my Meena time.

"Hi, Alex," I said, trying not to let my irritation show.

"Alex, this is my roommate, Rachael Donavan," Meena said.

"Nice to meet you." Alex shook Rachael's hand. Their grip lasted a little too long, and his eyes got wide. They made some small talk, but I wasn't paying attention. I wanted to know why Meena was going to spend the holiday by herself.

"Do you want to hang out during break?" I asked her in a low voice so our conversation was more private.

"You're not going home?"

"My mom's in Paris, so I'm staying here. Let's do something Wednesday."

Alex shot me a funny look. I gave him a nonchalant shrug as a nonverbal apology, and he gave me an approving head nod. My mom was in Paris, but both Alex and Darren had invited me to their houses for Thanksgiving. I'd been debating which invite to accept, but now I couldn't go to either. I wanted to be here with Meena.

Her expression turned ten shades of sad, and her eyes looked far away, like a shroud of misery was coming to claim her. "Not on Wednesday."

"Another day?"

"Maybe," she responded, looking down at her book. She didn't say if she had any plans, but I wasn't going to press it. *Back off, Callahan, she doesn't want you to know.*

My random thoughts took a backseat when Reese Denton joined us. I played rugby with Reese, and I didn't like him. He lived his life like he played the game. He was overly cocky without the passes or goals to back it up. He was tall but scrawny, and he wore skinny jeans—which I always thought made guys look like…girls. He had on a T-shirt that said "Rugby players have the biggest balls."

He sat down on the other side of Meena, and my jaw tightened reflexively as it always did when a guy was eyeing her. I especially didn't like it coming from Reese since he had a certain reputation. He greeted all of us, including Meena, pausing to give her what my mom called an "objectifying look."

Rachael groaned loudly, looking up from her laptop.

"What's wrong?" Meena asked.

"This majorly sucks. Reese, I can't go to your frat party on Tuesday. The flights are cheaper that day so I can't fly out on Wednesday like I wanted."

"Too bad. It's going to be a rager," Reese said, staring at Meena. "Are you coming, Ethan?"

I shrugged, trying to act laid-back, but every muscle was tightening. "Maybe." Those parties were notorious for casual hook-ups encouraged by the flowing alcohol and oddly placed couches. I usually went.

"I'll be there, Denton," Alex said.

"Good. Are you coming, Meena?" Reese asked, not even looking at Alex.

"I don't think so."

"Meena, I've invited you to every party since freshman year. This might be your last chance to come." He paused too long on the word "come." *Fucking dickhead.*

"Reese, you have a party every month." That was true. It was funny how we knew the same people, but I had never met her before. Then again, she didn't socialize much.

"True, but this is going to epic. You can bring someone with you if you want. I know how you girls like to travel in packs." It was obvious what he was getting at — don't bring a guy. "Come on, tell me what you like to drink, and I'll make sure we have it."

"I don't drink."

Everyone our age drank, but I wasn't surprised by her answer. It fit.

Denton picked up the energy drink she had in front of her, staring at the label. "I'll get this." It was almost comical how strong he was coming on to Meena, or it would have been, if my fists didn't have an uncontrollable urge to wipe that smirk right off his face.

"Thanks, Reese, but I'm busy. Next time."

I wanted to say something. To let him know she was off limits, but she wasn't mine to claim. Any verbal sparring between Reese and I would make her uncomfortable, so I let it go. Besides, Sunshine had done a good job of letting him down in her own gentle way.

I hadn't planned on going to Denton's party, but I was bored on Tuesday night. Darren was at Mandy's house, and all my other friends had either gone home for break, or were at the frat house.

I stood there with a red cup in my hand, hanging out with Claire Stevens. Claire and I dated last year. She was a cute girl, but boring. I knew she was super smart based on her honors standing, but she acted dumb, or at least she did in front of me. We hadn't come together, but she saw me and cornered me as soon I got there. She was droning on about the cons of certain kinds of liquor or some shit.

The Craftsman-style house, which was large, seemed claustrophobic tonight. Couples were making out on the couches, putting on a free soft porn show for the rest of us. There was an arm wrestling contest in one corner and groups playing beer pong in the other.

Someone was on the beer-cliner—a recliner the engineering students designed as a quick and stupid way to get drunk. I ought to know.

The latest participant, or victim, was leaning back in the chair. They'd inserted a tube down their throat that acted as the perfect delivery system for massive quantities of cheap alcohol. It was on a timer that would automatically fling them upright so that instead of choking, they downed the foul liquid without tasting it.

A group gathered around the chair, cheering the idiot on. Reese Denton was among them, yelling the loudest. I laughed because the beer-cliner, if nothing else, was entertaining.

The laugh died in my throat when I saw him pull her out of the chair and hug her as if she'd run a marathon. My hand tightened around my red cup so hard that some of the liquid spilled out. *What is Meena doing here?*

Shit. She was wasted, and there was shithead, Reese Denton, groping her, taking advantage of it. I walked over to them, leaving Claire in mid-sentence. It wasn't the easiest journey because I had to step on a few feet, bump some shoulders, and keep myself calm at the same time. I thrust myself forward as if I was in a freaking rugby scrum. Finally, I stood between Reese and Meena, creating a space that didn't previously exist.

I put my hands on her shoulder. "What are you doing here?" I demanded.

She blinked her eyes rapidly before registering me. Then she smiled. "Ethan, you're here! Friend number three is here." She wasn't slurring, but she swayed slightly.

"You said you weren't coming."

"She couldn't resist the lure of one of my parties," Denton said, sidling up next to her.

I ignored his idiotic comment and waited for her to answer.

"Raj wanted to come."

"And where is Raj?"

She scanned the room in confusion. I looked with her and couldn't find him either, although in this crowded space, he could have been a few feet away.

"How much have you had to drink?" I was yelling at her because it was so loud, but part of it was because I was so pissed off. Someone who never drank getting drunk at a frat party without anyone watching over her was a dumbass thing to do.

"I didn't count. I'm not a math person, you know?" She laughed, patting my shoulder.

"Relax, man, are you her mother or something?" Denton said, clapping me on the back a little too hard to be friendly. He came around to face me and put his arm over Meena's shoulder, pulling her away from me. *Fucking dickhead!*

"How much has she had to drink, Denton?"

"You think I kept track? Jesus, Ethan, she's fine. She's not doing anything illegal. She can definitely hold her own."

I wanted to smash my fist into his face. Instead, I gritted my teeth so hard it hurt. "She doesn't drink, asshole."

She giggled, like this was a joke. *She laughed at me.* "I'm fine, Ethan. Why do you look so worried? Guess what? It's a free country!"

"This has been fun, Callahan, but I promised this girl the tour."

I knew what that meant. His tours always ended in his bedroom, with an inebriated girl…or two.

"That's not happening," I said, stepping up to him. To his credit, he didn't back away.

"Are you telling me what to do in my own house?"

"I am—at least when it comes to her. Do we understand each other?" I said each syllable slowly, letting it sink in.

He opened his mouth to argue with me or maybe to punch me. I welcomed the physical contact. It would be the perfect excuse to pummel him. Meena interrupted us, though, like she got the situation even in her drunken state. "Reese, I don't want a tour right now. I don't think I can do stairs. I'm hot." The staircase was loaded with loitering people, probably all waiting for turns to get into a bedroom.

"Yes, you are," he said. *Shithead.* "It is hot in here. Let's go outside." He turned back to me, saying the words to me though he was talking to her. "Where we can be alone."

He would have shoved me out of the way, but I stood my ground as they walked toward the door. I glared after them, not sure what the right move was. I wanted to grab her and take her out of this place, caveman style, but it wasn't my right. Meena was an adult, and no one was forcing her. *Hell, maybe she wants to fuck Reese-fucking-dickhead-Denton.*

My hand hurt suddenly. I looked down at the red cup that no longer resembled any kind of drinking vessel. I'd managed to crush it into a tiny ball. Good thing it was empty. Better thing it wasn't made of glass.

I had no claim to her, but if Denton thought for a second I would allow him to be alone with her, then he was a bigger shithead than I'd estimated.

"What are we doing now?" Claire asked, putting her arm around my waist, hooking her finger through my belt loop.

"I'm going out outside," I said.

"Sounds good."

"Will you do me a favor?" I asked, moving her arm back to her side.

"I can do you a lot of favors, Ethan."

I ignored her come-on. "Do you know Raj Desai?"

"Yeah, I know him."

"Find him for me and tell him to meet me outside."

I left her there with her mouth hanging open. It was a dick move, but I couldn't worry about it now. She probably wouldn't find Raj, though. I was pissed beyond belief with him for leaving Meena in the clutches of a guy like Reese.

I walked outside and scanned the backyard for them. There were tons of people on the deck, hanging out and drinking. The music was louder out here than inside, but at least it was cooler and less crowded.

I marched to where they sat on the far side of the lawn. Denton was rubbing her leg. She wasn't encouraging him, but she wasn't pushing him away, either. I stood there, not sure what I was waiting for. Maybe for Raj so he could help me talk some sense into her. Or maybe a sign from her that I needed to step in.

Instead of Meena, it was Reese Denton that gave me the sign… when he kissed her. She didn't return his kiss, but she didn't exactly deny him. I no longer cared. My body moved on autopilot.

I cleared my throat. Meena broke their kiss, and they both looked up at me. She looked confused, and he was irritated as hell.

"We're leaving. Now."

She continued to stare at me, so I held my hand out. She took it hesitantly, like she wasn't sure if I was offering her a handshake. I yanked her up a little more forcefully than I should have.

"What the fuck is wrong with you? Are you seriously cock-blocking me right now, Callahan?" Denton yelled, standing up himself, wiping the dirt from his skinny jeans.

"Can't you tell she's drunk? Is this the only way you can get a girl these days?"

I moved Meena behind me so she wasn't in our crossfire. Reese and I stared each other down.

"She wants to be here."

"She doesn't know what she wants, asshole. She's drunk off her ass, thanks to you."

"I didn't force her. What are you going to do—drag her out of here?"

He shifted to walk around me, but I stopped him, grabbing a fistful of his shirt and pulling him toward me. I was a good foot taller, and I used that to my advantage. "Do not fucking test me. We both know how this will end. I'm bigger and stronger than you. I don't want to make you look like pussy in your house. I do that enough on the field."

He stared at me for a minute, weighing his options. The asshole didn't know there weren't any. He held out his hands and sighed. *Mission accomplished.* I let him go, giving him a good shove in the process.

I took Meena's hand, pulling her toward the front of the house. I was walking fast, and she was having trouble keeping up, but I didn't care. I just wanted to get her out of here.

"Ethan, stop. Where are you taking me?"

I stopped and took a deep breath, turning to her. I put my hands on her shoulders, peering down at her, trying to make my voice clear and slow so she would understand. "I'm going to ask you this just once. Do you want to be here?"

She stared at me in confusion.

I sighed and tried once again to penetrate the alcoholic haze of her mind. "Do you want to be alone with Reese Denton, in a bedroom where things might get out of hand, and you're not thinking clearly? Is that what you want? Because just say yes, and I'll leave your ass here."

She winced. It was a harsh way to talk to her. I had no right to be mad at her. Truthfully, I had no intentions of leaving her, but it would be easier if she believed it was her decision, not mine.

She shook her head slowly. It wasn't the clear answer I wanted, but fuck it, I'd take what I could get. I started walking again, pulling her beside me.

"I feel dizzy. Please stop."

I stopped, and she crashed into my back. She was swaying. I didn't trust her to make it across the lawn without falling, so I lifted her over my shoulder, ironically, caveman-style. It was the most efficient way. I ignored the whistles and murmurs of the other party people as I walked with Meena on my shoulder, looking like a total tool. I ran into Alex on my way out.

"Ethan? Is that Meena?" he asked in disbelief.

"She's had a lot to drink. I'm taking her to my place."

"Your place?" Alex raised his eyebrows.

"Yeah, there's no one at her dorm room to watch her, and I don't think she should be alone. Do me a favor." It wasn't a question, but Alex nodded anyway. "You know Raj Desai, right?"

"Yeah, I think so."

"Find him. Give him my number and tell him Meena's with me."

I didn't wait for Alex to answer. I knew he'd do this for me. I finally made it to my car. I opened the door and carefully placed Meena inside, pulling the seatbelt over her. She shifted and groaned, but she didn't protest.

I raced around to the driver's side. I started the car, putting it in gear. Her hand stopped mine from moving the gearshift.

"What?" I asked, ready to get into another argument with her.

"Are you okay to drive?" Her voice came out quiet and meek. My anger subsided instantly.

I stared at her hand on mine. It was trembling. I smiled to reassure her. "I've only had one beer." I didn't tell her that I spilled most of it. "I'm fine. I promise."

She nodded, turning toward the window, leaning her head against it. The ten-minute drive to my apartment consisted of her staring out the window as I clutched the steering wheel, replaying that fucking kiss in my head.

What the hell does he have that I don't? I'm a great guy. I'm a gentleman. Well, maybe not tonight, but I want more from her than some quickie. Hell, she knows that. She has to. By the time we got to my place, I was fuming.

Meena had trouble with the stairs, so I lifted her again, but this time in my arms, not over my shoulder. She was a perfect fit.

I took her straight to my bedroom, trying to be quiet so Darren wouldn't wake up.

Meena pointed to the lithograph poster on my wall. "Batman!" she exclaimed in a half-whisper-half-scream volume that only drunks could manage.

"Shh." Darren would be sleeping since he planned to take off early tomorrow for home. I laid her on the bed and sat on the edge of the mattress. I took her foot, putting it in my lap so I could get her shoes off.

"Your bed's so comfortable," she said in a quieter voice, stretching her arms.

"I know."

"You have a nice place."

"Thanks. It looks even better when you're sober," I said through clenched teeth.

She was trying hard to converse with me, but I was too pissed to be nice. More than that, I was hurt.

"What time is it?"

"A little past midnight."

"Happy birthday to me," she sang loudly.

I was too shocked to tell her to be quiet. I stared, not sure if she was playing a joke in her drunken state. "It's your birthday today?"

It was Wednesday, the day I'd asked her to hang out, and she'd said she couldn't. *Who is she spending her birthday with? Why wouldn't she go home to Mashpee?* She'd said her family didn't celebrate Thanksgiving, but they had to celebrate the girl's birthday. I knew enough about her religion to know it didn't preclude birthday celebrations.

"Happy Birthday, Meena." I tried to sound softer, but my voice still had an edge to it. I took her wrist in my hand. I had an urge to kiss the underside of it, but instead I just held it like I was feeling for a pulse.

"Yes, happy fucking birthday to me. It's mine, all mine now." There was a bitter quality to her voice. She sounded like she was pissed it was her birthday.

"Alex is going to look for Raj. I'm sure he'll come and pick you up."

"You're mad at me, aren't you?" She propped herself up on her elbows.

"Wow, you're very perceptive—even hammered," I replied sarcastically. "Don't worry. I'll get over it."

"Why? Tell me what I did wrong, friend number three." Meena had reached the slurring phase of drunkenness.

I should just tell her. After all, she probably wouldn't remember any of this. "Why did you do it?"

"Get drunk?"

"Why the hell did you kiss Reese Denton?"

"He kissed me."

"You didn't exactly stop him."

She stared at me, blinking several times, as if trying to comprehend my words. Finally, she swallowed. "I wanted to know what it felt like."

"To kiss Reese? Congratulations, you're one of many." I had no idea why I was acting like a total prude. In hindsight, I'd acted like an irrational psycho tonight, yet I didn't regret my actions. There was no way I was letting this girl get hurt. Not on my watch.

"To be kissed."

I dropped her wrist, trying to work my jaw closed. "That was your first kiss?" I'd figured Meena was a virgin based on the things she'd told me, but no boy had gotten to first or second base with this hot girl?

She nodded.

"Did you enjoy it?"

She laughed, surprising me again. "No, he tasted like warm beer, and he stuck his tongue so far down my throat I thought he was performing a tracheal intubation."

I laughed too, somewhat relieved by her confession.

"I was just pretending anyway."

"Pretending that you liked him?"

"That it was you."

My head swiveled toward her so fast I might have gotten whiplash. She scooted closer to me. Her brown eyes were calling to me. She trailed her fingers down my face.

My body reacted before my brain could register a single thought. I pulled her close to me and crushed my mouth to hers. Her hands fisted in my hair as she kissed me back. It was better than I'd imagined...and I'd imagined it *a lot*.

Her lips were as soft as pillows, and they molded to mine perfectly, like two puzzle pieces joining. I put my hand on her back, drawing her closer, feeling her small frame tremble against me. I went hard instantly. It couldn't go further than this, but right now, I needed her kiss.

I broke our contact before my hands roamed any further. We were both breathless. The lusty expression on her face must have matched my own. Then her eyes widened, and her jaw dropped.

"Sunshine?"

She clapped her hand to her mouth. "I'm gonna be sick!"

Meena jumped off the bed like she was on fire. It took me a second to register what was happening as she stumbled her way out of my room. I caught up to her as she rushed into the first closed door in the hallway. She fumbled for the lights and managed to find the switch.

Darren shot straight up in his bed, completely naked and cursing loudly.

I grasped Meena's waist and led her to the bathroom. "In here."

I walked her to the toilet. Luckily, we're boys so the lid was already up. She made it just in time.

"Everything okay?" Darren asked, appearing in the doorway.

I was holding Meena's ponytail away from her, rubbing her back as she puked up all of the liquor she'd consumed. "Shit, put some fucking clothes on, man!"

"Oh, yeah, I forgot I was in the buff," he said groggily, heading back to his room.

I sat there with Meena, next to the toilet, while she spent the next fifty-two minutes throwing up, gagging, crying, and apologizing.

"It's okay," I kept saying, trying to comfort her.

Thankfully, Darren put some clothes on and got me a few damp washcloths. I pressed them to her forehead and the back of her neck. I held her hair. I intermittently flushed the toilet. I whispered soothing words. I rubbed small circles onto her back. When it appeared she was finally done, I helped her up and steadied her while she washed her face. Darren couldn't handle the smell, but he helped in his own way. He found a new toothbrush for her and fetched a glass of water and aspirin.

"Here, she can wear this," he said, handing me one of his T-shirts.

I shook my head. There was no fucking way she was sleeping in Darren's shirt tonight. "I have a long shirt in my dresser. It'll be better, and grab a pair of my shorts."

Darren must have known what I was thinking, because he started laughing, but he got the clothes.

"Can you change by yourself?" I asked her, not wanting to let go of her waist.

"Yes, I'm fine." Her voice was clearer, which was a huge relief.

The shorts were falling off her, and she drowned in the shirt, but they had to be more comfortable than her jeans and sweater. When she was done, I led her back to my bedroom and laid her down, tucking the comforter around her.

I went to the kitchen to get her more water. Darren was fixing himself a snack. "Is she okay?"

"Yeah, she just had too much to drink."

"Apparently. What happened?"

I gave Darren a brief outline of the night's events. His eyebrows got incrementally higher with each sentence. "Shit, Ethan, you cock-blocked Reese Denton?"

"I don't care. He's a fucking asshole."

"Yeah, I know that. Hell, everyone knows that. Don't get me wrong, you're a good guy for doing it, but I've never seen you play the hero or throw a wrench in another guy's game."

"I'm not a hero. I'm as much of a tool as he is."

"Why do you say that?"

"I took advantage and kissed her too. After I fucking dragged her out of there when he did that."

"She told you she wanted it. It's not like you banged her."

I rolled my eyes. "Real classy, Jones."

"I don't get why you feel so guilty. Did she slap you or something when you did it?"

I chuckled cynically. "No—she threw up."

Darren laughed so hard, he had to clutch his stomach. "Fuck, that's funny."

"Actually, now that I'm thinking about it, she threw up after she saw you naked."

"Hey, don't push this on me. Maybe she came into my room for another reason? She wanted to see how a real man kisses."

I glared at him. "Shut up. I'm serious."

"Jealous much?" Darren grabbed his sandwich and made his way back to his room before I could respond. It was just as well. I didn't have an argument for him.

"I already had some," she whined when I brought her the water.

"Drink more. You'll be dehydrated otherwise."

She took the glass from me, but her hand was shaky so I held it for her. I sat on the edge of the bed next to her, allowing her to take small sips until it was the glass was empty. I took her wrist and undid her watch, setting it on the nightstand, and rubbed the place where it had been.

"Good night, Meena."

"Where are you going?" There was a fear in her voice I wasn't expecting.

"I'm going to sleep on the couch. I'll keep checking on you, though."

"Can you sleep here?" She patted the space beside her, looking so vulnerable and tiny.

I wanted to stay with her, but I didn't want things to get out of hand again. I didn't trust myself, and she was definitely in no position to be thinking clearly. One of us had to be the voice of reason.

"I don't think it's a good idea."

"Please," she pleaded. "Just until I go to sleep?"

How can I resist? I nodded, placing the water glass on the nightstand. I left the light on and moved to the other side of my queen-size bed, sliding in beside her. I had all my clothes on. At least they would serve as a protective barrier. I kept as much distance between the two of us as I could, lying down on my back and staring at the ceiling.

"I'm really sorry, Ethan."

"Don't apologize anymore. It's really okay. If that's the dumbest thing you do in college, you're better off than most people. I am curious, though, why you got so drunk. That's not like you, Sunshine."

Her back was to me, and she clutched the covers, moving into a fetal position. I wanted to reach out to her. Her hair was still in a ponytail. Would it hurt to sleep like that? I wanted to pull out her hair band and run my hands through it, but I stopped myself.

"I didn't want to be me tonight. I thought it would help me forget, but it didn't."

"Help you forget what?"

"That I'm not supposed to be here." She shivered, despite the heavy comforter.

"Where are you supposed to be?"

"Dead," she whimpered.

My heart froze in my chest, and I struggled to understand what she meant. She started crying soundless sobs that caused her body to shudder, like the emotion was too big for her small frame. I pulled her close. She turned and embraced me, and I held her tightly against my chest. I tugged out the hair band and stroked her silky hair while she cried in my arms.

I didn't say anything or encourage her to talk anymore. Truthfully, I wasn't ready for an explanation. I didn't even know if I wanted one. I just wanted…no…needed to hold her as much as she needed to be held.

She fell asleep like that. I kissed her forehead and whispered quietly, "If you were dead, I'd have no sunshine."

I fell asleep shortly after, with her curled up in my arms. It felt good…comfortable…right. That was, until the loud banging on my front door woke me from the most peaceful rest I'd ever had.

8

Meena

I woke up in the morning, blinking my eyes several times. The Palo Alto sun streamed through the blinds, casting patches of light and dark through the room. A room that was completely unfamiliar to me. The beige walls, mahogany furniture, and goose-down comforter were lovely, though.

I closed my eyes again, rolling over. A huge poster of Batman was staring at me. I squeezed my eyes shut again and forced them open. Nope, it wasn't helping. I flipped the comforter off and stared at the unfamiliar clothes I was wearing. They were loose but comfortable. They smelled like fresh linen and mountain spring…a familiar, pleasant scent. I stretched out on the large bed, deciding to go back to sleep. Whatever dream dimension I'd fallen into, I wasn't going to complain.

"Are you awake, Sunshine?"

The voice jerked me out of my thoughts immediately. In front of me, a freshly showered, shaved, and extremely handsome Ethan Callahan leaned against the doorframe. He was smiling, and his delicious aroma blanketed me. *I'm definitely dreaming.* He was sharply dressed in a pair of jeans that hugged his hips perfectly and a snug, black V-neck that showed off his sleek muscles.

"Ethan?" I croaked, not recognizing the quality of my own voice.

He handed me a lidded cup with straw as he sat on the edge of the bed. "Yes, it's me. Drink this."

"What is it?"

"It's hair of the dog that bit you. It'll make you feel better. I promise."

I sipped the drink slowly, thankful for the straw.

"How do you feel?"

I did a quick inventory. Despite my voice and confusion, I felt fine—relaxed, even. "I'm good. What happened?"

"You don't remember?" he asked with surprise.

"Not really."

He grinned his boyish grin. "Well, you went to a frat party, got wasted, let Reese Denton kiss you. I was there. I didn't trust him, and like I said, you were hammered, so I dragged you out of there and brought you to my place. Does that ring any bells?"

It started coming back to me in snippets and streams of haunting, hazy memories. "Ugh, I remember kissing him."

"Do you remember kissing me?"

I gaped at Ethan, confused because I was sure I would never forget kissing him, but I couldn't recall it.

"It's okay. I'm not offended you don't remember my kiss. I'm more insulted you threw up after. It's not a response I'm used to."

I gasped. "I threw up on you?"

"You managed to make it to the bathroom in time. I deserved it. You were drunk off your ass, and I shouldn't have kissed you in the first place. Do you forgive me?"

I imagined it must have been a friendly peck since I couldn't remember it. I was disappointed and relieved at the same time. "Ethan, it sounds like you saved me from a bad situation last night, which is what a really good friend would do. I'm in no position to accept your apology when the reality is that I owe you one. You obviously took care of me."

He released a breath and raked a hand through his hair, causing it to stick up for a second before falling back in place. "You don't owe me anything. In fact, you spent most of the night apologizing. Are you hungry?"

As soon as he asked, my stomach grumbled. "Yes, but you don't have to make me anything."

"It's not a problem, except, that is, if you tell me you don't like pancakes."

I smiled. "I love pancakes."

"Good, because that's the only thing I know how to make. If you want to take a shower, I washed your clothes. They're in the bathroom."

I looked down at the T-shirt and shorts I was wearing, recognizing they were Ethan's. My face flushed with embarrassment. "Did you—"

"You dressed yourself." He smiled impishly. "Not that I would have minded." He stood up and sauntered off, calling behind him, "Oh, the green toothbrush is yours."

The bathroom had many amenities, including stone tile, generous double sinks with a granite top, and a skylight. My favorite by far was the huge, executive-style shower encased with glass doors. I took a long, hot, steamy shower under Ethan's multi-shower heads, playing with each setting. His body wash smelled delicious. Even though it was a masculine scent, I slathered it all over myself. I did the same with his shampoo and conditioner making a note to buy him more.

I blushed when I looked over my neatly folded clothes—he had washed everything, including my bra and underwear. I tied my dripping hair into a tight bun. I brushed my teeth twice and mouthwashed three times. *How do I have a toothbrush here?* I assessed myself in the mirror. The dark circles under my eyes and blotchy skin made it easy to turn away. If only I had makeup with me, not that I ever wore it. I padded out to the living room, greeted by the sweet scent of hot pancakes.

"Have a seat. I'll grab you some coffee," Ethan said, waving his spatula. The space was open with a counter separating the kitchen from the living room. His apartment was ultramodern with eco-conscious concrete countertops and sculptural light fixtures. Exotic wooden planks covered the floors. A long, comfortable-looking, brown suede couch and a glass table faced a flat-screen television. The apartment was classy bordering on luxurious.

Besides the obvious expense of rent in Palo Alto, it was extremely neat and organized. It didn't seem like a college kid's apartment, but then again, Ethan wasn't the typical college kid. I sat on one of the modern, Eames-style chairs in the dining area. Everything was so designer chic. Perhaps my ass was sitting on a real Eames chair and not a replica.

Darren came out then, wheeling his suitcase behind him. "Good morning, beautiful. How do you feel?"

"I'm fine, thanks," I said, smiling brightly. He met my smile, except there was something mischievous in his.

"You were pretty drunk last night."

"I've heard," I said shamefully. I had a sudden memory of seeing Darren's naked butt. I winced as the heat crept into my face. "Sorry."

He started laughing, bending down so we were face-to-face. "Don't be sorry. Just one thing, though. The next time you come into my room in the middle of the night…plan on staying awhile."

"Don't you have somewhere to be, or are you letting her know where your hair straightener is in case she wants to borrow it?" Ethan barked from the kitchen entry, startling both of us.

Darren laughed. "Whatever. I'm going. You sure you want to stay here and miss Mom's turkey?"

"Yeah, give her a hug for me, and tell her I'm sorry."

They exchanged a hearty pat on the back that resembled some sort of awkward man-hug. It made me smile.

"You kids have fun." Darren turned to wink at me. Ethan groaned, and I did my best to smile and wave.

Ethan set a plate of before me with the most perfectly circular pancakes I'd ever seen, along with a bowl of fruit. He poured each of us orange juice from a carafe. It tasted freshly squeezed.

"This is really nice. Thank you," I said, placing the napkin on my lap.

"I wanted to do something nice for you."

"Do you do this for all the girls that spend the night?" I regretted the question immediately. *Why do I act like such a fool around him?*

He smirked. "No." As I took my first bite, he said, "I usually make them waffles."

I laughed.

"Just kidding."

"It's delicious." How did he get the pancakes so round?

"I really hate making pancakes."

"Why?"

"I'm kind of OCD. It takes me forever, because if it's not a perfect circle, I throw it away."

"Why did you do it for me then? I certainly don't deserve it."

He stared at me so intently I had a hard time meeting his gaze. "You do."

We continued eating in silence while I contemplated his statement.

"It's so weird. I remember going to the party with Raj and then bits and pieces of the night, but…" I slapped my hand to my forehead suddenly. "Oh God, Raj. He's going to be worried."

"Calm down. I had Alex find him. He knows where you are."

"Oh, that's a relief."

"Yeah, he tried calling me, but I'd left my phone in the car. He got my address from Alex and came over here."

I winced at the thought of Raj coming to find me. "I'm sorry."

"Don't be. He actually redeemed himself in my opinion. He left you alone and drunk with Reese." Ethan said Reese's name like it was a dirty word. "He wanted to take you back to his place. He didn't want to leave you here…with me."

"He did?"

"Yeah, but I finally talked him out of it and convinced him he could trust me." Ethan looked down at his watch. "Besides, he's getting on a flight to Ohio right about now, so it didn't make sense. Just make sure you call him soon so he knows you're fine."

"I'm glad he didn't give you too much trouble."

"Well, I wouldn't say that. He was okay, but before he left, he called friend number one."

I paused mid-bite. "He called Rachael?"

"Oh, yeah. She's a firecracker, huh? She had Raj make me go to my car to get my phone so she could call me."

"What did she say?" I braced myself for his answer.

"She made some very detailed threats to parts of my anatomy I value very much if I dared take advantage of you in any way."

I exhaled, imagining the ridiculous scene. I had imposed on Ethan way too much. "Did you even get any sleep?"

"Some."

"I'm sorry. They're very protective of me, and I'm usually not this stupid."

Ethan chuckled. "Stop saying that. I'm glad they are. They've earned their places."

I bit my lip, uncertain if my words were appropriate, but I wanted to say them. "You have too."

He smiled, but it was soft and sad. A thinking smile, not a feeling one. "Meena, there is something I've wanted to say since you woke up. I don't know how you'll react though."

"You can say it. You can say anything."

He took my hand, rubbing it gently. It felt intimate, but comfortable. He met my eyes and smiled brightly. "Happy birthday, Sunshine."

I snatched my hand away and covered my face. "I told you it's my birthday?"

"Yeah, you did, and I have a ton of questions about that. I've never met anyone who didn't like their birthday, at least not anyone our age. Why is that, Meena? And, while we're on the subject, why don't friend number one and two know it's your birthday?"

I moved my hands down to my lap and stared at him in horror.

"Don't worry; I didn't tell them. I just assumed they didn't know because I suspected they would have mentioned it to me…you know, between all the yelling and threats."

I swallowed hard. He deserved an answer to the mystery of why I was so fucked in the head. I would give him one. "I had a twin brother. He died when I was sixteen. I don't celebrate my birthday because it's a sad day for me. It's his birthday too."

He nodded, digesting my words. "I'm so sorry."

"I haven't celebrated it since he passed away. None of my family has."

We sat quietly for some time with only the sounds of scraping forks and knives filling the air. Finally, Ethan broke the silence with his soft, commanding voice. "There's something else. You said you were supposed to be dead. Why would you say something like that?"

I gulped, close to tears. "Don't worry, I'm not suicidal."

He exhaled, and his pinky flexed around mine under the table. I had no idea why that small touch comforted me so much.

"Then why?" he whispered.

"My brother's death was my fault. I was supposed to be where he was."

"That doesn't make much sense to me."

I took a deep breath, readying myself to tell a story I had never told anyone in my life. Raj and Rachael knew about Vijay's death, but they didn't know all the sordid details. Rachael had heard rumors, but she'd moved to Mashpee a year after the tragedy. "I wasn't always like this. I wasn't so uptight. In fact, I was a troublemaker."

He cocked his eyebrows in surprise.

"At least for my parents I was. My brother, Vijay, was perfect. He was like you. Math and science came naturally to him. He knew from the age of six that he was going to be a neurosurgeon like my dad. I wasn't a bad kid, but I talked back to my parents and disobeyed them. Not in huge ways, but enough so it caused them a great deal of anxiety. Vijay was the total opposite. He was respectful and obedient. He was their favorite. When I was sixteen, I started hanging out with a group of kids my parents disapproved of. They weren't awful kids, but they weren't exactly saints either. Vijay warned me they were a bad influence, but he kept it from my parents. He knew I had a hard enough time earning any praise from them."

I found myself smiling, remembering how overprotective my brother could be, but then I realized I was crying as hot tears slid down my face. Ethan handed me a napkin and tightened his pinky grip.

"We skipped school. Vijay invited himself along. No one wanted him there, but he didn't care. We hung out at the beach all day. My brother had never missed a day of school, and there he was, skipping... because of me. Some of the kids got drunk. I didn't, but not because I didn't want to. Vijay was watching me like a hawk. He didn't want me to ride on the back of Matt Stapler's motorcycle, so he insisted on taking that seat. I didn't see the whole thing. I just heard the crash, and we crashed too...into them. Vijay and Matt died instantly."

"I'm so sorry, Meena."

I laughed bitterly. "I just had a few scrapes, but I should have died that day. I should have been sitting where he was. He shouldn't have been there at all."

Ethan moved so fast, I didn't register what he was doing until his arms surrounded me in a tight hug. It was as though he was trying to take my pain.

"Listen to me. It wasn't your fault. You didn't force him to come. It wasn't as if he didn't have choices that day. He could have refused to get on that bike with a drunk driver. He could have called your parents, the police."

"He could have not cared so much for his stupid sister," I sobbed.

"You didn't cause his death, and he didn't take your place that day. It's called an accident for a reason. Nothing was intentional."

I sniffled, trying to catch my breath, and Ethan released me. "I didn't mean to lay all that on you."

"I'm glad you told me."

"I should go. I can walk home. Thanks for everything."

I started to pick up my plate to place it in the sink, but Ethan reached for my elbow, stopping me. "Can you do something for me?"

"Sure, I owe you."

"You don't, but I'm not above taking advantage of that feeling. Let's hang out today." I shook my head in protest, but he held up his hand. "I'm serious. Not for your birthday, but because, like you said, you owe me. We'll just enjoy this vacation day together…as friends. It's a beautiful day."

"Every day in Palo Alto is beautiful," I said, a smile playing out on my face, despite the fact that I'd just cried harder than I had in years.

"Yes, but it's not every day we have free. I want to take you somewhere."

"Where?"

"One of my other favorite places. Don't do it for you. Do it for me." He shook the hand with our conjoined pinkies. It felt so natural that I hadn't even realized he'd grasped my finger.

"For you?"

"Yeah, what the hell else am I going to do today?"

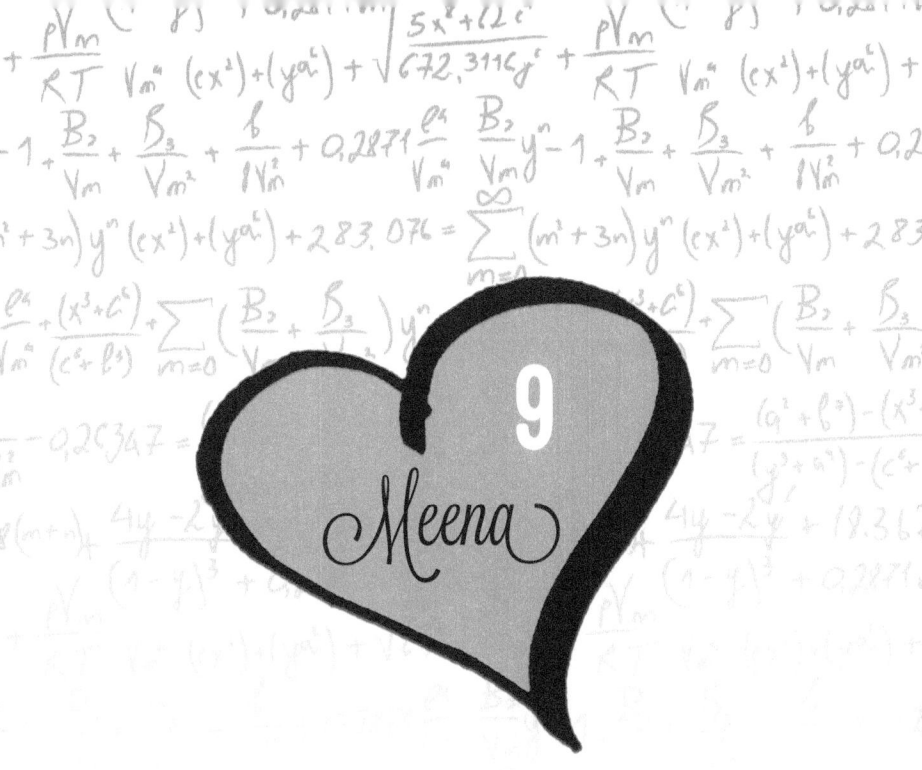

9

Meena

I didn't ask Ethan where we were going. I actually hadn't spoken to him since we entered the car. He wore dark sunglasses. It turned me on. Also, the interior of the car flooded with his scent. It was on him and on me. I was having a hard time not sniffing myself like a dog.

I spent the first ten minutes of the ride talking to Rachael, re-assuring her about my well-being. I didn't tell her I was still with Ethan to avoid a ruthless slew of questions. The next forty minutes, I talked to Raj. He accepted my explanation right away, and then told me about his night.

"Everything all right?" Ethan asked when I hung up.

"Raj had a tough night. That's why he was gone so long."

"What happened?"

I hesitated, but since Ethan already knew Raj's secret, it wouldn't really matter. "He was seeing this guy who was at the party last night. He found out the jerk had a boyfriend the whole time."

"That sucks."

"This is the first time Raj put himself out there."

"He'll learn soon enough."

"What's that?"

Ethan shrugged his shoulders. "Men are pigs."

I laughed, enjoying the cool ocean air that permeated the landscape. We had been driving for almost an hour, and we were by the coast. Ethan parked in a large lot on the Santa Cruz boardwalk. I had never been here, despite living so close.

"What are we doing?"

"Do you have a weak stomach? You know, when you're not drinking, that is."

I chuckled. "No."

"Have you ever ridden a roller coaster?"

"Not since I was twelve."

"Well, it's time you rode one again."

I stared at the high tracks above me, wincing at the screams of the other riders as they flew by us on another coaster. "Why is it so high?"

"It won't fall as fast otherwise."

We sat in the cozy car, and Ethan pulled the restraint across us. "You can hold on to this," he said, gesturing to the lap bar, "or here." He patted his arm.

I gripped the bar tightly.

"You know, that's not really holding us. It's the gravity."

"Are you trying to freak me out?"

"I'm just letting you know why my arm is the better choice."

The ride took off, and somewhere between the steep dips and inclines, I clutched his arm and buried my face in his chest.

When the ride came to a sudden halt, Ethan put his hand over mine. "You okay, Sunshine?"

I lifted my face, smiling widely. "Can we go again?"

Ethan

We made our way down the midway where the carnival games were. I stopped at a pitching game and laid down some money.

"What are you doing?" Meena asked.

"I'm going to win you something."

"Ethan, these games are shams," she whispered, like she was afraid she would offend the man who ran the game. It was so cute I had to laugh.

"I can win this one." She stared at me with those beautiful brown eyes, giving me a doubtful look. "Eight years as starting pitcher in little league says I can win."

I really wanted to get her a present, but she wouldn't like that. She didn't want any reminders that it was her birthday, and I didn't want anything to ruin our day, so this was a good compromise.

I weighed the wooden ball in my hand and threw it at the target of stacked balls. I missed, not once, but twice. Meena chuckled next to me.

"What?"

"I thought you said you were good at this."

I smirked at her, shaking my head. "Look at you, little Miss Smack-Talker." I pointed to the two remaining balls. "You try."

"Oh, no, I couldn't do that."

"Just try. I'm giving you free use of my balls." I didn't even get the double meaning until she started giggling. The man behind the counter laughed too. I smiled sheepishly. "Just humor me," I coaxed, pressing the wooden ball into her hand.

I showed her how to stand and aim, enjoying how close we were. She smelled like my body wash, but more feminine. Meena threw the ball fast and hard, which was impressive, but her aim was off. It missed the target entirely, hitting one of the stuffed prizes, which landed right on the guy behind the counter.

She bit her bottom lip. "I'm so sorry."

"Were you trying to do that? Because that's a really cool parlor trick," I remarked.

She shot me a cynical glance.

"Come here, little Miss Smack-Talker." I moved her off to the side, leaning down so my mouth was next to her ear. "Let me handle this. You stand here and pick out your prize."

I readied my last shot, trying to clear my mind and concentrate on the target. I threw it with accuracy and just the right amount of strength, knocking down the target. She squealed, patting me on the back in congratulations. I was hoping for a hug, but this was nice too. I was just happy my cocky attitude hadn't backfired on me.

"Which one?" the counter man asked.

"That one," Meena said, pointing to the strangest stuffed animal I'd ever seen. It looked a bit deformed, like the factory had made a mistake. It was the oddest shade of green, and it had two different kinds of ears. One was floppy and the other pointed. Even the counter guy asked if she was sure.

"Yes, is that okay?"

"Are you kidding? That's great. I've been trying to get rid of this thing for years," he said, getting it down for her.

She stared at the stuffed toy in her hand with crazy adoration as we made our way to the car.

"Thank you, Ethan. I love it. I've never had a stuffed animal."

"Not even when you were a kid?" It was hard to imagine. I thought it was a rite of passage for all kids.

"No, only learning toys. It's beautiful."

Beautiful was the last word I'd use to describe it. "Is it a bear or a dog?"

"Maybe it's a bog. See what I did there?" she said, laughing. I loved that laugh. It was innocent and sexy at the same time.

"Very clever. Aren't you going to be scared of it? I mean one eye is like twice the size of the other, and the ears don't match. It looks like it came out of a horror movie."

"Nope, I'll love it, not in spite of its differences, but because of them."

I shrugged, but I got what she was saying. She picked it because no one else would, and that said a lot about the kind of person she was.

"Are we going home now?" she asked when we reached the car.

"No, we're going to leave Bog here and go to the beach. We can't come to Santa Cruz and not say a passing hello to the Pacific."

I wanted to pull her close and take her hand as we made our way to the beach, but I restrained myself. I settled for keeping step with her, watching in fascination at the way the wind snapped strands of her hair loose from her ponytail.

"Why Batman?" she asked me as we walked along the edge where the sand and water greeted each other.

I stuffed my hands in my pocket. "I'm a math geek, so of course I like comic books."

"I wouldn't consider anything about you geeky."

"Batman is the best superhero, you know."

"Why?"

"He was just a guy. He didn't have any superpowers. He just used his brain and some kickass tools. I like all of them, though. I collected a ton of comic books as a kid. I still have them at my mom's house in Los Angeles."

"You're so mysterious, Ethan."

I'm mysterious? "What are you talking about? I'm an open book."

"Well, for one thing, I have no idea where you really live or where you're from. You've mentioned New York, Los Angeles, and Texas. For another, you've mentioned your mom, but you never talk about your dad." When I didn't respond right away, she added, "You don't have to talk about it if you don't want to."

"I grew up in Austin, Texas, until I was twelve, and my mom moved us to Los Angeles for her job. My father always lived in New York, and I would stay with him during summer and Christmas vacation. I love all three places, so I consider all of them my home."

"It must be hard dealing with divorce."

I hesitated answering, wondering how she'd react, but as usual, I deferred to the truth. "My mother and father were never together. I was the product of a one night stand."

She stopped in her tracks, staring at me. "Your parents told you that?"

"When I was old enough. They were always honest with me. Does that make you think differently of me?"

She shook her head so hard her ponytail flew along. "Not at all. I'm just surprised they told you. I already know you're an amazing person, so there's really nothing that can change my mind about that."

I smiled coyly at her compliment. "Thank you."

"What is your father like?"

"He was great. He died of a heart attack right before I came to college. I don't talk about him, but not because I didn't love him. It's actually the opposite. I really miss him."

"Oh, I'm sorry, Ethan."

I gave her a reassuring smile. "It's okay, you didn't know. My mother met my father when she was in Mexico on spring break. He was there for a business conference. He was a successful entertainment attorney. They were kind of opposites. He was older than her and very conservative. She was in grad school. It's funny—even though they never had a relationship, my father was always in my life. He was the kind of dad that would fly out to surprise you when your baseball team made the championships. He called me every night, too, and sent me letters. He was a busy man, but he wrote me actual letters on paper."

"It sounds like he loved you very much."

"I know it's not a common story. My parents never loved each other, but I never questioned that they both loved me."

We walked silently for a while. She curled her pinky around mine. It was my usual move, meant to comfort her, but right now, it was having the same effect on me.

"Why did you pick Stanford?" I asked. "Don't get me wrong—I'm happy you're here—but it seems so far away."

"That's why I picked it," she replied solemnly.

I couldn't blame her for not wanting to go home. Why would she want to if they didn't even celebrate her birthday?

"I don't want you to get the wrong idea," she said. "I love my parents. They're wonderful. But ever since Vijay died, something in our family broke. We mostly ignore each other. I don't give them any reasons to worry, and we just go through the motions."

"The motions of what?"

"Life, I guess. Why did you pick Stanford?"

I knew she wanted to change the topic, and I was glad to do it.

I grinned. "I actually really debated it. I got into MIT and Harvard, but I wanted to come here. Funny, isn't it? We could have ended up on the opposite sides of the county in each other's home states."

"But why not MIT? Isn't it math heaven?"

I laughed. "This time you will think less of me."

"No, I promise I won't. Tell me."

"I like to surf. It's hard to surf in Massachusetts."

"Seriously?"

"Yeah, there's nothing like swimming in the Pacific."

"I wouldn't know."

This time I stopped walking, "You've never been in the ocean? What about the Atlantic?"

She shook her head. "No."

"Why?"

"The emotional impairment I suffered from watching *Jaws* at the tender age of six resulted in exaggerated fears of the ocean."

I bit back my smile. "You're kidding."

"I know it's irrational. I can swim, but I just prefer pools. I had nightmares about sharks eating me for a long time after I watched that movie."

"You realize the fact you weren't in the ocean protected you from any attacks, right?"

"I was six. Cut me some slack, Swan Boy."

"Fair enough, but you're not six anymore." I sat down on the sand and began taking off my shoes. "I'm going to prove you have nothing to fear."

"How?"

"We're going in. This time we'll dip our feet in. Next time more."

"More?"

"You can't go through life being a toe-dipper, Sunshine. Come on, Meena, prove something to yourself."

"Why do you care about my stupid fears, Ethan?"

Because I care about you, I wanted to say, but instead, I grinned. "I'm no shark hunter, but I'd fight one for you."

She laughed, and what a great laugh it was — enthusiastic, genuine, and so very sexy. "That's quite possibly the sweetest thing anyone's ever said to me. I accept the challenge." She sat next to me and took off her shoes and socks. We both rolled up our jeans.

I took off my sweatshirt and took her cell from her front pocket and threw it down next to mine. We walked toward the water with our hands clasped.

"It's not so bad, is it?" I asked, as much to comfort her as anything else. She didn't act nervous except for her tight grip on my hand.

"No, but it's colder than I thought."

"We won't go further than this."

I turned to her, holding both her hands. The wind whipped through the strands of her hair. Her eyes met mine. I could get lost in those eyes…drown in them. I inched closer. She parted her mouth. The crashing waves surrounded us.

"Ethan," she whispered or maybe she shouted. Hard to tell with all the other sounds.

She crashed into me, the impact so sudden and strong that we both stumbled back. I fell on my ass, taking her with me. It took a second to realize the turbulent surf was to blame for capsizing us.

She was on top of me, lying against my chest. I wanted to keep crashing with her. To kiss her senseless right there.

Instead, I sucked in a deep breath, lifting her gently off me, breaking the moment. I deserved a medal for my restraint, but I promised myself when she agreed to come that I wasn't going to do anything to make her uncomfortable.

"Are you all right?"

"I'm okay." She headed toward the beach, her steps fast.

Our jeans clung to us. She took her sweater off, revealing a tight black tank top. My eyes pretty much popped out of my head. She crossed her arms, covering herself and fighting off her shivers. *Dick move, Callahan.*

I threw her my sweatshirt. "You can wear this."

"Thank you."

Pieces of hair stuck to her face, and her jeans tightened around her perfect ass. I forced myself to look away. Thank God she put the sweatshirt on quickly. I retrieved our cell phones and smiled apologetically at her.

"What are we going to do now that you've gotten me all wet?" she asked.

I choked at the question. She must have caught the double meaning because she blushed.

"I have an idea," I said, taking her hand.

The Beach Water Shed was a misleading name for the store. It was actually a high-end place, selling beach clothes and swimwear at outrageous prices, but it was convenient. I was familiar with it; I'd been there a few times. We walked in, dripping water all over the spotless floor.

"Are you sure this is a good idea?" Meena asked, hiding behind me like a child afraid of getting caught.

"Yeah, they're used to this kind of stuff." Even as I said it, the disapproving looks we were getting made it obvious I was talking out of my ass.

I headed for the first dress I saw. It didn't hurt that it was a short, white, lacy thing. "Will you wear this?"

She approached hesitantly. The first thing she did was look at the tag. I tore it off before she could see the price. "It's on me. It's my fault you're wet. It's only right that I should take care of it." *Fuck, did I just say that?*

She smiled and took the hanger, holding up the dress. She probably thought it was too revealing.

"We can find something else," I said.

"I like this, but I have money."

"You have to let me pay, or I'll feel like a total dick."

"Fine, but does that mean I get to pick your outfit?"

I shuffled my feet. "As long as you don't make me look stupid."

She walked over to the men's section. It was mostly swim trucks, but she found a pair of khakis and a white linen shirt.

"Can I help you?" the salesclerk asked. He was short and stocky, but I could tell from his build he worked out. His scowl changed to an instant smile when he turned from me to Meena.

"We're sorry. We're ruining your floor," she said, tilting her head toward the puddle marking our path in the store.

"No problemo, sweetheart. Are you getting this?" he said, taking the dress from her.

She nodded shyly.

I took out my dripping wallet and handed the guy my Amex card. I knew they worked on commission, and I was hoping it would distract him from staring at her. "We'll be wearing these out."

He pretty much ignored me as he looked over Meena. His gaze slithered down her body. My fists clenched. "This isn't your size. You're a small or maybe extra small."

"I didn't look at the size." *Why didn't I? Oh, probably because I was a dude.*

"Don't worry. I'll get you the right one. Just go ahead and get into the dressing room before you catch a cold."

My jaw tightened, and I wanted to deck this guy, but he was right. She was shivering, and it was my fault.

I finished changing before she did and stood outside the door. It irked me that the stocky sales boy waited beside me. "What are those?" I asked, staring at the box in his hand.

"Shoes. She's going to need shoes, unless she wants to wear tennis shoes with a dress." He said it as if I was stupid, and I pretty much was.

I sucked in a deep breath through my teeth when she came out. The dress hugged her curves, showing off her shapely figure and those long, lean legs. Her hair tumbled down her back, framing her face in rich, silky strands that curled at the ends. I swallowed, trying to form the right words, the ideal compliment, to match what I was feeling. Unfortunately, stocky sales boy beat me to it.

"You look like an angel."

"Thank you." She rewarded him with a bright smile.

Dickhead.

"Very nice," I muttered.

"I have the perfect sandals for you right here," he said, bending down on one knee, getting ready to take her ankle in his beefy hand. *That's not happening.*

I practically shoved the guy out of the way. "I'll take care of that. You can start checking us out. We're in a hurry." I handed him the tags I'd taken from our purchases. He mumbled something incomprehensible, but he left us. I bent down, mimicking his position. "Your shoes, ma'am."

Meena placed her hand on my shoulder to steady herself as I slipped the shoes on her dainty feet. They were that beige color girls referred to as nude, but they were a few shades lighter than her. I didn't know anything about women's shoes, but I knew that these shoes on her feet were turning me on something fierce.

"They're comfortable, but they seem really high."

I stood up, my hand hovering over her waist, struggling to keep it from touching.

"I'll never let you fall."

She took in a deep breath, keeping her eyes on her feet. "I broke my rubber band. My hair's a mess."

"It's beautiful. You're beautiful."

"Thank you for the dress."

"Thank you for wearing it." A thought occurred to me, and I fumbled with the collar of my shirt, trying to form the right words. "Do you need anything else, you know, to wear underneath?" Everything was wet, so it would stand to reason she would, and this store didn't sell those things.

She shook her head and smiled. "I can forgo for a night." She walked away from me.

Fuck. I discretely readjusted myself. The sight of her ass sashaying in that dress, and knowing she wasn't wearing any panties, wasn't helping the cause.

I caught up to her before we got to the register, handing her a button-up sweater I'd found. "This too," I said. She looked at it curiously. "I don't want you to get cold." I hoped I sounded sincere; I didn't want to tell her I was a stark raving jealous loon when it came to guys ogling her, and that dress was exposing just a little too much…sunshine for my liking.

We left with two plastic bags containing our wet clothes. I was glad to be carrying the bags because it kept me from putting my arm around her.

"Are we going home?" she asked.

"Do you want to?"

She was quiet for a moment, and I held my breath waiting for her answer. "Not unless you want to."

"Hungry?"

"Starving."

"There's a place on the boardwalk with a ton of vegetarian options."

She seemed surprised that I would think of her dietary restrictions. This girl had no idea I thought about her all the time.

Not only was the line out the door at the restaurant I'd chosen, it stretched around the corner. It was the day before Thanksgiving, and no one was cooking at home today. I checked my watch, happy it was as waterproof as claimed and was still ticking away. I mentally patted myself on the back for my perfect timing.

"Ethan, we don't have to eat here. It's going to be hours before we get seated."

"Or no time at all." I took her hand and led her inside.

"Reservations for Callahan, party of two," I said to the hostess.

We were seated in the quiet corner as I'd requested.

"When did you make reservations?"

"This morning after you agreed to come."

"What if I had wanted to leave?"

I shrugged. "Then I would have canceled them. It's not like they couldn't use the table. Are you mad?"

"No, but it's weird that you were keeping us on a schedule this whole time, and I didn't realize it. Did you plan the ocean?"

"Walking along it, yes. Making you wet, no." *Shit,* I coughed, trying to cover up the stupid thing I'd said.

She lifted the menu so I couldn't see her face.

"I made the reservation because the restaurants here get busy. I wanted to take you somewhere nice."

Although I couldn't see her, I knew her voice well enough to know she was smiling. "There is a lot of stuff I can eat here. Thank you for being so thoughtful."

We shared a nice dinner over candlelight and laughter. It made me happy to see the joy in her face and know I had a part in that. I liked making her happy. I'd debated the whole day about bringing up her birthday, but I decided to go through with it. I hated the fact it depressed her. I wanted to give it back to her. It was the present I most wanted to give her.

"Sunshine, I know you don't celebrate your birthday, but do you mind if I do?"

"What do you mean?"

"I want cake…Will you have some with me?"

She was thoughtful for a moment as she always was when weighing things. "Dessert would be nice."

When the waitress left, Meena looked at me quizzically.

"What?" I asked.

"She didn't ask what we wanted."

"I know."

They brought out the small chocolate cake I'd ordered. "Happy Birthday, Meena" was iced on top in pink cursive with one long candle in the middle.

"You did this?"

I nodded. "The birthday wish is the strongest wish there is. You've wasted so many of them. It's time you made one."

I relaxed when she smiled. The candlelight reflected off her face, illuminating her gorgeous eyes. She closed them to make her wish. I wanted to grant whatever it was. She was silent for a moment, pursing those perfect lips, before blowing out the candle.

"What did you wish for?"

"It won't come true if I tell."

"If it's meant to come true, it will. That's just an old wives tale."

She cut the cake and doled out the pieces. The math guy in me appreciated the perfect, even pie shapes.

She laughed, skimming the icing off her cake and licking her fork. "So, let me get this straight. You believe the birthday wish is real, but the telling part isn't?"

"I guess so."

"Fine, I'll tell you. After all, we wouldn't be here if it weren't for you. I wished we didn't have to leave. This has been such an unexpected, fun day."

"I can make your wish come true."

"What do you mean?"

"Let's spend the night."

She dropped her fork.

I rubbed the back of my neck, trying to explain myself. "Sorry, that's not what I meant. There's a nice hotel along the beach. We can get separate rooms. I thought we'd just hang out tomorrow since it's Thanksgiving and all."

She didn't believe me.

"I didn't make a reservation, if that's what you're thinking. I'm sure they have rooms. If not, there are tons of places here, but hey... we don't have to stay. I just...I want to make your wish come true."

She didn't answer for a long time, concentrating on her cake.

I waited like I always did, but I ran out of patience. "Meena, it was a bad idea. I spoke before I thought."

"It's okay. It was my wish after all."

After dinner, we strolled along the boardwalk. There were a ton of couples, walking hand in hand. Street vendors were selling an assortment of snacks and souvenirs. The stores were all lit up and busy. A man on a microphone was encouraging people to come inside a theater to watch some kind of macabre show.

"Thank you, Ethan. It's been a long time since I've celebrated my birthday. Thank you for today. Also, thank you for not making the restaurant sing happy birthday to me. That would've been embarrassing."

I stopped walking and smiled coyly at her. "I'm curious. How long has it been since someone's sang that song to you?"

She swallowed. "Seven years."

"I think we should make up for that."

I walked over to the guy with the microphone. "Can I borrow this?"

He scowled at me, not letting it go. I took out my wallet and peeled a few bills. They were still damp. I was smart enough to remember the cell phones, but not my wallet. He snatched them, handing over the microphone.

I started singing the birthday song. She was far enough away so it wasn't obvious I was singing to her. I was no great singer, but this song didn't require that. It was also infectious, and soon, all the people walking along the crowded boardwalk halted and joined in.

Meena's eyes darted around, taking it all in, but I only had eyes for her. She was embarrassed, but damn it, she deserved to hear this song, and now she had at least a hundred people singing it to her. We sounded awful, but that wasn't the point.

Everyone clapped when it was over. Even though I tried to make her anonymous, it was pretty obvious I was singing to her. Several strangers stopped to wish her a happy birthday. She smiled politely but self-consciously.

"Come here," I said, crooking my finger. She stepped toward me hesitantly, but when she was in reach, I put my arm around her and held it tightly. I hugged her and whispered in her ear, "Are you ready to beat the shit out of me yet?"

She laughed. "You're lucky I like you."

"Yes, I am."

I opened her door for her when we got to the car. She flashed a brilliant smile at me, pausing before stepping in. "If you still want to make my wish come true, I would like that. I'd like to spend Thanksgiving here with you as long as we get separate rooms."

"Absolutely," I replied with a huge-ass grin.

Meena wasn't playing a mind game with me. She was honest, and I liked that about her. The truth was I wished for something more, but she didn't, and I would respect that.

We had done so much that it was hard to believe it was just one day. It was equally hard to come to grips with the fact I'd been hung-over and exceptionally sad this morning and now I was deliriously happy. Ethan had done that for me. I usually spent this day sulking, crying, and always alone. It hadn't been a good day for me in a long time. Not until today.

I expected a small motel near the beach, not a luxurious seaside resort with gleaming chandeliers, polished marble floors, and a concierge desk. My jaw dropped at the room prices. Two rooms would be over a thousand dollars! "Ethan, we can go somewhere cheaper," I suggested when we stood in line at the registration desk.

He shook his head. "This is on the beach. Don't worry. I can afford this."

Judging from his lifestyle, he could, but it still seemed like a waste of money, and he'd spent so much today...on me. "Get one room." He cocked his eyebrows, so I quickly added, "One room, double beds. Friends can do that, right? Spend the night in the same room?"

"I don't mind getting two rooms."

"One room, two beds," I repeated.

Ethan paid for our room, and the lady in reception asked if we had any luggage. I looked away, embarrassed that we didn't. She would think this was some sort of sordid booty call, but Ethan wasn't flustered at all. In fact, he didn't seem to care what other people thought. I admired that quality about him.

"No luggage, but we need these laundered please." He slid the plastic bags with our damp clothes to her. She stared at them questioningly, but took them.

We headed to the hotel store. There wasn't a great deal of selection, but Ethan found ridiculous T-shirts embossed with flourishing script stating "Santa Cruz was made for lovers." He grinned lopsidedly as he handed one to me. We bought simple cotton shorts and a few toiletries too.

The room was amazing, done up in neutral colors, with a large balcony that framed the beach like it was a work of art. There were two beds broken up by a nightstand. A small, striped settee sat in front of a flat screen television. We looked at each other, and for the first time, we both seemed lost for words. It was a spacious room, but it felt claustrophobic. This was a bad idea.

I blurted out the first question I could think of just to fill the empty space. "Are you rich?"

He laughed. "Why do you ask?"

"I'm sorry, that came off so…tactless."

"You can ask me anything."

"I was just wondering, because you don't come off as the typical college student. You live in a very posh apartment in one of the highest-rent districts in the world. You drive a nice car, and this hotel… Well, it's not something I would have picked. I hope I'm not taking advantage of you, economically. I know today was very expensive."

"It's nice of you to be concerned about that. The answer is yes. My mother's well off, but I have my own money. My father was very successful. He left me a lot of money when he died. So much, I don't need to worry about it. I invested the bulk of it and budget myself, but yes, you could say I'm wealthy. I don't usually tell people, but they figure it out."

"That must be hard for you."

"Why do you say that?"

"Well, for one thing, I'm sure people treat you differently when they find out, and even if they don't, you'd wonder if they were. But, mostly, I think it would be hard because of the way you obtained it. I'm sure you'd give it all back to have your father."

A wistful smile spread over his face. "That's exactly right. I would—even if it were just one more day. You know, the thing that hurts the most is the absence of him. Whenever I hear a funny joke or the Yankees win, I want to pick up the phone and call him, but there's no one to call."

He sat on the one of the beds. I remained standing, wanting to comfort him but not trusting myself to be close to him. "Ethan, I hope you're not offended, but I think it might be easier if you believed in God."

"It's hard for me to believe in things I can't explain. My mind is rooted in science and math and the belief that there is an answer to every question. The moment you explain the answer with God, you stop trying to find the truth. I can't accept that."

"Sometimes it's not about thinking. It's just feeling. I didn't always believe like I do now."

"What changed?"

I swallowed the lump in my throat. "I have to believe my brother went to a better place than this, or maybe he's back here again, starting over."

"Reincarnation?"

"The ultimate recycling program, don't you think?"

He shrugged. "It's an interesting thought, especially when you consider energy doesn't die."

"I'm sorry. I didn't mean to start a philosophical conversation that is very unlikely to result in consensus. I just wanted you to know it's helped me."

"Did you ever go to therapy after he died?"

"No."

"I think you should. It'll help."

"Would you consider going to church? Or synagogue? A temple?"

He laughed. "That's a lot of choices."

"All paths lead to one place, in my opinion. In fact, spirituality is not limited to a place. I felt it at the beach when we were walking. I felt it this morning when I was talking to you."

"I felt it too, Sunshine. I'll consider it. Would you consider therapy?"

I was surprised he was willing to compromise at all. I nodded, at a loss for the words to tell him how special he was—how amazing, perceptive, and kind. He looked so handsome in the linen shirt and khaki slacks I'd chosen. He had left a few buttons undone, and it was becoming my undoing. His hair was disheveled, making it even sexier, and his face had a bronze glow. I desperately needed to get away from him.

He stood and walked toward me. I thought he might kiss me, but he did something equally intimate. He clasped my wrist and took off my watch, staring at it before setting it on the dresser.

My throat went dry as he rubbed my wrist. "It's broken from the water. I'll get you a new one."

"It's just a cheap watch," I said in a cracking voice I didn't recognize.

He released my wrist, taking off his own watch. He set it next to mine. I stared at the odd pairing. They would never share the same shelf or even be sold at the same store. They were so different…like us.

"What are you thinking?" he asked, interrupting my internal conflict.

"I need to take a shower."

He nodded, strolling over to the television, sucking in some breath. "Want to watch a movie after?" he asked, flipping through the channels on the flat screen. He was trying to sound flippant, but his voice was husky.

"Sure, you pick."

"*Jaws*."

"Very funny."

I didn't take cold showers, but a hot one wouldn't be the right choice. When I came back into the room, he had a movie set up for us. I wore the ridiculous tourist shirt and shorts, but his lusty stare made me feel as if I were wearing scandalous lingerie.

The temperature in the room was comfortable, but it felt unbearably hot like there was a tangible quality to the air between us. He must have felt it as well, because he jerked his gaze away from me suddenly, announcing he needed a shower too.

I opened the balcony and breathed in the fresh ocean air. I could not let my emotions take over. This was wrong, I kept repeating to myself like a mantra. Why had I agreed to spend the night with the only man I was attracted to in the most romantic place in the world? Surely, I was a masochist and enjoyed tormenting myself. There was a knock at the door, interrupting my self-deprecation.

I opened the door to a room service guy. Ethan had ordered snacks for us. I scrounged around in my purse, but I had no cash on me.

His wallet sat on the dresser. It was damp, but each bill was in neat sequential order. I peeled off a bill, almost ripping it, and gave it to the room service attendant. Even though it was just popcorn and licorice, the hotel was so luxurious they placed it all under a silver dome in fine crystal bowls. I headed back to Ethan's wallet. All of his money was going to be a huge clumpy mess in the morning. I separated out the bills, placing them on the high wooden dresser so they would dry. That's when I felt the small wrapped package in another compartment. This was definitely an invasion of privacy, but I took it out, reasoning whatever it was would also need to dry. I stared in shock at the square, gold-foiled package in my hand.

"Hey, whatcha doing?" Ethan asked, startling me. I felt an immediate heat with his presence, but I continued to focus my energy on the tightly wrapped package in my hand.

"I tipped the room service guy."

"Okay."

"I thought I'd lay your money out so it could dry. What's this?" I held up the package.

I thought he might be mad or contrite, but he laughed instead. "It's a condom."

"I know that."

"Then why are you asking?" His voice was authentically curious.

"Did you plan for us to end up like this? Was it contrived?"

Ethan's face transformed as he considered my statement. First there was shock, then he looked hurt, but his eyes finally narrowed into irritation. "No."

"Then why do you have this?"

"I always carry one in case of emergencies."

"An emergency? Like your dick accidentally falling into a girl's vagina?" I asked haughtily.

He took a step forward, and I naturally took a step back until my back was against the wall. He stayed at arm's length, but it still felt too close. I threw the condom on the dresser. It slid to the end, teetering near the edge.

"I've had it in my wallet for a year. It has nothing to do with you."

"Are you telling me you haven't had sex in a year?" I asked in disbelief.

"No, I'm telling you I haven't had an emergency in a year. In case you forgot, it was your idea to spend the night here and to get the same room."

I held up my hand to cut him off. "I know what you're trying to say. You think I want this. That I'm leading you on like some kind of... cocktease."

He shook his head, letting out a cynical laugh. "That's not what I was thinking. Your acting like...like a—"

"Like a complete bitch," I offered.

"Thank you."

My eyes widened, and he immediately looked sorry. He made an attempt to touch my hair, but I moved further away.

"Meena, I know you wanted to spend the night because you were having a good time. I know you wanted to get one room because of the expense. I believe you at your word when you say things. I wish you'd offer me the same courtesy."

He walked over to the couch and sat on it, placing his head in his hands. "If you want to leave, we can. Or we can just go to bed. Just to be clear, so there's no misunderstanding, I mean our separate beds. I don't feel much like watching a movie anyway."

I *was* a bitch. Ethan didn't deserve this. I was acting like an ungrateful child, throwing a stupid temper tantrum. I walked toward him, taking a seat next to him. My voice was barely louder than a whisper, but it cracked with emotion. "I'm sorry. I shouldn't have assumed. I know you're not that guy. You've been nothing but a very good friend to me, and I just proved I don't deserve it. This was the best birthday of my life. Sadly enough, I think it was the best day of my life. I'll always be grateful to you."

He looked up, and his features softened into a reassuring smile.

"Being with you is hard for me," I said. "It conflicts and confuses me at the same time."

"Why?"

"It's very easy to talk to you. I've told you things I've never told anyone, but at the same time, it's very difficult too."

"That makes no sense."

I gripped my knees to keep them from shaking. "You really need me to say it?"

"I do."

He was going to make me spell it out for him. I sighed in frustration because I knew he was not this dense. "I'm attracted to you, Ethan Callahan. Isn't that obvious?"

"I wouldn't say it was obvious, but I'm glad you admitted it."

"Well, I am, and that makes it difficult because I feel like I'm constantly fighting my feelings. It's a struggle, and truthfully, it's exhausting."

He was quiet for a moment. I was breathing hard, but I had no idea why, except that he was close to me. He leaned toward me. His eyes were intense and turbulent like the ocean itself, and his voice had a husky quality. "There's a very simple solution."

"What's that?"

"Stop fighting." He leaned in closer.

I closed my eyes, preparing for his kiss. I could feel the heat of his breath against my face. He smelled delicious. But he stopped just shy of my mouth—he wanted me to complete the kiss. He wanted it to be my decision, and in that moment, I made the only decision that felt right.

His lips felt soft but demanding against mine. I ran my fingers through his hair. He parted his mouth, and I let my tongue explore. He groaned and pulled me onto his lap so I was straddling him. His arms tightened around me.

My hands skirted tentatively under his T-shirt, trailing along his defined abs. I tasted his mouth and felt the intake of his breath. I felt the hardening of his other muscle beneath me. I tugged at his shirt impatiently. He broke us apart and took it off in a quick, fluent, one-handed method. I stared wide-eyed at his bare chest, trailing my fingers over it. He was patient and let me take my time exploring his body. It was impressive.

"You work out." It was a statement not a question. He grunted in response, which turned me on even more. "You have a tattoo," I remarked, tracing the four-leaf clover that graced his upper bicep.

"Do you have any?" he asked, but before I could answer, he covered my mouth. "Don't answer that. I'll find out on my own."

Of course, he knew I was too conservative for a tattoo, but I didn't object to the idea of his exploration. In fact, I encouraged it. He placed his hands on either side of my shirt and stared at me, waiting for permission. I lifted up my arms so he could remove it. He stared at my naked breasts with pure intensity. I should have felt shy about this, but I didn't. I wanted him to see me. All of me. It felt natural.

His thumbs flicked my nipples before taking one into his mouth. I moaned at the heat of his tongue as his lips encircled it. I shamelessly pulled myself up on my knees to give him better access. He sucked on it in a slow, precise rhythm before moving onto the other, providing the same luscious treatment. "You're so beautiful, Meena," he whispered against my chest.

"You too," I said, tugging his hair.

His laughter quickly tapered off. He pushed me back down to his lap and trailed hungry kisses over my neck and shoulders.

When we broke away, coming up for air, we were panting, but I didn't want to stop. He swallowed hard. "I have to say something before I lose my nerve."

I tried to press myself against him again, willing him to shut up, but he wouldn't let me.

"I need you to listen. We can go as far as you want. There are other things we can do to make each other feel good without having sex. I'm okay with any of it, and I'd settle for just kissing you all night if that's what you want. You draw the line. I just ask you tell me where it is now—"

I wiggled out of his grasp and covered his mouth with mine, inhaling the last of his words. When I sat up again, I looked into his eyes and said very clearly, "Ethan, I think this constitutes an emergency."

He grinned with happiness, but it changed to a hooded look as he growled in pleasure. He picked me up, carrying me without any effort to the nearest bed, laying me down, easing himself on top of me. He suckled my earlobe, his hot breath washing over my skin. The feeling was so pleasurable, I shivered.

He peppered hot, soft, wet kisses down my body until he reached my shorts. Slowly, he peeled them back, sliding them down my legs. Then he started kissing my ankles, calves, and moved upward until he reached the most sensitive part of me. He wrapped his arms around my thighs, pressing kisses on each and pulling me close. The delicious wetness of his tongue pierced me in soft thrusting motions.

I writhed and moaned, calling out his name. Rachael had told me about oral sex in great, gory detail. It sounded disgusting when she described it, but it wasn't. It was amazing. I leaned up on my elbows and watched Ethan's gorgeous head of sandy brown hair bob between my thighs. He lifted his eyes to meet mine. Something in my expression must have turned him on because he moaned so deeply that the vibration traveled through my body.

I couldn't look anymore and fell back against the bed, succumbing to the divine heat of the act. He licked, sucked, and flicked with his talented tongue. An intense building sensation filled me, followed by an unfamiliar current coursing through my body, waking every molecule.

I was so far gone, I didn't even realize he was on top of me again, kissing my neck and chin. I encircled him with my arms, drawing him closer, relishing the feeling of the hard planes of his body against my softer ones.

"You're so wet," he said in that husky voice I loved.

"Your fault," I replied, breathlessly.

"I should take care of that, don't you think?"

I laughed, but it came out choked. "Take care of it, please."

"I'll be right back."

I tightened my grip, "Where are you going?"

He laughed and kissed me again. "To get our emergency gear."

"Oh." I laughed, letting go of him. He walked over to the dresser area. *Holy shit. When did he take off his pants?* I stared at his beautiful ass with a sudden desire to sketch it. I wondered if this was how Michelangelo felt when he first saw David naked. Ethan's butt was sculptural.

"Are you checking out my ass, Sunshine?"

Does he have eyes in the back of his head? "Yes," I said honestly.

"I'm glad you like the view." *Like? I was in awe of it.* "Do you know where the condom is?"

"It's on the dresser."

"It's not here."

"Yes, it is."

"Well…I don't—"

"Ethan, I swear I put it there. Look harder. I'm going to help you look." There was a crazy, hysterical panic in my voice.

He laughed loudly and in a few swift steps, he was back on top of me, leaning his weight against his elbows.

"You're so mean." I pouted, gently slapping his chest.

"I wanted to give you another chance to back out."

"Why would you do it like that?"

"Because I didn't want you to feel guilty about turning me on."

It was ingenious of him, in a way. If I'd had any doubts, he'd given me an opportunity without worrying about his feelings. I couldn't believe he thought so deeply about my needs. He brushed his lips down my neck, instantly calming me.

"Do you have it on?" I asked.

"Yes, feel."

He took my hand and guided it to his erection. I think he did it to calm me, like the way a nurse might show a nervous patient a needle before injecting it. I doubted that worked, and this didn't either. He was hard and long. I moved my fingers up and down his length. He slapped my hand away when I tried to do it a second time.

"That's enough," he groaned in frustration. Then, much gentler, he whispered in my ear, "We only have one. Let's not waste it."

He bent my legs so my knees were in the air. He moved them outward, spreading me. "As far apart as you can go, baby."

I liked the new nickname. It made me wetter.

"You work out too, don't you?" he asked, trailing his hands up and down my legs.

"Yoga and Pilates," I answered, pleased with the impressed look on his face as I moved my thighs out as far as I could.

He kissed the top of each knee and chuckled. "We're going to have so much fun."

He leaned over me and penetrated me. "Are you okay?"

"Yes, fine." It actually wasn't painful at all. Then he moved deeper.

"And now?"

"Yes," I answered, turning away from his intense gaze.

"Meena, look at me…please."

"Why?" I cried out, not capable of more than a syllable.

"I need to see you so I know if you're in pain."

"Are you going to make it not hurt?"

He smiled softly. "I'm going to try my best." He moved deeper still. Ethan winced like he was in pain. "Fuck…you're so tight, baby."

"That's good, right?"

He managed some sort of half laugh, half-grunt response. He leaned in and kissed me passionately. "It's awesome…for me. For you…I'm not so sure. At least, not the first time."

He was pressing in incrementally. Each movement was slow and deliberate as I stretched to accommodate him. I wrapped my legs around his waist and encouraged him.

"No," he commanded.

I loosened my legs instantly, feeling guilty that I had done something wrong.

He shook his head, kissing my neck and whispering in my ear. "I love it. I really do, but I need to be in control, and right now I'm struggling."

It suddenly occurred to me why he was in pain. It wasn't from what he was doing, but from what he wasn't. He was holding back… for me. He pushed in more, and I gasped at the feeling of him inside of me.

"Okay?"

I nodded, incapable of speaking.

"That's it."

"It's over?" I cried, in a garbled voice.

He let out a strained laugh-grunt. "We haven't even started yet. I just meant I'm all the way inside you. I'm going to move now." He slid gently back and forth, staring down at me, occasionally closing his eyes and wincing in a mixture of pain and pleasure.

I moaned each time he thrust, feeling the slow contentment of his movements.

"I need to move faster."

I nodded, tightening my grip on his arms.

"You can help me now."

Instantly, my legs encircled his hips again, clenching tightly. He pulled out and rammed back into me in a rhythmic pattern that left me demanding more. He wanted me to set the pace of his thrusts, and I set it for high. I screamed his name, and he screamed mine, along with moans and grunts of pleasure.

His body got slicker with sweat as he moved against me. The momentum started building again, but stronger this time, until the sweet release of climax came. When I opened my eyes, he was staring at me intensely, like it was part of his pleasure.

He kissed me before lifting up. Then he squeezed his eyes shut, drawing his head up, murmuring my name, and increasing his movements, gliding with effortless beauty until his face contorted, frozen in a moment of incredible ecstasy. He fell on top of me, and I embraced him closely until our breathing returned to normal.

"Am I hurting you?" he whispered.

He was heavy, but his weight was distributed evenly enough that it wasn't unpleasant.

"No."

"Did I hurt you?"

"No." I wanted to say more, but I couldn't articulate anything else.

"Good," he said, pressing his lips against mine, before pulling out.

I missed our connection.

"I'll be right back." And then, as if he wasn't ready to go, he kissed me several more times before leaving the bed and making his way to the bathroom.

I had brought my shorts into the bathroom, thinking she might be more comfortable not seeing me completely naked. It was hitting me that I'd just taken her virginity. I discarded the blood-tinged condom in the toilet, a little shocked by its weight. That was the hardest I'd come since I was a teenager—I couldn't believe what she did to me. It wasn't like I was turned on by virgins, but Meena had the ability to make me feel the raw intensity of everything, like I'd been looking through a filter before her.

I washed my face and stared at myself in the mirror, a little pissed I had only one condom. I wanted her again. It was for the best, though, since she'd be sore. We'd have to wait. I took a washcloth and dampened it with warm water for her.

A sudden panicked thought gripped me. *Will she want me again?* We hadn't talked about anything. We'd just acted…completely spontaneously. *Will she regret this? Can we just be friends again?* Fuck, did I even want that? Hell no—I wanted to make her come again…and again.

Meena sat up, biting her lower lip nervously. She covered her naked body with the top sheet from the bed, clutching it as if it offered her some protection.

I sat next to her. "Are you okay?"

"I have to take a shower," she said, and she jumped off the bed in a swift movement, taking the sheet with her, but I sat on it. She yelped as it fell away before stumbling into the bathroom. She slammed the door in my face.

"Meena, talk to me," I urged, but the only response was the shower starting.

I sat on the edge of the bed and put my head in my hands. I had my answer. She regretted it. She regretted me.

She came out a short time later, wrapped in a towel.

"Do you want to get dressed?" I offered, getting up to leave the room and offer her privacy.

She shook her head. "In a minute."

I sat back down, unsure how to start this conversation. "I'm sorry."

"For what?"

I gave her a questioning look. "Because you obviously regret it."

"Why would you think that?"

I sighed. "What else am I supposed to think when the first thing you do is jump in the shower to wash it away." I turned to her. "To wash me off you." My voice was full of hurt that even I was not expecting.

She opened her mouth in a perfect O and shook her head. "Ethan, you're wrong. It was wonderful. I know you were very gentle with me, and you didn't have to be. I will never regret that you are my first."

I felt my muscles relax, and I exhaled a long deep breath. "Why the hell did you jump in the shower?"

She bit her lower lip nervously. "I was bleeding. It was kind of gross."

I laughed and tucked a damp strand of hair behind her ear. "You didn't know you were going to bleed?" I said more disbelievingly than I meant it to sound. It didn't put her at ease.

"Of course I knew. It was just a shock." She darted her eyes around the room nervously. "I can't look. How bad is it?"

I turned and lifted the top sheet back into place. The one we had been lying on. "I don't think housekeeping's going to love us, but I'm sure they've seen worse. Looks like we'll make use of the second bed."

"Ugh."

I turned back to her, shifting closer, putting my arm around her. "Sex is messy. It's natural and dirty and hot and beautiful."

She nodded. "It was all of those things and more. I wasn't prepared for it."

"It's different from that stupid birds and bees talk our parents have with us, eh?"

She bit her lip again nervously. "My mom hasn't had that talk with me yet." My jaw dropped open, and she quickly added, "She will. She just hasn't yet."

"What the hell is she waiting for? You're twenty-two years old."

She smiled half-heartedly and shrugged. "My wedding day."

I suddenly felt all the blood rush out of my face as my muscles all tensed up. I released my hold on her.

"What's wrong? You look like you've seen ghost." She actually put her hand to my forehead to check my temperature.

I swallowed, trying to find my voice. "Is it going to be a problem that you're not a virgin anymore?"

She laughed and bumped my shoulder. "No."

"Be honest with me."

"Ethan, you know how I say this is a free country? Well, so is India. You can't believe everything you read. My parents are old-fashioned, but people my age know it's not realistic to expect a virgin bride. Trust me when I say that no one is going to be looking for blood on those sheets."

I relaxed instantly, although it was strange to be talking about this with her after what we'd just shared. "Was this a one-time thing, then?"

She looked down. "It's an experience I'll always cherish, but I can't do this casually with you. As it turns out, I'm a very jealous person when it comes to you, Ethan."

"Who said anything about casual?"

"You want a relationship?"

I placed my finger under her chin, guiding her face up to my mine. I nodded slowly.

She looked pained as she stared up at me with those beautiful, brown eyes. "I can't do that either."

"Why?"

"I care for you, and I loved this," she said, gesturing to the bed. "But, I'm still going to have an arranged marriage. It's the way I was brought up."

I tried not to let my disappointment show. It wasn't like I wanted to declare my eternal love or anything, but I wanted more than a one-night stand, which is what this would be if she let it end like this.

She stood up with her back to me. Her voice was shaky. "I could never have a future with you, Ethan."

I encircled her waist with my arms and pulled her down to my lap. I sucked on her earlobe before I whispered into it. "What about the present? Can we have a present together, Sunshine?"

"What do you mean?"

"We have the rest of the school year before we go our separate ways. Let's spend it together."

"Do you think that's a good idea?"

"Yes, if we're honest with each other, which we are." I moved her hair aside and kissed the nape of her neck. She moaned softly. I knew her body well already.

"Don't you think it'll be difficult?"

I tightened my grip on her. "No, it'll be easy. I promise."

"Why?"

"Most relationships are all about figuring out if you have a future together, and we'll already know. We don't. We won't have that pressure."

I said it to reassure her, but I was also convincing myself.

than declared we shouldn't have sex for forty-eight hours because I was sore. I insisted I wasn't. He insisted I was. We spent another great day in Santa Cruz. He tried tofurkey and did his best not to gag. I tried to give him a blowjob with similar results. It was enough to excite him into forgetting about his stupid rule. That's how we found ourselves driving around for twenty minutes until we found a store. We were in desperate need of contraception.

Ethan stood in front of the boxes of prophylactics. I started walking away to get other supplies, but he grabbed my belt loop and pulled me back against his chest. His arms encircled me, his mouth hovering over my ear. "Which one?"

"You want me to pick?"

"No, I want you to guess."

I stared at the assortment of packages, utterly confused. "Why are there so many kinds?"

"Variety, taste, supply, and demand. Stop stalling."

He pressed into me, and I could feel his hardness. The aisles were empty, but there were cameras. The idea of a public display like this, standing in front of a rack of condoms, would normally have freaked me out, but I didn't care. I craved his touch, and each time a new heady rush of adrenaline would course through me. This thing we had should be bottled up and sold on one of these shelves. We'd make a fortune.

I tried to hide my wry smile as my hand paused on the box advertising the smaller sizes.

He smacked my butt. "You're mean."

"I'm just kidding, but that's what you get for picking out a dress that was two sizes too large for me."

He laughed and nuzzled my neck.

"Touché."

I went to the other side and picked up larger size condoms. "Is this right?"

"That's my girl," he said, rubbing the area he'd smacked, "but grab two."

His girl? My heart leaped and flipped right in my chest. "Two?"

"Or three?"

He took the packages from me, tossing them into the cart without looking. Then he took a few more and did the same. "Would you consider going on birth control? I've been tested." He kissed my earlobe, whispering salaciously in my ear, "and we don't have to worry about you."

"I get the feeling that turns you on a little."

"You're wrong…it turns me on a lot, and I don't know why."

"It turns you on that I was a virgin?"

He sighed, but I felt him smile when he pressed his mouth to my cheek. "Do you need everything spelled out? Yes. Yes. Yes. It turns me on like crazy that I popped your cherry. Wait, that was insensitive. Let me rephrase. I deflowered you."

Once I controlled my giggle, I pressed my hand against my chest and fluttered my eyelashes. "That's very romantic."

"I try."

"Okay."

"Okay, what?"

"I'll go on birth control."

"Good."

I struggled out of his grasp, but he still held me there.

"I need your approval, baby. We'll need this too." He gestured to the bottles of lubricant on the top shelf. I turned my face to stare at him. "It's for you. It'll help you."

There were a ton of bottles there, and I had no idea what to look for. I shrugged. "You pick. I trust you. I'm going to get snacks. Anything you want?"

He released his hold on me, picking up a package to study it. He was a label reader. It made me laugh to know he was going to spend some serious time picking the right lubricant.

He found me a few minutes later in the snack aisle. "We have a winner," he said, tossing a black box into the cart. "We need to get out of here…like now. Please tell me you're done?"

I gave him a knowing look as I held up the jumbo pack of energy drinks, displaying them like a game show hostess. He raised his eyebrow in amused curiosity.

"It's for you. It'll help."

Ethan laughed so loudly it echoed through the store.

13

Meena

*E*than and I spent the entire break in Santa Cruz. It was magical and special. Not just the sex, which was awesome in itself, but the long walks on the beach, the intellectual conversations, and the silly movies. I didn't care what we did as long as I was with him. In fact, it was so hard to leave him that Rachael beat me home. I hadn't been to my room since the party. So much had changed since then. I wanted a chance to get my bearings before facing Rachael's scrutiny, but no such luck.

She sat in her bed, legs crossed, arms folded. "You had sex with Ethan Callahan."

I had no idea how she could be so perceptive. "Why would you say that?"

"You were evasive the last time we talked."

"You're making an assumption."

"It's an educated guess. You're wearing the same clothes that you were when I left on Tuesday."

"I've done laundry, you know," I replied haughtily, although I had no reason to be since she was correct.

"Not here. Your quarters are still lined up." She had me. I always lined up my quarters on the corner of my desk in neat rows and perfect increments, ready for the laundry, and it was always exactly enough for two loads.

"I had sex. Are you happy now?"

"I want to know if you're happy, karma girl."

I sat on my bed, grinning so widely it hurt. "Yes."

She squealed and dashed out of her bed to jump onto mine. "Details," she screamed.

I gave her an abbreviated version of our first night. I left out what Ethan had done for my birthday. Rachael didn't know it was my birthday, and she might be upset about that. I told her how gentle he was, but sexy and commanding at the same time. How much it turned me on. I felt guilty for spilling all of our intimate details, but I was bursting to tell her.

"I'm glad your first time was so good. It's rare to have an orgasm your first time."

"What was your first time like?"

"Awful," she spat out. "It was in the backseat of Mike Pulaski's pickup. It was over before I knew it. That asshole actually complained I stained his upholstery."

"That's horrible."

She shrugged. "It's okay. I've made up for it. Anyway, so now you know what it's like, are you going to do it again?"

"We did. Again and again. We're in a relationship."

"That's great."

"Not really. My plans haven't changed or anything. We're basically enjoying each other in the short term."

"Meena, I haven't seen you look this happy since…well, since ever. People do this all the time. You have to grab what happiness you can in this life. When you're done, you'll be able to be that traditional, married, Indian woman who'll look back with no regrets."

I stared at her with skepticism. "I don't think people do this all the time, Rach."

"Sure they do. There's a reason 'friends with benefits' is an actual phrase."

"That's just it. We're not friends with benefits. We're in a committed relationship with an expiration date. It's different. Like there's a greater risk. We're renting space in each other's lives."

"What's wrong with renting? Who owns at our age anyway? You think too hard, Meena. Just enjoy his company and banging him. You're both smart, realistic people, so you'll be able to do this and say goodbye when the time comes."

"Bang him? Did you really just say that?" I asked, rolling my eyes.

She giggled. "Would you rather I said make love, fuck him, sex him, coitus, snake in the jungle?"

"No," I replied, giggling. "Isn't it funny how many words exist for one act in the English language?"

Rachael pondered my statement for a while. She had a minor in communications so she always enjoyed conversations about… conversation. "Why do you think that is?"

I didn't need to contemplate the answer. "It's because it's so prevalent in the culture. I think any language creates the most words for what's important to them."

"Huh, I like that idea. Like how there are a million words for snow in Eskimo."

I didn't think there were a million words or that the language was called Eskimo, but I nodded because she got the gist of it.

"What are there the most words for in Hindi?"

Ironically, I spoke broken Hindi, the way some immigrants mangled the English language. I used the wrong tenses and pronouns, but I knew the answer anyway.

"Family."

There were words to describe one grandparent as opposed to the other. Older siblings, younger siblings, father's brother versus mother's brother were all different. But I didn't want to dwell on that because what I was doing with Ethan would be devastating to my family. Of course, they would never find out. I'd been so careful with my parents' trust since Vijay died, they never questioned me anymore.

"Hey, have you talked to Raj?" I asked, desperately wanting to change the subject.

"Yes, we talked for a long time."

"How's he doing? I haven't talked to him since Wednesday."

"Good. He said that although this didn't work out, he's ready to get back on the horse again. I'm assuming that's some kind of gay sexual position."

I laughed. "Rachael, you know it's not. You know more about sex than Raj."

"Yeah, I know more about it than most people." Her expression turned sullen, which worried me. Rachael was always vivacious and lively. It was rare to see her sad. I didn't press, though. She would tell me when she was ready. She always did.

14

Ethan

Text from Ethan to Meena:

> I want to see you tonight.

> Me 2. Cant.

> Why? Also, please write out your messages. I hate text shorthand.

> Seriously? You write out your texts and use punctuation? That's very anal.

> We're talking about anal...already?

> Shit! You made me drop my phone.

> LMAO (abbreviations are allowed). I want to see you. It's been forever.

> It's been three days.

That's my point.

I want to but I have plans.

What are you doing?

You sound like an overbearing boyfriend.

Because I am one.

I'm hanging out with Raj and Rach.

Is there a reason I can't tag along?

It's not your kind of scene.

Will Raj and Rach mind?

No, but I don't think you'll have a good time.

Won't you be there?

Yes.

Then I'll have a great time…smiley face.

You wrote out smiley face? Who does that?

I do, and look, you did it too, Sunshine.

You win. I'll text you where to meet us, but just remember I tried to warn you.

I sat in the booth next to Meena and across from Raj, sipping my beer and cringing a little. "I can't believe I'm in a gay bar."

Meena giggled. "I'm sorry—I should have told you. You don't have to stay. I promised Raj I would come for moral support."

"Yeah, go ahead and bail on me like Rachael did," Raj interjected.

"Raj, it wasn't personal. Alex asked her out, and besides, she wouldn't like it here," Meena replied.

"You're here, aren't you?" Raj asked, gesturing to Meena. It was interesting seeing them interact. They acted like brother and sister.

"Yeah, but Rachael would have hated this. All these hot guys and none of them looking at her," Meena said, gesturing around the room.

I laughed because I had a feeling she was right.

"How come you're fine with it?" Raj asked her. I knew the guy was a bundle of nerves. Hell, I was a straight guy in a gay bar, and I looked more comfortable than he did.

"Because I only care if one guy is looking at me," she responded, grasping my arm. I put my hand on her knee and squeezed. She got uncomfortable with public displays even in a place like this, so I did my best to put her at ease, although I really wanted to sit her on my lap.

"Rachael's going out with Alex, as in my friend Alex?" I asked.

"Yes."

"When did that happen?"

Meena shrugged. "They exchanged numbers and texted each other during break."

"Cool." I knew Alex liked her, so I was happy for him. I just hoped it wouldn't color the relationship I had with Meena. I didn't want anything to jeopardize it.

"Do you want to go, Ethan? I can meet up with you, later?" she asked me.

I rubbed her knee. "No, I'm comfortable enough in my sexuality to stay and support Raj." I lifted my beer to him in salute, but he just darted his eyes nervously. "Raj, you know, the guys in here probably think you're with me, so you'll have to make the first move."

His eyes got huge. "I have no idea how to do that. You want me to make a move?"

"Yeah, unless you only planned on window shopping."

Raj stared at Meena hopelessly. "Don't look at me," she said. "I've never picked up a guy in my life."

"I wish Rachael were here. Her expertise would be valuable," Raj said.

Suddenly I felt their eyes on me, expectantly. I looked back and forth at them and gaped as what they were thinking hit me. "You want my advice…with this?"

"You're the only one of us who has any experience," Raj pleaded.

"Trust me man — I've never picked up a dude."

"It can't be that different. Come, Ethan, show us your moves," Meena said, rubbing my arm.

"I don't think it's a good idea." How weird was this. *My girlfriend wants me to show her gay friend my so-called "moves."*

"I don't mind, and besides, you have a high success rate, don't you?" She had a challenging look in her eyes.

I turned to her, not hiding my proud grin. She looked so sexy tonight, with her long hair loose and shiny, spilling over a tight lacy purple top and hip-hugging blue jeans. For the first time that night, I was relieved to be in a gay bar.

"Ninety-two percent," I replied.

"What?"

"My success rate — that's the number of times I've successfully picked up a girl when I've initiated the process. Now, it's not entirely accurate, because I haven't accounted for the girls that had boyfriends already that I didn't know about."

"It's kind of freaky that you have that number in your head," she replied.

Raj looked impressed and tilted his beer to mine in a toast.

I shrugged. "I'm a mathematician. I like to keep track of things."

"Am I in that total?" she asked.

"No, I sort of stopped counting after I met you." Normally, a girl would have gushed at a statement like that, but Meena looked worried. She didn't want me to want her as much as I did. It was crazy, to hold back on the only girl I'd felt this way about. "I don't think I picked you up…not traditionally, anyway," I added, for her benefit, not mine.

"Are you both just going to talk, or is someone going to give me some advice over here?" Raj interrupted.

I turned away from her sheepishly, realizing I was just staring blankly into her eyes. She was doing the same.

"Sorry. Okay, what do you want me to tell you?"

"Don't tell him, Ethan. Show him."

I almost choked on my beer. "What the hell? You want me to try to pick up a guy?"

"No, silly, pick me up. You know…traditionally," she said wryly.

"Yeah, that's actually a good idea. Show me, Ethan," Raj insisted.

I took a deep breath, but I nodded in agreement. "Fine. The thing that's worked for me is to be honest. The more special the girl is—and when I say girl, you can interchange that with guy. Anyway, the more special the girl is, the more of yourself you want to give her. Let her know that. Don't be afraid of telling her what you're feeling. You don't have to explain why you're feeling it. Feelings don't need explanations; they just exist, and it's okay to let yourself be vulnerable in that way. It's a rare trait for a man, and I think girls like it. You know what I mean?"

"Fuck, no. I have no idea what the hell you're talking about. Show me," Raj said as he finished his beer off.

"Fine. I would buy her a drink." I slid Meena's beer closer to her, and shifted so I was facing her. I tilted her chin so our eyes were locked. "You have the most amazing eyes. I used to think brown eyes were a little boring until I met you. I could look at your eyes all day and never blink once because they're always changing. When they're sad, they remind me of the soaked earth after a fresh rain in Austin. When they're happy, they twinkle like the sun-bleached sands of Santa Cruz. When they're excited, they glow like firewood burning from within." *Yeah, she had me spouting like an idiot poet.* I could hear Darren calling me a pussy right now, but I didn't care. It was all true.

She opened her mouth, but nothing came out at first. "Wow," she finally said.

"Am I freaking you out?"

"You don't need to explain your feelings. They just are."

Raj cleared his throat, breaking our trance. "What the fuck? You want me to say all that shit to a guy I just met? What if his eyes aren't even brown?"

"You could always ask him if he dropped his pen," Meena said.

I did a double take. "You knew?"

"Yeah, you were smooth and all, but I figured it out." We both laughed until Raj pounded his fist on the table to get our attention.

"I hate couples," he said with an exasperated sigh.

I felt bad, because we weren't really supporting him, which was what tonight was about.

"Sorry, man. Just buy him a drink and be yourself."

"That's your advice?"

"It's too much work to be anyone else. If you're not yourself, who else will you be?"

He nodded, considering my words. I gave him my full attention, and then I said my next statement slowly so it would be impactful. "Here's the thing. I'm not a gay man, but if I were, you wouldn't be a bad catch."

"Don't patronize me," he said in a mocking tone.

"I'm being honest. You think that's easy for me to say that to another dude? Trust me—it's not. I'm comfortable enough to admit you're a good-looking guy. You're obviously intelligent, successful, and although I don't know you well, I can tell you have a dry sense of humor that appeals to people. This is a two-way transaction. You're not selling yourself as much as buying into someone else. If he doesn't like you for you, then he doesn't deserve to know you."

Raj nodded and made a move like he was going to stand up. Then he sat down again and looked around. The guy had been so worried about himself, he hadn't even figured out if there was any-one worth picking up. He snagged my beer and drank it. I didn't object. He needed it more than me. He did the same with Meena's. He wiped his mouth, stared at us, and fuck me if he didn't salute before marching off.

"Thank you," she said so quietly I almost didn't hear her.

"For what?"

"You gave my friend the perfect pep talk when he needed it the most. You found the words when I couldn't. Thank you for that." It was obvious she loved Raj, so I was glad I could do this small thing for him...for her.

"I think I can consider him a friend too now," I responded, clink-ing her empty beer glass with mine.

"I think so too."

"How come you're drinking?"

"I decided everything in moderation. It's not so bad to try new things, although I'll admit I don't like beer."

I laughed. "I'll introduce you to wine. It's very sweet...like you. Want to dance?"

"Sure, I love this song." It was "Ho Hey" by the Lumineers. I liked it too.

I led her to the dance floor. We were the only heterosexual couple, so it was almost comical, but I didn't feel uncomfortable. In fact, Meena was the only girl in the bar. This was probably the only place where I felt at ease with that thought. She held out her arms, placing one on my shoulder and the other in my hand. We were so far apart another person could have fit between us.

"What the hell are you doing?"

"Isn't this the right form?" she asked innocently.

"If I were dancing with my sister. Get over here." I pulled her to me, practically embracing her. "Do you think I just wanted to dance?"

"Didn't you?"

"Hell no. Dancing was just an excuse to feel you." I kissed her head. Her body seemed to mold perfectly to mine even though I was so much bigger. We just fit.

"I feel you too. I have to feel you to make sure you're real."

"What does that mean?"

"I don't think a lot of guys would come to a gay bar to hang out with their girlfriend or give advice about picking up guys with such patience. I'm a lucky girl."

"The real question is am I going to get lucky?"

She giggled against me, and I felt myself go hard at the vibration. I had no idea how she had the ability to get such a physical response from me without trying.

"Spend the night with me."

"I don't think it's a good idea." She said that because Darren was a flirt, and despite the conversations I'd had with him, he continued doing it. It never bothered me before now.

"Darren's staying at Mandy's tonight. In fact, he's moving in with her." He was staying with her tonight, and he'd eventually have to move in with her when I kicked him out, so it was truthful in a way.

"Ethan, you know Darren's flirting doesn't bother me. I get that it's just part of his personality. What bothers me is the way it affects you. I don't want to ruin your friendship."

"You won't. Let me worry about that. Besides, you're right, his flirting bothers the hell out of me. It's disrespectful to both of us."

"Don't kick him out because of me."

She was smart the way she picked up on things. "It's something I've been thinking about for a while. It'll be the best thing for everyone. Mandy wants to keep a closer eye on him, Darren's been thinking about moving in with her, I want you to spend as many nights with me as you want, and I won't punch him if he's not there to piss me off, right?"

"It's really amazing how convincing you are."

"So, I've convinced you to have a sleepover?"

"You have." She leaned her head against my chest.

A tap on my shoulder interrupted our dance. In fact, the song had changed to some fast-paced number I would never dance to, but I didn't want to release her.

"Can I cut in?" asked a tall, blond, Thor-looking guy.

I sighed in aggravation. I couldn't catch a break. "She's with me buddy."

He smiled. "I wasn't asking her."

I stared awkwardly, unsure how to handle the situation.

"He's flattered, but he's straight. And, most importantly, he's mine," Meena answered for me, patting my chest. Her possessiveness was a total turn on. *Yep, that's my girl.*

"Can't blame a guy for trying," Thor muttered before rushing off.

Meena and I stared at each other and started laughing. "We should go," she said, taking my hand.

"What about Raj?" I asked her.

"We'll let him know we're going, but he's doing just fine on his own." She pointed to a table where Raj was in an animated conversation with an eccentric looking guy in a long wool scarf and black-rimmed glasses. "I have to get you out of here," she said.

"So you can get lucky?" I joked.

"That's part of it, but honestly, having a guy like you in a place like this…well, it's just cruel and, worse, false advertising. You can't expect me to fight every guy off."

I laughed, hooking my pinky with hers. I was getting lucky too—and not just in the bedroom.

15

Meena

We had been dating for a few weeks, and every day felt special whether we were doing something mundane like studying, or exciting like when he gave me surfing lessons, or special like when we walked to Baylands and watched the swans…our swans. I stayed over frequently on weekends, but I drew the line at school nights. It was hard enough to get motivated, and I didn't want to be a burden since Ethan or Raj had to drive me to school. I'd made an exception for today, though.

I was waiting for Ethan to come out of the shower. Raj would be here soon, but I wanted to say goodbye. We would see each other in Advanced Statistics later today. It was our last class together before winter break, but I was flying out soon after. We would be apart for almost three weeks.

He came out smelling clean and fresh, wearing a pair of low-slung jeans and a black button-down shirt that outlined his muscular build. I had no idea how he made clothes look so good. His hair was a damp, disheveled mess. I resisted the urge to run my hands through it.

"Hey, Sunshine," he said, pulling me into a kiss.

"Hi. Raj is going to be here soon, but I wanted to say goodbye."

"I can drive you."

"He's already on his way."

"I have something for you."

"A present?"

"Not quite."

"Show me," I urged.

He grasped me by my waist and led me over to his dresser. He opened the top drawer, gesturing to its emptiness.

"I'm confused."

"I'm giving you a drawer. It's all yours." He smiled, but I could tell he was nervous, and that was rare for him.

I turned and hugged him. "I love it. Thank you." I turned back to the drawer, carefully extracting it from the tracks of the dresser. "This will fit perfectly under my bed. It'll be great for storing my old notebooks."

"Meena, that's not—"

My cell phone beeped. "That's Raj. Gotta go. I'll see you later." I grabbed the drawer with one hand and my duffle bag with the other, managing to make it out the door.

"Meena, wait," he called out. "You don't understand."

"Gotta go…see you later."

I slammed the door shut, but I knew he was standing behind it, confused and startled by my reaction. I texted Raj to give me five minutes. We had time. I counted—five, four, three. Ethan flew through the door and almost knocked me over. I burst out laughing.

"You were playing a joke on me?" he asked, smiling with relief.

"Yeah. I'm not off the boat you know." I handed him back the drawer. "Look, I know what you're trying to convey with this."

"What do you think that is?" He seemed a little hurt, and I guess I couldn't blame him. I had meant to make him laugh.

"I know you're trying to say that I have a place in your life. A little niche that's mine, but I don't need it. It already exists here." I pointed to his head. "And in here." I rubbed the left side of his chest, where his heart beat rhythmically. "I don't need a physical reminder of it."

"It's not just that. Don't you want to keep some stuff here? I mean for convenience?" He set the drawer down.

"I have everything I need in my duffle bag."

"What about pajamas?"

I smiled coyly. "We always sleep naked, or I wear your shirts."

"True."

"Ethan, this is very sweet, but I'm fine, really. I like all my stuff in one place. In case you haven't noticed, we're both a little OCD."

"I've noticed."

I kissed him, and he pulled me closer, picking me up until I squeaked, "I have to go."

"I just need to kiss you again. I won't see you until next year."

"We'll see each other in Malkin's class."

"Yes, but the good professor might frown on me making out with you during his lecture," Ethan said, pressing his lips to mine.

"I'll see you this afternoon, and then I'll see you next year. I'll call or text you every night, okay? Or is that too much?" I asked him, not sure what the protocol was for something like this.

"It's never too much, Meena."

I had just put on my seatbelt when I received a text from Ethan.

> Move in with me.

> I wouldn't take your drawer so you're asking me to move in?

> Yes, after break. It's perfect. Darren will be gone by then, and as far as I'm concerned, you're more than a small niche. I want you here all the time.

> It won't work.

> Why? Name your cons and I'll pro you.

"You just spent the night with him, and he's texting you already?" Raj asked as he pulled out of the parking lot.

"He just asked me to move in with him. Is that crazy?"

Raj was quiet for a moment, then he said, "I like Ethan a lot. He's a really great guy."

"But?"

"But you're going pretty strong for what's supposed to be a casual thing."

"I know it doesn't make sense. The whole thing is a catastrophe waiting to happen."

"But you don't care?"

"The sane part of me that's full of coherent thought and reason does care. But the part that just feels can't really explain it. It's like I wouldn't want to give up this time with him for anything."

"And when we graduate?"

"It'll be over. We both know that, but doesn't it mean I can't have this right now. I'm happy. I think I make him happy, and we're not hurting anyone." The last part was a downright lie.

Raj chuckled, which was odd considering I was spilling my fears to him.

"What's so funny?"

"Just thinking of what your father would say."

The idea filled me with instant dread. Raj had met my parents when they came out to visit. Raj's parents were here too, and they all became friends, which wasn't unusual in our community. Indians tended to gravitate toward other Indians. It was some sort of special bond. Ironically, I never really did. My opinions were sometimes controversial, and I had a problem keeping them to myself. I was a bit of an oddball, but so was Raj, which was why we felt comfortable with each other.

"*Beta*," Raj said, using the Hindi word for daughter in his best fake *Gujarati* accent, which was more Hollywood's portrayal than Bollywood's. "What are you doing with your life? You know how these Americans are. This boy is just using you for sex." He was doing the Indian head shift thing, which was somewhere between a nod and shake.

Despite my fears, I had to laugh. "My father doesn't sound like that."

Raj tousled his thick black hair and turned to me with a coy smile. "They all sound like that."

My father's accent sounded more British if anything, but the words were accurate. It was what he would be saying and, even worse, was what he would think. Ethan was the horny American boy who wanted to use me for sex, and I was the slut who'd let herself be used.

"How's Phillip?" I asked, wanting to change the subject. Phillip was the man Raj had met at the bar. I had met him a few times, and he seemed very nice, but more importantly, very committed to Raj.

"He's good. We're good. I guess you and I are sort of in the same boat."

"I just hope it's not the *Titanic*," I joked, except there was an undeniable truth to the statement.

"If this is the *Titanic*, he can be my Leo DiCaprio."

"Raj, have you guys, um…"

"What?"

"You know?"

"Say it, Meena. You're asking if I've fucked him?" Raj smiled salaciously as he always did when he got me to blush.

"Yeah, I was just wondering."

"Yes, we have."

"And?"

He was quiet for a while, and I felt stupid for asking the question. "Let's just say, I'm definitely gay. There's no doubt about it."

"I don't know if I should say congratulations, or I'm sorry."

He nodded, understanding my meaning. Raj and I had conversed about this many times. It was a bittersweet realization for him. He was free from the burden of questioning who he was, yet he wasn't free to be that person. At least not if he wanted to keep his family intact.

I was in my dorm, getting ready for class when the next text came.

> I assume you have no cons since you haven't replied.

> Con: my parents would kill me.

> Don't tell them. It's not like they know about me anyway, right?

We texted like that throughout the day. I would find time between classes, or he would. I had never been much of a texter, but I found myself sneaking glances at my phone to see if I had a new one.

Con: I can't afford rent at your place.

Pro: I wouldn't expect you to pay rent. I didn't plan on getting another roommate after Darren anyway.

Keep your dorm room. If you don't like it here, you can move back.

Is that a pro?

Sorry, forgot that part. Pro: My apartment is pretty sweet, right? I know you love the shower, and I love the shower with you in it. That's a double PRO!

I laughed and blushed at the same time. I did love it there.

Con: I don't have a car.

Pro: I live close to the campus. You can ride your bike so that's a pro. Plus, I can give you a ride or Raj can. This is just a logistic issue. A very small con. I'm disappointed you even brought it up in this debate.

Con: It's too soon. We've only dated for a short time.

Yes, but we're only dating for a short time period. I don't care how long we've been going out. You shouldn't either.

I clutched the phone tightly, not sure how to respond to that one.

Time is a system for distinguishing events, not an accurate method for judging them.

You're too damn smart, Ethan Callahan! And to use your phrase, it turns me on "something fierce."

> LMAO.

> Con: I have dietary restrictions.

> You have to do better, Sunshine. You're not even challenging me. Pro: We'll go shopping together at Whole Foods. Pro: I'll eat better. Major PRO: You can COOK.

I sat next to him in Malkin's class, expecting him to distract me, but he didn't. He just slid a neatly folded piece of paper to me.

"What's this?"

"My last pro. Don't read it now. Think about it. I can wait until after break for your answer. If you really think this is moving too fast, we'll slow it down. You can draw the line—just let me know where it is." He'd said that to me before, when we first made love.

We were just going to be apart for three weeks, so why was this so hard? How difficult would it be when things were really over?

Rachael slept during the plane ride. I took out the paper Ethan had handed me. The boy had folded it into a precise square. Ethan had the neatest penmanship. It was block writing, and almost every letter was equal in space. It was so perfect that, at first glance, it looked like a computer font. I'd had a glimpse of his scratchpad, though. That writing was legible, but definitely not as neat. This note he'd written was a combination of the two. Like he was trying to be neat, but the words came too fast.

MY LAST PRO — WE ONLY HAVE A SHORT TIME TOGETHER. WE SAID NO REGRETS WHEN THIS IS OVER, BUT I WILL REGRET IT IF WE DIDN'T MAKE THE MOST OF OUR PRESENT. I WANT TO WAKE UP WITH YOU EVERY MORNING AND GO TO SLEEP WITH YOU EVERY NIGHT. MOST OF ALL, I WANT TO COME HOME TO YOU.

P.S. PRO — WE CAN HAVE SEX IN THE MIDDLE OF THE NIGHT WHENEVER WE WANT! MIDDLE OF THE NIGHT SEX IS THE BEST.

YOURS, ETHAN.

I laughed, folding his note back up into the perfect square. My heart was thumping with crazy trepidation. Ethan wasn't shy about his feelings. Maybe it was because his mom was a psychologist, or maybe he just knew himself better than most people. It was scary because it made me believe in us too much.

I spoke to Ethan a great deal over break. He never asked me about moving in with him. I appreciated that, because I had no idea what I was going to do yet.

We talked about philosophy and religion in that poetic college way that people our age did, as if conversations by themselves could change the world. With every revelation, I felt hungry for information about him.

Eventually, he asked me about Vijay. I found myself telling all kinds of stories about my brother. The tales where he managed to annoy me as brothers often did and the ones where he surprised me with an unexpected gesture. I'd blocked out so many things about him because it was painful, but I could talk openly to Ethan.

For his part, Ethan listened. He talked about his father too and how much he missed him and the things they used to do together. We were both still grieving, but through those conversations, I started healing.

My parents drilled me about school and my grades, but as usual, they never asked about anything else. My father worked most of the time. He had an apartment in Boston where he usually stayed when he had surgeries scheduled, which was quite often. My mother also worked, but from home. She'd be on the computer for twelve hours a day sometimes, writing code, negotiating contracts, or in e-meetings. It was the way our house functioned, or at least the way it did now. My parents had always worked long hours, even before Vijay died, but they'd made time for us. We'd all eat dinner together, go shopping in Boston, or take in the occasional movie. There were jokes and laughter too. These days, we lived like three strangers occupying the same house.

On New Year's Eve, I went out to lunch with Rachael. We hadn't hung out much over break. We usually didn't since we ran in different circles, or rather, she had a circle and I didn't. I was surprised to come home and find my mother making *jalebis*, the sweet Indian dessert of deep fried dough. It wasn't an easy recipe, and she rarely made them.

"Do you need help frying them?" I asked her. It was usually my job, and I enjoyed cooking with my mother.

"They're for tomorrow. I'll fry them in the morning." She hummed as she moved around the kitchen. "We're having company."

"Who?"

"Chetan Malhotra is coming over for dinner. You remember him?"

I did—our families were old friends. He'd lived in Boston before moving to Canada. We were close to the same age, so as kids, when they visited, we'd played. Actually, Chetan and Vijay had played together. I'd stayed out of their rambunctious games as much as I could.

"Is he coming with his parents?"

"No, by himself. He graduated last year with a business degree. He's going to be in Boston for a conference. He came a few days early to spend New Year's with friends, but he's stopping by to pay us a visit."

"Why?" My heart was beating wildly at the implications of what she was going to say.

"He wants to see you."

"Why?" I narrowed my eyes, already knowing the answer, but wanting confirmation.

"To see what you look like and how you turned out."

"You should send him a picture, then. I told you I wasn't ready to do this yet. We agreed we wouldn't start looking until after graduation."

"*Arey, Bachcha,*" she said and then repeated in English, "calm down, child. This isn't an official request, but Chetan has started his search, and I think you're his first choice."

"I haven't started, though."

She put her hands on her hips. "Listen to me. Do you think it's easy to find a suitable Punjabi boy living here? You'll be done with college in May, and it doesn't hurt to view suitable candidates, especially one like Chetan."

"I'm not ready," I remarked solemnly.

"I think you're mistaken how this process works. These things require careful planning. You think this is like one of those American TV shows where we parade fifty suitable boys around you, and you whittle them down by giving them a flower?" I laughed at my mother's example, but she wasn't joking. "This is serious, *Beta*. You have many positive traits. You're pretty, smart, educated, and you come from a good family, but you're also westernized, insolent, and you can't make a decent *chapati* to save your life. We need to find a boy who not only has the same traits, but is tolerant of the things you lack."

"Don't you think this is too soon?"

She pinched my cheek. "No time like the present. Can you put this stuff away for me? I have a conference call in a few minutes."

I nodded, taking the wooden spoon from her and placing it in the sink.

"By the way," she said, "a package came for you today. It's on the table."

I stopped what I was doing and went to the table. The parcel was in a long, unmarked postal box. I tore into it, staring at the most beautiful telescope I'd ever seen. It wasn't a traditional, scientific one, but handheld, long, and gold-colored. It looked old-fashioned, but the dials and description indicated it was technologically advanced.

"Who sent you that?" my mother asked, coming up behind me. I almost dropped the package. I had forgotten she was still there. He didn't list a return address, but there was only one person who would send me a gift like this.

"It's for school," I replied absently. My mother didn't ask any more questions. She wouldn't — not when she had a conference call to attend, and she'd already told me everything she needed to say. If it wasn't about school or my impending marriage, my parents seldom engaged in conversation with me.

I texted Ethan as soon as I finished tidying the kitchen.

> I got your present. It's lovely.

> You're lovely.

Even in a text, that boy could make my heart flutter. Ethan texted me back a series of numbers, and I stared at them with confusion, until I realized they were longitude and latitude markers.

> I'll call you at 11:45 pm your time. Or do you have plans for New Year's Eve?

> No plans, but aren't you supposed to be at a party?

> Yes, but I really want to kiss my girlfriend before the New Year.

> How do you propose we do that since you're a million miles away?

> I'm approximately 3100 miles from you, and don't worry about that. Just set it up with the directional I gave you. I'll talk to you soon.

That night, I set my iPod on low, letting The Band Perry mimic my sentiments when they sang "Don't Let Me Be Lonely." I braved the frigid temperatures and sat on the balcony in my parents' room with the telescope. My mother had gone to Boston to meet up with my father so they could shop at the Indian grocer. It was obvious from the menu that my mom wanted to impress Chetan.

I ran my fingers down the telescope's length. He'd spent a great deal on this gift. The ringing of my cell phone almost made me drop it.

"Hi, Sunshine. How are you?" he asked with that sexy southern inflection in his voice.

"Good. Where are you?" I heard a cacophony of voices in the background.

"I'm at the party." The hint of southern drawl in his voice was more prominent tonight. It immediately turned me on, but it also alarmed me.

"Are you drunk?"

"Very much so, but I'm not driving if that's what you're worried about." He knew me well. "I'm still inside, but I'm making my way to the roof."

"Be careful. I don't want your drunk butt falling off the roof."

His laugher boomed through the phone. "My drunk butt is just fine, but thank you for your concern." *His butt is very fine.*

"Why are you going to the roof?"

"So, we can have our New Year's kiss."

"I don't get it."

"Do you have the telescope set up?"

"Yes, do you have one too?" Although Ethan claimed to be a science geek, I highly doubted he brought a telescope to a New Year's Eve party at UCLA.

"I don't need one where I'm at, but I knew you would." It suddenly got quiet on his end and a heavy door slammed. "I'm on the roof. Where are you?"

"I'm on the balcony in my parents' room."

"That's kind of weird."

"They're not home."

"You're alone on New Year's Eve?" He sounded sad for me, and I didn't want him to be. The truth was I would have been alone even if my parents didn't leave. They fell asleep by ten at the latest.

"I'm with you, aren't I?"

"Yes, baby, you are. You must be freezing."

"I have a coat on." I was also wearing my warmest flannel pajamas, my robe, wool gloves, and a scarf. I resembled a very large jellyroll, and although Ethan couldn't see me, I was upset I didn't look more appealing. I hoped he wouldn't ask what I was wearing. I'm sure he looked gorgeous. He always did.

"If it gets too cold, go inside. I don't want my kiss to make you sick…again."

"Can you please explain this to me?"

"Patience, Meena. Do you see the star pattern in the telescope?"

I looked through it at the cluster of bright stars. The magnification on the scope was very good.

"Yes, I see it."

"What does it look like to you?"

"Stars," I replied dryly.

"Don't be a smartass. What does the pattern look like?"

I stared at it for a minute, trying to figure out the answer. I'd never been good at those puzzles where there was a picture in a picture, so this wasn't coming easy for me. After a few minutes, Ethan gave up on me. "It's a bird, Meena. It's the constellation Cygnus."

"That's Latin. It's the Northern Cross, right?"

"Very good, baby. It means swan."

I saw it right as he said it, like a blurry photo coming into focus. It was a graceful swan, diving into flight. "I see it, Ethan."

"I want you to concentrate on the brightest star. The one at the tail. Do you see it?"

"Yes, it's bluish."

"Right, I'm looking at it too. It's amazing isn't it? We're three thousand miles apart and looking at the same object in the sky."

"It's pretty cool, but how are you going to kiss me?"

"It will be a mental kiss. We have most of the senses. We have sight because that star is connecting us. We have sound, and trust me when I say your voice is turning me on something fierce. We can conjure the other ones together."

"Are we going to have phone sex?" I asked, giggling, but he would want to video chat if that's what he had in mind.

"I'm on a rooftop at UCLA. I don't want to risk arrest for indecent exposure. Although, with the drunken idiots here, I don't know if I'd get noticed. Besides, I don't want you taking any clothes off in the freezing cold. I had something more cerebral in mind. Just listen to me. We don't have much time."

"I'm listening."

"Are you comfortable?"

"Yes," I said, sliding onto the chair, repositioning the telescope, and suspending the phone between my ear and shoulder.

"We've established clear sight and sound. We're looking at one of the most luminous stars in the Milky Way. That's the reason I chose it. It reminds me of your eyes. It's two hundred and fifty thousand times brighter than our sun, and almost as beautiful as you, Sunshine. Do you know how much I love listening to the sound of your voice? It doesn't matter if you're reading aloud, or laughing hysterically, or even just having a normal conversation. I especially love it when you're screaming...my name.

"I don't need taste or smell. I remember how you taste. It's like a combination of honey and milk and sugar. I remember your scent too. Like vanilla and a million different spices. I can't name all them, but the flavor of you is my favorite thing. It's innocently sexy, and for the life of me, I don't know how that's possible."

His voice had a hypnotic quality to it, and I found myself visualizing him, even while focusing on the bright star trillions of miles above my head. The more he spoke, the easier it was to imagine him with me. Then the visuals turned tangible as I imagined the delicious things I wanted him to do.

"The touching is the easiest. When you're in my arms, it feels perfect. I don't want to let you go, especially when you shiver or laugh." His voice dropped to whisper...an enticing, lusty whisper, dripping with yearning. His words were so visceral that my breath hitched. "Most of all, I love kissing you. Do you know you moan when I kiss you? I don't even think you're aware of it. I want to earn every one of those moans. I want to bite your lower lip. I want to trace the outline of your mouth with my finger and then my tongue. I have such a craving for the honey and milk and sugar of you. I'm kissing you...right...now. Can you feel it?"

I moaned loudly. He laughed softly.

"Happy New Year, Sunshine."

I checked my watch. He had planned it perfectly. It was exactly midnight for me. "Happy New Year, Ethan."

Ethan made me go inside, but we stayed on the phone for another three hours until Ethan's New Year happened. I tried to illicit the same sensual response from him, but I knew I wasn't as good. The man was some kind of mathematic Casanova.

I planned to sleep in the next day, but my mother returned from Boston very early and woke me so I could help her cook. We spent the day working together, preparing an Indian feast, but we barely spoke unless it was a command from her or a question from me. I didn't know why it was so difficult to talk to my mother now, but neither of us could find the right words.

If my mother and I were considered strangers, my father was a ghost. When he was home, he would choose to eat in front of the television, watching CNN. He said it relaxed him, but I had no idea how watching the news did that. My mother ate in her office. I was the only one that ate at the table anymore.

When Vijay was alive, my parents insisted we have dinner there every night. We talked and laughed until we eventually argued over who was going to do the dishes. My father made it a competition, asking Vijay or me an SAT question. Whoever got it right was excused from dish duty. Vijay often won, but my father was smart, and he would make sure he asked questions about English and grammar that favored my interests. It was so long ago that it felt very strange to see the table set up again on this night.

Chetan arrived promptly at eight. Indians usually didn't eat dinner until nine. It was something Rachael freaked out about since her family ate at five. At school, I ate at a normal time or the cafeteria would close on me. When I came home, I had to force myself to get used to the later meal hours again.

I hadn't seen Chetan since I was ten. He was my height, with thick black hair, a thicker belly, and a goatee. The first thing he did was bow to my parents, as was custom. Then he gave me an awkward hug. His eyes raked over my body before proclaiming, "Little Meena, all grown up and so beautiful!"

I instantly disliked him.

Dinner conversation was an animated affair where my parents conversed more than they had in the past year. They asked Chetan all sorts of questions about his job and life in Quebec, his parent's health, his extended family, and his goals. Hell, if it would have been appropriate, my father would have asked his blood type. There was no doubt they already had a clear idea of how much money he made. These things were discernible character traits that floated through the figurative grapevine connecting all Indian families.

They extolled my virtues as if they were sales men attempting to unload a luxury automobile. Meena's going to graduate *summa cum laude,* my mother boasted. Meena has always been a good student, my father explained. Meena made this entire dinner, my mother bragged, although it was a false claim.

For his part, Chetan answered all their questions with the required respect, calling my parents Uncle and Auntie, again as was the custom. However, he arrogantly went on about his accomplishments, garnishing every sentence with flourishing hand gestures. He emphasized graduating in the upper percentile of his class at the University of Toronto and his senior position in the acquisitions firm he worked at. He even broke into French and made a few statements none of us could comprehend. I squirmed in embarrassment when my mother clapped as if he was giving a Noble Prize acceptance speech.

He offered frequent compliments toward the meal, using adjectives that were only appropriate for the Food Network. He told my parents how much he missed them, how *magnifique* our house was, and how wonderful I was, even though he didn't know me. There was a strange silence among all of us when he expressed his condolences regarding Vijay. Instinctively, my parents and I turned to the empty chair as if Vijay would suddenly appear. It didn't hurt me to see it empty the way it used to. I silently thanked Ethan for that.

The guilt hit me. Could this be construed as cheating? I didn't think so, but Ethan wouldn't be happy to know what I was doing. That was an understatement. Should I give permission for Ethan to see other people? As soon as I thought it, my fists clenched and a jealous heat crept into my face…and it wasn't from the spicy curry. That wasn't an option. Besides, he wouldn't want to.

"So, Meena, are you always this quiet?" Chetan asked, taking a third helping of cauliflower curry.

"She talks all the time," my mother chirped. It was comical that she'd actually answer this question for me that I would have giggled if I weren't so annoyed.

"I don't have anything to say."

"I'd like to hear about your interests," Chetan said, plinking his fork on my mother's good china. It irritated me as it did when he spoke. He talked with his mouth full.

"I'm an economics major."

"I know that. Do you plan on working?"

"I'm getting a degree, aren't I?" I folded my arms, feeling the heat of my mother's gaze without even looking at her.

"I know, I, ah…meant what will you do?"

"Do you think women shouldn't work? Is that why you asked me?"

"Meena, stop that," my father admonished.

"It's all right, Uncle. I asked her; let her talk. No, Meena, I think women should work. Of course, I'm a modern man. They should do whatever they want. That is until it's time to have a family, and then maybe they stay at home or work part-time. What are your thoughts on that?" *Damn, he is interviewing me.*

I shrugged. "That's fine for some woman, but I plan on working. I think the traditional ideas of women staying at home are a bit archaic."

Chetan seemed to be pondering my statement. "I don't have any issues with it. I guess I come off as old-fashioned, but I'm not. I have very modern opinions, and the ability to view things openly."

"What are your thoughts on legalizing gay marriage?"

My mother gasped, my father slammed down his glass, and I silently cursed my stupidity.

"It's immoral," Chetan answered without hesitation. "What are your thoughts?"

"I agree," I said, to which Chetan's shoulders relaxed immediately. "It's immoral to keep two people who love each other apart."

"Meena, that's enough. I'm sure Chetan doesn't want to hear about your California radicalism."

Chetan surprised me by smiling brightly. "You always spoke your mind, and I always liked that. I remembered that about you. That and all the games of tag I let you win."

Just like that, I instantly felt remorseful. Chetan, Vijay, and I played tag when he came to visit, and I always won. It was obvious now he'd let me. Hell, they'd both let me. They were tall, athletic boys, and I was a clumsy little girl. In hindsight, it was pretty cool they even let me hang out with them at all. "You let me win?"

"Yes, but you always beat me fair and square at chess."

The conversation eased up after that. I made an effort to be civil, bordering on cordial. Chetan didn't ask opinions about my world-views again, and I didn't give them. My parents relaxed somewhat, and even my father smiled a few times. Overall, the evening wasn't a complete bust, but I knew one thing for sure. *I will never marry Chetan Malhotra.*

Chetan spent the night with us. I excused myself after dinner and read in my room until I heard everyone go to bed. I made my way downstairs to grab a snack. I was so uptight and upset, I'd barely eaten my dinner. My father was in front of the television, watching CNN. There's no news like twenty-four-hour news, he'd often say.

"*Beta*, come sit with me," he said so quietly I might have imagined it.

I sat on the recliner adjacent to him. He kept watching the television, and I wondered why he'd asked me to join him. Finally, he spoke over the serious but pleasing voice of Anderson Cooper.

"You don't like him, do you?"

I smiled softly. "No, I'm sorry."

A small smile played on my father's lips. It was sad, though, like all his smiles. "He's somewhat conceited."

I jerked my head up, surprised my father had noticed this. The way my mother extolled Chetan's virtues, he could pass for the reincarnation of Gandhi.

"We won't force you into anything, Meena. But I would like you to keep an open mind. A good woman can change a man."

No woman is that good.

It was ironic that he was asking me to keep an open mind about this when Chetan seemed very close-minded. "I'm not ready to consider anyone."

"I don't expect you to be married tomorrow, but you should be serious during events like tonight's dinner. This is not a game. You are the most important thing in the world to me."

My heart tightened to hear my father say that. We all loved each other, but it was rare that our mouths could channel those emotions into words.

"I know, Papa," I said, calling him by the name I used when I was little. His smile brightened.

"Meena, I worry about you. We moved here to provide more opportunities for our future children. So...you and...you could have more, do more, be more." He was about to say Vijay, but he couldn't bring himself to finish the sentence. "But I question that decision all the time. I see evidence every day of the disrespectful attitude that is common in this society. Mostly, I see the contemptuous way marriage is treated here. It's a mockery. People make bets on it. Celebrities become even more popular when they divorce after a month of marriage as if it was a joke to begin with. It's easy to get confused between what makes a lasting union and what doesn't."

"What is that?"

"There's that stupid adage that opposites attract, but in reality, being with someone of a similar background, someone who comes from the same cultural ties and moral belief system, is what creates a lasting union. People get confused with these small sentiments of excitement, but they don't understand that when the heart burns, it's really heartburn."

"Huh?" I asked in utter confusion.

"That romanticized notion that's on every TV show, movie, or book. The one that says love is like a sudden burning in your heart. That's really just heartburn. You feel it for a short time, and then it naturally goes away, even if you do not medicate. It's not meant to last, and it never does."

"Dad, I understand what you're trying to say."

"I'm not finished. I want to tell you a story about our family. Do you know why your mother and I settled in this small town?"

"I thought it was to get away from the overpopulated chaos of Boston."

My father laughed. It was such a rare sound that I joined in, though I had no idea why it was funny. "Meena, we're from India. We're used to crowds and chaos. That never bothered us. We moved here because we thought Mashpee would be less distracting for you and…"

Why can't he say my brother's name?

"Well, also because it was surrounded by water, and it reminded us of home in that way. We wanted to move back, though…to India. We talked about it, and I even inquired about positions in hospitals at home." His admission shocked me, but it disappointed me that he referred to India as home since I'd never lived there.

"When was this?"

"When you got suspended for smoking in the bathroom at school."

I straightened up, shuddering. My father had never been so angry with me. I'd been twelve, and I'd thought I wouldn't live to see thirteen. His eyes were so huge and his anger so apparent that a vein jutted out of his neck when he screamed at me that he couldn't understand how a daughter of a brain surgeon could be so stupid.

"But you changed your mind?"

"We were talked out of it."

"By who?"

"Vijay." His voice choked.

I swallowed back the lump in my throat. He finally said my brother's name. How could a twelve-year-old boy talk two stubborn adults like our parents out of such a decision, especially one as docile and obedient as my brother?

"He heard us talking one night. He pled with us to reconsider. He said you were a smart girl, and you had learned your lesson. He argued neither of you would be able to acclimate to India, and we'd be horrible parents for forcing you to move. Mostly, he just promised us that you would never disappoint us again."

I had no idea any of this had happened. The crazy thing was Vijay would have been fine with the move. He was introverted but self-sufficient. He could have lived anywhere. Me...I wasn't so sure. Vijay's appeal was for my sake not his. A gut-wrenching thought hit me. If we had moved, he wouldn't have died. If I hadn't skipped school that day, he wouldn't have died. If I hadn't been born, he wouldn't be dead. How many ways had I killed him?

"Why are you telling me this?" I asked, willing myself not to cry. My parents never said they blamed me for Vijay's death, but I didn't need them to voice it. I saw the blame in their faces.

"Because, *Beta*, I want you to honor your brother's memory. Don't disappoint us again." My father stood up and turned off the television. He paused where I sat and started to bend down as if he were going to kiss or hug me, but then he stopped himself and settled on patting my head instead.

Like clockwork, the salty, hot tears fell down my face as soon as his bedroom door closed. I sobbed for an hour, until there was nothing left but shuddering gasps. My father missed my brother dearly. He wanted me to be married for all the reasons he stated, and one he didn't. He wanted a son again, but he'd settle for a son-in-law as long as the man I married met the qualifications. I renewed my vow to honor Vijay's memory by not disappointing my parents again. I would provide my father with some relief in the form of a new son-in-law. I would provide my mother with some happiness in planning a wedding and creating an extended family. I would do all of these things because Vijay's blood would always stain my hands.

17

Meena

"I thought Raj was picking us up," I said to Rachael when I spotted Ethan's tall, lean frame heading for us at the airport. I wasn't ready for the sight of him, and as usual, he took my breath away.

Rachael shrugged. "Don't look at me. He's your boyfriend. I have no idea why he's here."

"Hey," he said, placing my bag and Rachael's on his broad shoulders. "Raj had car troubles so he asked if I'd get you guys. Hope that's okay." It didn't surprise me that Raj and Ethan talked. I knew they had hung out occasionally and were real friends. It made me very happy.

"Sure," I replied, but neither of us moved. We just stared at each other, smiling like idiots at San Jose International.

"Jesus. Just hug or kiss or something so we can go," Rachael demanded.

I took a step forward, and Ethan put down our bags. I embraced him, wrapping my arms around his neck tightly. He picked me up and spun me around. "I missed you, Sunshine."

"Me too," I replied against his neck.

"Can we go now? This is too much PDA even for me," Rachael said dryly, but she was smiling in approval.

Ethan and I sat in the car in silence while Rachael prattled on about her holiday from the backseat. The Christmas presents she'd received, her resolutions, and finally, the crazy New Year's Eve party she'd attended, adding for no reason that she'd invited me but I'd refused.

Ethan turned to me raising his eyebrows.

"It wasn't my scene."

Rachael didn't know the wild, free-spirited me that existed when Vijay was alive. She only knew the meek, morose, quiet me that surfaced after his death. Somewhere during our time at Stanford, she'd found the real me. The girl that existed somewhere between the other two, and I loved her for that.

"Will you come over?" Ethan asked.

I nodded, but I didn't trust myself to speak. I wanted to talk to him in private. Of course, Rachael already knew what I was going to tell him. We reached the dorms. Rachael hopped out of the car, grabbing her luggage before either of us could say anything.

"Want help taking your luggage upstairs before we go?" Ethan asked me, making a move to open his door. I reached for his arm to stop him.

"Why move it twice?"

He grinned widely. "Really?"

"Yes, let's go home," I replied, threading my fingers through his.

My conversation with my father and my resolve to have an arranged marriage did not deter me from Ethan. In fact, it did the opposite. My justification was that I should enjoy this time before my impending nuptials. I couldn't think of anything I enjoyed more than the boy sitting next to me, with the too-long, brown hair and brilliant blue eyes. I knew we both cared for each other, and it would be difficult when this ultimately ended, but there was no reason to start the painful process of healing just yet. Ethan and I were adults. I had been honest with him, and he'd accepted the limitations that came with me. This was, in a manner of speaking, my way of sowing my wild oats.

Ethan

I had my back to the door, and she was pressing her body against me, kissing me hard and fast. I tried to get the key in the lock, but it was impossible from this angle.

"Baby, I can't open the door," I said, gently pulling her away from me. *Yes, we are going to have some really good I-missed-the-fuck-out-of-you sex. We are totally going to fuck the miss out of each other.*

Once the door was open, I had a strange desire to carry her over the threshold, but I quickly blocked it. I brought in her suitcase, and she headed for the couch. It was disappointing she didn't go straight to the bedroom, but I could wait. I sat next to her and pulled her legs over me. She went a step further and shifted onto my lap.

"We're home," I said, not hiding my grin.

"Yes, we are."

"What should we do first? Or should I say, where should we do it first?"

She giggled against my chest. "First, I want to give you my gift."

"You got me a gift? You know atheists don't celebrate Christmas, right?"

"Think of it as more of a thank you for letting me move in with you gift."

"That's cool, since I have a gift for you too."

"You know I'm not Christian either, so I don't need a gift. Besides, you gave me the telescope."

"That was just so we could spend New Year's together. This is a welcome home gift." I smiled coyly. "It's pretty awesome you agreed, otherwise I would have felt like a total dumbass about it. I was really taking a gamble on this one."

She stared at me curiously.

"You first, Sunshine."

She got that excited look on her face and jumped off my lap. She came back with a long manila envelope and placed it in my hand.

"What is this? A roommate agreement?" I joked.

"Open it."

I undid the clasp and felt her tense on my lap. I didn't have to look at her to know she was biting her lower lip as she always did when she was nervous. I stared in disbelief at the comic book inside the envelope. A Batman vintage collector's comic. "You shouldn't have spent this much."

"It wasn't that much. There's a store in Boston that has good deals on stuff like this."

"I know exactly how much this costs, Sunshine. Don't lie to me."

"Do you like it?" she asked tentatively.

"It's the best present I've ever gotten. Thank you."

"Really?" The surprise was apparent in her voice.

"Yes," I answered honestly, kissing her forehead.

"Are you going to read it?"

I laughed. "Hell, no. I'm going to lock it away in an airtight box and admire it from afar."

"Hmm, seems like a waste."

"I already know what it says, anyway. He wins. He always does. Now, it's my turn. Stand up."

She stood up, and I placed my hands on her hips and led her to the other bedroom. She looked at the closed door and back at me. "You're giving me Darren's old bedroom? Not exactly the sleeping arrangements I had in mind."

I laughed, putting my arms around her. "You won't be doing any sleeping in here. Close your eyes."

I looked to make sure they were closed. I opened the door and led her in, positioning her in the middle of the room for the best view.

"Open," I ordered and realized I was very nervous now. I didn't know how she would react to this, and it could go either way. She was very quiet, taking in the room. I'd covered the carpeting with linen drop cloths. There was a drafting desk in the corner and an adjustable artist's easel stood in the middle of the room with a blank canvas. A comfortable swiveling stool was in front of it. A few more blank canvases and sketch pads leaned against the far wall and shelves lined with baskets of various artist's tools and mediums took up another wall. Meena walked toward the shelves, exploring each basket.

"I didn't know what you'd like so I got some of everything. There are paints, pencils, and charcoal." I jabbered on about everything, trying to get a read on her expression. She seemed shocked.

"You did this for me?"

I rubbed the back of my neck and nodded. "I thought you'd like to explore your passion. Do you like it?"

She jumped into my arms so unexpectedly that I stumbled back. She kissed every inch of my face. "I love it. I love it. I love it."

The tension flowed out of me with her touch.

"This is the nicest thing anyone's ever done for me. Thank you, Ethan."

I wasn't expecting that. I was losing control as I often did when she touched me.

"I can't wait to get started. It's been so long since I've painted and—"

I covered her mouth with mine and enveloped her lips in a long kiss. When we broke apart, she was breathing hard, staring at me with that lusty look I loved. "You're gonna have to wait," I said.

She nodded, tightening her embrace. I cupped her ass and lifted her. She wrapped those long, sleek legs around my waist, and this time I did carry her over the threshold. The threshold to our bedroom. I sat us down on the bed, with her still in my lap.

"I love this bed," she murmured in a whisper against my neck.

"Our bed."

She started unbuttoning my shirt. I wanted to throw it over my head, but Meena had a look of stern concentration that was too cute. Her fingers shook a little with each button, but she finally got the last one open. I took off my shirt and then hers, running my fingers over the curves of her lacy pink bra. I removed her hair band, liberating those long, silky curls.

She pushed against my chest, not enough to move me, but I lay down anyway, expecting her to lie on top of me. She surprised me again by moving down my body, flicking her tongue against my chest and torso. She removed my belt with more confidence, unbuttoned my shorts, and unzipped them. Then she slid them down along with my boxers.

"What are you doing?" I asked her.

"Pleasuring you," she answered sexily.

I took her arm to stop her. I didn't want us to start off with a bad experience. In my estimation, no blowjob was better than a bad blowjob. Plus, I really didn't like the idea of her forcing herself to do something for my benefit.

"You don't have to do that."

"You don't want me to give you pleasure?" she asked, pouting.

"You do in other ways. I know you don't like it."

"You like it."

I couldn't believe we were verging on a potential argument about this. "I don't need it. Besides, you're really bad at it." I chuckled, but she just narrowed her eyes at me, and I cursed myself, hoping I hadn't *blown* my chances.

"I'll have you know I've been practicing."

I pulled her up so we were face-to-face. The intensity of my jealousy was like a vice grip tightening every muscle. "With who?" I wasn't hurting her, but there was no doubt I was demanding an immediate answer.

Meena just smiled and patted my chest, calming me with her soothing touch. "Not who, but what. Cucumbers."

"Cucumbers?" I asked with amused curiosity.

"Yes. Now shut up, and let me do this." She slid back down, repeating the trail of kisses. I propped up on my elbows and watched her path. She slid her tongue up and down my shaft several times. I was already hard before we started, but her tongue was doing some amazing things to me. I moved her hair so I could watch her face, but it was too much. I laid my head down on the bed, and started relaxing. Then she covered the head of my dick with her mouth, sucking me. I spoke her name in some sort of incoherent grunt. Her advance became more feverish until she took more of me in her mouth. Then all of me.

I choked back a gasp as she moved with the perfect balance of wetness and pressure. The heat of her mouth, the swirling of her tongue, the hold of her luscious lips — well, it was pure ecstasy. I wasn't conceited, but I could say with certainty, which only experience could bring, that very few girls could take all of me. Meena had, and somehow her gag reflex was gone. I felt the vibration of her moan in the back of her throat, and I almost lost it. I was actually clutching the bed sheets, battling the desire to watch her as she performed this intimate act, but knowing it would make me lose what little control I had.

"Stop. Now," I gasped, barely recognizing my own voice.

"You're not done," she said, pausing for just a moment.

"I will…that's…the problem." The lusty anguish that caused my words to sound gruff and strangled would have been funny, but I didn't want her freaking out about the eventual outcome of what she was doing to me.

"I hope so," she said simply.

"Fuck yeah," I said in a sort of gasping, choked cheer.

It only took a few more minutes. I came hard and fast. She didn't gag or gasp as I'd expected. Instead, she swallowed. I stared down at her, running my hand through her hair. She wiped her mouth seductively, smiling widely, obviously pleased with herself, but definitely not as pleased as I was. She crawled back up my body and laid her head on my chest. I stroked her hair and kissed her forehead as my breathing returned to normal.

"What are you thinking?" she asked, trailing her finger across my chest.

I grinned, staring into her eyes. "I love cucumbers. They're my new favorite food of all time."

We laughed so hard, the sound must have echoed through the sunny streets of Palo Alto.

18

Ethan

We'd been living together for several weeks now. I didn't know how she made me laugh, think so much, or get so hard. In general she just made me feel more than anyone else I'd been with.

I was surprised when she set up a small temple in our bedroom, but I respected it. She prayed every morning, and I did my best to leave her alone at that time. She did little things to make my life easier too. As simple as setting up the coffee maker the night before, or sewing the missing buttons on one of my shirts. Buttons she had ripped off in the heat of the moment.

I entered the apartment with two sacks of groceries. Meena was a great cook and made some pretty fancy meals. I compromised by buying groceries and doing the dishes, but she always helped. She brought up the rent thing a lot, feeling guilty she wasn't contributing, but I did my best to put her at ease with humor, which usually worked. I told her she could make it up to me by sharing showers, so we could save money.

"Hey there," she said when I entered. Rachael was over, and I waved at them, making my way to the kitchen. Both girls came in to help me unload.

"Jesus, how many cucumbers do you guys eat?" Rachael asked staring at the large plastic bag.

Meena and I both looked at each other. I expected her to blush or bite that luscious lower lip, but instead, she burst out laughing—that magical contagious laugh that left me with no choice but to join in.

"You guys are so weird," Rachael stated, placing the bag in the fridge. "I'm going to go."

"You don't have to go, Rachael. I was going to see what Alex was up to tonight anyway."

Rachael and Meena missed each other, and I didn't want to be that asshole boyfriend that took her away from her friends.

"That's why I have to go, Ethan. Alex and I have plans. He's picking me up. I'm going to watch his basketball game, and then we're going to the movies."

I wasn't exactly happy Rachael and Alex were still going out. I'd expected the relationship to fizzle out by now, but it just seemed to be getting stronger. Rachael was a heartbreaker, and Alex was my friend. I'd been there when a girl dumped him. He didn't handle it well.

I put away the rest of the groceries while they said their goodbyes. No, I didn't like the idea of our friends dating at all. It complicated things, and Meena and I were already complicated enough.

She came into the kitchen and stood so close to me that I couldn't help but pick her up. Okay, I could have helped it, but whatever. I sat her on the countertop, leaning into her. She was quiet, but she didn't push me away, so I naturally took it as sign that I should kiss her neck. It was one of her favorite places to be kissed. I could feel her body react to my touch, and I loved that I had that effect on her.

"Are you okay with Rachael dating Alex?"

Shit, she could always read me. "Not really."

"Why?"

"He doesn't rebound well."

"You're not talking about basketball."

"No, I'm not."

"I understand, but she's different with him. She's also one of the sweetest people I know."

"I know."

Meena stared at me suspiciously, since I hardly knew Rachael.

I bent down toward her ear, whispering the words. "She has to be if she's friends with you. Let's not fight."

"Is that what we're doing?" she asked, pulling me back to her. "I thought we were discussing."

"Discussions like this can get out of hand. If you want to fight, though, I'm game."

"You *want* to fight with me?"

"No, Sunshine, I want to have make-up sex with you. The fight is just a prerequisite."

She laughed. "Before you make me forget, you got a big package today."

I took her hand and placed it on my groin. "I have a big package for you."

She giggled and squirmed away. "Stop it." She put her hands on my shoulder, silently telling me to pay attention to her. "Come on, you have to open it. Rachael and I have been guessing what it is all day."

"Curious much?"

"Yes, that's me. Don't keep me in suspense. It's personal, and it's from a girl, so I think I deserve to know." It was funny that she was jealous, although she had no reason to be. *How does she not get that I only have eyes for her?*

I turned around so my back was to her. I took her long legs and wrapped them around my waist. "Where is it?"

She immediately put her arms around my shoulders, preparing for a piggyback ride. "In the bedroom."

"You put it in the bedroom?"

"Rachael kept threatening to open it, so I thought it was best if the temptation was out of sight."

I laughed and carried her to the bedroom. Our bedroom. I dropped her on the bed next to the large box. She fidgeted impatiently as I tried to open the package. Finally, she sighed and ran out of the room, returning with a knife. I went to grab it from her, but she backed away suddenly, placing it carefully on the bed next to the box. Her odd reaction surprised me.

"I know it's weird. It's just a superstition. If I hand you the knife, it's bad luck," she explained, biting her lower lip.

"I've never heard that one."

"It's an Indian thing."

I nodded, used to this explanation from Meena. Whenever she did things that were strange to me, she'd explain it away with that sentence. I picked up the knife and opened the package. "This is from my mom. She sends me care packages once in a while."

Meena put her hand over her heart. Her face reflected a mixture of guilt and relief. "That's really sweet."

I shrugged. "It is. She's a great mom."

"What did you get?"

I opened the box and started removing the contents. "She baked me cookies like she always does," I said, dropping the decorative tin on Meena's lap. She opened it and took one.

"That's so nice."

"You should reserve judgment until you try one."

She took one and bit into it. I laughed watching her try to chew it. Meena was doing her best not to look disgusted.

"It's okay. You can be honest."

She choked down the small bite she had taken. "I think she forgot to use butter…or sugar."

"Let me try." I brought Meena's hand with the cookie to my mouth. I took the smallest bite possible. "Nope, that's just about right."

"Why does she make them for you if you don't like them?"

"I've never told her. She likes making them, so I pretend to like eating them."

Meena stared at me for a moment. Then she stood up and combed through my hair. "You're a very good boy, Ethan."

I shrugged, embarrassed by her compliment. "The rest of this is just the typical stuff. School supplies, socks, jelly beans, epoxy resin." Her face scrunched with curiosity as I handed her the tube. "For my surfboard." I continued to dig deeper. "More shirts. My mom thinks I don't own any clothes."

I threw the folded shirts on my bed, where they landed with a heavy thud. Meena unfolded them, revealing the small hard-cover book hidden inside. I snatched it out of her hand.

"Let me see it," she said, trying to reach around my back.

"No way."

"Ethan, let me see it." She tried to grab it from me.

I held her back, but she stood up on her tiptoes, putting her arms around my neck. She nibbled on my ear and ran her tongue down my neck. Her hair was down today, and it brushed softly along my arm while her breasts crushed against my chest, and her delicious mouth continued to make me forget what we were doing. I was defenseless. When she backed away, she grinned with triumph, holding the book in her hand. I hadn't even realized I'd relinquished it to her.

"Very sneaky," I muttered.

"*Sex Acts for the Modern Couple?*" That was the title, but she was definitely asking a question. When I didn't respond, she asked, "Your mother sent you a sex manual?"

"Yeah, she did," I replied, concerned about Meena's reaction.

Meena looked at it, turning it in her hands. Then she looked at the postmark on the package. "Shit, your mother is Dr. Rosemary Love? The world's premier sexologist? Oh my god. She wrote this book."

I moved the stuff from the edge of the bed and sat down, suddenly wishing I'd never opened the stupid box. "I take it you know who she is?"

"I think everyone knows who she is. She's written, like, ten books."

I laughed because she said it like I didn't know that. "Twelve. She's written twelve books including this one. It's her newest one. She always sends them to me, but I never read them. She wrote a few chapters of the book Raj was reading too. That's why I knew what it was about."

Meena slid into my lap. I put my arms around her.

"It must be so cool to have a famous mom."

I didn't expect her to be so excited about my mother's identity. "It wasn't that cool."

"What do you mean?"

"My mom's always been open about sex." She stared at me curiously, and I quickly added, "Not in an inappropriate way or anything. She just always explained everything. Even things that didn't need to be. You have no idea what it was like."

"It couldn't have been that bad, Ethan."

"I love my mom, she's the best, but you didn't have to deal with your mom telling you it's okay to masturbate when you're twelve, or demonstrating how to properly put on a condom using a carrot. I still can't eat carrots. Or worse, explaining the importance of pleasing your partner before yourself. Shit, let's stop talking about this."

She laughed, tightening her grip on me. "Well, it worked. You definitely know how to please a woman."

"You have no comparison."

"Ethan," she said sharply as if I'd insulted her. "I know what my body feels without needing a comparator. I know you please me in a way that's not typical or common."

"Thank you," I said simply. "You please me too, Sunshine."

"Why didn't you tell me? You talk about your mother a lot, but I just thought she was a normal therapist."

"I wasn't exactly keeping it from you. No one knows except Darren, and he only knows because he practically lived at my house in high school. He says my mom's the ultimate MILF."

"MILF?"

"Mother I'd Like to Fuck. Everyone thinks she's some kind of nymphomaniac, but she's not. At least, I doubt she is. I don't know…I don't like thinking about it too much."

"I'm sorry. I didn't mean to make you feel uncomfortable," she said.

"It's fine. After all, didn't your ancestors write the original sex text?"

She giggled. "You're taking about the *Kama Sutra*? Yep, we wrote the book and then closed it forever. Sex is a taboo topic for us."

"Well, then, your mad skills are even more impressive." I cupped her ass and kissed her neck, hoping we were done talking.

"You know what's strange? Almost kismet in a way?" she asked between moans.

"What, Sunshine?"

Her lips curved in a bright but mischievous smile. "The cucumber thing. I learned about that from—"

"Don't say it!" I didn't mean to scream it, but I did.

"But, I wanted to tell—"

I moved my hand over her mouth, but she still seemed determined to tell me the exact words I had no desire to hear.

"Meena, do not finish that sentence."

"You don't know what I was going to say," she replied with an irritated pout.

"I do. I don't want to hear you tell me that you learned to give me the best blowjob in the history of blowjobs from one of my mother's books."

"Oh," she said with obvious surprise. "It was the best one, really?"

"Yes, the best one ever, and unlike you, I have a point of comparison. But you'll ruin it for me, so please do me a favor and don't mention it again."

"Okay, I promise." She nodded, wearing a huge smile. "You know, it's so ironic."

"What is?" I cringed, hoping she wouldn't belabor this topic of conversation.

"Your mother talked to you about sex too much, and my mother never talked about it, yet we both managed."

I laughed at her correlation, feeling less tense about revealing my mother's profession. "I think some things just come naturally. The human body was designed to fit together, after all."

She tightened her grip on me, kissing my cheek, whispering, "I think our bodies fit better than most."

I had to agree with her on that one. She was a smart girl, a beautiful girl, and she was mine.

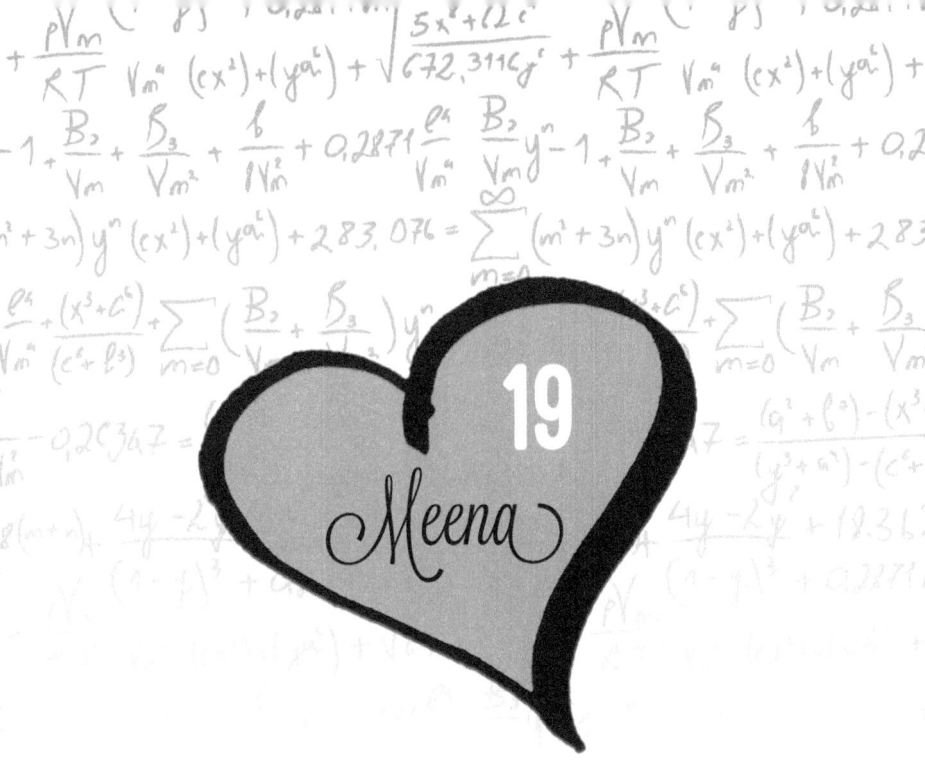

19

Meena

 sat facing Rachael and Raj in a corner booth of an Irish pub, sipping on what Ethan called a "girly" drink. Ethan and I had made a deal that we would hang out apart from each other at least once a week. Neither one of us wanted to be complicit in ignoring our friends.

"What's Ethan doing tonight?" Rachael asked.

"He's having dinner with the Math Department professors, and then going out with some of the guys after. I think Alex is going." It was rare for an underclassman to be invited to prestigious dinners with professors, but Ethan was a rising star.

"Alex isn't going. He's working at Pala Mia's."

"He works there?" Raj asked, surprised. Pala Mia's was a pretty extravagant restaurant, and it was hard to imagine Alex's casual style being associated with it.

"Yeah, he got a job as a waiter. It helps with his student loans," Rachael answered. I knew Alex struggled to stay on a budget. He didn't have Ethan's wealth or the deep pockets of parents like Raj and I did. Rachael received a scholarship from her church and other associations to pay for her schooling. Sometimes it was easy to take that for granted.

"How's Phillip?" I asked Raj.

Raj smiled. "He's good, but we fight a lot."

"Why?"

"He thinks that everyone should be themselves, free to announce to the world who they are. He doesn't understand that it's not so easy for someone like me."

"I'm sorry, Raj. I know it's got to be a difficult situation," I said.

"It's okay, Meena. I could say the same thing to you."

He was absolutely right.

"Yeah, my guy is the wrong race, wrong religion — although he has no religion so I don't know if that counts — and he has no caste status." I left out his mother's occupation to respect Ethan's privacy, but that was an issue too. "You're so lucky, Rachael."

"Why do you say that?"

"You can introduce Alex to your parents at least."

Rachael laughed so hard, she almost spit out her drink. "I'm in the same boat as you two idiots."

Raj and I stared at her incredulously. "What are you talking about?" Raj finally asked her.

She cast her eyes downward. "Jesus, you guys are so dense. His name is Alex Goldberg."

"So?" I asked.

"He's Jewish. I'm the daughter of a Protestant preacher. I'm as much of a loser as you two."

Neither Raj nor I spoke. We had been so busy with our own issues, we didn't even think about this.

"I'm so sorry, Rachael, but wouldn't your parents be more accepting?"

"I don't know. Maybe, if he converted. We're not really at a place where we need to have that talk, but I don't think it will turn out well if we did. His parents are religious too. His uncle is a rabbi, for God's sake. Our relationship sounds like a pathetic joke. What happens when the slutty daughter of a Christian pastor winds up with the noble nephew of a Jewish rabbi? I have no idea what the punch line is, but it can't be good."

"Don't call yourself slutty. Only we get to do that," Raj chimed in, trying to make her laugh. She laughed, but it had a bitter quality.

"Have you guys discussed it?" I asked her.

"Have *you* guys discussed it?" she repeated, staring at both Raj and me.

"Ethan accepts it. He knows I'm going to have an arranged marriage no matter what. He's not looking for a long-term relationship anyway. This is our senior year of college, and we're just…" I didn't know how to finish the sentence. I had no idea what we were really doing.

"I try to avoid it. Phillip can be a real bitch sometimes."

I had to giggle at Raj saying "bitch" — the word sounded foreign on his tongue, like he was trying it on for size.

"So, we all suck," I summarized.

"If this is a competition, I suck the most," Raj proclaimed. Rachael and I gaped at him, waiting for an explanation. He cleared his throat for emphasis. "My guy is the wrong caste, the wrong religion, and born in the wrong country to the wrong parents. Did you know he dropped out of school to pursue poetry?" Both Rachael and I shook our heads. We knew very little about Phillip. "Can you imagine what my parents would think if I told them I was dating a…a…poet, let alone sleeping with one?" I cringed, imagining exactly how the stern conversation would go, because it wouldn't be much different from what my parents would say to me. "Oh, and worst of all, he's the wrong gender."

Rachael held up her glass. "Rajesh, I officially announce you the winner of the Losers in Love Club." We toasted to Raj's sad accomplishment, commiserating as only close friends could.

"Is that what we're calling it, the Losers in Love Club? It seems like no one would want to win," I asked Rachael.

"It's not about who wins or loses, folks. It's what our gym teachers always told us — it's about how you play the game. In the end, we're all playing with honesty and integrity, so that counts for something, right? It has to."

I knew Rachael well enough to know she was trying to justify it to herself, but her statement helped me too. I was about to comment that our lives weren't a game when Rachael interrupted my thoughts.

"Meena, check out who just walked in." Rachael angled her head toward the door. Ethan stepped in with a bunch of guys. He didn't see us since we were in a dimly lit corner of the bar. His group made their way to a table in the front. I felt my heart quicken as it always did when he was in the room. He was wearing black fitted trousers, a white oxford shirt, and red polka dot tie. The suit jacket was probably in his car. He hadn't liked the idea of wearing a suit to the dinner, but he looked so scrumptious in it. His brown hair had been swept to the side when he left, but now his bangs had fallen on his forehead in that way I loved so much. I stared at Ethan so hard I almost didn't notice the statuesque blonde sit next to him. *Almost.*

"I should tell him we're here," I said, scooting out of the booth.

"No," Rachael commanded, gripping my arm. She eyed the blonde too, sitting a little too close to Ethan with her head propped in her hands in a gesture of demure but obvious flirtation.

"Why?"

"This is a rare opportunity."

"For what?" Raj asked.

Rachael gestured her arms wildly, feigning her best Aussie accent, in a surprisingly good imitation of the late, great Steve Irwin, "Ladies and gents, we have the extraordinary privilege of viewing the most mysterious species in all the land — the North American boyfriend. We can view him out on a stroll without the protection of his mate. Let's see how he reacts when he's pounced on by a ruthless predator of the blond variety."

Raj and I both laughed, but I had to admit, despite the funny way she put it, I could see Rachael's point. I hated myself for being such a jealous girl. It was a feeling that was completely foreign to me until I met Ethan. I saw the way girls looked at him, like they would have sewn themselves to his hip if given the chance. It made me even more conflicted about us. Part of me thought it was unfair to him that we had this committed relationship when it couldn't go anywhere, but I knew I couldn't give myself to him if he were with anyone else. We'd talked about this. Ethan had assured me he wouldn't want us any other way.

"Watch as the prowler stalks her prey, preparing to attack at any moment," Rachael narrated.

The blonde giggled at something he said, rubbing her hand over Ethan's arm. I clenched my fists so tightly they hurt. He continued to smile at her, but eased away, taking his arm out of reach, in a gesture that was effective and easily understood. I fought with the urge to slap the girl senseless.

"What do you think they're saying?" I asked. It was obvious they were having some sort of animated conversation despite Ethan's physical rebuke of her advance.

"She's saying, 'Ethan, you're, like, such a total hottie, you know?'" Rachael said, switching to an exaggerated but equally accurate rendition of a Valley girl accent. "'I want you to pour some of that international microbrew on my nipples and then totally suck it off.'"

"Rachael, be serious," I said with an agitation in my voice that surprised me.

"Why the microbrew, sugar?" Raj asked in what I imagined was his Ethan accent. He failed miserably to get the subtle nuances of California surfer tone, mixed with slow, southern drawl, peppered by the clipped East Coast inflection that was uniquely Ethan.

"He never calls me sugar," I replied sarcastically.

"Sorry, Sunshine," Raj corrected.

"Don't," I warned both of them. I had no intention of sitting here while they applied the sweet pet name Ethan called me to this blond bimbo.

"Sunshine fits her more than you, Meena," Raj said, toying with me.

"Because she's blond? I'll have you know I'm so fucking full of sunshine that it's coming out of my pores." These fruity drinks had a way of sneaking up on me, and my voice was so dramatic it was comical, even to me. Thank God, Raj was our designated driver. They looked at each other, laughing nervously, before staring back at me with apologetic smiles.

"Relax, Ethan doesn't like international beer. He only buys American, right?" Rachael asked. It made no sense, but it somehow comforted me. "I've never seen his eyes stray from you, Meena."

"Besides, what kind of girl gets off on having beer poured on herself? You know how messy and sticky that can be?" Raj exclaimed, and it was so funny I cracked up, especially since we didn't know this girl. "If a girl asked me for that, I'd be totally turned off."

"Raj, you're turned off by all girls, remember?" We all laughed at that. Rachael went to put her arm around Raj, completely missed, knocking his beer into his lap. It was so ironically funny that I cracked up harder.

"Shit, Rachael," Raj admonished.

"Sorry, I'm such a klutz," she said, gathering napkins and wiping his lap.

Raj grabbed her wrist and took the napkins from her. "Stop, I can do it."

Rachael smiled slyly. "Is it turning you on?"

"If it was turning me on, I wouldn't have asked you to stop, you wench."

We all cracked up again, absorbed in our private joke, until Ethan came to the table. Of course, we'd made such a scene with our uproarious laughter and beer spilling that he would notice us. We all regarded him like children caught in the middle of a mischievous act, which was exactly what we were.

"Hey," he said smiling. "I didn't know you'd be here."

"Hi, there," I replied nonchalantly, although I was anything but.

"Can I join you guys? I'm getting kind of bored over there talking about math." He didn't fool me. Ethan loved math. He could expound on equations and theories like they were philosophical arguments, full of passion. At the same time, I didn't like him on the other side of the room. He belonged next to me.

I scooted over to make room for him, but before he could sit down, the blond harlot walked up, handing him a beer, causing the otherwise dark room to take on a red color for me.

"Ethan, you forgot your beer," she said amicably. She didn't have a Valley girl accent at all. In fact it was British, which made her sound quite brilliant, causing my unfounded dislike to strengthen.

"Thanks." Ethan took the beer from her and gestured to us. "This is Annabelle. She's a math major too. Annabelle, these are my friends, Raj and Rachael." He paused as if for emphasis when his eyes met mine. "And this is my girlfriend, Meena." A pleasant shiver coursed through my body hearing him introduce me as his girlfriend.

"It's nice to meet you," Annabelle said, offering her dainty hand embellished with perfectly polished pink nails.

I took it, forcing myself not to squeeze too hard. "You too," I exclaimed a little too loudly, pasting a fake smile on my lips.

"Ethan's been talking about you all night. Although he's shown me pictures, it's nice to meet you in person. I feel like I know so much about you already."

I'm an idiot. I had no reason to be jealous. Ethan was the most honest and loyal person I knew, and he would never do anything to diminish my trust in him.

"Would you like to join us?" I offered.

"Sure," she answered good-naturedly, sliding in next to me. She seemed nice, and as long as she kept her paws off my man, there was no reason we couldn't be friendly.

"I'll get the next round. What's everyone having?" Ethan offered.

We gave him our orders. He laughed salaciously when I told him I wanted a "sex on the beach."

He smiled and winked at me. I could read his dirty thoughts because they matched mine. *That can be arranged, baby.*

When Annabelle ordered an international microbrew, Raj, Rachael, and I exchanged a quick glance before doubling over in laughter.

"Something funny, Sunshine?" Ethan asked, arching his brow.

Thankfully, Raj was quick with a reply. "I spilled my drink, and I should go clean up before people start wondering."

I tipped my own drink back, thankful that laughter had a place in my life once more.

20

Meena

$\mathcal{I}$t wasn't lost on me that Ethan had introduced my friends as his friends. That's kind of what we all became after that. We rarely went out separately anymore. We'd meet up in big groups. Philip joined us too, and I found his eccentric attire and witty personality charming. I could see why Raj liked him.

A temporary cease-fire was called on Darren's flirting, and that's when I really got to know him. He was sweet, funny, and I knew why Ethan and he were so close. But, his girlfriend, Mandy, deserved a Medal of Honor for putting up with him. She was shy and totally enthralled with Darren, to the point that I worried about her. Ethan told me I worried about everyone too much. It was true, but what he didn't know was I worried about him the most.

Our relationship seemed to be subtly shifting into deeper waters. I didn't want to bring up the arranged marriage thing, but I did occasionally in the smallest ways, as a reminder. I felt like what we were doing was wrong, but it felt so good and right that I didn't care. I would marry an Indian man and live the life my parents wanted. I would fulfill my destiny and honor my brother, but in the meantime, I could at least look back on this time of my life with joy at all the happy memories I was making with Ethan.

My body was on top of his. He was hard and lean, but it was a comfortable position for me. He gently trailed his fingers on my back, while I stared into his piercing blue eyes. It was the first day of spring break. He was leaving for Hawaii today for a surfing trip with some of his friends from Los Angeles. It was planned before he'd met me, and although I knew about it, it came too soon.

"I could still cancel and spend the week with you," he said, twirling a piece of my hair. It was a conversation we'd had several times, and he was tempting me to change my mind, but I wouldn't let my selfishness destroy his plans.

"I won't let you. If you cancel, I'll refuse to spend any time with you."

He laughed. "Well, I guess it would be stupid since that would be my motive." He lifted his head, planting a soft kiss on my forehead. "I'll miss you."

"Me too."

"Will you reconsider coming with me? I have more than enough airline miles to get you a ticket. Think about it—you, me, the beach. I'll buy you all the girly drinks you want. I promise to protect you from sharks."

"I'm not going to dominate your time with your friends. Besides, what would I do there?"

"I taught you how to surf, remember?"

I almost agreed because even the thought of watching Ethan on a surfboard riding a wave made me wet, but I shook my head. "Go and have fun. Don't worry about me."

"What will you do?"

Rachael and I had both decided to forgo going home for spring break, choosing to stay at Stanford since this was our last year here. We wanted to walk the beautiful campus, take pictures, and reminisce about our time here. We also wanted to spend some good old-fashioned girl time together.

"I'll probably stay at the dorm and hang with Rachael."

He shook his head. "Stay here. This is your place whether I'm here or not. You can invite Rachael or Raj whenever you want. Besides, it'll probably be more comfortable than the dorms." He was so right about that.

"Maybe. We'll see. Raj is staying until tomorrow, so we'll probably hang with him tonight."

"I'll miss you," he said, fixing a stray strand of hair behind my ear.

"You already said that."

"I know." His smiled widely. "We only have a little time left, and I feel like I'm wasting it."

This was dangerous territory. We avoided speaking about our timeline. "Ethan, don't," I pleaded.

His smile turned impish, and I knew he was going to try to make me laugh. He had an ability to disarm my melancholy before it took root. "You know what I think, Sunshine?"

"What?"

"I think you should marry Raj."

"Huh?" I was completely baffled, but his smile didn't fade.

"Don't you get it? You can be Raj's beard, and I will be your lover. We'll all live happily ever after."

I laughed and then contemplated his statement, tapping my fingers against his chest.

"I was joking." His tone was completely serious now.

"It's not a horrible idea, Ethan." I narrowed my eyes, upset he'd come up with a brilliant idea only to dismiss it.

"It's stupid."

"Why?"

"Because we'd all be living a lie. None of us would be happy."

He was right. It was enough that Raj and I would have to live a lie. Why force Ethan? He was the most well-adjusted person I knew — someone who was comfortable in the truth of who he was. Blanketing yourself in lies was something weak people did. People like me. "You're right. It would never work anyway."

"I'm glad you see that."

"Yeah, Raj is Brahmin."

He stared quizzically. "So?"

"Different castes. It's all part of the social hierarchy in our society."

"So, your parents wouldn't let you marry him?"

"Intercaste marriages are more common these days. Mine would probably favor the union, but I doubt his parents would. He's a higher caste." I started laughing. It was true, not really a joke, but I wanted to make him smile.

"Why does it matter so much?"

I took a deep breath. "I guess to keep the bloodlines pure." There was an inflection in the statement, which made it sound like a question.

Ethan's jaw dropped, and he just stared at me with awe. "Shit, did I set my watch for a different century?"

"I understand it's a hard concept for you to grasp."

"It's a crazy concept for anyone living outside of a Dickens novel."

"It's the way this works, Ethan. You're being a bit ethnocentric, don't you think?"

He arched his brow. "Let me get this straight—you're talking about purity of bloodlines and accusing me of being ethnocentric?"

"Yes, I am. This is the way things are done."

I moved to get up, but he embraced me and crushed his lips against mine. His mouth was unrelenting, passionate, and demanding. I surrendered to it as I had to every moment with Ethan. The kiss communicated both apology and challenge. I stared at him, breathless and surprised by his gesture. Ethan smiled, but there was little humor in it.

"Sunshine, your pool of applicants is so small I doubt you'll get married at all." There was something hopeful in his voice, and I wanted to encourage it, but I stopped myself.

"You know what's small? Your luggage limitations. How are you going to fit all your surfing gear?"

"I'm a math guy. I'll make it fit, but first, we'll walk to the park and visit Suzanne and Isaac."

I missed Ethan terribly that whole week, even though he texted and called every night. Rachael practically moved in, but I still longed for him. I slept in one of his T-shirts on his side of the bed. Rachael slept on the couch. Even though I offered her my side, I was glad she refused.

It was Friday, and Ethan would be home Sunday. Rachael and I sat on the couch, watching some sappy, modern-day version of *Romeo and Juliet*, a tale that seemed overly done but never out of style. We painted each other's toes wild colors.

"You and Ethan remind me of this movie," Rachael said, pouring us both some more wine as the credits started rolling. Her voice was a little choked like she was trying to hold back a sob. Crying was a very rare thing for Rachael.

"It's a redo of *Romeo and Juliet*."

"That's why I said it."

I laughed. "You realize how that turned out, right?"

"Oh, yeah, I forgot. It was a bad metaphor."

"I guess it's like you and Alex too, huh?"

"Not really. We're dating. I like him a lot, but I don't know where this is going to go. I have so much I want to do, and he's a junior so he'll be here for another year. The timing is all wrong."

"Time is a system for distinguishing events, not an accurate method for judging them," I said, surprised that Ethan's words had come so naturally off my tongue.

"Look at you, a regular Plato," Rachael said, impressed with me, but her expression turned sad. "I've never felt this way, Meena, and I know I told you to do this thing with Ethan like it was casual, but I see how you guys are together. It doesn't take a Mensa membership, which I happen to have, to know you're good for each other."

I regarded her skeptically. Rachael had changed so much this year, and I had a feeling it was more than just because of Alex. "Rachael, what's going on with you?"

"What do you mean?"

"You've changed your views about so many things. Not just Ethan and me, but you're in a committed relationship, which I've never witnessed. You're more sentimental and softer. It's not a bad thing at all, but why the shift?"

She slammed back her wine, as if to give herself courage. "I had an epiphany of sorts over Thanksgiving break." She was quiet for a moment, touching up her toes.

"Are you going to tell me, or should I leave this alone?"

"Do you remember Jonathon Hall?"

The name sounded familiar, but I couldn't place it. "Did we go to school with him?" It wouldn't be surprising if I didn't know him. Our high school was small, but I pretty much kept to myself after Vijay's death.

"We did. In fact, we both had class with him."

"I don't remember him."

Rachael sighed. "Mr. Hall."

I shouldn't have taken a sip of my wine just then because I choked so hard Rachael had to smack me on the back. "Our AP English teacher? Rachael, you didn't!"

"I didn't plan it or anything. I was with some friends at a bar, and he was there. We waved to each other. After my friends left, he walked over. We had a few drinks and talked about school. You know, he's only ten years older than us. Besides, I reasoned with myself that I wasn't in high school anymore so there was nothing wrong with it."

"So, you slept with him?"

She nodded. I cringed. "The sex was really good. The man can quote Keats for God's sake."

"Well, he is an English teacher," I replied dryly.

"I know, but it was romantic and sweet. I almost wondered about a relationship with him."

"What happened?" I debated if I really wanted to know.

"Afterward, I turned to him and said in my sexiest voice, 'You know, I always had a crush on you in high school.'"

She was quiet for a moment, but my patience was strained so I asked, "And?"

"He said, 'Me too.'"

"Gross." It was skeezy to me. There was nothing romantic about a grown man being attracted to a sixteen-year-old.

"Yeah, it freaked me out too, but not as much as what he said after that. He talked about how he knew I wanted him back then. How I'd wear those short skirts to his class, and he imagined I was an easy lay. He called me Lolita, for fuck's sake."

"That's awful, Rach."

"It was a good thing."

I stared at her, bewildered how she could consider it a positive experience.

"Mr. Hall taught me more that night than he ever did in his class-room. I realized I'd always played the slut. I was so worried my father's profession defined me that I went out of my way to be the opposite of everything I'd been taught. I reasoned I could seek forgiveness later. After all, Jesus forgave Mary Magdalene. Surely, he would do the same for me. But, it occurred to me that night with Mr. Hall — crap, that sounds weird — with Jonathon, that my choices were not because it was who I wanted to be, but who I didn't. I didn't want to be the goody-goody preacher's daughter who was never invited to parties or asked out by boys. Does that make sense?"

"It makes perfect sense, Rach. You were being someone that you weren't. You were living a lie."

"Yes, that's it. I was living a lie. And now, with Alex, there are times when I can see us together forever, but other times when I question what kind of girl I really am. Is there something wrong with me?"

I hugged her. "You don't have to justify your feelings. Figuring it out is not a product, but a process. You're still…processing." It was weird how I'd adopted so many of Ethan's philosophies. I wondered how different my reaction would have been to this story before Ethan.

"Your boyfriend has good taste," she said, patting my back.

"Thank you," I replied.

"I meant the wine."

Rachael and I fell asleep on the couch. I dreamed I was floating, but I wasn't scared. I was safe and surrounded by the most delicious scent. "Shh. Sorry, Sunshine. I'm just putting you to bed." How I longed for that deep, raspy voice.

"Why are you home early?"

"I missed you."

"Where's Rachael?"

"She's fine. I got her a blanket. You're drunk, huh?" There was a hint of amusement in the question.

"I don't think I'll hurl this time."

He chuckled. "That's a relief."

"You should have left me on the couch. I'll probably snore or something."

He laid me on the bed and pulled the sheet over me.

"You snore every night."

"Do not."

"Do too. Actually, it's more like a purr. It's cute. You sound like a kitten." He bent down and whispered next to my ear, "There's no way you're not sleeping next to me. I really need to hold you."

"No complaints here," I replied sleepily as my lips curved into a smile. A few minutes later, he slid in next to me, embracing me, and I asked, "Did you have fun?"

"No," he said.

"Why not?"

He didn't answer for a long time. I thought he'd fallen asleep until his voice punctuated the quiet. "No Sunshine."

I sat on the bed with my notebook, trying to concentrate on Abouab-dillah's antichains, but it was proving difficult with Meena doing yoga on the floor. Each pose turned me on more than the last—it was fucking exponential. Her long legs, firm ass, and flexible body mesmer-ized me. I liked watching her do everything, but I loved it when she got out the purple mat and put on those tight yoga shorts. I silently thanked the man who invented them—pretty sure it had to be a guy.

"Ethan, are you watching me?" she asked from her downward dog position.

"Hell, yes. You think I could look at anything else?"

She laughed. "Should I leave so I don't distract you?"

"Don't even think about it." I was getting hard, looking at her round, plump ass, just waiting for me. "How long do you think you can stay in that position?"

"A long time probably. Why?"

"Could you stay like that if say, there was forceful pressure against you?"

"What kind of pressure?"

"Me."

I couldn't see her face, but I knew she was biting that lower lip. "We can always experiment."

"Seriously?"

"Yes, but you should hurry." She didn't have to tell me twice. I threw down the notebook and practically ripped off my clothes with one hand, while rubbing her ass with my other. It was so perfectly voluptuous that I felt the urge to smack it, and then I did.

"Did you just spank me?"

"Yes." I hoped she wouldn't freak out, but I just couldn't help it.

"Do it again," she said excitedly.

I grunted in excitement and complied with her command, slapping her a little harder and then rubbing the area gently. It was turning me on something fierce. She hardly moved, though I had a protective hand under her waist in case she fell. I expected her to be struggling in the pose since she'd told me to hurry.

"You should stand and stretch first."

"I don't need to." She was being cocky, and I loved it, but there was no way I was going to make it uncomfortable for her.

"Meena, you told me to hurry, remember?"

"I didn't tell you to hurry because I'm afraid I'll fall."

"Then why?"

"I'm very wet, and you should take care of it since it's your fault."

I laughed, rolling her shorts and panties down. My fingers penetrated her and confirmed she was soaked. She took off her sports bra, still maintaining position. This girl was nothing short of amazing. My hands cupped her breasts, fondling them while my thumbs flicked her nipples. I bent over her, punctuating my kisses with gentle bites. Her moans told me she liked it. I traced her spine with my tongue and spread her legs. I entered slowly, but once I was inside her moist, tight, delicate walls, I couldn't stop from pounding into her. She screamed in a mixture of pain and pleasure.

"Are you okay, baby?"

"Don't stop," she commanded.

I didn't. This was I'm-going-to-fuck-you-hard sex, and both of us were all in.

After a few minutes, her legs started to wobble. "Ethan, I can't," she panted.

"Hands on the bed," I said, lifting her so she could reach without breaking our connection.

I slowed down the tempo, caressing her back and ass with my hand. "Ethan," she moaned, causing me to jerk harder. My name on her lips like this, well…it was just too much for any mortal man.

"Sunshine, please…tell. Close." I couldn't even form a complete sentence.

"Close," she said with great urgency, obviously having the same problem, but understanding what I was asking.

"Get there," I commanded.

And then she did. Just like that. I only moved inside of her once more before my own release. We were both panting. I leaned my head against her back, freshly slick from sex. I loved it.

I loved her.

It was the first time I'd acknowledged it, but I had known for a while.

I moved out slowly and massaged her legs, trying to work out any kinks. I lifted her to the bed and got in beside her. I lay down, moving her against my chest where I could hear her heartbeat and she could feel mine. I removed the clip in her hair, fanning it out. We were both quiet as our breathing returned to normal. I wanted to express what she meant to me. I wanted to have the conversation we'd avoided for so long.

"Choose me," I said simply, regretting the word selection instantly. It didn't convey what I was really feeling. It was an instruction, not a true explanation of how deeply I needed her.

"Choose you for what?"

I tightened my arms around her, pissed at myself for not being clearer and irritated with her for not understanding. "For a tennis partner. What the fuck do you think?"

"Ethan —"

I shifted so I could look into her eyes. "Meena, stop this. I make you happy. Don't throw your life away because you feel guilty about something that isn't your fault."

There was a great sadness in those chocolate-colored eyes. "I'm not trying to hurt you. This isn't a choice for me. It's something I have to do."

"You're wrong, Sunshine. I see couples like us all the time. It's not uncommon."

"In my family, it is."

"This is why religion is evil," I yelled, exasperated.

"It's not just religion. It's a cultural expectation. It's my promise to my parents. It's my promise to myself never to hurt them again."

"So, you'll just settle for hurting me, then?"

She winced, and I instantly felt guilty. This wasn't easy for Meena. She had experienced so much pain, and my vow was to take it away, not add to it.

"What do you want from me, Ethan?" she asked in a sad whisper.

I was quiet for a moment, although I knew the answer.

"A future."

She shook her head, and I saw the tears start to form. I went to wipe them away, but she slapped my hand. "Don't." She flipped off the bed, quickly putting on her bra, shorts, and a T-shirt.

"Meena—"

"Just stop," she said, holding out her hand like she was trying to hold me back. "I was honest with you. I told you we couldn't be anything more. You promised me you accepted that. Don't make me feel guilty about it now."

"Where are you going?" I asked as she headed out the door.

"For a run. You interrupted my workout," she said, slamming the door.

Meena

My loose hair whipped around my face while my feet pounded the sidewalk. It wasn't helping because what I really wanted to do was run away from what he'd said. I hated hurting him. He had to see that. He had to know that. So, why did he throw it in my face? Didn't he know I was hurting myself just as much, probably more?

It wasn't long until he reached me. Ethan was fast, and although he was breathing hard, he could outpace me. I slowed and then stopped, bending down to catch my breath. I placed my hands on my knees choking back the sobs. I felt his hand rubbing my back, but I didn't want the comfort right now. I wanted the pain. I started walking briskly, and he kept pace beside me.

He held out a bottle of water. A rubber band was around the base. I took it and quickly tied up my hair, grateful and mad at the same time. I chugged the water, cursing him for being so damn thoughtful all the time. I slowed down some more. He did too, matching his footsteps to mine, until his pinky curled around mine.

"Where are we going?" he asked softly.

"I'm going for a walk. I have no idea what you're doing." I was a hot, sweaty mess, and my voice betrayed me by cracking.

"Obviously, I'm going with you."

"I don't recall inviting you," I said, stopping and turning my head to him.

He stared at me for a few seconds before smiling softly and shrugging. "It's a free country."

I sighed and continued my walk, but I didn't disengage our fingers. I had no destination in mind when I started, but we ended up in the right place anyway. We headed straight for the lake where our swans lived. He sat next to me, but he didn't say anything.

I spotted Isaac and Suzanne first and pointed to them. He nodded. We sat. We contemplated. We watched. "Suzanne looks sick," I finally said.

"Swan flu?" he replied.

"Funny." I let out a cynical laugh. "What are we doing?"

"Watching our swans," he said, gesturing to the lake.

"I mean with each other."

"I thought we were solving for C."

"There is no solution, Ethan." My hands shook. He took them in his, pulling me gently so I would meet his gaze.

"Do you know how I feel about you?"

"Yes."

"So, you understand that I lo—"

"Don't!" I screamed before he finished the sentence. I tousled his hair and said more gently, "Don't say it, please."

"Why?"

"Because it's a wasted sentiment."

"So, you don't care."

"It's because I care that I don't want you to say it. It won't change my mind. That's what I'm trying to tell you. Maybe if my brother hadn't died, things could be different." Ethan opened his mouth, but I pressed my hand to his lips to stop him. "I'm not telling you that so you can talk me out of it. I'm telling you because it's a fact for me. I'm so sorry, but I can't be the girl you need—the one you deserve that's strong and loves you with an open heart. This is not a choice for me, but you have a choice, and I promise I'll respect it."

"What choice do I have?"

I swallowed, feeling the tears roll down my face. He wiped them away. "We can end things now."

"Why would I want to do that?"

"So we can stop procrastinating and start healing."

He was thoughtful for a moment, and my whole body tensed, waiting for his response. He shifted toward me, placed his arm around me, and pulled me against his chest. "I choose us for as long as I can."

"Ethan, you can't talk me out of this, so you have to promise to stop trying."

"You know I'll never agree with it." I opened my mouth, but he gripped me tightly, stopping the words from forming. "I won't try to change your mind. I promise."

I started crying, and he held me against his chest. When the sobs were nothing more than breathy gasps, he spoke. "Come on, let's go home. I believe you owe me something, Sunshine."

"What?"

"Make-up sex," he said.

I had no idea how he could make me laugh, as emotional as I was, but he did.

We never discussed the fight we had a few weeks ago, but it still hung in the tension-filled air around us. I was careful with her. I knew she was hurting. I had a feeling it was mostly because of what she was doing to me and not herself. So, I did as I promised and left it alone.

The adult dinner party was my idea. It started when I was looking at her latest painting. She had done three so far. I loved them all, but this one was my favorite—a Rembrandt-inspired piece with the silhouette of a man and woman on opposite sides of the canvas, looking at each other against a backdrop of dark blue sky and golden stars. I was no art connoisseur, but her work was good.

I told her she should exhibit her paintings somewhere. She reacted as if I'd suggested she strip in public. Maybe, in a way, I did. I was the only one who'd ever seen her work, and that seemed like such a waste.

I suggested we throw a dinner party since we were going to be adult college graduates soon. I figured we'd invite our closest friends and display her art. She hated the idea at first, but I finally wore her down. In a way, it was a good distraction for both of us.

I came out to the kitchen where she was slicing the garlic bread on the counter. I stood behind her, wrapping my arms around her waist. "It smells good."

"You smell good," she replied, turning her head to kiss me.

I moved her hair away from her neck. She had it down, and it was driving me crazy. "You smell good," I replied, running my nose down her neck. "Don't wear your hair like this again."

"You don't like it?" She adjusted it self-consciously.

I took her hand and kissed her wrist. "I like it too much. That's the problem."

I backed up, gesturing to myself so she could inspect me.

She grinned and adjusted my tie. "You look hot."

"I can't believe you made me wear a suit."

"You said adult, so I told all the boys they had to wear a suit and all the girls to wear dresses. Otherwise, they would get no wine."

"Oh, if you threatened the alcohol, I'm sure they'll be in appropriate attire."

"Speaking of that, I think we might need another bottle. Would you mind?"

I looked at the two bottles on the counter. "With this crew, we're going to need more than one."

She nodded, taking off her apron. I sucked in a deep breath between my teeth. She was wearing a new rust-colored dress that tightened around her curves and formed a deep V on her neckline, showing off the slightest bit of cleavage. She looked gorgeous, and it was making me horny as hell. "You look beautiful," I said as I kissed her neck and nibbled on her earlobe.

"Ethan, you should go. They'll be here any minute."

"I don't want to go. I want to come. You in that dress is turning me on something fierce. Come on, baby, we can do this quick."

She giggled against my chest. "Ethan, seriously."

"Fine, but…you. Me. Later." I punctuated each statement with a hard kiss to her mouth. I headed toward the door, but added, "Dress is optional."

"I'll be there," she said, winking at me.

"That's good because I'd hate to start without you."

"*Go!*" she said, throwing a dishtowel at me.

"Going."

Before I left, I glanced at her paintings displayed in the living room. I turned to her and smiled reassuringly. She was looking at them too.

"They are really good, Sunshine."

"Of course you'd say that. You're sleeping with the artist and totally biased."

I laughed. "True, but I'm being honest here. Besides, this is a risk for both of us."

She stared at me in confusion.

"If it doesn't go well, you might blame me and withhold yourself. I think I'm actually betting higher stakes here." I shut the door as she threw another dishrag, even though it was nowhere close to me. "Your aim could use improvement, though," I yelled through the closed door.

Meena

There was a knock on the door as soon as he left. I thought Ethan had forgotten his keys, but it was Raj and Phillip. Raj looked handsome in his traditional charcoal suit and red power tie. Phillip looked nice too, but in an unusual way. He was wearing overalls with a plaid shirt. Granted he did have on a lime green bow-tie and suit jacket, so technically he was in code.

They both kissed me on the cheek. "*Mia bella*, good to see you," Phillip exclaimed with flourishing hand gestures.

"So, how come I didn't know you painted?" Raj asked pointedly.

"It's just a hobby," I replied sheepishly, making my way to the kitchen.

"Where are these paintings?" Phillip asked.

"In the living room."

I heard them both chat quietly while I filled their wineglasses in the kitchen. My hands were shaky. I wished I hadn't sent Ethan out. He had the ability to relieve my agitation with his mere presence.

I brought out the wineglasses, careful not to spill any liquid. "These are damn good, Meena," Raj said, but I didn't put as much merit in it as Phillip's reaction. Raj was my friend after all.

"They're beautiful, just like you," Phillip said, grinning as he extolled the virtues of each one. He finished with the painting on the couch. I soaked in his words, feeling foolishly giddy.

"Thank you," I said, exhaling the breath I'd been holding since they walked in. "I'm just getting dinner finished."

"Can we help?" Raj asked.

"I've got it, but could one of you get the second easel? It's in the closest in the guest bedroom. I think we might need the couch space."

"Let Raj go," Phillip chimed in with a cynical smile. "He loves being in the closest."

I stared at both men, noticing the tension between them for the first time. Raj's irritation was apparent, as was Phillip's annoyance. *This isn't good.*

There was another knock, though, and I went to answer it, grateful to give them a minute alone after a comment like that. Rachael and Alex both hugged me.

"These are great, Meena," Alex said. He asked me questions about technique, lines, and shading that I was embarrassed I couldn't answer with a true artist's knowledge.

"They are awesome, karma girl. I can't decide which one I like the best," Rachael claimed.

"Do you always have issues making up your mind?" A question that loaded coming from mild-mannered, friendly Alex was a shock.

"I like this one the best, Meena," Rachael said, pointing to my rendition of swans in flight. She turned back to Alex, smiling sweetly. "See, it's easy when I'm not being pressured."

I stared between the two of them, confused and uncomfortable with their unease with each other. I took Rachael's hand. "I need your help," I said, leading her toward the guest bedroom where Raj was. "Alex, can you please stir my sauce?" I didn't wait for his reply, practically dragging Rachael with me.

Raj was coming out of the bedroom, easel in hand, when I pushed him back in. I shut the door and stared at both of them.

"What's going on with you and Phillip?" I asked Raj.

"Is he hurting my sweet Rajesh?" Rachael asked, putting her arm around Raj. "Because if he is, I'll bust his balls."

Raj laughed. "If you're going to hurt him, do it above the belt, please." It took a second for his meaning to dawn on us, but when it did, Rachael and I let out a simultaneous groan. "He's just pissed that I'm not like him. His parents are so fucking supportive it's sickening. They actually want to throw him some kind of gay pride party or something. He doesn't understand that not everyone's family is like that."

"Make him understand, Raj," I said, clasping his hand.

"I don't know if I want to. I won't come out to my family for him. I won't for anybody. Whoever I'm with has to respect that because this is my choice."

I nodded, totally understanding his predicament. There was no real solution. Raj was also going to have an arranged marriage, but unlike me, he had been able to keep his parent's from starting a search.

"Rachael, what about you and Alex? What did he mean you have a problem making up your mind?"

She smiled, but there was an innate sadness in it. "I got the internship in London."

"That's great," Raj exclaimed, hugging her. I was happy too, except I could see from Rachael's expression she wasn't. She had been dreaming of this internship since freshman year.

"He doesn't want you to leave?" I asked.

"He's actually very supportive of it. He wants us to continue our relationship while I'm abroad."

"I don't understand the problem," Raj said.

"I love him, but I don't think we can make it a whole year apart."

"They say absence makes the heart grow fonder," I replied, knowing it was cliché, but I had no other words.

"They also say out of sight, out of mind," she muttered.

"He loves you. He's not going to cheat on you, Rach."

She sighed deeply, adjusting a stray red hair. "Meena, I'm not worried about him."

Oh. "Oh."

"Sunshine, are you going to stay in here all night?" Ethan asked, opening the door. As soon as he saw the three of us, his expression changed to guilt. "Sorry, did I interrupt?"

"No, we're done," Raj said. "There's nothing left to say."

Raj was right. There was no magic cure to solve our problems.

We went on like nothing was wrong. Ethan, God bless him, did his best to be the perfect host, refilling everyone's wine and conjuring conversations that passed as amicable. He turned on music, choosing "99 Problems," not Jay Z's version but one by an artist named Hugo that Ethan had introduced me to. Somehow the lyrics were soothingly ironic for all of us. Ethan sang the words to me, spinning me around in his arms while we were setting the table.

Darren was the last to arrive. His appearance only added dangerous sparks to the tinder in the room.

"Hey, beautiful," he said, pulling me into a long embrace. I could smell the alcohol on his breath. "Not a lot of girls could get me to wear a suit, but I did it for you."

"Started drinking early, eh?" Ethan asked, coming behind me and placing his arm protectively around my waist.

Darren shrugged.

"Where's Mandy?"

"We broke up," he announced.

Although he didn't treat her right, he had really cared for Mandy and had to be heartbroken. "I'm sorry, Darren," I patted his arm, all the while feeling Ethan's grip tightening.

"What are you going to do?" Ethan asked. I almost wanted to tell him to shut up. This wasn't the time.

"Relax, Callahan. I'm not asking to move back here or anything. We decided to live together until the end of the school year."

"That must be awkward," Ethan stated, but I could hear the relief in his voice.

"I live with a girl that hates me. It's not so crazy. You should know, we can learn to live with a lot of messed up stuff," he replied, gesturing toward us.

I instantly felt cold. Ethan confided in Darren, just like I confided in Rachael and Raj, but I had no idea Darren knew the detailed intricacies of our relationship.

"Cut it out," Ethan warned sharply.

"Something smells good," Darren commented, ignoring Ethan.

"Meena's been cooking all day," Ethan said proudly.

"Oh," Darren didn't hide his obvious disappointment. "So, we're having curry, then?"

I could feel the muscles in Ethan's chest tighten. I gave him a pleading look and turned back to Darren, smiling so brightly it hurt. "You couldn't handle the curry." I took his hand. "Come see my paintings," I said enthusiastically, leading him to the living room. "Ethan, please get Darren some wine." Ethan groaned, but went to the kitchen anyway.

I pointed to each painting and made some awkward small talk about them to relieve the tension. Everyone chatted away, but we were all on edge. The subtle things gave it away like an irritated eye roll from Rachael, Alex clutching the stem of the wineglass too hard, Phillip and Raj trying to avoid each other. Darren listened with rapt attention as I droned on about nothing of consequence.

"What do you think?" I asked when I had run out of things to say.

"I'm impressed, but I have to admit I'm disappointed too."

"Why?"

"I was hoping for a nude — particularly a self-portrait," he answered, smiling salaciously.

I felt Ethan before I heard him. He practically shoved Darren's wineglass at him. He clasped my waist, pulling me against his chest. "If such a painting existed, it would be for my eyes only."

Darren laughed like Ethan had made a joke. He held up his wineglass in a mock toast. "Not for long. Right, Sunshine?"

Everything moved in slow motion. The harsh sound of flesh connecting to flesh as Ethan's fist hit Darren's jaw. "Get the fuck out of my house!"

Darren was sprawled on the floor, the shattered wineglass lying in pieces around him. The blood oozing from his split lip mixed with the wine staining his white oxford. Raj and Alex moved swiftly, holding Ethan back from attacking again. Phillip helped Darren up.

"Fuck, it was a joke, man," Darren said, touching his mouth.

"It wasn't funny, shithead," Ethan snapped, trying to free himself from the tight hold Alex and Raj had on his arms.

"Don't, Ethan. It's not worth it," Alex warned.

"I'm sorry, Meena," Darren said to me.

"Shut the fuck up. Don't talk to her. You don't get to talk to her," Ethan screamed, struggling against the restraint. I wasn't sure what to do, but Ethan was going to break free any minute, and it looked like he wasn't done with Darren.

I turned around and put my hands on his chest, trying to block his view of Darren. "Stop it." Amazingly, he did stop struggling, but his blue eyes were cold and hollow, full of fury. "Get a hold of yourself."

"You're telling me to get a hold of myself?" he asked in disbelief.

"Yes." The demanding-yet-calm tone in my voice surprised even me. "This isn't you."

Ethan took a deep breath and yanked himself free, stalking away from us.

"Where are you going?" Raj asked.

"To get a fucking hold of myself," Ethan announced, slamming the bedroom door.

Rachael found the first aid kit, and we fixed Darren up the best we could. Raj and Phillip cleaned up the mess. The wine had spattered on one of my paintings, but I didn't care. I only cared about the boy I'd sent to his room for all intents and purposes.

"I'm sorry, Meena," Darren kept repeating.

"At least he didn't break a tooth," Rachael offered as if it was a great consolation. Darren nodded, but he kept repeating his apologies to me like a skipped record.

Rachael left to put away the kit and take care of my dinner, which I was pretty sure was a complete mess.

I glared at Darren. "What's wrong with you?"

"I'm an asshole."

"No, I think you just play one on TV," I retorted.

"Say what?"

"I know you're a nice guy. This isn't you. You've had too much to drink, and you're upset because of Mandy, but you shouldn't have said that."

"You're right. I doubt he'll forgive me this time."

"I'll talk to him."

"You know he loves you, right?"

I stared at Darren's gray eyes in disbelief. "He told you?"

"He didn't have to."

"It doesn't matter, Darren."

"You don't love him?"

"I didn't say that. Raj is going to drive you home."

"Meena, I can — "

"Raj is going to drive you home," I said more forcefully. "I'll talk to Ethan. He'll calm down, and we'll bring your car to your place tomorrow."

"But — "

"I swear to God, I will punch your nose if you don't listen to me right now."

He chuckled. "Okay, Sunshine. Thanks."

"Don't call me that again," I said.

Darren's eyes widened, but I gave him a comforting smile and squeezed his hand to let him know it was okay. Only Ethan could call me that.

Raj took Darren home, promising to return shortly. Rachael asked me if they should all leave. I asked them for a few minutes to sort things out.

I walked into the bedroom, not knowing what to expect. The room was dark, and Ethan was sitting on the bed, shoulders hunched with his head in his hands. I thought he might be angry with me. I stood in front of him for a few moments, hoping for some clue. He completely surprised me by grasping my waist and leaning his head against it. Then he gently pulled my body down so I was sitting in his lap. He put his head on my shoulders and held me tightly.

"Ethan — "

"Shh, just let me hold you. Please."

I did, and we sat like that for several minutes. I could feel the tight muscles in his body relax, like I was some sort of remedy for them.

"Did Darren leave?" he asked after a while.

"Raj took him home."

"What about everyone else?"

"They're still here. Should I ask them to go?"

"No, you made a lot of food. We should eat it." He released me. I stood up and held out my hand toward him. "I'm sorry. I meant this to be a good night for you."

"Every night I'm with you is a good night. Don't be sorry. He was being a total ass, and if it wouldn't have ruined my manicure, I'd have punched him myself." Ethan laughed, but it sounded hollow.

Raj came back, and we served the food. Dinner was a tenuous affair. The meal was definitely not worthy of any favorable Food Network adjectives, but it was flavorful and edible. Unfortunately, the conversation was not. We were stiff and uncomfortable with each other. This should have been a happy time for us. Most of us were going to be graduating soon and starting our lives, but instead, we carefully stayed away from any conversation of substance. The things we did say were poor substitutes for the things we omitted.

Ethan was talking to Alex and Phillip while I said my goodbyes to Rachael and Raj.

"Well, you sure know how to throw one hell of a party, karma girl," Rachael said sarcastically as I hugged her goodbye.

"Yeah, it should win the award for worst dinner party ever," I replied.

"If this is an adult dinner party, maybe we can just stay kids for a while longer," Raj interjected, kissing my cheek.

"Thanks for coming, but most of all, thanks for staying."

"Is he going to be okay?" Rachael asked, gesturing toward Ethan who had been unusually quiet during dinner.

"I think so."

"Are you going to be okay?" Rachael asked me.

"Are any of us?" I said, looking at both of them.

Rachael shrugged. I shrugged. Raj shrugged. It was amazing that with all that shrugging we didn't get neck cramps.

Ethan insisted on doing the dishes and cleaning up. I decided I needed a long, hot shower. I sat on the built-in seat, adjusting the nozzle to the rain function. I'd never seen Ethan that angry. I had never seen him become violent, and although Darren was out of line, Ethan shouldn't have punched him. It was still my fault. Everything was my fault. I was hurting the person I loved the most.

"Can I join you?" Ethan asked, staring at me. I hadn't heard him enter the room.

"I was hoping you would."

He took off his clothes, revealing the hard-packed muscles of his chest and torso. I stared at the thatch of sandy hair that formed a perfect V-pattern, leading to that other muscle which had given me so much pleasure. My eyes lingered on the long, sinewy legs that carried me with no effort. The strong arms that held me in their embrace and always made me feel safe. He was beautiful.

"Sunshine, if I knew you were going to watch me, I would have done a strip tease for you," he joked, opening the large shower door.

"What you did was just fine."

He squirted soap in his hand and began rubbing my shoulders. The hot water washed over us. I never imagined being so comfortable with my nudity with any man, but Ethan made it easy for me. He always looked at my body with carnal lust and desire, giving me courage to be open with him. His hands slid up and down my sides, settling at my hips.

"We really suck at throwing parties," he said after a while.

I embraced him. "I think it had to do more with our guest list than our abilities as hosts."

"Good point." He took my hand in his. I stared at the knuckle that was a little bruised from colliding with Darren's face. I rubbed it with my fingers.

"He was out of line, but you've heard him say stuff like that before. Why did you punch him?"

"I was jealous."

I kissed the corner of his mouth. "You have no reason to be jealous of Darren."

He chuckled cynically. "Who said I was jealous of Darren?"

"Then who?"

His voice was quiet, but it pierced straight through my heart. "I haven't met him yet. I probably never will."

I bit my lip so hard it hurt. Of course, he was thinking of the man I'd marry. A man I hadn't even met yet. "I'm sorry." It was all I could think to say.

"I promised you I wouldn't waste my time...our time, talking you out of it, and I won't, but there's something I have to know. I need to ask you a question. Be honest with me."

"What?" I asked, placing a hand on each side of his face.

His hands traveled down my back. "What happens if the man you marry is cruel to you? What if he's a drunk, or a loser that can't keep a job, or worse...what if he hurts you?"

"Ethan, it's not like that. I'll know him."

"Through an interview?"

"It's much more than that. I'll know his background, his family, and the engagement process is a long one. We'll be engaged, but I'll be able to date him before we're married." I didn't want to go into all of these details with Ethan, but I could tell from his questions and the way his muscles tightened around me that he needed clear answers.

"Even if you do know him, people can change and not always for the better."

"That can happen in any marriage."

He swallowed, his hand stilling at the small of my back. "You mate for life, remember?"

I'd forgotten I'd told him that at the pond, but it was obvious he hadn't. "I won't let anyone abuse me, if that's what you're asking."

"Promise me."

"What?"

"Swear it to me right now, Sunshine. Promise me that if he hurts you, you'll get out, and if it's difficult, you'll call me. No matter how much time has passed between us." He took my hand and pressed it against his heart.

"I don't think you understand. Divorces are possible. It's not like someone will—"

"Don't justify it. I know you're from an educated, modern family, but I also know social stigmas exist. You've told me that. I just want you to swear it to me. Say it like an oath."

"Why?"

"I need this."

I was touched, but surprised by what he was asking. My culture wasn't one where women were killed, stoned, or beheaded for being independent. Ethan knew that, but I guess the whole idea of arranged marriage would cause him to wonder, and it was more difficult for a woman to stand up for her convictions than the western norm.

"I promise you, Ethan Callahan, that I'll leave my future husband if he hurts me."

"And if you can't?" I shook my head, but his whisper was so powerful it sent a shiver down my back. "You owe me this. I need to hear you say it."

"I will call you no matter how much time has passed between us."

"Thank you," he said, exhaling.

I turned around and reached for the shampoo. He took it from me.

"Let me," he said.

I closed my eyes and surrendered to his touch as he washed my hair. "What if it's ten years from now, and you have to explain to your wife why some weird, obnoxious woman is calling you in the middle of the night?" I meant it as a joke, but as soon as I said it, the words sounded bitter and fell flat.

His fingers stilled, and he leaned down, his mouth hovering above my ear. "I'll tell her the truth. I'm friend number three, and I always will be."

$\mathcal{T}$he closer we got to our expiration date, the more complicated things became. The dinner party didn't help, although it served as an opportunity for me to ask her the questions, which yielded the promises I needed. I told myself I could handle it. Meena had always been honest with me. She wasn't cheating on me. She wasn't lying to me. She wasn't even breaking up with me. In some ways, I wish she were. It sounded crazy, but at least then I could hate her. I could have a focal point for my anger, frustration, and sorrow, but I couldn't hate her. Her heart was too pure. She was my sunshine.

I don't know how she did it, but she convinced me to forgive Darren. It helped that he groveled a lot. It also didn't hurt the cause that he had a fat lip. He'd finally crossed the line with me, but we had a long history. Darren's father was a drunk who beat his mother. Darren wasn't anything like his dad, but it haunted him, and that fear came out in assholish ways like flirting with my girlfriend.

I returned from a pickup game of rugby to find Meena chopping vegetables in the kitchen. I came up behind her as I always did. I never surprised her. She always sensed my presence as I did hers. Something was wrong, though. Her fingers were shaking as she held the knife, and her shoulders shook like she was crying.

"What's wrong, Sunshine?"

She sniffled. "I went to the park today to watch our swans. Isaac was by himself."

"So?"

"Suzanne wasn't with him. They don't travel alone. I ran around the whole lake looking for her, and then I found her." The tears started flowing freely, falling on the cutting board. "She's dead."

"You're crying because of a dead swan?"

She stiffened. Fuck, I shouldn't have said that. She was moving the knife so fast I was afraid she was going to cut her finger. It seemed like some sort of coping mechanism for her.

"I know you're upset about Suzanne, but it's okay." I placed my hands on her shoulder and rubbed them.

"You think I'm crying because of her? I'm not. She's gone. I'm crying for Isaac."

"Why?"

"He'll be all alone now, Ethan. He won't have anyone. She left him all alone. How could she do that to him?" She sounded hysterical.

"Meena, you're being ridiculous. You need to calm down."

She was chopping so fast, it was difficult to distinguish between the knife, the carrots, and her fingers. I stilled the knife in her hand and took it from her.

"What are you doing?" she yelled, backing away from me.

"Relax. I don't want you to chop off one of your beautiful fingers."

"You know you're not supposed to touch it when I am." She backed into the far corner of the kitchen. How could she possibly feel this much…for a swan?

"What happens when we touch the same blade? What's the worst that could happen? Fucking tell me." I didn't mean to sound so pissed, but all of the emotions broke through the carefully constructed damn I'd built.

"It means we'll fight, and look, that's exactly what we're doing, isn't it?"

I laughed sarcastically. "You can't honestly believe in this stuff." I threw the knife in the sink. "Your father's a doctor, for God's sake."

"That's pretty hypocritical coming from a man who has a four-leaf clover tattooed on his arm."

I narrowed my eyes at her. "It was a drunken dare on St. Patrick's Day. I don't believe it brings me any kind of luck. I don't believe in any of that silly superstitious crap, and I have no idea how you do."

"That's it, isn't it? You think I'm stupid. Just tell me. I give you permission."

I didn't consider my words because I wanted to hurt her. "Yes, I think you're stupid. I think it's the most fucked-up idea I've ever heard to marry someone you don't even know in hopes that you'll fall in love with him eventually. You're going to throw away what we have for some…some fucking unknown variable. You're an idiot."

"I don't owe you a justification, Ethan."

I swallowed the burning lump in my throat. I shook my head at her. "No, you don't owe it, and you can't give it because you don't have a justification." I stomped toward the door, needing to escape this fucked up mess we were in.

"Where are you going?" she asked in a shaky voice.

"It's none of your business. I don't owe you anything, either." I slammed the door so hard on my way out that the sound followed me down the hallway.

Meena

He had been gone for a long time. I texted and called him, but he didn't return any of my messages. It was late when I finally called Alex and Darren. They hadn't seen him, but they both went to search for him. He'd left so angry. All the signs were there that we'd have a blowout. That was what happened when there were so many unsaid things between people. Even on simmer, the pot always boiled over.

Darren and Alex brought back a very drunk Ethan. "Honey, I'm home," he said, with the full southern twang that came out when he drank too much. I'd seen Ethan buzzed, but never witnessed him falling-down drunk.

They placed him on the bed. I thanked them, hugged them, and sent them away so I could take care of him. I took off his shoes and socks. I removed his watch, rubbing his wrist. I thought he had fallen asleep, but he surprised me by sitting up and staring at me with those piercing blue eyes that looked as tumultuous as the waves of the Pacific.

"You're drunk," I said, hoping he'd take it as a warning not to speak.

"No shit, Sunshine. And you're a fucking coward," he spat, slurring the words.

"Stop it."

"Do you even care that you're breaking my heart?"

There was such anguish in his voice that I felt the transference of his pain like a physical force wrapping itself around me.

"Ethan, you know I care. I wish it didn't have to be this way."

"Yeah, but you won't do anything about it because you're a coward."

I stared at him, shaking my head. He was being so mean, but in some ways I deserved it. I went to tousle his hair, but he slapped my hand away.

"I want you out of my life. You're occupying too much space."

"Ethan—"

"You're taking up too much space in here," he said, gesturing to his head. "And way too much in here." He moved his hand over his heart.

"Let me just take care of you tonight."

"You're the reason I'm in pain. You'll just make it worse. I need you to go. I'm fucking blinded by all your damn…sunshine. I need it to be dark so I can breathe again."

I choked back a sob, but I got up and walked out. I called Darren and Alex and asked them to come back. Ethan needed someone to stay with him. They didn't question it. They must have heard it in my voice. I called Raj too. He helped me pack. I was quick and quiet, but Ethan had passed out by then, so it really didn't matter.

Ethan

I woke up to the worst headache I'd ever had. It took me a minute to get my bearings. The first coherent thing I did was grope her side of the bed. When I didn't feel her, I called out her name. The door opened, and I expected it to be her, but it was Alex instead. He brought me a tall glass of water that I gulped down.

"Where's Meena?" I asked him.

He avoided my gaze. "You were wrecked last night."

"Yeah, I got that part. Where is Meena?"

"You should sleep it off some more."

"Why aren't you answering my question?"

"She's not here."

I swallowed, waiting for more of an explanation, but he offered none. "Where is she?"

He took the water glass from me and made a move like he was leaving the room.

"Where the fuck is my girlfriend, Alex?"

"She moved out."

I didn't believe him. She wouldn't leave me. It was too early anyway. We still had a month. We had more time. She owed me more time. I had no idea how I managed to find the strength with my pounding head, but I flung off the covers and ran to her set of drawers, pulling them so hard they dislodged from the track. They were all empty. The closet was devoid of her clothes as well.

I ran to the other bedroom. All the supplies were where they should be, but there was only one painting. It was my favorite one with the starry background. *She left it for me.*

I was free of any rational thoughts. The last conversation I remembered was about a dead swan and her crying. Did she leave me because a stupid swan died? I grabbed the wooden easel and flung it against the wall. It broke into a dozen pieces. I grabbed what had been an easel leg and used it like a bat to fling all of the baskets off the shelf. Pencils, tubes of paint, and charcoal littered the floors. I smashed them with my feet, not caring about the mess I was making. I was breathing hard, my head was pounding, and my whole body hurt. The emotional pain was the strongest, though. She betrayed me. How could she leave me? The lone unscarred object in the room was the painting, and I wanted to destroy it. I took the wooden stick in my hand, preparing to rip through the canvas the way she ripped open my heart.

"Don't do it, Callahan," Darren warned.

"Why?" Just hearing another voice calmed me somewhat, but I was still determined. He reached for the stick, but I held it tightly.

"I'm not going to fight you. We've already established you can beat the shit out of me, but don't do this."

"What difference will it make?"

"You'll regret it."

He was right. I dropped the stick and settled for punching a hole in the wall. It was stupid. My mother had written papers about unfounded anger in young men, but the physical assault on the inanimate objects still made me feel better.

"She left me."

"I think you helped her make that decision."

I gaped at him, completely confused.

"I don't know what you said to her last night. She wouldn't tell me, but I saw her. She looked…wounded. She looked like my mom after my dad beat her."

"Are you saying I hit her or something?" I started shaking, realizing I had been so wrapped up in her leaving, I hadn't thought about what I might have done to cause it. The cold grip of fear took hold on me as I realized I couldn't remember.

"I know you didn't. You don't have that kind of evil in you, but you definitely injured her. She loved you. She left you. She had to."

"I wasn't ready."

"You were never going to be ready, man. She knew that."

He was right. I slumped down to the floor. Darren waited, making sure I was okay before he left the room. His words soaked into my hazy head. He was right. She loved me, so she left me. She did it for me, not her.

25

Ethan

texted and left her voice mails. I looked for her on campus. I never found her. She was avoiding me. I knew her whole schedule, and it was apparent she was taking different paths to class and eating at odd times in the union. I called Rachael and Raj too, but they both warned me to leave her alone. I couldn't, though. I racked my brain in the weeks since she'd left, wondering what I'd done. What had I said?

> Sunshine, I'm sorry. Please talk to me.

> Meena, I don't know what I did. Let me make it right. Smiley face.

> Baby, I miss you. Please just let me know you're okay.

> I know I was an ass. I was drunk. If you recall, you said things you didn't mean when you were drunk. Please forgive me.

> This can't be our goodbye. I need a proper goodbye. We need closure. Can't you give me that?

> You're making me feel like a stalker. I guess that's what I am now. I went from friend number three to stalker number one.

> Sunshine, if you cared about me at all, you would talk to me.

That one did it. A simple text came back.

> I'm trying to get out of your head. HELP ME.

That's when the rattling, fragmented, bitter words came back to me. I couldn't remember them with clarity, but I knew Darren was right. I'd wounded her. Meena cared so much she cried for dead swans and Mandy, a girl she barely knew whose boyfriend was a jerk sometimes. She absorbed guilt like a sponge, even when it wasn't her burden to bear. She felt guilty about what she was doing to me, and I'd encouraged it.

I tried to leave her alone, but it was a few nights before graduation, and I had to see her. Even if it was just to say goodbye. The end of us had happened, but I didn't want the bitterness clouding all of the good memories we had. I waited in the lounge area of her dormitory. It took a few hours until she finally came down. She'd lost weight in the time we'd spent apart, and she looked sad but beautiful…always beautiful, warm, and bright…like sunshine.

"I need to talk to you," I said, clasping her arm before she made it to the door. She hadn't seen me and jumped back.

"This is a bad time." She removed my hand. I let her.

"We're out of time. I know that. Just talk to me."

"Meena, who is this?" asked an elegantly dressed woman coming through the door. The similarity in features was undeniable. *Meena's mother.*

"Um…this is…"

"My boyfriend," Rachael chimed in. I had no idea where she had come from. She'd probably been there the whole time, but my eyes were locked on Meena. Rachael held my hand.

Meena had explained this to me once. Her parents were okay with her being friends with Raj because he was Indian, but they would disapprove of friendships with other boys. Rachael was doing her a favor by acting as a decoy.

"This is Meena's mother, Mrs. Kapoor," Rachael introduced.

"Hi, I'm Ethan Callahan. It's nice to meet you Mrs. Kapoor."

Mrs. Kapoor shook my hand, regarding me somewhat suspiciously. "I didn't know you had a boyfriend, Rachael."

"It's a real recent thing," she replied.

I offered a smile. "Very recent."

"We should go, Mom," Meena said.

Two men came through the door. I saw the unpleasant look on Meena's face. The taller, stern man could only be her father, but there was also a younger guy with a goatee.

Rachael squeezed my hand in some kind of warning gesture when he placed his hand on Meena's shoulder. *Fucking dickhead.* At least she jerked from his touch.

"Ethan, this is Dr. Kapoor, Meena's father. And this is Chetan, a family friend who came to watch Meena graduate."

I shook hands with both of them. Chetan winced in pain when I shook his hand. My grip was way too strong for a friendly handshake, but I couldn't help it. Passive aggression was my only means for alleviating my anger. I almost laughed when he rubbed his palm after.

"Would you like to join us for dinner, Ethan? Rachael's parents are at the restaurant, and I'm sure they would love to meet you," Mrs. Kapoor offered.

"He can't," Rachael interjected before I could answer. "He just came to pay me back for the textbook I picked up for him." I had no idea what she was talking about, but Rachael held her hand out to me.

I stared at it dumbfounded. She wiggled her fingers. "Pay me back, Ethan," she said. It was probably the first viable excuse she could think of as to why I was waiting at their dormitory. I had to admit, she sounded convincing. If the degree in communications didn't amount to anything, she could always take up acting.

I took out my wallet and stuffed a fifty in her hand, wondering how Rachael managed to extort money from me. "Thanks, Ethan. We have to go."

I watched them all leave. I stiffened when Chetan placed his hand on the small of Meena's back, leading her out. This felt like some sort of horrible punishment—granted, it was one I deserved. I left, drove around for hours, but ended up right back at her dorm.

A girl exiting the building held the door for me so I could sneak up to Meena's room. I just needed to talk to her face to face. I needed her to hear my apology even if she didn't accept it. Hell, I really just needed to hold her one more time.

She answered the door on the first knock. She was wearing her yoga shorts and a T-shirt embellished with Einstein's field equations. My T-shirt. Her hair was tied up in a ponytail. My fingers twitched, wanting to free it. She was listening to "This Ain't Goodbye" by Train. The lyrics eerily echoed what I was feeling.

"Can I talk to you?"

"Yes," she said, opening the door. I was expecting some resistance, but she seemed to want the conversation as much as I did.

"Who is he?" I asked, trying keep my voice level.

"He's a family friend. My parents invited him."

"Is he a contender?"

If a laugh could be defined as sad, then that's what she did. She laughed sadly. "I suppose. I'm sure you don't want to talk about this."

"No, I guess not. Where's Rachael?" I was procrastinating. I didn't want our time to end.

"She's staying at the hotel with her parents. My parents are there too."

"Why aren't you there?"

"I wasn't done packing. I was hoping you'd come."

I swallowed, feeling a mixture of relief and sadness. The room was pretty bare, except for a few boxes and miscellaneous items.

"Let me help you," I offered.

She shrugged and pointed to the packing tape. I took the cue and started closing up the boxes for her. "I told Rachael she needs to give you back your money. I think she was trying to make me laugh."

"Did it work?"

"Yes."

"Then it was money well spent."

We worked in the thick tension of silence. I kept glancing at her. Meena was a small girl, but she'd definitely lost weight…too much weight. My shirt was falling off her shoulders, revealing the pink, lacy strap of her bra.

She misunderstood my gaze and stared at me contritely. "I stole your shirt. Do you want it back?"

I laughed and strode over to her. I tugged at the hem of shirt. "Yes, take it off right now. I insist." She giggled as my fingertips tickled her sides, but she didn't push me away.

"Ethan, will you do something for me?"

"What do you want, Sunshine?"

She laughed. "I know what you're thinking, you naughty boy, but what I'd really like from you is a letter."

"A letter?" I asked in disbelief.

"I want a tangible piece of you that I can have. I remember how you said your father wrote to you. I always thought it was very sweet. I left you the painting so you could have that part of me. I want something of you that's personal."

I sighed. "Not exactly what I had in mind, but I will."

"Thank you." She rifled through a box and handed me a pen and notebook.

"Now?" I asked, not hiding my disappointment.

"No time like the present," she said, trying to smile, but failing.

"What do you want me to write?"

"Anything. You can tell me you hate me—I don't care. Memories have a way of becoming faded, and I don't want us to fade. I just want to remember the realness of you."

"I could never hate you."

"Then say that, Ethan. I don't care if you scratch or scrawl, or pen it in that neat block writing you have."

I really didn't want to write her a letter. It seemed too final. I took the items from her and sat on her bed. I couldn't think of what I wanted to say to her—it was too much emotion to put into words. All I could do was watch her as she moved around the room.

She walked up to me after a while. "Did you finish my letter?"

"Yes, in fact I wrote you twenty-six letters," I replied.

She regarded me curiously, taking the notebook from me, staring at it with narrowed eyes. "I can't believe you wrote the alphabet. Are you making fun of me?" She threw the notebook across the room.

She sat on the edge of the bed with her shoulders hunched. I gripped them and leaned against her neck. "I'm sorry. I can't express what you mean to me in words. I want to show you not tell you."

"I have to finish packing." She stood up and walked over to the far corner of the small room. She picked up a box that was too heavy for her. I raced up to her, trying to take it from her, but she wouldn't relinquish it. It tipped spilling items to the floor. We both bent down to pick them up.

"I never wanted to hurt you," she choked out, holding back a sob.

"I know that. I didn't mean those things I said that night."

"Yes, you did, but it's okay. I'm glad you had a chance to say them. I needed to hear them."

I wasn't sure how to respond to that, especially since I couldn't remember exactly what I said. So, I just held up an odd-looking object wrapped in a long velvet pouch. "What's this?"

Her eyes widened, and she immediately snatched it from me. "It's nothing."

There was a small impish smile on her face, and it was the first one I'd seen today. She bit her lower lip anxiously, but there was a bit of excitement in her eyes.

I couldn't give up so easily. "Show me."

"It's nothing," she said, scrambling to her feet. She backed away toward the bed.

I matched her backward steps with forward ones, like a predator after its prey. It was turning her on. "Obviously, it's something you don't want me to see."

"It's one of those woman things that would freak you out, Ethan."

"I know it's not a tampon, Meena. Now give it," I growled, narrowing the space between us.

She jumped back on the bed, trying to crawl to the other side, but I leaped on top of her before she could. I stared down at her face, inches from mine. I knew what she wanted. What she needed. What we both needed. I kissed her long, slowly, passionately, tracing her lips, tasting her mouth, sucking her tongue. When I moved away, we were both breathing hard. I stared at the object I'd taken from her during the exchange, turning it around and shaking the pouch. It fell out with a thump right next to her head. It was long and pink with a couple of settings.

"Have you always had a vibrator?" I asked, amused.

She bit her lower lip. "No, I never even masturbated before."

"Before what?"

"Before I left you."

"Why do you have it?" I knew the answer, but I wanted to hear her say it.

"Rachael said it would help with the physical needs. She took me to buy it."

I chuckled, imagining innocent Meena in a sex shop. "Has it helped?"

"I can't believe we're talking about this. It's so embarrassing." She covered her face with her hands.

I moved them away. "You can tell me anything. I just want to know."

"I think I'm doing it wrong."

I laughed. "Show me what you do."

"Ethan, are you crazy?"

"I want to help you with this. There's no reason to be embarrassed. Do you think I don't masturbate? Granted, I don't need any tools, but I do it, a lot, recently."

"I can't show you. It's weird."

"There's nothing weird between us." I kissed her neck and tugged at her shirt until she sat up. I took it off her. "I'll make it easier for you."

"How?"

"I'll get you wet."

I ran my fingers over the lacy outline of her bra before removing it, revealing her perfect round breasts. I took my time suckling each one, letting my teeth graze the nipples. She moaned. I trailed kisses down to her waist, removing her yoga shorts and the lacy pink panties underneath.

She tugged on my shirt. I reached behind me, ripping it off with one hand. She moved her feet up, curling her toes around the waistband of my jeans. I stood up and unzipped them, shrugging them off along with my boxers. I stared at her lying naked on the twin bed, ready and waiting for me. I wanted to take her right then, but I needed to make this last. I made a slow path, kissing her ankles up to her thighs, before diving in with a deep thirst, needing to taste her sweetness.

She tugged my hair and screamed loudly as I licked, flicked, and thrust with my tongue. Her thighs shook, and her body writhed with my every movement. I sucked on her clit, devouring her while driving her to the edge. I felt her let go, moaning my name over and over.

I moved up to her neck, marking my path with my lips, wanting to touch every part of her body. My fingers trailed down, moving into her soaking pussy. "You're so wet."

"Your fault," she said breathlessly.

"Then take care of it." I put the dildo into her hand and shifted so I was at her side. The surprise on her face made it apparent that she'd forgotten about it. She seemed uncertain, but she wouldn't be satisfied with the orgasm I'd given her. She needed the relief that only penetration could provide. She took the tool and glided it down her waist until she reached her opening where she inserted it.

"What do you think about when you masturbate?" I asked her.

"You."

I smiled. "Right answer."

"What do you think about?" She wasn't even moving it. No wonder she couldn't get herself off.

"You."

"Really?"

I knew by her expression she thought I was lying, but I wasn't. "Yes, you. Just you."

"Just me?"

I smiled sheepishly. "Well, sometimes you have two sets of boobs."

She laughed.

"What can I say? I'm a sci-fi nut." She continued to laugh until I clasped the hand that was holding the vibrator and turned it on. "Get on with it, baby."

She moved it slowly with hesitation.

"Meena, you like it rougher than that. Let me show you." I tightened my hand around hers and moved it with force.

She moaned in reply.

"I really like this," I whispered against her ear.

"Why?" she asked in a half-moan, half-scream.

"Usually, I'm preoccupied when you're in this state, but right now I can just concentrate on you. You make the most beautiful faces when you're about to come." I trailed kisses down her cheek and neck while thrusting the vibrator.

"Ethan, I don't want this."

"What do you want?"

She moved her hand to the back of my head, pulling me toward her. I didn't budge. She grunted in some frustrated, garbled command.

"Use your words, Sunshine."

"I want you."

That was enough. The statement drove me crazy with lust. I removed the plastic toy from between her legs and positioned myself on top of her. I entered her, propelling wildly. Her arms clung to me. Then she scraped her nails down my back so hard she drew blood. I loved it.

I growled in response, unable to articulate my appreciation any other way. I rolled us so I was on my back. She sat up and moved the length of my erection. Her pussy claiming me like a vice-grip. I sat up, removing her rubber band, letting her silky locks surround us. I embraced her tightly, grazing her shoulders and neck with my teeth. I bit more roughly in the sensitive skin on her breast. She screamed out in pleasurable pain and raked those long nails of hers across my back again. I clasped her hips and guided her, working toward our mutual release. I took her lower lip in my mouth and massaged it between my teeth. She yanked my hair.

"Fuck, do it again." She did.

"It's always your fault when I'm wet." She leaned her forehead against mine.

"You'll never know how much I needed to hear that," I gasped, drawing her into me.

The sex was completely frenzied and primitive, but it was also the perfect expression of who we were in that moment. We desperately needed to leave our marks on each other.

I choked out her name. All of her names. Meena. Sunshine. Baby. My girl. That was who she would always be to me. I felt her release, and I immediately let go, unable to hold on to my control. We were both panting, covered in slick sweat, and our hearts were beating to the same tune, loud, conflicted, but passionate all the same.

I cradled her back and laid her down gently onto the bed. I dislodged myself in an excruciatingly slow motion, knowing this was the last time I'd be inside of her. I ran my fingers over the patterns my teeth made on her beautiful body, and I kissed every one of those areas. She rubbed my back.

"I hurt you. I'm sorry," she said between sobs.

"I hurt you first. I'm sorry."

We weren't talking about the sex, and both of us knew it. Then I remembered the thing I had to tell her. The last conversation where I'd said she was being irrational that I'd replayed in my head until I finally figured out what she was telling me. The information would give her some peace.

"Baby, guess what I found out?"

"What?"

"Swans don't mate for life."

"They don't?"

"No, I looked it up. There's some new research on it. They found out by performing DNA testing on the offspring. It turns out there were many sets that had the same mother, but a different father. Sort of a swan version of 'who's my baby's daddy.'"

"Why are you telling me this, Ethan?"

"Don't you see, Sunshine? You don't have to feel bad about Isaac anymore. He's going to be just fine. He'll be in a lot of pain for a while, but he'll move on. Suzanne didn't abandon him. Not really."

She wiped a tear from my eye. I hadn't realized I was crying too.

She swallowed and nodded. She pulled me close and kissed my lips softly. Then she moved her mouth toward my ear. She whispered the words, full of choked gratitude and warmth, "Thank you, Ethan."

26

Meena

$\mathcal{D}$espite the intensity of the past school year, we were both studious, and we both walked with the gold cords of *summa cum laude* honors. I clapped loudly for him as I knew he did for me. I had thought that would be it. We had our proper goodbye, and I was satisfied with that. I never expected to break bread with him in the most uncomfortable dinner in the world. It made our little attempt at a dinner party look like the White House Inaugural Ball in comparison.

My parents made reservations at Pala Mia's to celebrate my graduation. They invited Raj's and Rachael's families as well, reserving a huge table for us. It was extravagant, and the last thing I was in the mood for. I sat next to Chetan, who had managed to annoy me more than I thought possible as he extolled the virtues of Canada versus America.

"Isn't that the boy we met the other day?" my mother asked.

"Who?" My heart started beating wildly as my eyes darted around the room. Sure enough, Ethan sat at a table adjacent to us with a beautiful brunette I recognized as his mother. He looked incredibly handsome in his charcoal suit and emerald green tie. A tie I had bought for him.

"You know…Emmitt."

"Ethan," I corrected.

"Who's Ethan?" Rachael's mother asked. I shot Rachael a troubled glance, noticing her skin turned the same color as her fiery hair.

"Rachael's boyfriend," my mother announced.

"You have a boyfriend and didn't tell us?" Rachael's mother admonished.

"We…uh."

I sent a silent ESP signal to my best friend. Surely, we were so close she would read my thoughts. *Tell her you broke up. Tell her it was over*, I pled silently.

"Yeah, my boyfriend," she answered.

I shut my eyes tightly, willing the nausea to go away. I knew Rachael's mother. She wouldn't let this rest.

"You should invite him to join us, Rachael," my mother offered.

"No!" I said way too loudly. "He's with his mother. He's busy."

"Well, if he's dating my daughter, he'd best make some time," Rachael's mother proclaimed, standing up and walking in their direction.

It wasn't five minutes later that two more chairs were brought in. Ethan and his mother sat next to Rachael and across from me. I couldn't help but stare at his mom. I never expected to meet her and certainly not like this. Her hair was up in a tight chignon, she was wearing a sophisticated but feminine pink suit, and she looked completely polished. She smiled at all of us and shook hands as introductions were made. She had very kind blue eyes that matched her son's.

Ethan looked uncomfortable. I'm sure he protested, but I knew Rachael's mother. Rachael had been so private about her exploits that her mother was afraid she was going to be a nun. Verna Blackwell had no intention of letting this opportunity pass. I tuned out the other conversations around the table as Verna asked Ethan all about himself. He was uneasy, but he answered politely.

"What is your faith, young man?" Rachael's father, Pastor David Blackwell, asked Ethan. I stiffened in my seat.

"I'm non-practicing at this time," he replied. Pastor David didn't look pleased, but he didn't press.

"What are your plans for your future?"

"Mom, don't you think you've asked my boyfriend enough questions?" Rachael said, gently punching Ethan's arm in what was supposed to appear as a friendly gesture, but I knew it was a little too strong. *Why had she told the whole boyfriend lie in the first place?*

A glass of water slammed down so hard in front of Ethan that some spilled over the side. We all stared up at Alex.

"Hi, I thought you weren't working today," Ethan said.

"They called me in. They needed help with a big party. Nice party, man." He looked at Rachael pointedly. The poor guy had no idea what was going on. The jury was still out on Rachael's decision to continue their long-distance relationship. Rachael's parents still didn't know about him.

I couldn't even imagine what he was thinking when Rachael referred to Ethan as her boyfriend. Alex straightened up and maintained a semblance of calm amicability while he took our drink orders. "Are you having the same as him?" Alex asked Rachael, his eyes darting suspiciously between both of them.

"She's not. Trust me, on that," Ethan offered.

"Why not? Rachael loves lemonade too," Verna stated.

"The lemonade here is very bitter," Alex replied.

"I don't want lemonade, Mom. I don't like it."

"Yes, you do," Verna insisted.

"I'll have ice water."

Alex left to get our drinks along with the other waiter. "I'm going to check and make sure he has the drink order right," Rachael announced. Ethan stood and pulled her chair out.

"It's a drink order. I'm sure he can manage that," my father said.

"I want to make sure he knows I don't want lemonade."

"But—"

"She's right, Dad. Let her make sure it's clear," I replied, patting my father's arm.

Ethan smiled at me. I tightened the scarf around my neck. Of course, he knew I had worn it specifically to cover up his love bites. He rubbed his back against his chair, and I couldn't help but giggle. He did it to put me at ease, to make me smile like he always did. Everyone glanced at me like I was crazy. Everyone but Ethan.

"So, Mrs. Callahan, what do you do?" Verna asked Ethan's mom. "You look familiar to me."

I sucked in a deep breath, preparing for the impact of the bomb Dr. Love would ignite when she explained her occupation to this conservative group.

"It's Love. Miss Love. I'm a psychologist," she said simply, and I exhaled.

"Oh, that must be interesting."

"It is."

"I didn't even know Rachael had a boyfriend," Verna explained.

Chetan was jabbering in my ear about something. I nodded and murmured to let him know I was listening, but I was completely disinterested.

"I didn't know either," Dr. Love replied.

Rachael returned to the table. "Did he understand about the drink order?" I asked her.

"He was confused, but he understands now," Rachael replied, staring at Ethan's mom, her eyes blinking with comprehension. Rachael had lent me the book in the first place, after all. She was about to blurt something stupid out. I wished she was closer to me so I could kick her, but Ethan realized it too, because he turned to her and shook his head in warning. A warning she heeded.

"It's so strange how American kids keep things from their parents. It's like they enjoy being secretive," my mother said. I flushed with embarrassment, fighting the urge to bang my head on the table at the bitter irony of the moment.

"I don't know about that. I think it has to do with trust and taking ownership for your own decisions. They always tell us when they're ready as long as we're willing to listen." Dr. Rosemary Love seemed like such a genuine person. Unfortunately, I was a fraud.

"What are your plans after graduation, Ethan?" Verna asked.

He looked at me and then to her before answering. I leaned forward, wanting to hear this. Chetan was talking about the benefits of outsourcing or something. I'd written many papers on the subject and normally might find it an interesting topic, but right now, I was fighting the urge to shush him.

I wasn't sure what Ethan's plans were either. The last we had talked, he was being heavily pursued by many companies. They'd sent him expensive gifts, took him to fancy dinners, and flew him out for interviews. He had narrowed his choices down to three, but I didn't know which one he'd picked. There was a major Internet company right here in Silicon Valley, a high profile Wall Street firm in New York, and...NASA. *The man is being courted by NASA.*

"I'm going to work at a Wall Street financial firm. I used to live on the East Coast, and I miss it," Ethan announced.

We would be close to each other, and yet so far. It didn't seem fair. I wondered if he was thinking the same thing.

"New York is so crowded and dangerous. I have no idea why anyone would live there," Chetan blurted out. I had no idea he was listening.

"It's the best city in the world," Ethan answered, narrowing his eyes.

"What are you going to do when Rachael goes to England?" Verna asked. I wondered if she would ever run out of questions.

"I'll be sad," Ethan answered.

"Well, it's only for a year. I'm sure you'll work something out."

"Are you ready to order, or *do you still need time to decide?*" Alex asked only Rachael. It was clear he'd overheard.

We all ordered quickly. This whole situation was ridiculous and uncomfortable for everyone. Everyone but the parents who seemed completely oblivious to all the secret conversations that were taking place.

"Meena, your mom was telling me you are interested in graduate school. There are some really great schools in Quebec," Chetan said.

I wouldn't have even paid it much attention, except Ethan shifted in his chair, staring at me, waiting for my reply.

"I don't know where I'm going to graduate school or if I'm going yet," I replied.

"I could get you some pamphlets."

"That's very nice of you, Chetan," my mother said.

"You know, if you're interested in graduate school, you should consider New York. They have some impressive choices," Ethan said a few decibels louder than necessary.

It was the first time he'd spoken directly to me. He was asking me to move to New York so we could continue our charade. To live some more in the present with him. My heart lurched at the thought of spending a few more years with him, negotiating our clandestine romance, but it was stupid. As long as I was around, Ethan wouldn't live for his future. He'd live in my present.

"Quebec is the financial epicenter of Canada. There are great opportunities there," Chetan said, interrupting my rampant thoughts. God, I wanted to elbow him.

"New York is the financial epicenter of the world. Besides, you don't speak French, do you, Meena?" Ethan asked me.

I shook my head.

"I can teach her," Chetan said, and then he said some phrase in French, which sounded ridiculous since I had no idea what he was saying.

Ethan laughed cynically, eyeing Chetan closely. "*Le pensez-vous est-vous celui facile à acclimater? Il sera difficile pour elle.*"

Ethan speaks French? Why didn't I know this, and why did it sound so sexy coming from his lips and so lame coming from Chetan?

"You speak French? How wonderful," Verna said, clapping her hands.

"His pronunciation is incorrect," Chetan chimed in.

"I just speak conversational French. Meena, do you really think you could learn to speak French? That you could manage the cold winters of Quebec? That you could live in a foreign country?"

"Canada is hardly foreign," Chetan spat, obviously offended.

"Last time I checked, it wasn't part of the United States," Ethan said, raising his eyebrow at me.

Damn him.

I gulped down my water. "Actually, I don't think either Quebec or New York is in my future. I wouldn't fit in, and you shouldn't live somewhere you don't fit. It would just be living a lie." I said it to Chetan, but the words were for Ethan.

"You have plenty of time for that decision, Meena," my mother interjected. She was irritated by my snub toward Chetan, but I didn't care.

"Raj, what are your plans?" I asked, realizing he'd been unusually quiet. He was sad from his breakup with Phillip, but he'd hardly said a word. He'd already told me he was going to Ohio State for graduate school, so I didn't need to ask the question, but I wanted a distraction from the Chetan/Ethan-French pissing contest.

"I actually just had a change of plans. We're moving to India."

I think Rachael, Ethan, and I all gasped at once. I peered over, trying to get a good view of Raj who was at the far end of the table on my side.

Raj smiled sadly. "It's a good thing. There will be tons of *closet* space for me."

"Raj, I told you we need to pack light," his mother said.

Raj's father started explaining how he had a chance for a transfer to Hyderabad. My father congratulated him profusely, telling him what a wonderful opportunity it was. It was more than he'd talked throughout the entire dinner.

All of the graduates spent the rest of the meal in stony silence, while our parents chatted amicably. We were all in mourning. Not just for ourselves, but for each other.

I excused myself when dessert came, hoping Ethan would follow me. He did. I pulled him into the women's restroom and then into a stall. We stood in the small space, pressed intimately together in a way we both craved.

"I can't move to New York. We can't keep doing this," I whispered with quiet urgency into his ear so no one could accidently overhear me.

"I figured. You're not going to marry that tool, are you?" he whispered back, his warm breath sending chills over my skin.

"No, I'm vetoing him."

He exhaled. "Thank goodness."

"I like your mom. She seems nice."

"I hate your parents."

"Ethan—"

"Sorry, I shouldn't have said that. They are wonderful people." He didn't say it sarcastically. It sounded like he meant it.

"Why the sudden change of heart?"

"They have to be. They made you." He started undoing my scarf. He trailed kisses along my neck. "Shit, this looks really bad. Did I make a problem for you?" he asked, running his finger over the dark spot on my neck.

"I can cover it. I didn't know you spoke French."

"I didn't know you were going to graduate school."

"I didn't know you were moving to New York."

"We can do this all night. There are things we will never know. Why did you pull me in here?"

"To say goodbye. My last conversation with you can't be about the merits of New York versus Quebec. It's not the way I want to remember it."

"You want to have sex?" he asked, raising his eyebrows seductively.

I giggled and slapped his chest. "Hardly. You realize your mother could walk in here any minute."

Ethan shrugged. "It's not my mom I'm worried about. Let's not say goodbye. We're getting too good at it. You believe in reincarnation, right?"

I nodded, wondering what he was getting at.

"That's one religious notion I might be able to support. Let's just say, see you in the next life."

"See you in the next life, Ethan Callahan."

He crushed his mouth to mine, drawing me into a passionate kiss I wasn't ready for. My arms encircled his neck, and my toes curled inside my pumps. It lasted a long time, and when he finally pulled away, I was completely breathless.

"See you in the next life, Sunshine. I'll be looking for you."

27

Ethan

$\mathscr{M}$y mom insisted on helping me pack, but it was annoying. I didn't have the heart to tell her, but the OCD side of me kept rearranging her boxes. I was almost done anyway. The apartment I'd lived in for the past four years was now empty. Darren was coming to get all the furniture. He had decided to stay in Palo Alto and found a place with Alex. I was driving to New York and only wanted to take what would fit in my car. I was glad to be leaving. Everywhere I looked, I saw her. Her painting hung over the couch. It would be the last thing I packed.

My mother set down the textbooks she was carrying. She put her hands on her hips, regarding me with disapproval as she caught me rearranging the box she'd just packed.

"Are you going to tell me what's going on?"

I picked up the box to stack it with the others. "Sorry, Mom, I just like things in a certain order. You know that."

"Not about that, Ethan. Tell me about how you're in love with your girlfriend's roommate."

I dropped the box on my foot. "Ouch," I shouted, hopping on one foot.

"Sit," she said, leading me to the couch. "Are you hurt?"

"Yes," I said, rubbing my toe.

"I wasn't talking about your foot, young man."

I laughed uncomfortably. My mother had a sixth sense, or maybe it was part occupation and part mom-sense. "How did you know?"

"Ethan, I am a psychologist. I saw the way you looked at Meena was not the way you looked at Rachael. In fact, I have never seen you look at any girl that way."

"Rachael is not my girlfriend. Meena is, or I guess I should say… Meena was."

I gave my mother the whole beautiful mess of us so she'd understand why I was so conflicted. It didn't seem right to describe it as a fling or affair. It was so much more than that. My mother listened with rapt attention as I went on about how this girl came into my life and made me feel things that my cynical, scientific mind didn't think were possible. And then how she left me, and now I was struggling to feel anything but empty. It helped to talk about it.

"You've been keeping a lot from me, son."

"I didn't think it would matter if you knew. After all, it was just supposed to be a temporary thing."

"Sometimes it's those temporary things that leave the biggest impressions on our heart." She stood up and pointed to the painting, "She painted this?"

"Yes."

"It's very good."

"I know. She's talented. I've told her, but she doesn't believe me."

"It's a sad painting."

"Sad? I wouldn't say sad. It's a couple looking at each other. I would say…it's romantic?" I asked.

"No, Ethan, they are not quite looking at each other. They're looking past each other to a point that's beyond the canvas. Do you see?"

I stood next to her. I'd examined this painting so much, studying every color, curve, and line. How had I not seen that? The heads were tilted in such a way that it was apparent they weren't staring at each other like I'd thought.

"You're right, and you know what? That's really perfect." I sat back down.

"Ethan, I know you're heartbroken, but you have to understand she didn't do that purposefully."

"I know that. She was honest about everything."

"Cultural ties are some of the strongest bonds there are. I knew enough sitting at that table that it was best to not bring up the focus of my occupation. Every one of you seemed to be struggling with some kind of pain. It's funny how modern and archaic we are at the same time. Ethan, you have to forgive her, or you won't be able to move on."

"I'm not angry with her."

"You are. I can see that. Anger is a useful tool at times, but it never really solves the problem."

She was right. I was angry with Meena for abandoning me. For not choosing me when it seemed so simple.

My mother moved on into a litany of how the heart was the most amazing organ, and it could mend its pain. She was speaking metaphorically, but I wanted to correct her and say the heart was the weakest organ. Typically, it was the first to go and the most complex to fix, but I didn't. I was quiet and nodded. My mom could usually make me feel better with her words—she was a psychologist, after all—but right now, I just wanted to be sad. It seemed like the best emotion for me. It fit.

"I know you hate my cookies," she said suddenly.

"What? Why would you say that? I love them."

She laughed. "I wanted to make sure you were paying attention, but it's true. I know you hate them, and I love you for that."

"Is this some sort of reverse psychology?" I asked in complete confusion.

"Hardly. I bake them because it makes me feel good to do something for you no matter how small. You pretend to like them because you know it makes me feel good. You're a very good man, Ethan, and I'm a very lucky mom. I know you're hurting right now, but I also know there's a horizon. A point beyond the canvas that you need to focus on, so you can get past the pain and live for your present."

"You mean the future, right? Live for the future."

"No, Ethan, I said it right. Live in the present. That's where we all need to live."

28

Meena

I enrolled in a few graduate classes at Boston College. I stayed at the apartment with my father. He ignored me, and I helped him in the illusion by being invisible. He didn't start conversations with me unless it was about school or a possible marriage candidate. I would only ask him about work or what he wanted for dinner. Those were the acceptable topics of discussion and allowed us to function with each other.

I emailed or texted Raj and Rachael all the time, but it wasn't the same. Raj was in India, and Rachael was in England. I was all alone. I missed my friends, especially friend number three. I thought about Ethan constantly—what he was doing and, more specifically, who he was doing it with. I remembered how girls threw themselves at him. He was the intelligent, sweet guy who was incredibly handsome and unassuming. He was the perfect guy, at least to me. *Who am I kidding?* He was to most girls.

I vehemently rejected Chetan, and my parents finally accepted that. They arranged new prospects for me, but I found excuses why they weren't a suitable match. I was putting off the inevitable. My mother lamented that I was being too picky. My father said it was the most important decision of my life, so he understood my high standards, but I could see he was becoming increasingly frustrated as well. What both of them couldn't understand was that I was in deep mourning. I was grieving like they were for a boy who had been taken from our family before his time, and also for the boy I left behind.

The summer days passed in slow, miserable agony, leaving me consumed with sadness. At the end of the semester, I moved back to Mashpee, deciding I needed a break from school to start life. My parents disapproved, but they figured I was young and should make the decision on my own. It was irony at its best.

Mashpee was beautiful all the time, but I especially loved the fall, when everything smelled fresh and clean. The trees boasted bright canopies of color in hues that were so vibrant they didn't seem real. I sketched them, but I didn't do them any justice. I didn't have the right mindset to appreciate the beauty that surrounded me, although I knew it was there.

I spent most nights with the telescope Ethan sent me, trying to find Cygnus. It didn't appear as bright or beautiful as it had last New Year's Eve. I wondered if he was looking at it too. I slept with Bog, the bear-dog Ethan had won for me at the carnival. My mother threatened to throw it out, saying I was too old for stuffed animals. It was funny since I'd never had one, but I managed to save him from her threats. I clutched that poor imitation of an animal every night because it was the only thing that let me sleep.

One day in late September, Raj called me on my cell. He told me all about living in India. I knew most of it from his emails, but it was so good to hear his voice. He seemed to be making a life for himself, going to graduate school there and learning to find his way in a culture that was ironically foreign to him. We never discussed Ethan, but Raj and he still kept in touch, so I almost dropped the phone when he mentioned Ethan's name.

"What did you say?" I demanded.

"Ethan was in the hospital…" Raj repeated.

"Why?"

"He—" The line went dead, and I felt my heart did too. Fucking dropped call.

I screamed Raj's name into the phone, willing him to answer me although our connection was broken. My mom banged on my bedroom door and told me to be quiet so she could work. I called him again, but a cold voice recording told me the circuits were all busy.

Was Ethan hurt? Was he sick? He was so healthy and vibrant. I had to know. My heart was beating wildly in my chest, and my mind was racing with all the terrifying possibilities. I'd sworn after I said I would see him in the next life that I would never contact him again. Any communication, no matter how small, would be unfair — not to me, but to him. This was an emergency, though, and my heartbeat wouldn't return to normal until I'd heard his voice.

I punched number three in my contacts. I'd meant to delete his number, but I couldn't bring myself to do it.

I expected to get his voice mail, but he answered on the second ring. "Sunshine?"

I was breathing so heavily he probably thought it was a prank call. His voice sounded weak and distant although the line was clear.

"Ethan, are you okay?" My voice quivered, giving away my emotional state. I didn't care. All I cared about was the answer to my question.

"I think I should ask you the same thing. You sound like you're hyperventilating. Take some slow, shallow breaths, Meena."

I couldn't believe he was trying to comfort me right now. "Why were you in the hospital? Please, don't lie to me."

"I've never lied to you. Just calm down first."

"I can't. Tell me." I sounded hysterical, and he was completely calm.

"I broke my leg playing hockey."

I exhaled. It wasn't life-threatening at least. "You don't play hockey. You're a really bad skater." It sounded stupid that I was explaining this to Ethan like he didn't know.

"Hence, I broke my leg," he replied. I had no idea how he could make me laugh when I thought I was having a heart attack, but he did.

"Is there someone taking care of you?"

"Yes, my mother came. She's staying with me. I'm fine, Meena. Breathe."

He was silent while I controlled my breathing. I felt ridiculous. "I'm glad you're fine. I'm sorry I bothered you. I just…Raj told me, but the line went dead. I wanted to make sure. And I'm really sorry for bothering you. Goodbye." It was a litany of excuses, but I couldn't think of anything else to say.

I was about to hang up when he said, so softly I almost wondered if I'd heard it or imagined it, "Don't go."

"Ethan—"

"I miss you. Just talk to me."

"What should we talk about?"

"Anything. I just want to hear you again." There was a pleading in his voice that melted my heart, but it also made me come to my senses. It was wrong to put him through the emotional mess of me again.

"I don't think it's a good idea."

"We were friends once. Remember me? I'm friend number three. We can be again. Just tell me what you did today. Just talk."

"I had an interview." There was a whooshing sound as Ethan inhaled, and I quickly added, "A job interview."

"What was the position?"

"Bank teller."

"Really?" he asked with clear surprise.

"There's nothing wrong with being a bank teller, Ethan." I didn't mean it to sound haughty, but it did.

"No, there's nothing wrong with it, if that's what you want to do, but I don't think it's right for you."

"Why?"

"Meena, you graduated *summa cum laude* from Stanford. It just seems like a waste of your education."

"There aren't a lot of choices in Mashpee, and the commute to Boston is brutal." I didn't want to tell him about the failed experiment of living with my father in that rented apartment in the city. "Besides, I really don't want to start a job that will be difficult for me to leave. I don't know what my future plans are."

"Because you might end up moving to Quebec?"

"I'm not moving to Quebec for sure, but you're right. I don't know where I'll be."

"It sounds like you're putting your life on hold, Meena."

"I should go. I'm glad you're okay."

"Wait. I'm sorry. I didn't mean to sound judgmental. Let's not talk about you anymore. Let's talk about me. I'm far more interesting."

I laughed. He always had an uncanny ability to make me laugh when I needed it the most.

We talked for an hour about his injury, his exciting job in New York, and his horrible attempts at becoming a decent hockey player. He told me about Darren and Alex and what they were up to as well as a few other mutual friends. He filled up the empty space, and I listened to him, enjoying every word until we were interrupted by call waiting.

"Raj is calling me on the other line," I said.

"You should answer."

"Bye, Ethan."

"Are you busy on Thursday night?"

"No." In truth, I wasn't busy on any night.

"I'll call you at eight."

"Nine. I eat dinner around eight."

"That's pretty late for dinner."

"It's an Indian thing."

"Nine o'clock then."

We never talked about it officially, but Thursday nights became our night. He'd call every week. We'd talk for hours about everything and nothing at all. We stayed away from any tense topics. Ethan never told me he was dating, but I suspected he was. I never told him about my other interviews, the ones I dreaded.

He'd tell me about New York, his colleagues, or just interesting people he encountered on the street. I'd tell him about my job at the bank, which wasn't very interesting, but he listened and asked questions as if I were building a rocket. My colleagues didn't like me very much. They thought I was stuck-up because I was standoffish. Truthfully, the sadness followed me around like a shadow that threatened to envelop me. But on Thursday nights, I smiled and laughed just enough to make up for the rest of the week.

It was mid-November, and Ethan sounded different tonight. He was telling me about a lucrative deal he'd brokered when he stopped mid-sentence. "What kind of questions do you ask?"

"What are you talking about?"

"During your interviews for potential mates. What do you ask?"

"You don't want to know this."

"I do, or I wouldn't have asked. I'm curious."

"I have a working list of questions."

"Such as?"

"What is your favorite color, for one."

Ethan laughed. "You can't acquire any information from someone by asking that."

"I think you can. I mean, your favorite color is brown so I know you're earthy and appreciate nature."

"I said that because I was looking at your eyes at the time. You need to ask something more meaningful. Otherwise, you won't know this guy."

"Why do you care?"

He ignored the question. "Ask him what he would do to make you feel better if you had a bad day."

"That's a good question." I couldn't believe we were discussing this after we'd carefully avoided the topic for so long.

"You like your feet rubbed, a plate of fresh cut fruit, preferably pineapple and strawberries. And watching *Austin Powers*. It always makes you laugh, especially the third one."

"Ethan, what are you doing?"

"I was just giving you the answer. It's stupid to ask a question without the answer key."

I laughed nervously. "Why would he know that? He doesn't know me."

"Yeah, I guess he'd never say something like that, huh. Your questions need to be refined. You need to take this seriously. It's the most important decision you'll ever make."

"I have to go, Ethan," I said. I could hear the melancholy in his voice, and it was contagious. This was a bad conversation for us.

"Your birthday's coming up," he announced, swiftly changing the topic.

"Thanks, but I knew that."

"Do you have plans?"

"Um…I'm sure I'll go out with some friends from work," I said nonchalantly.

"You don't have any friends from work."

"How did—"

"I can read between the lines."

"I'll figure it out. I should go. Good night."

"Sweet dreams," he stated as he always did when we ended these conversations.

I settled into bed, clutching Bog. I was almost asleep when the text message came.

> Come to New York for your birthday.

> That's a horrible idea.

> Tell you what. I'll pro your cons.

I smiled, remembering this game fondly.

> Con: My parents would freak if I told them I was going to visit a boy.

> Don't tell them. It's not like they know about me anyway. Tell them you're going shopping or visiting a girlfriend. It's just a short train ride away.

He was right on all accounts.

> Con: It will be too difficult for us.

> I promise we will be platonic—Friends only. We can do that. We have before. PRO: I'll help you with your interview questions. It will only be weird if we make it weird.

> Things are different now.

> I promise I no longer have any physical interest in you. I realized you are way too skinny for me and your ass is bony.

I laughed.

> Very funny. You know what comments like that do to a woman?

> Yeah, it makes you want to beat me up, so there's another pro for you. You can't beat me up unless you come here.

Sorry, I'm not a violent person so that won't work on me.

Pro: You won't spend your birthday alone. Pro: I won't spend Thanksgiving alone. It falls on your birthday this year. Pro: I want to see you. I miss my friend. Do it for me, not for you.

For you?

What else have I got to do?

29

Meena

I arrived at Penn Station in the early afternoon, anxious but excited to spend three days with Ethan. We hadn't seen each other in almost six months. My heart twisted and my pulse quickened when I spotted him.

He was wearing a crisp black suit in a modern cut that emphasized his sleek physique. He had a green and white polka dot tie that was formal enough for business, but whimsical too. His hair was shorter, but his bangs still forked over his forehead, creating a focal point toward those brilliant blue eyes. I had said goodbye to a boy back in Palo Alto, but this was definitely a man standing in front of me. I smiled as I approached him, but faltered when he didn't return it. He looked…angry.

"You look nice," I said to him.

He took my bag and gave me an awkward pat on the back as if any other greeting would have been too much. "I came from work."

"The suit suits you," I commented, trying to make him laugh. It failed.

"You've lost weight."

"Thank you," I replied as we walked toward the exit.

"It wasn't a compliment. How much have you lost? Ten? Twelve pounds?"

He was eerily close. I hadn't been skipping meals on purpose. I just wasn't hungry. He was doing a damn fine job of pissing me off.

"You shouldn't ask a woman about her weight, Ethan. It's very rude. If you have to know, I've been on a diet, and it's working."

He laughed cynically. "This isn't a diet. This is you not taking care of yourself."

"Did you just invite me so you could pick a fight?"

He stopped on the busy Manhattan street and stared at me for a minute. "I'm sorry. It's good to see you, Meena. I'm glad you're here."

I nodded and followed along, although I was less enthusiastic about the trip than before.

"Let's grab some dinner."

"It's only three," I said, glancing at my watch.

"I eat early, you eat late. We'll compromise, we can have two dinners."

Ethan didn't eat this early—he wasn't geriatric, for God's sake—but I didn't argue with him. We stopped at a café close by.

He scanned the menu intently. "You can have the vegetable stir fry, the eggplant parmesan, or if you're feeling adventurous, the grilled artichoke with kumquat salad." This felt more familiar to me. This was what Ethan always did. It was such a small thing, I'd forgotten about it. He always looked for items I could eat before choosing his own meal. I never realized how sweet that was.

We ordered, and he filled me in on the plans for the weekend. We were going to a Broadway play and visiting the Statue of Liberty, the Empire State Building, and the Guggenheim. He had planned our itinerary methodically so there was no free time. I had a feeling he did that on purpose.

"Ethan, that's so much stuff. We don't have to do all that. We can just hang out."

"We will be hanging out," he replied. This felt weird. We had never been this stiff with each other, even when we were fighting our growing attraction in Stanford.

We ate. It made me nervous that Ethan watched me. He asked me several times if I wanted more food. Finally, I blurted out, "What's wrong with us? This isn't us."

He smiled softly at my outburst. "This is the new us. We'll make it work. We'll be okay."

I nodded, unsure if he was right. I ordered dessert, more to please him than myself. I scraped away at the decadent cake before me.

"Do you still sketch?" he asked.

I smiled at the first real thing he'd said to me. "Sometimes. Do you still scratch?"

He laughed. "Sometimes. I'm on medication again. I'm having trouble concentrating."

"Really?"

"Isn't that ridiculous? A grown man on ADHD medication?"

"Does it help you?"

"Yes."

"Then it's not ridiculous."

I wanted to say more, but a svelte woman in a stylish black dress approached our table. I saw her before Ethan did. She had shiny blond hair and translucent skin that made men stare at her as she sauntered to our table. "Ethan, is that you?" she asked, placing a hand on his broad shoulder.

He stood to greet her. "Ronnie. Hi," he said, somewhat uncomfortably.

"I thought you'd be out of town. You said you had plans for Thanksgiving."

So, Ethan did have an invite. Or course he did. I hid my hands under the table so the shaking wouldn't be apparent.

He adjusted his tie, although it was perfectly placed. "I have company. This is my old friend Meena," he said, gesturing to me.

"Nice to meet you." Ronnie shook my trembling hand, barely grasping it. "I'm Ethan's new friend Ronnie." The warning in her voice was very clear.

I nodded, unsure of what to say. It didn't matter because she turned her attention right back to Ethan. "Are we still on for Saturday night?" It was the day I was leaving, and she wanted me to hear their plans.

"Sure, sweetheart," he replied. At least he didn't call her sunshine. *At least I have that.*

"Good. I can't wait." Then my heart dropped into my stomach when she kissed him. It wasn't a casual kiss either, but something that should have been reserved for the bedroom. It was worse because Ethan let her. He didn't encourage her, but he didn't exactly push her away either.

They exchanged a few more pleasantries, ignoring me. I sulked like a small child, willing the ground to open up and swallow me. It wasn't that I didn't want Ethan to move on and find happiness, but I really didn't want him to move on in front of me. He sat back down and ordered us some more coffee. *Maybe he wants to prolong my torture.*

"Just ask. I know you're curious. I have nothing to hide."

"How long?"

"We see each other once a week or so. She wants a commitment, but I'm very honest with her. I've told her I'm not ready for that."

"You kissed her in front of me. That was mean."

"I didn't kiss her. She kissed me."

"You didn't exactly stop her."

"Maybe I was pretending." This conversation seemed vaguely familiar, but I couldn't quite place it.

"Pretending what?"

"It's not important. Look, I'll just spell it out. Do you want to know what my life is like? All the stuff I don't tell you? I work…long hours. They say I'm the most driven associate at the company and describe me as ambitious, and it's true that I am those things, but mostly I welcome the distraction of it. I drink too much."

I started to open my mouth to comment on his revelation, but he stopped me.

"Don't worry, I never drive when I'm drunk, and I'm no alcoholic, but it numbs things. I like the numbness. I crave it. The majority of my meals come in cardboard boxes or containers that can be delivered to my apartment or office. I have sex with a few different women, including Ronnie. It helps too."

I fought back the tears that were threatening to spill.

"It's not all bad news, though. I have Thursday nights."

I twisted the white linen napkin in my hand. "This was a bad idea."

"I didn't tell you all that to make you feel sorry for me. I just wanted you to know my truth. I'm going to be fine. It's just taking longer than I thought. You're going to be fine too. We just need to figure this out."

"What?"

"Being friends again. It's going to be hard, but I want to try."

"Why? It's just torture for both of us."

He laughed cynically, finishing off his coffee. "A little bit of sunshine is better than none at all."

"I would tell you about my life and how I love Thursday nights too, but I suspect you already know. I will tell you that I know how to use the vibrator now. Thank you for your tutelage on that."

Ethan laughed. It was a more genuine laugh this time. "I'm glad I could be of assistance."

He opened the door of his Denali, and I climbed in. I kept thinking of the things he said. But that kiss was all I could see in my head. Ronnie was not just gorgeous—she was stunning. She could be a model...maybe she was. His text was almost a self-fulfilling prophecy—he was no longer attracted to me. He missed me, but he wouldn't even touch me. He couldn't even make eye contact with me.

It was for the best. We could be friends. It would be easy to be platonic when he no longer had physical desires for me. I only wish I could turn off the way my heart quickened or my skin broke out into tiny goose bumps when he was near.

His apartment was huge. It could fit the Palo Alto apartment inside of it several times. The floors were an exotic wood, the surfaces were polished marble, and the furniture was extremely high-end and modern.

"Ethan, when you said you had a park behind your house, I had no idea you meant Central Park," I said, staring at the view outside his balcony window. "This was your father's apartment, right?"

"Yes, it was part of my inheritance. I was going to sell it, but the market's not so great right now. It's really too big for just me. Do you like it?"

"It's amazing."

"There are two guest bedrooms. I gave you the bigger one, but the other one has a nicer view if you want to switch."

I expected the sleeping arrangement. In some ways, I insisted on it, but I was still disappointed. I didn't care if he slept with other women, but I still couldn't get over the lump that rested on my chest, heavy and unyielding, invoked by a jealousy like I'd never known, or the fact that I craved his body as if it was an antidote for my ills.

"I'm going to take you there tomorrow," Ethan said, coming behind me and pointing to the park.

He didn't wrap his arms around me like he used to. He didn't cup my butt or kiss my neck. It was wrong of me to want those things, but I did anyway.

We spent my birthday exploring the city. It was Thanksgiving, but Ethan had planned for that and made sure all the places we went to were open. We chatted amicably, and I thanked him profusely, not wanting him to think I was ungrateful.

There was something missing, though. I was there, and Ethan was there…but *we* weren't there. Not together. We were two strangers posing as friends trying to make something work that seemed impossible.

We ate dinner at the Russian Tea Room. They brought out a cake that was far too big for the two of us. I made a wish. Ethan didn't ask me what it was, and I didn't divulge it this time.

Friday was no different. We hit all the sights on his list like tourists, even though I had seen them all on previous trips to the city. He pointed out things like a tour guide, and I asked appropriate questions or made comments.

We stopped to eat a lot. Ethan said he was hungry, and there was this great deli with huge sandwiches I had to try or this Italian eatery with the perfect pizza or this bakery with cannoli that was to die for. Ethan always had a big appetite, but the man couldn't be this hungry unless he had tapeworms. He was trying to fatten me up like a Thanksgiving turkey.

"I'm not anorexic. Stop treating me like this," I said when he suggested an Irish restaurant that featured vegetable stew, explaining it would be a great snack for us. *Who eats stew as a snack?* I still had the take-out box from the last restaurant we ate at, for God's sake.

He swallowed hard. "I know that. I'm just not sure what else I can do."

"Do?"

"Do for you. I don't know what else I can do to be a friend. I thought I was in pain, but I saw you, and well…I can see I'm not the only one suffering. In fact, I don't even think I'm the worst off of the two of us."

"I'm fine, Ethan. I'm an adult. I'm capable. And most importantly, I'm full. Now, I want to take my bony ass back to your place and go to bed if that's okay with you."

He winced, adjusting the collar of his jacket. I just walked past him, wondering if I could catch a train back tonight. I heard his clipped steps behind me, but I walked faster, praying I was going the right way and fighting the tears that were burning my eyes.

That's when I saw her. We had seen many homeless people in the city, but she seemed different. She was sitting on an old blanket, wearing about ten layers of clothes, probably her whole closet. She smiled at me with kind gold eyes. I smiled back — something about her spoke to me without words.

Ethan came up behind me. "I know what you're thinking. You shouldn't give her money. If you really want, there's a shelter I donate to that helps people like her."

"I have no intention of giving her money," I replied, walking toward her. I bent down so we were at eye level.

"Hi, I'm Meena." I held out my hand to her. She seemed surprised by the gesture as if she had no idea what the proper reply was. I took her hand and shook it. "Are you hungry?"

She smiled softly and nodded. I figured she was in her sixties, but it was hard to tell since the streets probably aged her faster. Her face was lined, and her hair was long and white, but I imagined she was beautiful not so long ago. Hell, there was something beautiful about her right now.

"Amelia," she said in a raspy voice.

"Amelia, what would you like to eat?"

"I'll take whatever's in the box," she said, pointing to my take-out box. I looked down at it, forgetting I still had it.

I put my hand on her shoulders as gently as I could. "I know you'll take it, but what do you want?"

"I miss Thanksgiving," she said. It was yesterday, but it wasn't lost on me that she used the present tense, not the past. She probably hadn't had a real Thanksgiving in a long time.

"All right. I think I know." I marched into the deli. Ethan followed me. I ordered the turkey, mashed potatoes, corn, and any other side dishes that made sense. I ordered a slice of pecan pie too.

"Are you going to clue me in on what you're doing?" Ethan asked.

"You wanted to eat, so we're going to."

"This isn't exactly what I had in mind, but whatever." He took out his wallet, but I held my hand up.

"Let me. It was my idea. I want to." I paid for the meal and walked back out to Amelia.

She seemed surprised as if she thought I was going to disappear in the deli forever. I handed her the food and utensils.

"Thank you, Meena," she said gratefully.

I bent down again and looked her in the eyes. "Would you like some company?"

Her eyes got wide, but she gestured to a bare spot on her blanket. Ethan stood, looking uncomfortable. I knew on some level I was being rude to him as my host. More than that, he was the boy who didn't want me to spend my birthday alone, but I couldn't face him anymore. I wanted to be sitting next to Amelia right now and breaking bread with her. She ate. I opened my take-out box and picked at my food so she wouldn't feel odd.

"We always had big Thanksgivings. My father owned a turkey farm," she said. Her voice sounded less raspy, like she was getting used to it again.

"Where?"

"Upstate. A long time ago. He always saved the biggest turkey for us. Do you like turkey?"

"She's a vegetarian," Ethan said, sitting down next to me. I hadn't expected him to do that.

Amelia stared at me, smiling widely. "We all have our faults."

I didn't know if it was Ethan or I that laughed harder. She told us stories about growing up on a turkey farm and the days of work to get ready for Thanksgiving. Ethan and I listened and asked questions. She was an interesting woman.

"Do you need help?" I asked her when she was finishing her pie.

"No, this is my choice," she said simply. I left it at that. I knew Amelia had more tragic stories in her, but tonight was not the time for those. She didn't want to tell those stories. I took the empty food containers to throw them away.

"Thank you," she said, clasping my arm.

"It was nothing," I commented. "It was really not much at all."

She shook her head. "Not for the food. For the company."

I nodded and hugged her. She was a very tiny woman under all those layers. Ethan and I started walking back toward his apartment, each in our own thoughts.

"I'm sorry. That was probably very strange for you. Thanks for not freaking out."

"I can't say I've ever done that before, but it didn't feel weird."

"I'm weird," I said, smiling at him.

He hooked his pinky into mine. A gesture I'd missed terribly. "You are a very good girl, Meena Kapoor."

In some ways, Amelia did more for us than we ever did for her. I felt some of our lost connection again. Whatever had flickered between us turned off as soon as we reached his house, though. Ethan went to straight to his bedroom to work. I went to the guestroom, took a long hot soak in Ethan's jetted tub, and went to bed.

The recurring dream or vision woke me shortly after. It was more vivid tonight than in the past, and I was breathing heavily.

I felt around on the nightstand for my watch and put it on, noticing it wasn't that late. I went to the kitchen to get a glass of water. I saw the thin white line under his door. The sounds of Barenaked Ladies' "The Old Apartment" softly floated through the closed door, calling me to him. I headed toward it, craving the comfort that only he could provide me. I knocked on his door tentatively, scared he would send me away, so I opened it before he could respond.

He was lying in bed with his laptop, shirtless and in boxer briefs. My heart began to stammer, and my mouth went dry. I thought my memories of Ethan's body were crystal clear, but now I knew I hadn't done it justice. His chest was broad, and his arms held just enough bulk so the muscles were visible every time he moved them. His hair was messy and damp. He smelled deliciously clean, like soap and linen.

"What's wrong?"

"Can I come in?"

He patted the side of the bed that was empty. I sat on the edge. "You're wearing my shirt."

I'd forgotten, but it was the shirt I'd taken from him with Einstein's formulas. The one I wore to bed all the time. "I have everything of yours still. I have the letter where you asked me to move in with you. Your last pro. I have Bog. I have this shirt. I even have the alphabet letters, although I'm still a little mad you didn't write me a real one that night."

"I showed you instead," he said, smiling.

I ran my hands over his comforter. "Your bed's comfortable," I said, taking in his large bedroom. It was huge, with a wall of windows and a separate sitting area. Everything was in neutral colors with small splashes of color. A crystal chandelier was suspended over the bed. The only artwork was…my painting. It didn't fit the fancy décor, but he had placed it where it would be the last thing he saw before he went to bed and the first thing he that greeted him in the morning.

"You always found my bed comfortable, but you didn't come in here to compliment my bed."

"I had a nightmare."

"Want to talk about it?"

"Yes and no. I'm pretty messed up as you can see."

"What do you mean?"

He got up and moved the laptop to a side table. I watched the muscles in his legs as he approached the bed again. He sat on the opposite edge. It was a king-size bed, but the chasm between us felt as wide as the Pacific.

"You don't find me attractive anymore. I get that. You live in New York. They practically breed supermodels here."

He looked at me as if I'd grown another head. "Why the hell do you think that?"

"You said my ass was bony and I'm too skinny."

Ethan laughed.

My hands balled into fists. "Go ahead and laugh."

He crawled to where I was, and my heart quickened with his slow advance. "Meena, you're the most beautiful girl in the room."

"Smooth, Ethan. I'm the only girl in the room."

He shook his head and moved a strand of hair behind my ears. "Sorry, that came out wrong. I meant to say you're the most beautiful girl in any room. You always have been. The most beautiful girl in the city, the country, the world, the universe."

I gave him a sarcastic glance. "You don't have to lay it on so thick. I wasn't fishing for compliments."

"You don't have to, Sunshine." It was the first time he'd called me that since I'd been here. It sent a chill down my spine. "There's something else you need to know."

"What?"

"I don't want you to have the wrong impression about things, so I need to tell you. It's been over six months since us. I didn't do anything for a long time, but I was dying a little more every day. Those other girls...they're just solar simulators for me."

"Huh?"

He chuckled. "They're a light source used to simulate sunlight. They're artificial sunshine. Do you understand?"

I smiled. "Only you could describe meaningless sex with science and have it make sense."

"Tell me about your dream, please. I want to hear it."

"It's stupid."

"Dreams usually are. They're not supposed to make sense."

"No, it made sense. I think it was a premonition, not a dream."

"Oh, you've developed psychic abilities? Now you have to tell me." He sat next to me, but kept enough distance so we weren't touching.

I swallowed hard. "I dreamed it was sometime in the future. I was with my husband, and we were shopping. We had a stroller so I assume we had a baby. We ran into you, and you were with your wife. You had a child too, but he was older." I turned and smiled at him. "He looked like you. He had sparkly, mischievous blue eyes. It was awkward because we greeted each other like long lost acquaintances. There was no real warmth. That's the part that makes me the saddest, I guess. I know I've lost you, Ethan. That was my choice, so what I'm feeling isn't right."

"Meena, I have a very important question to ask you. Will you answer honestly?"

I stared at him, slowly nodding my head. He scooted closer to me and looked into my eyes.

His voice dropped to a serious tone. "This dream of yours..."

He paused, and I nodded for him to go on.

"You remember it clearly?"

I nodded again.

He swallowed. "Did my wife have big boobs?"

He broke into a goofy grin, and I smacked his chest. "You always need to crack a joke?"

"I'm sorry. It's my coping mechanism."

He tucked a strand of hair behind my ear and kissed my forehead before hooking his pinkie around mine. "I know just what to do."

"What's that?"

"I have some fruit. You know strawberries and —"

"Pineapple?"

"Yes. We'll cut it up and watch *Austin Powers*, and you can make fun of my horrible British impressions, and I'll try not to be distracted by your shagedelic body. And tomorrow, I'll make you pancakes, okay?"

"I'd like that."

"I figured you might."

Somewhere between Mini Me and Ethan wrapping his hand around me, one of us — I'm not sure who — kissed the other…We didn't stop kissing for a long time. Ethan made love to me, and we fell asleep in each other's arms. It was the best sleep I'd had in a long time.

I woke up all alone. It was dark out but early morning, and I would be leaving in a few short hours. I dressed quickly and walked into the bathroom to wash my face and brush my teeth. Then I set out to find him. He was on the balcony, sitting in a comfortable-looking chaise wearing a terry cloth robe. I tiptoed outside in case he was sleeping.

"Morning, Sunshine," he said. The balcony was narrow but long, covering the length of the front room. The light from the living room spilled out in a soft glow on the stonework. I expected it to be freezing, but it wasn't. It was a brisk day, but not too cold. A heat lamp in the corner aided the pleasant climate. The city wasn't fully awake, but there were errant sounds of car horns and truck motors below us.

"This is nice," I said.

"Come sit with me." I went to take a seat on the other chaise, next to him, but he tugged my shirt hem. "No, sit with me."

He scooted over for me, and I lay next to him. Ethan's face had some morning scruff, and he rubbed it against my neck. It felt amazingly good. He enveloped me in his arms, embracing me tightly.

"Ethan, do you —"

"Shh. Please, Sunshine, just let me hold you for a minute."

I was quiet as he held me. I felt the tension of his muscles, the intake of his breath, the pulsing of his heart. It was a quiet moment, and it was ours alone.

"We never talked about your interview questions."

I tensed immediately, not expecting him to bring it up. He must have felt that because he moved his hands to slowly massage my shoulders.

"We don't have to talk about it. I don't want to," I said.

"It doesn't matter anyway. You can't know someone by asking them questions."

"That's not true. You can know the important things."

"Sunshine, everyone knows the important things about us. It's the unimportant things that make us who we are. Do you know what I mean?"

"No."

He turned me so I was facing him. He brushed my hair back and embraced me. "Everyone knows you're Meena Kapoor, *summa cum laude* graduate at Standford with a degree in economics, twenty-three years old, of Indian descent, a practicing Hindu, a vegetarian. That's the working knowledge of you, but it's hardly intimate."

With a weak smile, I dredged up the courage to ask him. "What is the real me?"

He put a hand on each side of my face. "You don't like cake."

I scrunched my nose in confusion. "I love cake."

"No, Meena, you love icing. You always skim off all the icing and take only a bite or two of the actual cake." As he said it, I realized it was true. It was so small and silly, but something he knew about me that I hadn't even realized. "When you wear high heels, you walk very slowly. You think you're clumsy, but you're not. You're very graceful. Your greatest fear is a shark attack. When you get nervous, you bite your lower lip. When you're confused, you scrunch your nose. When you're sad, you cry, but you always try to hide it. When you're happy…well, it's pure sunshine. You feel so much, baby, not only for yourself, but for others. That's you. Those are the unimportant things that really matter. The things I know."

My eyes went wide, staring at him. I buried my head in his chest and wept then. I wept, and he let me, holding me tightly. It felt like we were at some crossroads.

"I know, for instance, right now, you're crying more for me than you." He was right. He was always right. When I finally got control of myself, I looked up at him. He wiped an errant tear from my face. "I'm sorry I made you cry."

"I needed it. You're the kindest person I know, Ethan Callahan. I don't deserve you. Not as a friend and certainly not as anything else."

"Does that mean we're not going to have 'it's early morning, I have a woody, and I really want to fuck you' sex? I'm so disappointed."

I laughed and leaned into his ear. "I don't deserve you, but I'm certainly not a masochist. I won't deny you my body, and I'm fine with taking full advantage of yours."

He chuckled and slipped his hands under my shirt, caressing my breasts. My nipples hardened instantly. I felt his erection poke me as he jerked up.

"Sore?" he asked.

"No, I'm fine."

He undid his robe and pressed his body against mine. He clasped my waist and pulled me so I was lying on top of him. He kissed me passionately. His mouth tasted like fresh mint and orange. "Are you cold?"

"No."

"You're shivering."

"It's not because I'm cold."

He laughed softly, before pulling on the hem of my T-shirt, dragging it up.

"What are you doing?"

"I'm taking my shirt off," he replied with an amused grin.

"Not here," I said.

"Do you think I'd let anyone see what's for my eyes only?" he asked, shaking his head. Ethan grabbed a thick velour blanket from the back of the chaise and draped it over us like a tent. "Is this better?"

"Yes, but I can't see you."

"But you can feel me, right?" he said, grinding his erection into me.

"Yes."

"That's the only sense we really need."

He removed my shirt and pulled off my shorts with his feet. He sucked on my ear and neck. I had no idea how his mouth knew exactly where to go in our shroud of darkness, but it seemed capable of finding its way to the places on my body that needed it. I pressed my lips against his neck and felt my way down his chest, following with my mouth. I worked my way down to his nipple, flicking it with my tongue. He moaned and gently guided me the rest of the way. I took his full erection in my mouth, stroking it with my tongue. His legs squirmed, and his breathing intensified as he called out my name. I loved giving Ethan pleasure as much as I loved getting it from him. I tasted the first drops of his excitement before his strong hands encircled my arms and pulled me up.

"I want to be inside you. My favorite place. I want you to fuck the hell out of me, baby."

He handed me the foil wrapper, and somehow I placed it over him. I'm not sure how Ethan was able to guide me straight onto his erection in the dark, but he did. I gasped at the penetration. I moved forward toward him, kissing him wherever my lips landed. He wrapped his legs around me, helping me with the pushing, pulling motions.

I couldn't see Ethan, but I felt him, and in many ways that was more erotic, more sensual, and more intimate. I felt his unshaven face as it glided along my breasts. The tip of his tongue as it tasted my neck. His fingers as they threaded through my hair. His heated breath against my skin. The sound of my name from his lips, increasing exponentially with each thrust and combining with the sound of his name as I screamed it. I felt my release and his. I felt everything.

I fell into a slump on his chest. His arms embraced me like we were melting together. We were one…completely connected…completely entwined in that moment. He released me, and I slid off him, wincing not because of pain but the loss of our link. He moved the blanket and stared into my eyes for a long time.

"Why is it so hard to let you go?" he asked.

I didn't know how to answer. The truth was I was having the same problem.

We tried to make breakfast, but we just ended up having sex on his marble countertops. I took a shower, and he insisted on joining me, making an amusing excuse about water shortages in the city.

Finally, the time had come for me to leave. I folded his shirt and set it in my bag. I smiled at the two additional T-shirts he'd left on the bed for me.

I thought about how easy it would be to stay here in this beautiful city with him. But then I thought about my parents. I couldn't cause them any more pain.

We pulled up to the train station. He turned to me, smiling sadly. I stopped him before he could say anything. "Ethan, we can't do this."

"Do what?"

"We can't be anything to each other. Not friends and certainly not lovers. Although in our case, the two seem interchangeable. I know some people can, but we're not those people."

He was quiet for a long time as if pondering my words.

"Say something," I prodded.

He smiled again. "If I had known that was goodbye sex, I would have made it last longer." He tilted my chin so I was looking at him. "You're right, Sunshine. We can't do it. There was never anything casual about us." He moved a strand of hair behind my ear. "I love you. I'll always love you."

I stared at him, mouth parted. The words stuck in my throat caused such an ache, it hurt to swallow them down.

"I'm sorry. That was selfish," he said.

I shook my head. "How could that ever be selfish?"

"I didn't say it so you could hear it. I said it so I could say it, just once, out loud, to you."

I took his hand, "Ethan, I won't say it back to you, not because I don't feel it, but it would be cruel since this was my choice. But I do need to say some things to you that are long overdue. You told me once that I should go to therapy, and I think I'm going to, but I want you to know something. Talking to you, expressing myself in ways I never had, having you accept me for all my faults…it meant something. You were my therapy. I will always be grateful for that. You will always be in here," I said, pointing to my head, "and you most certainly are in here." I moved my hand over my heart.

He put his hand over mine. "Meena, it wasn't a one-way street. I'm not saying I'm going to attend religious services anywhere, but seeing your faith in people, even complete strangers, your trust and goodness, it changed me too." He pressed his forehead to mine. "Sunshine, you were my church."

We didn't kiss. We didn't say anything more. There was nothing to say. I stepped out of the car. He grabbed my luggage and walked me to the platform. Before he left me, I grasped his shirt. "See you in another life, Ethan Callahan."

He smiled and kissed my wrist. "Next life, Sunshine."

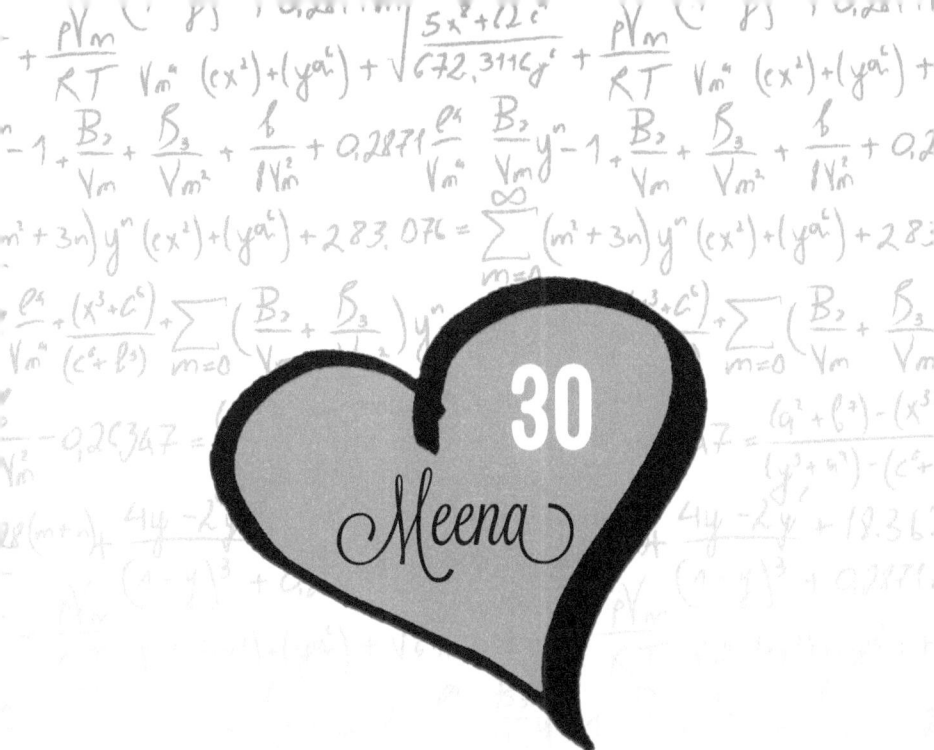

I sat in Rachael's pink bedroom with her and Raj, trying to tune out Frank Turner's song "The Way I Tend to Be." I loved the song, but it reminded me of Ethan. Six months had passed since I saw him last. We stayed true to our word and made no attempts to contact each other. I still slept with Bog, I still looked for Cygnus, and I still wore his shirts, but the days became more bearable as I moved through them.

I'd been so busy I was grateful for this afternoon with my friends. Rachael's internship was over, and Raj had come for my party. Their presence rejuvenated me, although the sadness still lurked.

"What are you doing?" I asked Rachael. She had her back to me and was hunched over her desk.

She turned around and held up a long, cigarette-like object.

"Are you crazy? My dad's going to kill us. Hell, we're in your house. *Your* dad's going to kill us."

"Meena, don't say 'hell' in a preacher's house. Besides, we all need stress relief right now, during this very sad occasion."

"You're calling my engagement party a sad occasion?"

"If it's not sad, then why do you look so depressed?"

She had me there.

"Whatever you're rolling, I'm smoking," Raj said.

"I'm not sad, Rachael. I'm marrying a doctor, and we're moving to Gloucester. I love Gloucester…it's wicked cool."

They both laughed at my lame joke. Rachael lit the joint and inhaled deeply.

"What if your brother walks in?" I knew Rachael's parents were away for the day, but Kevin was in the house.

"Where do you think I got it from?" she replied smugly. "He uses it for medicinal purposes."

"What ailment does Kevin suffer from?" I asked.

Rachael smirked. "Dry skin."

"Pot helps with dry skin?" I asked.

"Only in America, right?" Rachael asked.

Raj smiled, reaching for the joint. "Or as I like to call it — the greatest country in the world."

"So, what's up with you guys? You both look pretty depressed yourselves, and you can't tell me it's because you feel some misguided empathy for me," I said.

Rachael's smile faltered. "I broke up with Alex, or rather, he broke up with me."

"Why?" Raj and I asked in unison. The last I'd heard, he'd visited her in England and things were going well.

"I cheated on him. He never wants to see me again," she said, tearing up. I hugged her hard until she pushed me away. "Hey, it's okay. I knew it was going to happen. I told him as much."

"No, you basically had a self-profiling prophecy, Rachael," I said.

"I'm a slut. I know who I am, and that's better than you two losers. I hereby call this meeting to order of the Losers in Love Club," she said, pounding her fist on the desk like a gavel.

Raj passed me the joint. I regarded it curiously before taking a drag. I sputtered and choked on it so much that Raj handed me his water bottle.

"Rachael, you are a slut because that's who you think you are, but it's not the person you were meant to be," Raj said rather poetically.

She crossed her arms, staring him down. "That's interesting coming from you, Rajesh."

He laughed. "Let's just say I'm taking some steps in the right direction for once."

"How?" I asked.

"I'm not going back to India. I'm here for good."

Rachael almost dropped the joint, but she caught it and set it in the clay bowl on her desk. We both rushed to hug Raj.

"So, you told your parents?" I asked.

"Fuck no. They have no idea I'm gay. I'm not quite ready for that, but I decided I'm going to be ready one day. It's going to happen. Right now, they're still pissed I left."

"What made you decide?" I asked.

"It's funny, because India wasn't as bad as we thought. There is a decent gay scene. You'd be surprised. There were secret bars and lounges. No one would have pressured me to come out of the closet, either. The closet was a comfortable place for all of us there. I was actually enjoying it."

"So, why didn't you stay?"

"Because it wasn't me. I didn't like living like that, wondering if I'd be caught. My mother had started to talk about available girls, and I just kept thinking about it. It's one thing for me to pretend I'm someone else, but could I subject her to that? Some innocent girl, who marries a man who has no physical interest in her? It seemed wrong."

I shuddered at his words. In a way, it wasn't so different from what I was doing. I felt like a hypocrite. I slumped down in my chair and took another deep drag as the joint was past to me.

"So, that's it? You just woke up one day and made that decision?" Rachael asked.

Raj took a long drink of water. "I had a catalyst that drove me to it."

"What?" I asked.

"Mr. Mukopadhyay."

Rachael and I stared at him quizzically.

"Mr. Muko-who?" Rachael asked.

"Mr. Mukopadhyay. Remember when I came to the states a few months ago when my parents sold their house?"

Rachael and I nodded.

"I was the power of attorney so I spent the week there, packing up the house by myself, and I saw him. He was our neighbor. Our subdivision is mostly Indian families—it was nicknamed Little India. My parents chose it for that reason. Mr. Mukopadhyay was this guy who had moved into his parent's house after they'd passed away. Growing up, all the parents warned their kids to stay away from him. They called him peculiar. We all thought he was a pedophile, which was funny because, looking back on it, the guy hated kids. He would tell us to stay off his lawn, and he never passed out Halloween candy. But after I saw him, I just couldn't get him out of my mind, so I knocked on his door."

"What happened?" I asked, leaning forward.

"I thought it would be weird because I had no idea what I was doing there, but he knew right away. He said—" Raj switched into his Indian accent "—'Rajesh Desai, you've finally come to see me.'"

Raj shifted back to his normal tone and continued, "He made us tea, and I sat there trying to find an excuse to leave, but he said the answer to my question before I could even form it in my head. 'Yes, I'm gay,' he said. 'And so are you.' I stayed there for two hours while he told me his life story. How he'd fallen in love with a man when he was younger, but they had so many issues. Whenever they went out, they had to pretend to be friends. They couldn't go to certain places for fear of running into people. They couldn't hold hands, let alone kiss or hug. His partner was out and living freely and resented Mr. Mukopadhyay for keeping their relationship a secret. Despite that, they lived together for twenty years, until his partner died of cancer. He told me that, in the end, he wasn't even allowed in the room since the hospital said he wasn't family. He couldn't even properly grieve his lover's death."

We were all quiet for a minute, absorbing the sorrow of not being able to be with the person you loved when they needed you most.

"You know what he told me that really stuck?" Raj asked.

"What?" Rachael asked.

"He said I was lucky to live in this time, when a man could be free. I practically spat out my tea and told him that wasn't the case, not when you're Indian. He said he was too much of a coward to make it happen, but I was in a position to make the choice. That it wasn't easy for the first gay men to come out, and because of my culture, it wouldn't be easy for me. But if I didn't want to end up a lonely old man who people regarded as a hermit or, worse, a pervert, that I'd better stop hiding and start living."

"Wow, that's some story," Rachael said.

"Yeah, that's when I decided. I'm not ready to come all the way out, but I will. I know that now. Before, the idea seemed so scary I would break into a sweat just thinking about it."

"That's too bad," Rachael said.

"What is?" I asked.

"Raj is no longer a member of our little losers club. He's a winner."

"Raj, I'm so happy for you," I stated.

"Thanks, Meena. I wish you guys would consider joining me."

"And become gay? I don't think it's a club for just anyone," Rachael said, laughing.

"Become free," he said simply. "The three of us all have issues tying us down, whether they were self-imposed like you, Rachael, or part of our identity like Meena and I."

"I had no idea you were such a philosopher," Rachael replied dryly. "You're like a regular Deepak Chopra."

"We *are* free, Raj. Rachael will find someone, and she won't make the same mistake again. And me, I'm getting married, so we're going to be just fine."

They both stared at me with sarcastic expressions. They never mentioned Ethan, and I never told them I loved him, but of course, I didn't have to. They knew me like only close friends could, and I said, "Shut up and hand me the joint."

31

Ethan

I had no idea what I was doing. It felt like my body was on some kind of autopilot. We'd said so many goodbyes, but I couldn't let it end without at least fighting for her, for us, once more. Since we'd had our weekend together, I couldn't even deflect my depression with drink or other women like before. I'd found myself at the Tiffany's counter a few months after she left. I needed a new watch. The saleslady brought out a large assortment, but my eyes kept darting to the other items in the store.

Meena's name meant precious stone in Hindi, and I found myself mesmerized by all the precious stones. I ended up buying a watch, but something else too. Something that weighed down one side of my jacket but was counterweighted by the item in my other pocket. They were very different, but each one powerful, and I had no idea which I would give her.

Meena's house was a large Cape Cod that was cheerful and lit up. A valet driver parked my car. I walked in as if I were an invited guest. The house was large, but it felt claustrophobic with all the people. There were plates of food I recognized from when Meena cooked for me and some I did not. I grabbed a glass of champagne and swigged it for courage. Some people were in Indian dress while others wore western clothes. Many were speaking in what I imagined was Hindi, but there were many dialects so I wasn't sure.

I heard snippets of a conversation as I made my way through the rooms, looking for her. Two older women were gossiping, but they were speaking loud enough that it was apparent they didn't care who heard. "She gave her parents such a hard time. It is a miracle she found anyone at all. Girls today are so picky. Not like us." It was funny to me. It sounded like they were talking about choosing a dress, not a life partner.

I saw Raj and Rachael first, sitting on a couch in the living room. I took a seat between them. Raj smiled knowingly like he'd figured I'd show up even though I hadn't told him. Rachael gaped at me.

"What are you doing here?" she demanded.

"I guess I'm a glutton for punishment," I said.

"How did you know?"

"I told him," Raj interjected. "Maybe Meena needs her own catalyst."

I had no idea what they were talking about, but I didn't care. My eyes darted around the room, searching for her among the sea of people.

"Ethan, she made her choice. Being here is just going to hurt her. She's suffering enough."

"I'm not here to hurt her, Rachael. Don't you think it's funny that she's suffering at what should be a happy time for her?"

"Trust me; the irony isn't lost on me. I rooted for you guys more than anyone, but Meena made up her mind, and you need to respect that."

In many ways Rachael was right, but I wasn't going to stand by and not see her once more. Maybe hold her again, or give her one of the items in my pocket. Not both, but one. Which one, I didn't know. Before I could say anything, though, Rachael's parents approached us.

"Ethan, you came to see Rachael. How sweet," her mother said, making a move to hug me, which was very awkward since I was sitting and she was standing.

I stood up, and Rachael's father slapped me on the back, much harder than I was expecting.

"I…ah…" *Damn, why did we tell this lie again?* I couldn't remember.

"Come and meet Rachael's brother, he's…" Verna started scanning the crowd, but I felt a grip on my arm before she could find him.

"Right here. Kevin," he said. He had a hefty build, spiky red hair, and a myriad of visible tattoos. "Come with me. I want to talk to you, man to man."

I stared at Rachael, who shrugged her shoulders in a what-do-you-want-me-to-do gesture. I gritted my teeth.

"Rachael and I broke up," I blurted.

He was looking at me like he wanted to pummel me. "Then why are you here?" Kevin asked.

Fuck, I know why I'm here, but there's no way I'm going to tell this jerk. "I don't know."

"I know. He wants to get back together with Rachael," Verna chirped.

"Well, then, we definitely need to talk, bro." Kevin pulled me away, and I found myself following him. His parents followed us. I spent the next twenty minutes hearing about how special Rachael was from her mother while she accosted me with baby pictures and her brother cast stern glances in my direction. I mostly listened while they droned on about all things Rachael. I think I responded appropriately enough to satisfy them.

I somehow managed to escape them and found my way back to the couch where Raj and Rachael were perched. "What the fuck was that?"

"What?" Rachael asked innocently.

"Why the hell does your mom have so many naked baby pictures of you in her purse?"

"I was a cute baby."

"I thought your brother was going to hit me. What's his problem?"

"Be nice. He has issues," Rachael said.

"Yeah, like dry skin, for one," Raj muttered.

"What?" Rachael sighed. "I've been crying a lot. He thinks it's your fault."

"Rachael, it's your own damn fault you're crying."

Of course, I knew about what happened. Alex had spent many long nights lamenting—bitching—about Rachael's betrayal. In many ways, it was exactly what I had hoped wouldn't happen. Right now, though, wasn't the time.

"How is he, Ethan? He won't talk to me."

"Heartbroken, Rachael. He needs to heal, and you need to let him. I don't know if he'll forgive you, but you have to give him space."

She laughed bitterly. "You're such a hypocrite, you know that?" She was right, but she was wrong, too. I never cheated on Meena. She left me. I'd done nothing but give her space since.

"Look, you're Meena's friend so, for some reason, I feel an ounce of sympathy for you, but you hurt my best friend, and that's never going to be okay in my book. It's not just the cheating. It's the shame."

"What shame?" she demanded.

"You never told your parents about him. He feels you were ashamed."

She shook her head. "He never told his parents either."

I sighed, wanting to end the conversation. It was a huge detour in my true purpose here. "Yes, he did, Rachael. He told them."

Rachael's mouth dropped open in shock. It probably wasn't the nicest thing for me to tell her. It was just rubbing salt in the wound, and this girl looked wounded enough.

"Did you think your parents wouldn't accept him?" I asked. "Although we're not real, they seemed to accept me, and I'm an atheist."

"I guess they might have," she said, staring at her hands folded in her lap.

"I sincerely hope you get the chance to find out one day. I really do, Rachael."

I kept scanning the room for Meena, but I had the feeling she was in the room that had the most people and music flowing from it. I recognized the distinct sounds of the bhangra drums.

"What do we know about him?" I asked.

"Why are you torturing yourself, Ethan?"

I swallowed back my frustration. "Answer the question."

"I'll tell you," Raj said. "Meena declined all eligible applicants. She had many suitors, but she always found something wrong with them."

"So, why is he different?"

Rachael sighed and continued the story. "Meena's parents got pretty frustrated and asked her what she was looking for specifically. She told them if they could find a man who was scientifically minded, tall, stylish, and with a sense of humor, she'd marry him. Oh, and he had to have blue eyes."

"Blue eyes?"

"It's a rare trait, but some Indians have them," Raj explained.

I started laughing so hard, people turned in our direction.

"It's not funny," Rachael said.

"It's pathetic. She asked for an Indian version of me."

"Yes, I suppose she did, but guess what? He exists, and she's marrying him, so you need to back off."

That's when I saw her, and my throat went dry. She was in a traditional Indian dress, a sari. It was brightly colored in vivid hues of aqua and pink patterned paisleys. Her bare stomach was framed by the silky material wrapped around her. She'd gained weight. She looked healthy. Hell, she looked happy.

Her hair was down, and the soft, luminous black waves fell against her shoulders. There was the smallest diamond chip in her nose, which only shined when she turned a certain way. It was really hot. My fingers twitched, watching her move across the room, greeting people. Then I saw him. Then they saw me.

Meena approached with hesitation. He was right on her heels, placing a hand on the small of her back. He was smiling widely, but she looked frightened, and I had a feeling her lower lip would have a mark on it from the way she was chewing on it.

"Ethan," she said, but there wasn't much I could say because he was there too. I suddenly felt the weight of what I was doing, and it was too heavy for my shoulders.

"Hi, I'm Prem." He extended a hand.

"This is my boyfriend, Ethan," Rachael said. *Why are we still lying?* I stiffened at the introduction, but I shook Prem's hand. Some part of me wanted to meet him.

"Welcome," he said.

I thought he'd walk away or Meena would, but they both stood there. He started chattering on, asking me questions. I answered, but I found I had some questions of my own. I wanted to hate this guy. I had planned on it. At least then I would have a face to focus all my anger on, because I had never been able to successfully target it on Meena and I never would. An elderly lady pulled Meena away. She was hesitant, but she left. I was glad in a way. I needed to interview Prem.

The more I spoke to him, the more I had to admit he was a good guy. He was extremely intelligent, and the way he spoke about Meena was respectful, almost reverent. He was a heart surgeon who volunteered for Doctors Without Borders. He also seemed to have that dry sense of humor that Meena appreciated. My sense of humor. Fuck, he even told me his name meant "love" in Hindi.

He wasn't like the tool from Quebec. He seemed genuine and real. We were the same height and build too. We sipped champagne and talked for a long time, until I felt in my pocket, and knew for certain, which item I would give Meena tonight.

Raj found her for me and led her to the kitchen where I waited. "Hi, Sunshine," I said, rubbing my neck sheepishly.

"Ethan, what do you want?" she asked, adjusting her hair and biting into that lip.

"Is there somewhere we can talk?"

She was silent for a minute, and I readied myself for her wrath, but instead she said, "If you go out this door to the backyard, there is a playground adjacent to our property. I'll meet you there in a few minutes."

"See you in a few," I said, exhaling. I hadn't realized I was holding my breath.

Meena

I looked ridiculous, trekking across the soggy yard, squishy from recent rains, holding up the hem of my sari and wearing galoshes. He sat on one of the swings. I took the swing next to him.

"You have a park behind your house too," he said, breaking the silence.

"It's a playground. Hardly a park. Vijay and I used to play here when we were little."

"I'm sorry," he said.

"Don't be. It's a very happy place for me."

"Why didn't you ever wear anything like this for me?" he asked, tugging the border of my sari.

"You like this?"

He smiled mischievously. "It's turning me on something fierce."

I laughed. "To be honest, I don't even know how it's staying on. It took three women to help me dress. For that matter, it has so many tucks and folds, I have no idea how to take it off."

"I could have helped with that part," Ethan said.

I shuffled my feet, moving my swing closer to his. "Why are you here?"

"Do you love him?" he asked with urgency, like our time was short, which it was.

"I hardly know him," I said, looking away from his sharp gaze.

"Do you think you could love him?"

I shrugged. "Time will tell. He's a good man."

Ethan nodded as if agreeing with me. I knew he and Prem had talked for a while, and I had worried the whole time, wondering what they were conversing about.

"I don't know if I should be the honorable man I want to be and tell you that I hope you fall in love with him, or be the selfish man I am and hope you never fall in love with him."

"Ethan, you are anything but selfish."

"This is so hard…to find the right words. They don't exactly make greeting cards for this kind of thing."

I smiled. "You don't have to say anything. Just hold my hand for a minute."

He clasped my hand and squeezed it. We sat there for a few minutes, not wanting to let the moment go. Finally, he stood up and took out an envelope from his pocket. He pressed it into my hand with both of his. "This is for you. I wanted you to have it."

I looked at the fat white envelope with the perfect block script, showing a single word, "Sunshine."

"You wrote me a letter?" I asked.

"Sort of…but not exactly. I think you'll understand."

He bent down and whispered gently in my ear, "Maybe I'll just say, I hope he's worthy of you. Goodbye, Meena." He pressed a kiss to my forehead, and I watched him walk off.

"See you in the next life," I yelled, but I was all alone, and he was gone.

I stared at the letter in my shaking hand. I knew I shouldn't open it, should return to the party. People would be looking for me. Prem would be looking for me, but I had to know what it said right now.

The envelope was stuffed full, so I had thought it would be a huge letter, one that would take me a long time to read. I used the light from my cell phone and smoothed out the pages. They were written in Ethan's scratchy scrawl with random notes written in no particular order with no clear pattern. One said, "She always wears her hair up. Always." Another, "We like the same music." Another, "She is loyal and I like that. She is stronger than she thinks." As I read on, they became more specific and intimate.

I suddenly realized with alarming clarity what Ethan was doing. These were his errant observations about me that he had scrawled in his notebook. They were basically a litany of the thoughts he'd had throughout the year we were together. He'd told me once that he sometimes needed to get rid of the paper to get it out of his head permanently. That's what he was doing. He was telling me he could move on. He was saying goodbye for the last time. I saw the ink smear as big, fat, salty droplets fell onto the page. I sat and read and cried for a long time. I looked like I was grieving, but then, it was appropriate since that's exactly what I was doing.

"Hey, there you are," Prem said, jerking me from the letter clutched in my hand.

He took one assessing look at me and the letter. He didn't say anything. He only took the swing beside me. The one Ethan had occupied.

"The party's winding down. Your parents are looking for you."

"I'm sorry. I'll go in," I said, wiping my face, praying the kohl on my eyes wouldn't smear. He clasped my arm as I was about to get up.

"Let's take a minute," he said.

I nodded gratefully and sat back down. He didn't say anything else. Finally, I broke the silence. "I'm not what I seem." The confession was whispered, but it sounded like it echoed.

"Is anyone really?" he replied.

"We don't know each other."

"Tell me what I don't know."

I stared at him, the brilliant blues eyes played off his striking features and caramel skin with perfection. He was a very handsome man.

"I didn't make the rice pudding *kheer* that first night you visited us. I know my mother told you that, but she made it. To be honest, I don't even like it that much, so I'll probably never make it for you."

He laughed. "I can cook. I'll learn how to make it myself." He shuffled his feet and swung back and forth for a second. He was wearing an expensive suit, but it was obvious he felt at ease. "I lied. I'm not a vegetarian."

"You're not?" I said, amused by his confession.

"No, I like meat, especially steak."

I was quiet for moment. "That's okay as long as you don't cook it in the house."

We both laughed, and it sounded good to me.

"I love country music," I blurted out.

He chuckled. "That's okay, as long as you don't play it in the house."

I smiled. It felt comfortable with Prem. He was sweet, smart, and handsome. He was everything I wanted. *I have found the man for me, so why does it feel so wrong?*

"I'm in love with another man," I announced, not hiding my tears this time. "I'm sorry."

He was quiet for a moment. I expected him to be outraged, but he spoke very calmly. "Who?"

"Ethan. You met him tonight."

"You're in love with your best friend's boyfriend?" he asked, his eyes widening, like that was more of a shocker than telling my fiancé I loved another man.

"That's just a lie we told a long time ago, but it's time I told the truth."

He nodded, twisting his swing. "I'll help you get over him."

I gasped. "You would marry me knowing I was in love with someone else?"

Prem shrugged. "It's not a deal breaker."

"How could it not be a deal breaker for you?"

He didn't answer right away. He took out his cell phone and began scrolling through it. I waited patiently, wondering if he was going to call my mother or something.

"Look." He held the phone up to me.

I took it and stared at a picture of Prem and a gorgeous girl with shoulder-length black hair and an endearing smile. "She's beautiful. Who is she?"

"We were both volunteers for Doctors Without Borders in Haiti. She's a doctor too."

I took my fingers and expanded the photo so I could clearly see her. "Do you love her?"

"We had a summer fling. She was special to me, and I still think about her all the time. The point is, we're not so different."

"I don't understand."

"What?"

"She looks Indian."

"She is Indian."

"So, you could be with her, then. You could——"

"She's Muslim," he replied, and I needed no further explanation. That was a harder row to hoe than what was going on with me.

"I see."

"So, do we know each other well enough now? Has our little swing-set confession served its purpose?"

I handed the cell back to him. "Prem, you are a wonderful man, but I can't do this. I'm so sorry. If I hadn't met Ethan, then there would be no doubt."

"But there is doubt?"

"No, it's more than doubt. It's knowledge. I can be physically faithful to you, but I will never be emotionally faithful. Marrying you would be…" I was thinking of the phrase, and it hit me with such clarity, I almost bolted off the swing. "It would be living a lie." The statement was Ethan's, but in that moment, I completely understood and owned it.

He was quiet for a moment, but he eventually smiled at me. "I understand."

"My mother is going to kill me." I said it jokingly, but there was truth to the statement, and Prem knew it too.

"We'll tell our parents it was mutual. We weren't compatible. It'll be fine."

I took his hand and kissed it. It seemed like the right gesture for the gratitude I felt. "Will you try for her?" I asked, pointing to his phone. He was still looking at the picture.

"It's not just me I have to worry about. She has a family too. It's a lot to give up."

"But you'd be gaining so much."

"Come on. It's getting chilly out here, and we have some hearts to break." He helped me up.

"Hearts to break?" I asked him.

"Yes, our parents'."

We both laughed, but it was uncomfortable because it was so true.

32
Meena

*B*y the time we got back, almost everyone was gone. My mother looked at me with reproachful eyes and chided me for being so rude. They all looked at my tear-soaked face, blackened by the kohl eyeliner. Prem's father said it was obvious we'd had a little lover's spat. He said it was good we talked and made up, but it was far from what had happened.

Prem and I had worked out that we'd break the news separately so the combined wrath of our parents couldn't unite into an impenetrable force. Prem and his family left, saying pleasant goodbyes. I hugged his parents, knowing that they would hate me very soon.

I scrubbed my face, changing into jeans and a T-shirt. I helped my mother with the dishes and cleaning. The party had been catered, so there wasn't that much left to do. When everything was done, I took her hand and led her to the dining table. I asked my father to join us. He seemed slightly annoyed at having to turn off CNN just when Wolf Blitzer was warming up, but he came.

"What is it?" he asked. "Are you apologizing?"

"For what?" I asked.

"For being so rude to all the people who came to congratulate you on this auspicious night."

I bit my lip. It was now or never. "Prem and I are not getting married."

I let the words sink in. My mother gasped and my father scowled. "What did you say to him?" he demanded.

"It was mutual," I said, hoping that Prem's idea would help me. It didn't seem to have any effect.

"We can call him. We can go over there and talk to his parents. Make them understand," my mother said.

"Understand what?"

"That you are sorry for whatever you did," my mother answered as if I was a small child.

"This is brilliant," my father said, throwing his hands in the air. "We did everything you asked. You know that's not even the way this works, but we did it because you were so stubborn about it."

"I was stubborn because I didn't want this. Any of this."

"What the hell do you want, then?" my father asked through gritted teeth.

"I'm in love with someone else. We met in college. I have loved him for a long time. I want to be with him…if he'll have me." A sudden fear gripped my heart because, in a way, Ethan had broken up with me tonight. He had let me go, and maybe that's the way he wanted things. I didn't dwell in that darkness too long.

My father laughed cynically. "An American boy?"

"Yes, he's American…" I stared up at my father, narrowing my eyes defiantly, which was probably not the best attitude at this time. "American like me."

"I told you we should have moved back to India," my mother bellowed.

"Who is this Romeo you think is going to whisk you away to his Camelot?"

"Romeo and Camelot are not in the same story, Dad," I said.

My father stood up so fast, the chair fell behind him. "Don't be disrespectful to me, especially in my house. You know nothing. I've seen the way these people treat marriage and family. They don't have the same standards we do."

"You're wrong. Ethan is not like that. He loves me, and I love him."

"Ethan?" my mother spat. "You're in love with Rachael's boyfriend?"

I cursed Rachael for making me have to explain this preposterous story yet again. "He was never her boyfriend. She just said that so you wouldn't ask why I was friends with a boy. I'm not going to lie about it anymore. I don't want to hurt you, but I cannot and will not live by your rules."

My father straightened and sighed. "*Beta*, I understand the hormones of young people. I am a doctor, after all, but things are different when you're with someone full-time. You start seeing faults you didn't know existed. That's why in an arranged marriage you know what you're getting."

"I know Ethan's faults. All of them, and I love each one. He knows mine too. We lived together at Stanford, so I know him very well."

"Bloody bitch!" my father screamed, banging the table so hard, the centerpiece moved a few inches. I knew he wasn't saying it to me. I had only heard him say the term a few times when he was very angry. It was a curse remaining from his British schooling.

I stood up and walked toward the stairs, deciding I had given them more truth than they could handle for one night.

"Where are you going? This isn't over," my father said as he followed me.

I turned. "It's over. I'm sorry I'm not doing what you want. I know you think I'm disobedient."

"Disobedient is one word. I was thinking ungrateful."

"Maybe, but I can't live my life because of a mistake I made a long time ago."

"What are you saying?" He was so angry his face was red and his eyes huge.

"Leave her alone," my mother said, moving toward us. "She's emotional and not thinking clearly. She'll change her mind after a good night's sleep."

I laughed sarcastically. My mother's answer for my life was always a good night's sleep.

"I'm sorry Vijay died. I loved him too, and for a long time I blamed myself as you blamed me for his death."

"Shut up. Don't bring him into this," my father warned.

"Why? Because we never talk about him? He was smart and nice. He loved science. He annoyed me because he was my brother, and I annoyed him, but we loved each other. We all did once."

"Yes, he was all those things, and he wouldn't have done this. You are disparaging his memory."

"Dad, I didn't kill Vijay. It wasn't my fault. It was an accid—"

"Shut up."

"No, I won't. I didn't mean it to—"

I felt the sting of the slap before I could even comprehend the movement. I touched my cheek and stared at my father, a man who had never even spanked me in his life. Fresh tears invaded my eyes, but I didn't just feel them for me. My father stood in shock, staring at his hand like it had acted on its own. Clearly, he felt remorseful for his actions.

"I'm sorry," he said solemnly.

"I'm not."

Both of them gaped at me. My mother went to touch my cheek, but I backed away.

"That's the first sign of emotion you've showed me since he died. I'm glad you still have some in you."

I ran toward my bedroom. I flung myself on the bed and felt the wretched sobs take over my body. I cried for my brother, for my parents, and for myself. I didn't know what was going to happen, but somewhere along the way, some crazy instinct told me I was crying for Mr. Mukopadhyay too. All the Mr. Mukopadhyays of the world. There were so many of us. It was time to leave this club…time to stop hiding and start living.

33

Ethan

$\mathcal{I}$ had planned to take a flight out that night. Actually, I hadn't planned anything, since I purchased a one-way ticket to begin with, but I went straight to the airport from Meena's. All the flights were booked. I considered driving home in the rental car, but I was tired. I bought a T-shirt in the hotel store and some shorts to sleep in. Coincidently, the words "Lovers Choose Boston" were embossed on them.

Raj texted me and insisted we should meet up for a drink. The poor guy tried really hard to cheer me up, but I was horrible company and headed up to my room at the Airport Hilton after one drink. I shut off my phone, not wanting to be disturbed again, and had a fitful night's sleep.

I arrived at my gate much earlier than I needed to. I just wanted to get home so I could start. Start forgetting about her. In some ways, I was glad to have met Prem. He was a good man who would take care of her. We hadn't talked about her promise to me, but I worried about it constantly. I didn't know him very well, but he was a decent person. In other ways, I wish I hadn't seen her again. The image of her in that sari was something I'd never forget. I would dream of it.

A shadow fell across me. I jerked my head up. Meena's father stood above me. I instantly tensed. For a moment, I wondered if I'd fallen asleep and was having a nightmare. The man was tall with a thick thatch of salt and pepper hair. He had a demeanour that demanded attention. I felt like saluting him.

"May I speak with you?"

"Of course," I replied, sitting up in my chair. He took the seat across from me. He was wearing an expensive suit, and I looked completely crumpled in comparison with bloodshot eyes, an unshaven face, and messy hair. I wore the wrinkled shirt and pants from the night before. This was definitely not the impression I wanted to make on Meena's father.

"I hear you're in love with my daughter."

I was not sure what a heart attack felt like, but I was pretty sure I was having one. "Did she tell you that?"

"I think you should refrain from asking any questions before I get my answers. It took a great deal for me to get here. Raj told me you were leaving today, and I missed you at the hotel."

"I left early."

"Obviously." It was apparent this wasn't going to be an amicable discussion.

"Look, Mr. Kapoor—"

"Dr. Kapoor," he corrected.

"My apologies, Dr. Kapoor—"

"I would sincerely appreciate it if you stopped interrupting me." It was ironic since he was interrupting me, but I quieted.

He waited to make sure I wasn't going to say anything further. "As I was saying, it took a great deal for me to catch up to you. They made me purchase a ticket to come back here. And when you're a man that looks like me, purchasing a one-way ticket with no luggage... Well, let's just say I would have been here forty minutes ago."

I would have laughed, except I knew he wasn't joking.

"I have some questions for you, and I expect complete honesty in your answers. Can you do that?"

"Yes, sir."

"Do you think it was appropriate for you to corrupt my daughter? To have her turn her back on everything she had been brought up to believe?"

I gulped. I wasn't sure how to answer, especially since I had no idea how much he knew. The man was smart. It felt like he was interrogating me. "I wouldn't use the term 'corrupt.' I don't think she would either."

"Oh? How else would you identify it when you live with her and subject her to gossip in her community?"

"Meena's an adult. With the utmost respect to you, there was nothing corrupt about our relationship. I love her, and I give her nothing but respect." I had used present tense, but the past tense didn't feel right either.

"Is that so? So, if she were to leave with you today, what would you do? Take her away and make her part of your life as long as she suited you?"

I cleared my throat. I would not falter on this question. My answer rang true because it was in my heart. "Sir, if Meena had chosen me, I would not discard her. She would not be part of my life. She would *be* my life. But I will never ask her to make that choice, because that's how much I love her."

He paused as if considering my answer. "You would be all right stepping aside and letting her marry Prem?"

"The choice was never between him and me."

Dr. Kapoor raised his eyebrows questioningly, and I cleared my throat.

"It was between you and me. I won't make her choose."

They started boarding my flight. I stood, holding my hand out to Dr. Kapoor. "This is my flight."

He shook his head. "I'm not ready to shake your hand. I'm not done asking questions. So, you can either get on that flight, or you can answer all of my questions."

"What else could you possibly want to know? I promise you I'll leave her alone. You have my word as a man on that."

"I want to know if you are right for her. I want to give you an interview, and then I'll decide if I can shake your hand."

My eyes widened. I fell more than sat back in my seat, preparing myself for the most important interview of my life.

It was funny, I'd thought Rachael's mom had asked a lot of questions, but she had nothing on Dr. Kapoor. I was honest with him about everything including my parent's relationship. I made no excuse or apologies for it. This was me, and I wouldn't be anyone else.

He told me of Meena's confessions, her breakup with Prem, the fight they had gotten into. He even told me he slapped her. I had a hard time controlling myself for a minute, trying to hold back my anger, but it was obvious he regretted it.

Before we finished, I asked him a question of my own. One I never thought I'd get a chance to ask.

When we were done, he stood up and held out his hand. My hand was shaking as I took his.

"I'm not so scary, am I?" he said.

I exhaled the longest breath of my life. I think I'd held it the whole time we spoke. "No, it wasn't as bad as it could have been."

"Out of curiosity, what would have made it scarier?"

I was surprised by the question, but I smirked when answering, which was probably a mistake. "You know those cliché television shows where the boy shows up, and the father is busy cleaning his rifle while he talks to him?"

Dr. Kapoor smiled. The first smile I'd seen, but it didn't put me at ease. "Yes, Ethan, I'm not just off the boat."

I laughed because it was what Meena always said.

"I'm familiar with them," he said. My laughter disappeared as he gripped my hand tighter and spoke very quietly so no one would hear. "Listen to me, young man. I am Indian and typically nonviolent. I do not own a rifle, but I am also a brain surgeon and the things I can do with a scalpel will make you wish I owned a gun. Do I make myself clear?"

I gulped audibly. "Very clear, sir."

"Do not hurt my little girl."

"I never will." I had to shake my palm out when we were done. My hand hurt, but my heart and head felt so full and complete I did not care.

34

Meena

$\mathcal{I}$ came down to breakfast in my flannel pajamas. I had texted Ethan late last night and early this morning, but I'd received no reply. I called him, but it went straight to voice mail. I started assuming I had been wrong and he had, in fact, said his final goodbye. I prayed it wasn't too late. I had so much to say to him.

My mother was sitting at the kitchen table. I approached her warily, preparing for another lecture. She pushed out a chair and motioned for me to sit.

"Mom, I don't want to talk anymore."

"I need you to listen now."

I crossed my arms, waiting for her to begin. I owed it to her to let out her anger. I deserved it in many ways. She wouldn't be able to change my mind, but at least I could give her some catharsis.

"We never blamed you for Vijay's death."

The statement jolted me in my seat. "You know that they were my friends and not his. He was there because of me."

"Yes, of course we knew that. We never blamed you, though. In fact, if anything we blamed ourselves. For a long time, we kept saying if only we had done this or that, he would still be here. I am so sorry, *Beta*."

"For what?"

"Because I knew you blamed yourself for it. You were sad, and I never did anything to bring you peace. I failed as a mother."

"No, Mom, it wasn't your fault either."

"You're right. It happened. It was a tragedy in all our lives, but we were so busy looking for blame and living with the guilt that we never really grieved his death. We never moved past it. Do you forgive us?"

I started sobbing again. I had no idea how many tears a person could make, but I felt like I might have surpassed a quota. "Yes, I forgive you. I forgive myself. I love you."

We embraced, and she was crying too. It was in that moment that I realized how I had lost her as a mother. How much I missed her support and guidance. More specifically, how grateful I was to get it back.

When we released each other, she got up and came back with a box of tissues.

"I assume Dad doesn't share your opinions."

"He does. We talked about it all last night. He feels the same. I just couldn't wait for him to tell you."

"Did he go back to Boston?"

"Yes."

"So, he just ran away again to the apartment and job?"

"No, Meena, he went to Boston, but not to work. He went to meet someone."

"Who?"

"Another candidate."

I let out a horse scream. "Are you kidding me? You just tell me all that, and now you expect me to…to…just pick up…" I was so upset I couldn't even finish the sentence.

"No, *Beta*, calm down."

The front door closed just then. My mother rubbed my shoulders, and despite my tension, it calmed me.

"He's back," she said.

My father came into the kitchen a few minutes later. "Meena, you have a guest."

I stared at my father. He had an impish smile on his face, which was very odd for him in general but particularly on this occasion.

"Is it Prem? Because I already told—"

"Meena, please stop being insolent just once and come with me."

There was amusement in his voice that I hadn't heard in a long time. It prodded me to stand up and follow him. He led me to the living room where Ethan stood, shuffling his feet nervously. I had no idea why, but I ran back into the kitchen.

My dad sighed, following behind me. "Women really confuse me," he muttered.

My mother laughed, following behind him. "We always have."

"I don't understand. What is he doing here? Did you threaten him?" I hissed the questions at my father, imagining him asking Ethan here to tell him off in front of me.

My father laughed. "Yes, but not in the way you think." He placed his hands on my shoulders and turned me so I was looking at him. There was nothing but love in his expression. "I have already lost one child. I will not lose another. We only want your happiness. I have interviewed him, and I approve, but the final choice is yours, as it always was."

I nodded, feeling my pulse race. My father gave me a little push. I made my way back to the living room. I walked very slowly toward him, scared he might disappear if I was too fast. His sandy brown hair was a mess, his face was rough with stubble, his piercing blue eyes were bloodshot, his oxford shirt was crumpled, but I had never seen him look more handsome.

He grinned that boyish smile at me, and my heart melted. "Hi, Sunshine."

"You spoke to my father?"

"Yes, he had a lot of questions for me."

"I'm sorry."

"Don't be. I have some things to tell you."

"Before you say anything I have to tell you something first. Something I should have said a long time ago. I love you, Ethan Callahan. I've loved you for such a long time. I think I first realized it in Santa Cruz, and I have felt it every day since, growing exponentially. I'm so sorry for not expressing that to you and not fighting for us like I should have. I was weak, but now—"

He pulled me toward him and kissed me, long and slow. I heard a distinct gasp coming from the French doors and realized my parents were spying on us. He must have too, because he released me right away. "You were never weak. You are the strongest person I know. Now, I have to tell you something."

His eyes darted around the room, and he began pacing. I waited until he finally came back and stood in front of me. My heart was pounding in my chest, making it difficult to focus.

He took my hands in his. "I felt alone for so long. I didn't know why. I had friends and a family that loved me. I felt at home wherever I lived whether it was in Austin or Los Angeles or New York, but I never felt as whole as I did in Palo Alto my senior year where every day was full of sunshine. I wondered why that was, but then I realized it was because before then and after then I was homeless."

"Ethan, that doesn't make sense," I said, rubbing his arms.

"No, Sunshine, it really does. Because home is and has always been where you are."

I let out a raspy choke.

He hugged me. "As I said, your father asked me a lot of questions, but I had one for him. He gave me the right answer, so now I have a question for you."

I had no idea what he was talking about. I was still confused when he stepped away and fell down on one knee. He held out a velvet box in one hand. I regarded it with curiosity.

"Meena Kapoor, I love you. This precious stone is not nearly as precious as you, but I hope you will do me the honor of wearing it and becoming my wife."

I took the box from him, staring at the most beautiful ring I had ever seen. I looked back at Ethan who was staring up at me with hopeful eyes. I fell to my knees so I could talk to him without being overheard.

"What are you doing? This isn't exactly protocol," he said, now confused.

"Ethan, you don't have to do this. I don't want you to do something you're not ready for. I'm just happy we have a future together. I'm satisfied with that for now."

He smiled and shook his head at me.

"Sunshine, I no longer want a future with you."

I swallowed, unsure of his meaning.

He placed a finger under my chin and lifted my eyes to meet his. "I want a forever. Will you be my forever?"

I was sitting in a cab in rush hour traffic while it made its way to the restaurant Ethan had chosen in the Village. Part of me wanted to ask him to cancel and just spend the evening in his arms, but it was my birthday. Ethan always made a big deal out of it, and I wouldn't cancel because, in some ways, the day had become so much more than my day. It was our day. The day he gave back to me.

We'd been married for a little over two years now. Each day felt like a precious gift to me. We lived in that huge apartment, over-looking Central Park where we had found two new swans to stalk and make our own. I found a job as a senior data analyst. It wasn't exactly a thrilling job, but I liked my co-workers and I loved coming home…to him.

Ethan had made so many sacrifices for me. I would never forget how my mother insisted we have an Indian wedding. Although he wasn't religious, his mother wanted an American one. We ended up having both in what was now referred to by our friends and family as the longest wedding in the history of the world. He told me he loved me so much he married me twice. It was all worth it, though.

I laughed to myself in the cab, thinking of the moment when we finally told my mom what his mom did. She told me she already knew. I regarded her curiously, then with horror, when she admitted she owned several of Dr. Love's books. I instantly understood Ethan's embarrassed reaction the day I'd found out.

My mother came to love Ethan. She claimed he reminded her of Vijay in so many ways. My father didn't exactly love him, but Ethan definitely earned his respect. *Not an easy task.*

"This is it," the cab driver said.

I looked out the window. It was a busy area of the Village, but the restaurant looked deserted. "Are you sure?"

"Yep, that's the address ma'am."

I paid him and got out, wondering if Ethan's meticulous planning had somehow backfired and he'd given me the wrong address.

"Hello, Mrs. Callahan, or should I say, birthday girl?" Ethan said, coming up behind me and embracing me, making me gasp with his sudden appearance. "Did I scare you?"

"Yes, a little. I think you got the address wrong. This place looks abandoned."

"I don't know about that. Let's go in."

He pulled open the door. It was completely dark, and I turned searching for him, but he wasn't beside me anymore. A light switch came on and then I was surrounded by people yelling, "Surprise!" I backed up in shock, my mouth hanging open and my knees shaking.

Ethan immediately embraced me again, "Are you ready to beat the shit out of me yet?"

I laughed. "You're so lucky I love you."

"Yes, I am," he replied.

I didn't see him after that hug for a long time because people were dragging us in opposite directions. Ethan had invited so many people to celebrate with us. I greeted our families, our new friends from New York, his colleagues, my colleagues, and our neighbors. I spent the most time with our old friends, though. Rachael was with Alex. They had been apart for so long and moved on, but they started talking again after they were in our wedding. And, like weddings often did, it served as a catalyst to reignite their relationship.

"Look," Rachael said, holding out her hand. A marquee diamond adorned it.

I shrieked and pulled her in for a big hug. I saw Ethan give a manly-man hug to Alex on the other side of the room. "Your parents?" I asked, knowing she'd get the question.

She shrugged. "They're not jumping for joy. Neither are his. Both sets say one of us needs to convert, but we're happy. I'm finally happy, karma girl. Not only with him, but myself."

"That's great, Rach."

"Yep, glad you finally came out of the closet," Raj said, putting his arm around Rachael.

I hugged him and his partner, Daniel. We exchanged pleasantries, and they wished me a happy birthday.

"I came out to my parents," Raj exclaimed.

"Good, so we both came out of the closet!" Rachael shrieked.

"No more Losers in Love Club for us," I said. "How did they react?"

"They disowned me."

Rachael and I both hugged him.

"Hey, watch it, my guy might get jealous," he said, backing away. "It's okay. Not every story has a perfect ending. The important thing is that we all fought for our happiness, and we won. They'll either accept me for who I am, or they never will. Either way, it's okay. This is me, and if I'm not me, who am I going to be?"

I nodded, hearing the clear undertones of Ethan's advice from that gay bar that seemed so long ago. "I'm so glad you guys could come. It's so good to see you."

"We'll see how glad you are when the weekend's over," Rachael said.

"Why?"

"We're staying with you. I'm making Thanksgiving dinner this year. That poor husband of yours hasn't had a real Thanksgiving bird in years."

I laughed. "Well, that's true. He definitely deserves it."

I excused myself after a while. I searched for Ethan, but he found me first, pulling me inside an empty room. There was a couch in the corner, and he walked us to it, sitting me on his lap. "I just wanted a minute alone with my wife. Are you enjoying yourself?"

"I love this. Thank you. I can't believe you did this for me."

He kissed my neck softly. He moved the strap of my dress to plant a few on my shoulder. "Well, we had to properly redeem ourselves as hosts. Do you like this place?"

"Yes, I can't believe you rented it out for my birthday."

He smiled impishly, "I didn't exactly rent it." I regarded his suspiciously. "We own it."

"You bought this?"

"*We* bought it, Mrs. Callahan, and I thought it was a good location for, say…an art gallery? What do you think? You always thought an art gallery right here in the Village would be perfect." I stared at him in disbelief. "Come on, Sunshine, you know you don't like your job that much. This is what you're meant to do, and we can afford it. My job is more than enough to support us without even touching my inheritance. I took a vow to make you happy, now let me do that. And don't worry—when you become rich and successful, I'll stay home and be a man of leisure."

I laughed. "You, a man of leisure? You can't even stay in bed when you're sick. Plus, making me happy was not one of your vows. If I recall, it was love, honor, and cherish."

"I'm not talking about those vows. It's the vow I made to myself the day I saw you in Malkin's class. It's the vow that I made to your father that day at the airport. Now, come on, Meena. You know that man has an assortment of scalpels with my name on them. Don't make me break my vows."

"Well, since you put it that way, I agree."

"Great, then, one more question."

"What's that?"

"Did you drop this pen?" he asked, pulling a pen out of his pocket. "I thought I saw you drop it."

I tilted my head. "No, I don't think that's mine."

"Well, it's a good thing I found it, anyway, because you're going to need it."

"Why?"

"I want you to sign the papers too."

"Thank you, Ethan." I embraced him and whispered in his ear, "Not just for this present, although it's perfect and I love it. Not just for this party, although it's amazing just like you. Thank you for always believing in me. Thank you for being my best friend. Thank you not just for loving me, but liking me, even when I didn't like myself very much."

He pulled me up and looked into my eyes. "You're very welcome, Sunshine."

"I have a present for you too," I said, swallowing hard.

He smirked. "You bought me a present on your birthday? You are a good wife."

I bit my lower lip. "I didn't exactly buy it."

"Oh, you made me something? I love that."

"No, Ethan, we made it together."

He tilted his head in curiosity. "I'm confused now."

I took his hand and placed it on my tummy. His eyes widened, and I could feel his muscles tense.

"You can't see it for a while, but I know you'll really love it. You're going to be such a great dad."

He stared at me and then at his hand. He rubbed my belly in slow circles, and because it was Ethan, they were perfectly round circles.

We had been trying for so long that we were ready to make an appointment with a specialist. Both of us thought there had to be something wrong. We had experienced several false alarms, so I didn't even want to tell him until I knew for sure.

"Ethan, say something."

He embraced me tightly, holding me in his arms. His voice was quiet when he spoke, "Let me just hold you…both of you."

He held me. His shoulders trembled, and I knew he was crying. I was too. His muscles started to loosen up eventually. His voice came out choked, full of emotion. "Do you remember how I said the comic book was the best gift I ever got?"

"Yes," I said.

"This is now the best present in the world. Thank you, Meena. Thank you for helping me solve for C and finding the sum of us. Thank you for being my wife, my friend, my life, my present, my future, and my forever. I love you…something fierce."

The End

Acknowledgments

Ethan and Meena's story is very personal to me. I hope you enjoy reading it as much as I loved writing it. This book would not be possible without some very special people. Thank you to my beta readers Roberta, Etheleen, Darshana, and Hiral for adding the perfect touches of spice to this story. Also, a big thank you to my family, Pat, Justin, and Nix for enduring every variety of take-out delivery known to man. Thank you to Ominfic for believing in my work and my awesome editor, Robin, for trimming in just the right places… no more split ends!

Finally, a big thank you to you, the vigilant reader for choosing this work among all the amazing choices out there. I hope you enjoy it and consider leaving a review or recommendation.

About the Author

I am a hopeless romantic in a hopelessly pragmatic world. I have a full-time life and two busy teenagers, but in the dark of night, I sit by the warm glow of a computer monitor and attempt to conjure up passionate, heartwarming stories with plenty of humor.

I started imagining stories in my head at a very young age. In fact, I got so good at it that friends asked me to create plots featuring them as the heroine and the object of their affection as the hero. You've heard of fan fiction…this was friend fiction.

I hope you enjoy this book and always search for the Happily Ever After in every endeavor. I love hearing from readers, so please write to me!

www.mkschillerauthor.com

Paranormal Romance

The Light series: *Seers of Light, Whisper of Light* & *Circle of Light* by Jennifer DeLucy
The Hanaford Park series: *Eve of Samhain* & *Pleasures Untold* by Lisa Sanchez
Immortal Awakening by KC Randall
The Seraphim series: *Crushed Seraphim* & *Bittersweet Seraphim* by Debra Anastasia
The Guardian's Wild Child by Feather Stone
Grave Refrain by Sarah M. Glover
The Divinity series: *Divinity* by Patricia Leever
The Blood Vine series: *Blood Vine, Blood Entangled* & *Blood Reunited*
by Amber Belldene
Divine Temptation by Nicki Elson
The Dead Rapture series: *Love in the Time of the Dead* by Tera Shanley

New Adult Romance

Three Daves by Nicki Elson
Streamline by Jennifer Lane
The Shades series: *Shades of Atlantis* & *Shades of Avalon* by Carol Oates
The Heart series: *Beside Your Heart, Disclosure of the Heart* & *Forever Your Heart*
by Mary Whitney
Romancing the Bookworm by Kate Evangelista
Flirting with Chaos by Kenya Wright
The Vice, Virtue & Video series: *Revealed, Captured* & *Desired* by Bianca Giovanni
Granton University series: *Loving Lies* by Linda Kage
Variables of Love by MK Schiller

Young Adult Romance

The Ember series: *Ember* & *Iridescent* by Carol Oates
Breaking Point by Jess Bowen
Life, Liberty, and Pursuit by Susan Kaye Quinn
The Embrace series: *Embrace* & *Hold Tight* by Cherie Colyer
Destiny's Fire by Trisha Wolfe
The Reaper series: *Reaping Me Softly* & *UnReap My Heart* by Kate Evangelista
The Legendary Saga: *Legendary* by LH Nicole
The Fatal series: *Fatal* by T.A. Brock
The Prometheus Order series: *Byronic* by Sandi Beth Jones
One Smart Cookie by Kym Brunner

Historical Romance

Cat O' Nine Tails by Patricia Leever
Burning Embers by Hannah Fielding
Seven for a Secret by Rumer Haven

⋆⤙⤚→Anthologies and Sets⤙⤚→⋆

A Valentine Anthology including short stories by
Alice Clayton ("With a Double Oven"),
Jennifer DeLucy ("Magnus of Pfelt, Conquering Viking Lord"),
Nicki Elson ("I Don't Do Valentine's Day"),
Jessica McQuinn ("Better Than One Dead Rose and a Monkey Card"),
Victoria Michaels ("Home to Jackson"), and
Alison Oburia ("The Bridge")

Taking Liberties including an introduction by Tiffany Reisz and short stories by
Mina Vaughn ("John Hancock-Blocked"),
Linda Cunningham ("A Boston Marriage"),
Joy Fulcher ("Tea for Two"),
KC Holly ("The British Are Coming!"),
Kimberly Jensen & Scott Stark ("E. Pluribus Threesome"), and
Vivian Rider ("M'Lady's Secret Service")
The Heart Series Box Set (*Beside Your Heart, Disclosure of the Heart &
Forever Your Heart*) by Mary Whitney
The CONduct Series Box Set (*With Good Behavior, Bad Behavior &
On Best Behavior*) by Jennifer Lane

⋆⤙⤚→Singles and Novellas⤙⤚→⋆

It's Only Kinky the First Time (A Keyhole series single) by Kasi Alexander
Learning the Ropes (A Keyhole series single) by Kasi & Reggie Alexander
The Winemaker's Dinner: RSVP by Dr. Ivan Rusilko
The Winemaker's Dinner: No Reservations by Everly Drummond
Big Guns by Jessica McQuinn
Concessions by Robin DeJarnett
Starstruck by Lisa Sanchez
New Flame by BJ Thornton
Shackled by Debra Anastasia
Swim Recruit by Jennifer Lane
Sway by Nicki Elson
Full Speed Ahead by Susan Kaye Quinn
The Second Sunrise by Hannah Downing
The Summer Prince by Carol Oates
Whatever it Takes by Sarah M. Glover
Clarity (A *Divinity* prequel single) by Patricia Leever
A Christmas Wish (A *Cocktails & Dreams* single) by Autumn Markus
Late Night with Andres by Debra Anastasia
Poughkeepsie (enhanced iPad app collector's edition) by Debra Anastasia

coming soon from
OMNIFIC PUBLISHING

Redemption by Kathryn Barrett
The Brit Out of Water series: *Jazz Hands* (book 2) by Eleanor Gwyn-Jones
The Dead Rapture series: *Love at the End of Days* (book 2) by Tera Shanley
The Playboy's Princess by Joy Fulcher
The Jeweler by Beck Anderson
The Fatal series: *Brutal* (novella 1.5) by T.A. Brock
The Vice, Virtue & Video series: *Tied* (book 4) by Bianca Giovanni
The Divinity series: *Entity* (book 2) by Patricia Leever
The WORDS series: *The Truest of Words* (book 3) by Georgina Guthrie